DEATH TAKES
A BUGGY RIDE

DEATH TAKES
A BUGGY RIDE

A John Lapp/Sallie Stoltzfus Mystery

A Novel by
Ron Yeakley

iUniverse, Inc.
New York Lincoln Shanghai

DEATH TAKES A BUGGY RIDE
A John Lapp/Sallie Stoltzfus Mystery

Copyright © 2007 by Ronald Yeakley

iUniverse books may be ordered through booksellers or by contacting:

iUniverse
2021 Pine Lake Road, Suite 100
Lincoln, NE 68512
www.iuniverse.com
1-800-Authors (1-800-288-4677)

Because of the dynamic nature of the Internet, any Web addresses or links contained in this book may have changed since publication and may no longer be valid.

This is a work of fiction. All of the characters, names, incidents, organizations, and dialogue in this novel are either the products of the author's imagination or are used fictitiously.

ISBN: 978-0-595-40427-8 (pbk)
ISBN: 978-0-595-84803-4 (ebk)

Printed in the United States of America

Prologue

The bright lights and the long shrill blast of a car horn startled Jacob Stoltzfus and caused him to tighten his grip on the leather reins. The clatter of the buggy's steel-belted wheels and the steady rhythmic clop-clops of Blackie's shoes on the wet two-lane black macadam road were interrupted again, this time by a series of sharp staccato blasts.

"Where do they want me to go?" the bearded man, peering from beneath his broad brimmed black hat, wondered aloud. He searched for his tormentor through the side view mirror but was blinded by the reflected glare of the headlights. "Come on, come on," he urged, hoping for a break in the oncoming traffic, one that was long enough to allow the attacking vehicle, its horn still blaring, to pass. But the traffic coming from the opposite direction was continuous, cars, pickup trucks, those new sport vehicles, all spraying rainwater on the horse and the enclosed, square-boxed buggy. He reasoned that something, maybe a game, must have let out at the high school; otherwise the road would be fairly quiet at this hour.

Knowing that his horse and buggy were defenseless against a motor vehicle, the Amish man's concentration turned to finding a place where he could pull over, but the fields rolled right up to the edge of the road. On a dark rainy night like tonight, running the horse off the road was not an option. An unseen ditch could result in serious injury to his horse, not to mention the stability of the buggy and harm to himself. He could slow the standard bred to a walk, and edge into the field, but that would probably anger the menacing vehicle behind him even more.

"Go now," Jacob yelled aloud when he saw a break in the opposing traffic. A heavy jolt rocked the entire buggy, reverberating through the poles attached on each side of the horse, confusing Blackie, throwing him off his pace. "Gott in

Himmel! They chust hit me! Are they crazy?" Jacob snapped the reins and within moments, Blackie regained his normal stride.

A car, a red Mustang with three teenaged boys leering through the side window saluted him with raised beer cans. The car kept pace for a few moments before the driver hit the throttle and sped away.

A flush of relief swept through the Amish man's body until he noticed a heavy drag on the left rear wheel of his buggy. Blackie felt it too, causing him to break from his fast trot into an awkward gallop. Ahead, the reflected vehicular headlights on the otherwise dark, wet road revealed a driveway at the end of a field. The Amish man pulled on the right rein and steered the horse safely off the road. Blackie picked his way down an old cement driveway pitted with cracks and potholes and Jacob rode the bumping, rocking buggy until they pulled up beneath a portico that extended over the island of three abandoned gasoline pumps. Glad to be out of the rain, he sat for a moment, pulled the wire-rimmed eyeglasses from his face and wiped the lenses with a red checked handkerchief. When his pounding heartbeat had subsided to the point where he could think straight, he grabbed a battery-powered lantern from beneath the bench seat and pulled on the handle of the buggy's sliding door. He jumped out, eager to assess the damage. Blackie, shaken, nervously lurched forward. "Whoa," Jacob commanded as he wrapped the reins around the rusting gas pump and tied a half-knot to finish it off.

Circling the buggy, the small beam of light from the lantern revealed the problem. The wooden spokes and the steel rims of the left rear wheel appeared to be intact. But the top leaned out ten degrees to the left. The wheel's mounting to the axle was bent. Too much damage to continue.

Jacob Stoltzfus surveyed the area. A smile broke across his face when he suddenly realized where he was. This old gas station backed onto a field that was part of his father's farm. He would unhitch Blackie, walk the quarter-mile or so along the side road and up the lane to the barn where he would hitch Blackie back up to a new buggy and still be on time for his meeting at the Dutch Treat.

He was unsnapping the harness when a pair of bright headlights flashed across his face. A truck had entered the driveway and rolled to a stop twenty feet from the service overhang.

Shading his eyes from the glare of the headlights, Jacob picked up the lantern and walked toward the lip of the overhang. The truck was an ancient pickup with a squealing fan belt and a rough idle that rocked the engine from side to side. Inside, the driver flashed his high beams and held them for a few moments before returning them to low. The truck door opened and a man of medium height in a black raincoat stepped out.

The Amish man's mouth, open in welcome, was frozen when he saw that the intruder, silhouetted by the headlights, wore a red handkerchief over his nose and face. A shotgun was crooked over his left arm. The masked man, rain bouncing from his orange Fram Filter cap, moved closer, then stopped six feet away.

"I want the money," he demanded in a low growling voice that was intended to be a disguise. He raised the shotgun toward the Amish man's face. "Do what I say! I'm not screwing around here."

Jacob, at first mesmerized by the intruder, slowly turned, reached through the open buggy door and pulled out a blue-striped Nike gym bag. Using both hands, he carried it to the edge of the overhang.

"The money in there?" the gunman asked.

Jacob nodded, yes.

"Take three steps toward me and set it down."

Stepping into the rain, Jacob did as he was told, dropping it into a puddle of water.

"Now step back."

Jacob took three steps back.

Lowering the gun in his right arm, the attacker reached down for the bag's handles with his left. The handles were wet, and the weight of the bag surprised him. When the loosely tied handkerchief began to fall from his face there was not enough time to push it back.

The sag in Jacob's bearded jaw betrayed him.

Knowing he had been recognized, the gunman dropped the gym bag at his feet and raised the shotgun with both hands, aiming at the Amish man's chest. Jacob trembled and begged in a heavily German-accented voice, "take the money. It's all right. I won't tell nobody. You can have it. I can even get more."

The gunman shook his head. His voice quivered, no longer attempting to disguise it. "I wish this hadn't happened. Shit!" He spit in frustration. "I really wish it hadn't." Their eyes met through a veil of water falling from the Amish man's broad-brimmed hat. "But I can't let you go now. Dammit, I can't."

The Amish man's mouth opened in protest as the white blast of buckshot from the left barrel smashed into his stomach. The pellets knocked him back but not down. The second blast, square in the chest, sent his hat flying and his body sagged to the ground.

Blackie shrieked, reared his front legs, and bucked and kicked against the brace of the buggy behind him.

The gunman threw the shotgun to the ground and quickly snatched up the gym bag. His head whipped in the direction of the boarded up window of the gas station office.

"Who's there?" He yelled. His eyes searched for a repeat of the tiny red glow he was sure had been there. He bent down to retrieve the shotgun only to realize that both barrels were spent. He asked again. "Who's there?"

Still no response. A shudder of fear shook his body. He kicked the shotgun away, stepped back to the truck and jumped behind the wheel. The gears ground into reverse and the engine strained as the truck rolled back toward the highway.

The horse's hooves clattered on the cement and the buggy rocked back and forth for another twenty seconds.

Then, except for the splatter of the steady rain that fell in roped curtains over the sides of the tin roof, everything was silent.

Chapter 1

John Lapp stood on the back steps to his kitchen, sheltered from the light rain by the gabled roof above. Through the illumination from a 100 watt floodlight mounted to the white stucco plaster, he stared at the brown lawn and depleted vegetable garden that lay beyond. A single hooded sparrow, plump from a summer of seeds and berries, hopped, scratched and bobbed among the twisted tomato vines for bits it may have overlooked before. A few cabbages, a row of carrots and a dozen stalks of celery remained to be harvested before the first frost of the year. His crops had been unusually abundant this year, due primarily to the good soil which he faithfully amended with composted leaves, grass, table scraps and cow manure. The soaking rains had come on order. Over the winter months, he would miss the feel of the rich, loose black soil in his hands. Lapp, a farmer by birth, had been reduced to a backyard plot of five-hundred square feet.

In mid-October, daylight is slow to make an appearance through the low clouds and steady rain. He took a final sip from the coffee cup he held in his right hand and blew off a trace of grounds from his bottom lip before stepping back into the house, first pulling the aluminum and glass storm door, then pushing the wooden door with three square windows in the upper half, closed behind him. He switched off the floodlight.

At the kitchen table, he cleared the remains of his breakfast. The white plastic bottles of vitamin pills, ranging from A to E, that his wife, Betsy, had always arranged on the placemat next to his spoon, were left in place. He rinsed the traces of granola and bluish 1% milk from his cereal bowl, and placed the empty juice glass and coffee cup, on the dishwasher rack. He stowed the half-gallon plastic milk carton and cardboard carton of TreeSweet orange juice into the nearly empty refrigerator. Even though Betsy had moved out three weeks ago after determining that their marriage should no longer exist, he was still eating her healthy breakfasts. The hearty slabs of fried scrapple, fried eggs, and white toast soaked with butter, jelly or apple butter to go with his orange juice and coffee he had promised to reintroduce to his breakfast table had not yet materialized. Too much time and trouble.

The *Today Show* beamed from the 12-inch black and white TV set on the corner of the kitchen countertop. Katie Couric finished an interview with a rock music star he had never heard of, and a commercial for a local savings bank came on. Lapp tucked the plaid shirt into his green chinos, pulled on his ankle-high brown waterproof boots, and turned his attention to the local weather report. The weatherman, an aging icon with a fifties-style crew cut and a jovial voice pattern, reported that the current light rain would continue throughout the day and possibly turn to ice by tonight. To John Lapp, an eight-year veteran of the Pennsylvania State Police, the report meant that he was in for a long day filled with, responding to, investigating and reporting traffic accidents, most of which, with better driving habits, should never have happened. It would be a day of excuses from drivers who always found it easier to blame something or someone else for their mishaps, rather than exercise proper precaution and practice common driving sense.

The ringing telephone jarred his thoughts. He approached the telephone on the hallway table half-hoping that it was it Betsy saying she had made a mistake and was coming home. More likely, if it was her, she would be asking if he had found a place of his own so she could, per their agreement, move back into the house.

"Hello?"

"Lapp? Trooper John Lapp?"

The male voice was not familiar. He cleared the early morning frog from his throat before responding, "this is Lapp."

"This is Lieutenant Warren Moyer. Criminal Investigation. You on duty today?"

Lapp's pulse quickened as he tuned in on a muddle of distant voices in the background indicating the call was from the field. "Yes, sir. I will be. I was just leaving for the barracks to dress out." Why was a criminal investigator calling?

"I'm glad I caught you. Listen, maybe you can help us. We've got an unusual homicide on our hands."

Lapp remembered Moyer from his Academy training class lecture on basic criminal investigation work, and could picture his square, deeply lined, forty-ish face on the other end of the line. "A homicide? That's a little out of my line, isn't it, sir?"

"Normally, yeah. Listen, I'm over at what used to be Muller's Sonoco station. You know where that is? Over on the Old Philadelphia Pike? Route 340?"

"I know where you mean."

"The sooner you can get over here the better. I've already cleared it with your sergeant."

"Who's the victim?" Lapp asked.

"We're hoping you can help us out with that. The dead man's Amish. No ID. About your age. Late twenties, early thirties. Hard to tell with the full beard. Got himself blown away by a shotgun. Before we try to figure out whodunit, we'll need to find a way to identify him, and notify next of kin. Since you used to be Amish, and speak the language, we figured you could help us out."

"Most Amish speak English as good as you and I do." Then, Lapp added, hastily, "Don't get me wrong. I'm happy to help."

"They may speak English, but in my limited experience, they clam up around uniforms and badges. You might get more out of them if you talk Pennsylvania Dutch."

"Maybe," Lapp said. Then again, maybe not.

"How long will it take you to get over here?"

"Not long. Ten-fifteen minutes. It's prime leafing season, but the tourists usually aren't out this early."

"Good. I'll see you then. Have we ever met?"

"Not formally. I went through your class at the Academy."

"Then you're already halfway to being an expert homicide detective." Moyer chuckled.

"Yes, sir. I'm on my way." Lapp hung up the receiver. Drawn by the sound of the NBC chimes, he returned to the kitchen to see a News Bulletin interruption of the *Today Show.* A young Asian female reporter, flooded by a portable light, stood beneath a black umbrella in front of a yellow crime tape. As she spoke, the camera roamed the crime scene, panned across four patrol units and two ambulances with lights flashing, past the gas pumps to a horse and buggy and ended with three rain-coated men standing watch over a blanket-covered body. "No one from the State Police has been available for comment, but the horse and buggy seem to indicate that the victim is Amish."

Lapp hit the "off" button on the remote, lowered the thermostat to 50 degrees, shrugged on a hooded jacket, hit the kitchen light switch and pushed the button that rolled up the garage door. The five-year-old Ford Ranger roared to life. Backing down the driveway and turning down the street, a surge of adrenalin rushed through his veins. His pending divorce from Betsy was replaced in his brain by the unsettling question: what was he getting into?

Chapter 2

Nearing the crime scene, John Lapp's senses were heightened by the anticipation and dread of looking at the tortured face and body of a man with a beard, identified only as, "Amish, someone about your age." He had used his limited training in attending to and comforting injured drivers and passengers, including children, prior to the arrival of paramedics, but had never faced a fatality.

Peering through the light drizzle being efficiently swept away by newly replaced windshield wipers, he saw three satellite dishes cranked high above their TV remote vans. Three station wagons bearing the painted logos, call letters and frequencies of their radio and television station owners were joined by spectator cars, vans, pickup trucks with camper shells and SUV's, forming a virtual used vehicle lot along the roadside entrance to the gas station.

Since he was driving his own truck instead of a marked cruiser, he was forced to park on the first off-road shoulder space available, about one-hundred yards away, behind an old, green, Dodge pickup.

He pulled the hood over his head, and hurried past the lineup of two dozen curious gawkers who stood behind the yellow security tape gossiping and speculating over what happened here last night. Lapp stopped next to two middle-aged, overweight women in workout sweats sheltered by a black umbrella, and surveyed the scene. The black horse tied to the gas pumps was still harnessed to the buggy. A few feet away from the state-mandated fluorescent yellow safety triangle on the back of the buggy, lay the body, protected from the rain by a blue tarp. A patrol car, colored lights still flashing from the rooftop, was parked a dozen feet away. A mixed bag of a half-dozen rain-coated investigators milled around the scene speaking with lowered voices words not yet ready for press or public consumption.

Lapp stepped up to a young Sheriff's department officer and flashed the ID pinned to his wallet. "John Lapp. I'm looking for Lieutenant Moyer."

"That's him over there. The heavyset man in the black raincoat," the officer said while lifting the tape so that Lapp had only to bend down slightly to enter.

Moyer was issuing orders to two other plain clothed detectives, one short, one tall, both covered from head to foot in black-hooded rain gear. "We'll check every house and farm within a half-mile to see if anybody saw or heard anything. Also, we're only, what, twenty-five feet from the highway? Somebody must have passed by while the crime was in progress and saw something. I'll make a pitch to the media for witnesses."

The two men nodded their understanding and put their heads together to devise a plan. Moyer saw Lapp and yelled, "watch out for those tire tracks and buggy ruts. Lapp?" Moyer stepped away to greet him. He smiled through the drips of rain that fell from the bill of his fedora hat.

Lapp's face was flushed with embarrassment. "Yes. I'm sorry. I should have been more careful."

"Ah, hell, probably nothing there because of the rain. I'm a little touchy. Being called out of a deep sleep will do it to me every time. You made good time. Thanks for coming." Moyer extended his right hand and stared at Lapp's clean-shaven face.

Since they last crossed paths in the hallways of the barracks, Moyer had added more weight to his bull-shouldered upper torso. The jaw of his round reddish face was a prairie of grey bristles. "So you used to be Amish?"

"Yes, sir. Fifteen years ago."

With a chuckle in his voice, Moyer asked, "gave up the bushy beard and plain clothes and decided to defend and enforce the law."

"Something like that."

"Well, I'd like to hear how all this came about, but I guess we'd better take care of business first. You still stay in touch with your relatives? Or is that not allowed."

"It's allowed, but no, I haven't."

"I heard about shunning and was just wondering."

"I wasn't shunned."

"Good. So the Amish will talk to you?"

"If they don't, it will be because of who I am now and not who I was then."

"Good. I'm glad we got that straight."

A tall Trooper stepped next to them. "John?" The freckled-face young man, folded his arms across his chest against the cold, and acknowledged Lapp with a tired smile. They had gone through the Academy together and remained passing friends.

"Whitey?"

"Lapham answered the call. He's been here since 11:00 last night," Moyer said. "It was Lapham, here, who heard me pissing and moaning about an Amish victim. That's when he told me about you. Excuse me for a sec." Moyer stepped a dozen feet away to slap the back of a tall man in a blue jacket and a baseball cap with a State Police insignia on it.

"I don't know whether to thank you or not for getting me into this," Lapp said with a smile.

Whitey responded, "I'm glad to be relieved. I'll tell you, man, it was spooky out here. I kept the engine running and the headlights shining on my unit so it wouldn't be pitch black. And, all night long that damn horse kept banging and jerking on his lead looking back at the body and then at me with eyes that said, come on, man, let's get the hell out of here."

Lapp smiled. "You should have talked to him, petted him, made a new friend."

"I did that. He tried to bite me. Anyway, I'm out of here." Whitey extended his right hand. "I covered the body. He's pretty tore up."

Lapp nodded his thanks. His attention was drawn to two men in yellow slickers who were busily taking a series of measurements from the buggy to the tarp-covered body.

"You guys about done?" Moyer asked. He stepped next to Lapp and pointed to the black hat lying brim down next to the body. "You think there might be an owner ID inside?"

Lapp shook his head. "I doubt it. Amish don't write their names on their belongings. Is that the murder weapon?" Lapp asked, nodding at the shotgun lying in a puddle on the broken cement.

"A 12-gauge, double-barrel," Moyer confirmed.

Lapp shook his head in disbelief. "The killer just left it there?"

"Weird, huh? Either he wants to be found, or is convinced we can't trace it." Moyer paused. "You ready to look?"

Lapp's stomach tightened with apprehension. His dry throat allowed the words to pass through. "There's about 18,000 Amish in Lancaster County and maybe a thousand or two my age. But, I guess it's worth a try."

"Watch out," Moyer warned, pointing to the pair of wire-rimmed glasses, the lenses still intact, lying in a diluted puddle of blood next to the covered body.

"Over here," Moyer said, crouching on his haunches and pulling back the corner of the tarp to so that Lapp could see the victim's head.

Lapp rocked on his heels and gasped audibly when he saw the bearded face, the blue eyes still wide open. Fighting to maintain his balance, he crouched lower, his eyes focused on the victim's forehead. Lapp's face turned up to Moyer. "I do know him." He cleared his throat. "His name is Jacob Stoltzfus."

"You can make positive identification?"

'My God," Lapp's voice quivered. "That scar above his right eyebrow? I was there on the school playground when he got it. Hit by a baseball bat."

"Baseball bat?"

"Danny Smoker did it. It was an accident." Lapp's throat choked back a cry. "It's him. Jacob Stoltzfus. I think he still lives over by Leacock Road in Paradise" He gasped a deep breath. "I know his wife, Sallie. I know the whole family."

Moyer nodded, and pulled the tarp back so that Lapp could have a quick look at the coagulated blood, and the matted chest hair that poked through Jacob's shredded white shirt and black vest. He re-covered the entire body.

Lapp straightened from his crouch. Feeling a rush of vomit enter his throat, he turned away, swallowing it back. Moyer grabbed his left arm and shoulder to steady him. "You okay?"

Lapp reached beneath his canvas hood and swiped the sweat from his forehead with the back of his hand.

A short, stocky woman wearing a baseball cap with the letters SHERIFF above the bill, pointed a 35mm camera at Jacob's body and clicked away from different angles. Lapp winced with each camera flash. When she moved in for a close up of Jacob's face, he said in defense, "they don't want their picture taken."

The camera lady gave him a look, snapped two quick shots, shrugged and moved away.

Lapp felt silly defending a dead man's face.

Moyer patted Lapp on the back. "Sorry. It's required procedure."

A tall man in blue coveralls with the block letters CORONER across the back and ALBRECHT sewn in script over his heart stepped next to them and asked, "you guys done?"

"You check with the crime scene guys?" Moyer asked.

"They're done," Albrecht confirmed.

"Then he's all yours," Moyer said, as Albrecht and a shorter man in identical coveralls moved in to load the victim onto a gurney. Moyer turned to Lapp.

"Feeling better? Take some time? Tell you what. Why don't you look around a little? We've been over everything pretty well, shot all the pictures, but you might see something we missed."

Lapp nodded his appreciation. "What about footprints?" he asked. "Will I contaminate the area?"

"We found a few boot prints, but everything else is washed away by now."

Lapp shook his head. "I can't understand how this happened. What was Jacob doing here? Do we know anything at all?"

"Not much. The body was discovered about 11:00 last night by some teenagers driving by. 911 answered the call. They woke me up about midnight," Moyer said.

Lapp's eyes were drawn to the TV cameramen who swarmed like hornets around the gurney as it was shoved into the back of an ambulance.

Moyer continued, "there wasn't much I could do in the middle of the night. I called the coroner who established time and cause of death. I left Lapham here and went home for a few hours sleep.

"Those teenagers that found him. What did they say?"

"Not much so far. I'm bringing them in later this morning for questioning."

Lapp focused on the black horse and buggy. "Has anybody given that horse anything to eat or drink?"

"Good question. Probably not."

"There's a feed store just down the road, but they're probably not open yet. I could at least get him some water."

"I'll have someone take care of it. I got a thermos in the car. You ready for some coffee?"

"No, thanks." The idea of bitter coffee in his sour stomach was repulsive.

"I think I'll grab some. I could use a cigarette about now, too."

Lapp walked past the buggy and stopped beside the sleek black gelding that stood seventeen hands high and weighed over a thousand pounds. The shock and anxiety of Jacob's body had settled in and his heartbeat and blood pressure had returned to a normal rate. Standing eye to eye, he asked, "is that you, Blackie?" Saliva dripped from the horse's mouth as he ground his mouth around the bit. "Last time I saw you, you were a feisty three-year old training to be a buggy horse. You're thirsty, I bet. All this rain and none to drink. They're supposed to be getting you some water." The horse shook his head from side to side. Lapp stroked the white blaze on the horse's forehead. "Do you remember me? It was a long time ago." Blackie's ears flicked forward, indicating he was willing to listen. Lapp admired the strong hindquarters, heavier and stronger than a thoroughbred, with a better temperament, too. Jacob had always been a good judge of horseflesh.

He side-stepped a stream of urine draining into the rain and looked at the large pile of horse turds in the canvas catch back behind Blackie's tail. He pushed the windowed sliding door of the buggy so that it was fully open before climbing inside. The front and back bench seats were covered with a maroon crushed velvet. The front seat had a heating pad with a cord that he followed with his hand to a 12-volt battery that provided power for the exterior lights. Fancier than what he remembered. He smiled over Jacob and Sallie riding in style and wondering if Jacob had received approval from the church elders to use the fancy pad. When you're Amish, you should not get too comfortable.

Lapp lifted the maroon pile carpeting and examined the fiber-glassed bottom shell.

In his day buggies were all wood. The top of this one was covered with a sheeted black vinyl. An outfit like this could cost between two and three thousand dollars.

He walked around the back of the buggy to the left side where he grabbed a spoke in the left wheel and pulled to straighten it out. It was bent enough to reveal the ball bearings in the axle. The wobble in the wheel would have made it impossible to continue. Which, he concluded, was why Jacob had left the road and sought refuge here at the gas station.

He examined the rear of the buggy and was tempted to use his pocketknife to dig out one of the twenty or so shotgun pellets that were embedded there but that would be tampering.

"What do you think?"

Lapp did not turn to acknowledge Moyer. "The left rear wheel is all cock-eyed. It had to be hit pretty hard to be in that shape."

"You think we're talking road rage?" Moyer studied Lapp's face, curious and concerned over his mental condition.

"There's probably a car somewhere with a steel wheel scrape on the edge of its bumper."

Moyer nodded in agreement.

"The buggy was rammed from behind as well. There's a dent just below the safety triangle," Lapp observed.

"We better notify the next of kin. Ask a few questions. Since you know where they live, you navigate and I'll drive."

"What about the horse and buggy? Where are you taking them?"

"The buggy's going back to the barracks."

"What about the horse?"

"We'll send someone to the closest Amish farm and ask them to pick him up."

"Too bad that wheel's so bent," Lapp said pensively. "Otherwise I'd drive them home"

"You still know how?"

Lapp smiled. "I'm sure it would come back to me."

"We'll take my car. It's over there," Moyer said, pointing to a dark blue Pontiac Trans Am parked just outside the yellow tape.

'If you don't mind, I think I'll take my truck. After we notify the widow, I should probably drive her over to his parent's farm."

"Maybe so. Tell you what. I'll follow you," Moyer said. Then he added, "shit! We got to walk the press gauntlet to get out of here. Just keep walking and ignore them."

They did just that. One reporter, followed by a cameraman with a glaring spotlight mounted on top, gave chase, focusing first on Moyer who walked past, then on Lapp. A woman's voice yelled, "sir? Sir? Is there anything you can tell us?"

Lapp was on the street now, walking fast past the thinning line of spectators.

Climbing into his truck, Lapp pulled the hood from his head and sat for a moment. He was sweating profusely and his stomach turned in nervous apprehension over being thrust back into the lives of people he had, years ago, left behind. Particularly Sallie Stoltzfus. Sallie Yoder, then, back when he was nineteen and she was seventeen. At a crossroad in his life, he faced a life-changing dilemma: to pursue her within the strict teachings of the Amish church, or, give her up and make a new life in an uncertain world filled with endless possibilities.

Chapter 3

Responding to the streaks of sun that broke through the black clouds, Lapp twisted the wiper controls to intermittent. Moyer, driving the Blue Trans Am, followed closely behind. There wasn't much chance of losing him on the sparsely traveled, two lane, Leacock Road. The overhead lines on utility poles that followed the undulating ribbons of macadam rarely branched off to the distant farm houses and barns. This part of Lancaster County was pure Amish farm country. With winter coming on, the limestone soil in the vast empty fields had yielded bounties of wheat, corn, alfalfa, oats, barley and tobacco. The roadside produce stands sold grapes, apples and apple cider, squash and pumpkins.

In less than 15 minutes from the scene of the crime, the two vehicle caravan passed the unpainted wooden mailbox and turned into the rutted two-hundred yard lane that led up to Jacob Stoltzfus' house and barn.

The last time Lapp had been up this lane he was riding on the bench of his open-air spring buggy holding the reins and steadying the pace of his favorite horse, Bill. On that warm Saturday morning in September of 1984, Sallie Yoder, seventeen, radiant and alive with excitement, sat by his side. They had gone for an hour's ride prior to church services in the Stoltzfus barn. Holding hands, she spoke with great excitement and emotion about her upcoming baptism. She hugged his arm and urged him to begin his instructions so they would both be church members. Because he loved her, and wanted desperately to continue his courtship of her, he pretended to share her enthusiasm.

Now he would see Sallie again, not as a suitor but as a Pennsylvania State Trooper.

To the left of the narrow lane, the stubbled remains of corn stalks poked out of ten acres of rich soil darkened by three days of steady rain. On the right, in a pasture guarded by a split rail fence, Lapp counted twelve Holstein dairy cows, and, to his surprise, two huge wooly brown, humpbacked creatures that brought a smile to his face. Among the cows, completely integrated, stood two large buffalo, staring at the two vehicles with as much curiosity as Lapp did at them. Had Jacob bought them as a way to subtly torment the more strict old order Amish? Or, were they one of Jacob's dreams and schemes, perhaps seeking a new source of profit?

Halfway up the lane, the two vehicles encountered three small children walking toward them. Two boys and a girl. The boys that Lapp guessed were about ten and eight years old, wore black hats and sack coats, vests, and suspenders that held up cotton trousers above their black high-top shoes. The same outfit he had worn at that age, he thought, except for the black tennis shoes. He would have worn rubber galoshes in rainy weather like this. Each carried a pair of books tied by a black belt slung over their shoulders.

The little girl, about six, peered from beneath a wine-colored bonnet that covered her braided blond hair. Lapp recognized Sallie's full lips and round pink cheeks in the little girl's face. A hem of gray from her ankle-length dress showed from beneath her buttoned black coat. Her feet were covered with dark blue boots. Beautiful children, all three, as he would have expected from parents like Jacob and Sallie.

Standing aside, allowing the vehicles to pass, the older boy, with arms spread wide shielded the other two behind him. Had these children been taught, as he had at their age, to avoid the "English" or "non-Amish" from the outside world?

Lapp waved his hand as he passed. The children, their faces filled with curiosity, hesitated before returning his wave. They waved at Moyer, too, as he passed by. Through the truck's side mirror, Lapp saw the oldest boy take several protective steps back up the lane before being convinced by the other two they'd be late for school.

Three children. The Amish believed that children were a gift from God, so they did not practice birth control. He fully expected that one, perhaps two more younger children would be at home with their mother.

The tires from the two vehicles crackled and ground to a stop on the fine pea gravel parking area at the foot of a slowly grinding windmill. The white wood-sided, two story house, with its wide front porch and shingled roof faced to the west, away from the lane. Next to the south side of the house, a 10 x 10 foot bed of Fall flowers was in full bloom. More than any individual family could use, the yellow, orange, red and rust colored chrysanthemums were most likely being raised as a cash crop to be sold at local farm markets.

A paved walkway led through the flower beds to the door of a single-story addition to the house. Inside that door, Lapp knew, was the kitchen, the center of all activity in an Amish home and the place Sallie was most likely to be.

Stepping out of his truck, Lapp's heart beat faster. How much had she changed? Would she recognize him? What words would he use to tell her? How would she react?

Moyer stepped next to Lapp and waited for him to lead the way. Lapp was almost certain that if Sallie was in the house she would have seen and heard them coming up the lane and would now be standing inside the door, her eyes wondering the who and why of these intruders.

"You want me to tell her?" Moyer asked.

He was tempted to say, yes. "No. I'll do it."

Lapp cleared his throat twice so he could speak clearly. "Sallie!" He rapped on the door. He called and knocked again. When there was no response, he turned the door knob, peeked inside, but hesitated to intrude any further. "She's not here. She's probably down at the barn or one of the sheds."

They stepped away from the door while Lapp surveyed the farm. A weedy two-wheeled lane led past the buggy shed, the calf pens, the chicken coop, the pig pens and the milk house, all in need of a coat of white paint. The large red barn, banked into the hill, sat beneath a silver-topped silo. Lapp breathed deeply and relished the pungent smells of wet grass and bare dirt.

"You ever done this before?" Moyer asked, striding next to Lapp.

"You mean notify next of kin?"

"Yeah."

"Once. I was patrolling on graveyard and a teen-aged girl was crushed in a car wrapped around a telephone pole. Two o'clock in the morning, I knocked on the family's door. The mother answered, half asleep. When she saw my uniform, she began shrieking, and collapsed into my arms."

"I just wanted you to be prepared."

Lapp nodded. The Amish were not inclined toward hysterical outbursts, but he steeled himself for the worst.

Lapp decided that the pig sty or the chicken house would be the most likely places to find her at this time of day. They dodged water puddles and Lapp slapped at a mosquito buzzing in his ear. He called, "Sallie?"

"Ja?" A female voice answered his call.

They moved in the direction of the voice. Two Rhode Island Red chickens, flapping their wings, scurried ahead of Sallie as she stooped through the door of the four by eight-foot whitewashed chicken house. Shading her eyes from the sun with her left hand, she carried a wire basket of brown and white eggs in her right.

He cleared his throat again. "Sallie? It's Johnny Lapp." He took several steps toward her and saw in an instant that Sallie had thrived. She was still beautiful. Her oval face, slim nose, reddish cheeks and full lips were unchanged. The front of her brunette hair was parted in the middle. The back of her head was covered by a white net bonnet. Her greenish-blue dress, with its white apron, ended just below her knees. Light brown cotton stockings covered her legs down into the blue Keds on her feet.

A wide smile broke across her face. "Johnny Lapp? Is it you? I guess I didn't hear you. I was hunting eggs." Her smile faded when she saw he was not alone.

"It's me." Lapp took three steps closer while Moyer stood back.

"I almost didn't know you. I wasn't expecting to see you no how. It's been so many years now," Sally said, smiling nervously. "Somebody told me once you were a state policeman," she added, her eyes turning to Moyer.

"I am. I'm just not in uniform. It's been a long time, Sallie. About fifteen years now," Lapp replied. "Sallie, this is Warren Moyer. He's a criminal investigator with the State Police."

Moyer tipped his fedora hat and nodded a silent hello. Sallie nodded back.

Lapp took a deep breath. "We're here because we have some bad news. It's about Jake."

"Is he in any trouble?" She asked almost hopefully.

"I'm afraid it's more than that, Sallie. Jake was killed last night."

She gasped audibly. Her eyes snapped shut and her head dropped. The eggs in the basket jiggled beneath her trembling hand.

Lapp desperately wanted to wrap his arms around her. Instead, he reached for and held the handle on the basket of eggs.

Sallie understood the gesture and released the handles.

"I'm so sorry," Lapp whispered, gasping back an outburst of his own.

Although her lips didn't move, Lapp was certain she was praying. A minute later she raised her head. Her blue eyes were blurred, but no tears stained her cheeks.

"Where is Jake now?"

Moyer, feeling Lapp's distress, stepped forward and relieved him. "They've taken him to a place called the morgue. The police need to examine him."

"What happened? Johnny? I don't know what this … why this …"

"He was shot. It happened on the Philadelphia Pike just past 772. At the old Sonoco station that's closed.

"Why? Why was he over there?" She wondered aloud.

Lapp responded, "we don't know why. We were hoping you could help us with that. We want to find out who did this to Jake."

"We're sorry to bring you this bad news, Mrs. Stoltzfus," Moyer began, "but it's important that we know where he was last night. Anything that might help us in our investigation."

"Jake never came home," Sally said softly, using the corner of her apron to blot away the tears from the corners of her eyes. She directed her words to Lapp, knowing he would understand. "But I wasn't so worried. Sometimes he stayed at his parents house if he was over that way. It rained pretty hard, too."

Lapp became aware of the squealing and snorting coming from the pig sty at about the same time Sallie did. It was their feeding time and they were not shy about announcing it. "Can I feed the pigs first?" Sallie asked. "Then we can go up to the house."

"Can I help?" Lapp offered.

Sallie smiled her thanks, and led the way. Sharp slivers of sun sliced through the clouds and reflected on the puddles of water on the ground. A young tabby cat suddenly appeared and fell in step with Sallie. She glanced down as it tried to rub against her moving ankles, but did not acknowledge it.

"Maam," do you know where your husband was last night?" Moyer asked, his impatience showing.

Sallie did not respond. A glance from Lapp to Moyer told him it would be better to wait.

At the sty, the four fattened mud-slathered hogs—three reddish Durocs and a huge black and white Poland China sow—snuffled, grunted and bumped each other like Sumo wrestlers in anticipation of the feeding. Sallie, crossed her arms over her breasts as if to hold back an emotional outburst, and watched Lapp dump several large scoops of mash and oats into the long narrow pig trough. He filled a galvanized pail with water drawn from a wooden barrel and splashed it into the feed. .

Eat up, Lapp thought, examining the hogs. Your days are numbered. Six months old, and around 200 pounds, they were ready for butchering season, which was only a month or two away.

As Lapp finished the chore, Moyer's shuffling feet were tempered by Sallie's announcement. "We can go up now," she said, silently leading the way to the house.

They wiped their wet shoes on the burlap bags by the kitchen door and stepped onto the grey linoleum floor. The lingering scents of fried bacon and scrapple were still evident, but the table and counter were clean and clear of pots, pans and breakfast dishes.

Lapp extended the basket of eggs to Sallie. As she took them, their eyes met and held briefly. Sallie motioned for the men to sit across from her on a long wooden bench that served as seating for the rectangular kitchen table.

Moyer pulled the fedora from his head, revealing thin strands of brown hair combed straight back and began to unbutton his raincoat when he changed his mind. The room was cold. About 60 degrees. The Amish dressed warmly and did not waste fuel.

Lapp surveyed the modern, gas powered refrigerator and range, the stainless steel sink surrounded by walnut stained cabinets, past the open door to the parlor. His eyes settled on the wooden stairs that led to the second floor. There were no sounds or signs of other children in the house.

Sallie eased her body over the bench and sat opposite the two law officers.

Moyer began again. "To begin our investigation, it's important that we get as much information as possible about your husband's whereabouts last night."

Sallie, her face drawn, stared blankly at the two men.

"Where was he last night?" Moyer repeated patiently.

"He went off in his buggy. He never said where he was going."

"What time was that?"

"After supper. About 6:30 or 7:00, I think. He went out to the barn to the horses. I don't know when he left, exactly."

Moyer continued. "Did he say when he'd be home?"

"No. I never saw him after that."

"Did he do this often? Go out without saying anything?"

"Not so often. Two or three times a week, maybe."

Sallie caught Lapp's surprised reaction to her answer, then turned back to Moyer.

"Did he say where he went?"

"Sometimes he did. Sometimes he went to see his parents. Sometimes he said he had business to take care of."

"What kind of business?" Moyer asked.

"He never said much. If it was business, it was man's business. He didn't tell me."

"When he didn't come home last night, didn't that worry you?" Moyer's voice rose.

"It wondered me," she replied evenly.

"And did he do this often? Stay away overnight?"

"Not so often, no."

"How often? Once a week? Once a month?"

"Once a month, sometimes." Sallie walked to the windowsill and stared at the heavily blooming potted red geranium.

Moyer nodded for him to jump in.

"Sallie, back then, I knew Jake pretty good too. He was often up to something. What I mean is, he got excited about something and would talk about it day in and day out. Was there anything he talked about these last few days?"

Keeping her distance, she responded in a reluctant tone that was almost a sigh. "Horses. I guess he always talked about horses. He wanted more horses."

"Draft horses or buggy horses?"

"Buggy horses. Fast horses."

"Like Blackie?"

Sallie's voice rose. "Where is Blackie?"

Lapp answered. "Blackie's fine. The police were taking him to the closest farm. They'll bring him home."

Sallie nodded, satisfied with the answer.

Lapp picked up the line of questioning. "Do you know who Jake was talking to or where he was planning to get those horses?"

"He liked to go over to New Holland," Sallie said, brightening slightly.

"The horse auction over there," Lapp explained in an aside to Moyer.

"He wanted to raise horses and train them to sell."

"To other Amish?" Lapp asked.

"I don't know. He never said." Sallie walked back to the kitchen table. "When can I bring Jake home?"

Moyer answered. "As soon as the autopsy is finished. We'll let you know."

"The men will fetch him."

Moyer shrugged at Lapp. The questioning was over.

Lapp rose and edged around the long table until he was face to face with Sallie. He placed his right hand firmly on her shoulder. His voice was steadier now, his tone more professional. "I'm sorry to be the one to deliver the bad news. Jake was a good man. We'll find out who did this." He dug into his pants pocket and retrieved a wrinkled. business card. "Here's how you can get a hold of me. Will you do that?"

Sallie, avoiding his eyes, took the card and turned away.

Outside, leaning against the fender of his Trans Am, Moyer lit a cigarette. "If she knows what her husband was up to last night, she's not ready to talk about it. I didn't expect her to talk to me, but I hoped she might open up a little more with you. You got any ideas?"

"She's in shock. And she probably doesn't know much. An Amish woman doesn't question what a man does unless it affects the house or the children. If it's all right with you, I'll offer her a ride to Jacob's parents' farm and break the news to them."

"Good idea," Moyer said, squashing the cigarette butt into the gravel. "Maybe you can get her to open up a little more. When you're through, report back to me at the barracks. We'll go from there."

As Moyer drove down the lane, Lapp's attention was drawn to a shrieking red tailed hawk that circled the house. Its wings spread wide, the hawk soared and rode the thermals caused by the warm air rising from the harvested fields. The hawks from Hawk Mountain near Reading, 60 miles away, were frequent visitors during his childhood. As a boy, he watched them with curiosity and admiration. During his last days on the farm, they became his symbols of freedom.

Chapter 4

Sallie Stoltzfus sat tall in the passenger seat as State Trooper John Lapp steered his pickup down the lane and onto the two lane macadam road. They had not spoken since leaving the farm. The shoulder and lap seat belts were pulled across the black triangular cape that Lapp knew was cut and sewn with her own hands. A black bonnet covered her ears and half of her face making it easier for Lapp to sneak curious glances of her.

His love for Sallie had begun, he supposed, as soon as boys become aware of girls, at age ten or eleven. John Lapp was not alone in his admiration of Sallie Yoder. But, among the other boys, only Jacob Stoltzfus turned out to be a serious rival. During their school days, up to age fourteen, they competed for Sallie' attention with no clear winner. Sallie's closest friend, Mary King, put them in perspective by announcing that Sallie told her she liked the both of them, and considered Johnny Lapp the serious one and Jacob Stoltzfus the funny one.

Their competition reached a peak that summer, fifteen years ago, when Sallie was among the two dozen Amish boys and girls, between the ages of seventeen and twenty-one, who were candidates for church membership. Beginning in May, following the Spring Communion, and continuing for eight weeks, John Lapp and Jacob Stoltzfus were in the boy's instruction class, while Sallie Yoder, who would turn eighteen in October, was in the women's class.

During that same eight week period, both Lapp and Jacob vigorously courted Sallie, taking her for buggy rides, going to barn dances and "singings" vying for her time and attention at every turn. Then, just when he felt he was winning, John Lapp was put at a distinct disadvantage by the strictness of his father, who caught him in the hayloft listening to the radio and singing "night fever, night fever," along with the popular Bee Gee's song. Moses Lapp grabbed the small battery-powered radio from his son's hand, slammed it to the planked floor and crushed it with his boot. He raised his arm to strike the boy but backed off when Johnny defended himself with clenched fists raised in defiance.

It was the beginning of the end for young John Lapp. Moses tightened the reins on his son, forcing him to work night and day and restricting his movements. Lapp convinced his sister, Sarah, to get the word to Sallie that he was being kept prisoner on the farm. When Sallie arrived in a buggy and tried to visit him, his father turned her away. Worst of all, Abe Troyer, a hired hand, seemed happy to compound his misery by reporting sightings of the fast horse and buggy that carried Jacob and Sallie up and down the lane of the Yoder farm at all hours of the day and night.

The final blow came on a Sunday evening when he received a surprise visit from Jacob. Wearing his calf-high rubber boots, Lapp was washing down the milking stalls in the cow barn when he turned to see the beaming face of his friend.

"How did you get here?" Lapp asked.

"How do you think, dumbkupf. I cut across the fields. I heard you were penned up here."

"You knew I was."

"I had to come tell you. I asked Sallie to marry me," Jacob said excitedly. "Last night sitting in the buggy. I kissed her at least six times, good strong kisses. And then I asked her."

Lapp's heart sank. He asked warily, "what did she say?"

Jacob bounced on his muddy boots with excitement. "She said she would think about it after the baptism." Jacob responded to Lapp's lack of enthusiasm by adding, "don't you see? One of us is going to get her. You never said much, but I always knew you stayed Amish because of Sallie. Now you can do what you want."

"You took advantage of me being penned up," Lapp accused, angrily.

"I thought you'd be happy. You know you don't wanna stay. Now you don't have to."

"I haven't decided anything yet. Don't think you have her, neither. Not as long as I'm still around, you don't."

Jacob shrugged. "Be that way, then. You going to take the vows?"

"I'm still in bible class, ain't I?"

"Maybe you are, but you don't wanna be."

Lapp turned the patrol car up the narrow lane to Eli Stoltzfus' farm. Jacob had been killed less than a quarter mile away.

Jacob's younger brother, Daniel, plodding behind a team of four mules disking a field of corn stalks, paid no attention to the truck that ploughed through drifts of leaves from the huge bare-limbed walnut tree and came to a stop next to the hitching rail.

Since Lapp had last been here, a single-story "grossdawdy haus" had been added to the two-story main building. The entire complex was a white-sided affair with a new roof of bluish-green asbestos shingles.

Sallie unsnapped her seat belt and was out of the truck before the engine was turned off. At the kitchen door, Jacob's mother, a large-boned woman, who Lapp remembered for her teasing smiles and words, threw her hand across her mouth to silence the anguish of Sallie's words. A half-minute later, Lydia Stoltzfus pointed Sallie toward the barn. Then, lifting her skirts, Lydia ran toward the corn field to alert Daniel.

Lapp remained in the truck until a wave of Sallie's arm invited him to join her.

"Lydia said she thinks Eli's at the horse stalls." Sallie set a pace of quick determination. Lapp picked up his pace and fell in step with her. They passed the tobacco barn with the drying stalks visible through the alternate boards propped open for air circulation on the way to the faded white gabled barn with twin silos. Lapp pulled the iron ring to open the side door and were greeted by the pungent smells of fresh alfalfa hay and manure. Through the dusty, dim light, Eli Stoltzfus scooped up a large flat shovel topped with straw and manure from an empty stall. He dumped the manure on top of a heaping wheelbarrow and was startled when he turned and saw Sallie with a strange man. Lapp remembered Eli as being a head taller than other Amish men. He was at least sixty, but still powerful looking in his black sackcloth work jacket that was stretched tight around his chest and shoulders. The broad brim of his battered straw hat shadowed his eyes. His face sported a snowy white beard that fell, like a large bib, to his chest, but, in the Amish custom of avoiding vanity, had no mustache attached to it. He propped the shovel against the stall frame and stepped toward them.

Sallie choked on her words. "Papa? This is Johnny Lapp. Do you remember him?"

Eli stared through his thick wire-framed glasses until his brow showed a hint of recognition. "He brought me over here just now." She fought to control the tremble in her voice. "He says that Jake got killed last night."

"Was sagst? My Jake? You say he got killed?" His growling voice challenged her statement. "Is it so? How could that be?"

She looked to Lapp to answer, but didn't wait for him to speak. "He never came home last night. And now he's been killed and nobody knows why." Sallie's voice was still tight, but did not crack.

"What do you have to do with it?" Eli said, glaring at Lapp. "Ain't you Moses' boy?"

"I am. I'm a Pennsylvania State Trooper now. I'm just not in uniform."

Eli's harsh eyes continued to challenge Lapp's presence there. "A State Trooper?"

"That's right. I'm sorry."

Eli's shoulders sagged as the news sank in. "If this is so, how did something like this happen?"

"We don't know yet. He was shot and killed last night. At the old Sonoco gas station, on the other side of your woods."

Eli shook his head, trying to comprehend what he had just heard. He turned his words toward Sallie. "What was he doing over there?"

"He went out after supper. He never tells me where he's going."

"He doesn't tell you? He just goes out? In all that rain? Did you ask him?"

"I gave up asking," Sallie shot back.

Lapp stopped the attack on Sallie. "Sallie thought he might have come over here last night."

"Over here?" Eli bellowed.

"Last night. Did Jake come over here last night?" Sally asked.

"We never saw him. We ain't seen him for awhile now." Eli added woefully, "we don't have much to say to each other no more."

Lapp caught the confusion on Sallie's face. "I just thought ..." her voice trailed off.

"Where is Jake now, then?" Eli asked.

Sallie looked to Lapp for an answer.

He responded. "They're doing an autopsy on him. An examination. It's the law. They have to do it. By tomorrow they can release him to you."

Eli removed his straw hat with his left hand as a gesture of respect for the dead, while he scratched the deep circular indentation in his hair with the black nails on the fingers of his right hand.

"Does the wife know?" He asked Sallie.

"I told her. She went to get Danny."

"Ich vorstei net," Eli said. He looked hard at Lapp as his memory reconstructed John Lapp of a decade ago. "You used to come here. You knew Jake."

"I was here many times."

Finally, when he concluded in his mind that this man who was Jacob's age, clean-shaven, with light brown hair in English clothes standing before him had never joined the church and therefore need not be shunned, he lowered his eyes and asked, plaintively, "are you sure it's so?"

Lapp nodded, sadly. "I'm sorry. In the next few days it will be the job of the police to ask you some questions that might help us determine where Jacob was last night and why someone might want to kill him. We don't know much of anything right now, but we're committed to bringing his killer to justice."

The old man put his hat back on and pondered, "justice? You do what your laws say you must do. But it will not bring Jacob back to his mother and to his wife and children. If God wants you to find who killed Jacob, he will do so. It is not for us to do. God decides. We live by God's will."

Chapter 5

Stepping outside, John Lapp and Sallie Stoltzfus were met by the alarmed faces of Jacob's mother, Lydia, and his brother, Daniel.

Sallie stepped into and was swallowed by Lydia's heaving breasts and ample arms.

Daniel, with sweat beading on his forehead, gasped to catch his breath. "Is it true about Jake? What happened to him?"

Lapp gave the wiry man of twenty-five a quick explanation of what they knew and what steps would be followed to get Jacob, Blackie and the buggy back to Jake's farm.

Lydia gently pushed Sallie back and asked, "how is Eli?"

Sallie said, "he's at the horse stalls."

Lydia disappeared into the barn. Daniel, angry and at a loss for words, followed behind.

The ride back to Sallie's farm was a replay of the ride to Eli Stoltzfus' farm. They rode in silence. No talk of the pain and grief that was on Sallie's face, and no words of consolation or comfort from John Lapp.

Lapp stopped his truck at the top of the lane. "Would you like go to your parents house? You might not want to be alone."

Sallie shook her head, no. "Alone sounds good right now. When will people know about Jake?"

"I would think in the next hour or so. The newspapers and TV cameras are probably waiting at the Police Barracks for whatever we can tell them."

"I was thinking about the children. I don't want them to hear about it at school. They probably won't," Sallie concluded, her head lowered toward her lap where her fingers twisted a crease in her apron.

"Do you want me take you to the schoolhouse?" Lapp asked.

"No. I'm all right."

"You sure?"

"I'm sure." She raised her head and their eyes met. "Thank you, Johnny."

For what, he wondered? For disappearing for fifteen years and then showing up to tell her husband was dead?

She sensed his silent thoughts and said, "for being the one and knowing how to tell us about Jake."

"I'm sorry."

Sallie nodded in agreement, pulled the handle on the truck door and jumped out.

When she disappeared through the kitchen door, Lapp turned his truck around and rumbled back down the lane feeling the warmth of knowing that Sallie's house would soon be filled with friends who would take over the arrangements for Jacob's funeral. Although the Amish did not own television sets, radio receivers or telephones, the word of Jacob's death would spread through their English and Mennonite friends and neighbors. In fields, kitchens, barns, blacksmith shops. sheds, roadside stands, cabinet shops, craft shops and other cottage industries, small units of men and women would be shaking their heads over Jacob Stoltzfus' death. And like Eli, most would not question the what or the why of it. They would agree it was a shame for his family and friends, but it was God's Will.

The Lancaster Barracks of the Pennsylvania State Police, a two-story yellow brick building consisting of two square wings with triangular roofs, a rectangular center, and an oval driveway in front, is situated on the corner of Highway 30, the old Lincoln Highway, and Oakview Street. With Department Headquarters in the state capitol of Harrisburg, local enforcement is divided among six area commands. Command VI covers the southeastern part of the state and consists of Troop J in Lancaster County, Troop K in Philadelphia, and Troop M in Bethlehem.

John Lapp parked his truck in the rear area designated for employee vehicles, and felt a stab of apprehension over how he would hold up his end in a criminal investigation.

He punched in the code to the back door and took the stairs to the locker room on the lower level. While twisting the combination on his lock, a strong grip squeezed his right bicep. Bill Buckner, the shift sergeant said, "don't bother changing, Moyer's waiting for you upstairs in the interview room."

"Lapp. Come on in," Warren Moyer said, seated across a small rectangular table from three teen-aged boys. Stripped down to a white shirt with sleeves rolled up above his elbows, and the brown tie pulled away from his neck, Moyer looked ten pounds lighter. "These are the boys who found the Amish man's body. We were just getting started. Why don't you sit in and hear what they have to say." He pointed to the padded desk chair. "You want coffee or anything?" he asked, pointing to the large Styrofoam cup in front of him and the Pepsi cans that sat on the table in front of each of the boys.

"No, thanks."

Moyer turned to the boys and said, "I'd like each of you to introduce yourselves to me and to Trooper Lapp. Start with your name, age, and what you do for a living. We'll start with you," he said nodding to the boy on the far left.

The stocky youth, a spectacle of short curly permed hair dyed the color of vanilla ice cream, a left ear that sported a line of small rings and a nose stud in the left nostril, turned slightly toward Lapp. "My name," he cleared his throat and continued, "is Randy Miller. I'm nineteen and I work part-time at the Turkey Hill store in Ronks."

All eyes turned to the boy in the middle.

The shaggy youth with stringy orange-colored hair that fell to the neck of his royal blue nylon 76er windbreaker spoke up. "I'm Tim Holtzman. I'm eighteen. I'm looking for work. There's not much around here," he added, forcing a smile. From the length of his torso, Tim looked to be the tallest of the three, close to six feet. Tim turned his head to the younger one on his left.

The baby-faced teenager with curly shoulder-length dirty brown hair, and a tiny blonde goatee that stuck out from his chin like fine pubic hair said, "and I'm Ryan Holtzman. We're brothers, me and him," he said nodding at Tim. "I'm sixteen and still in school."

"High school? Where do you go?" Moyer asked.

"Manheim Central High School. I'm a junior."

Lapp thought of the three as the all too common type of teenager that he dealt with for traffic violations. Smart mouthed, surly and unrepentant.

Moyer took a sip of his coffee and that acted as a signal for the boys to each take a few gulps from their Pepsi cans.

"Well, that's a good start," Moyer said with an edge of mockery to his tone. "Now who wants to do the honors and tell us how you happened to be out there and found the Amish man last night."

Randy Miller and Tim Holtzman shrugged and, with their eyes, elected Ryan Holtzman to be their spokesperson.

Ryan Holtzman, unzipped his dirty blue and white Dallas Cowboys padded jacket, leaned back in his chair and began cautiously. "We were driving on the old Philly Pike and we saw what looked like lantern lights coming from the old Sonoco gas station. So we said to Randy ... Randy was driving, let's go see what's up."

The expressions of confirmation from his two friends bolstered his confidence so he continued, spilling out the words. "We pulled up and saw the Amish buggy and the horse and then we saw the body laying there behind the buggy and we drove off and called 911. That's how it happened."

"Whoa. Not so fast. What time was that?" Moyer asked.

The three looked at each other and Ryan said, "around 10:30. Don't you think?"

The other two nodded and Randy mumbled, "yeah", and "it sounds about right."

"And it was just curiosity, that's all?"

"Well," Tim Holtzman said with a smirk. "Maybe it was a little more than that."

Lapp and Moyer caught the alarm that spread across the other boys faces.

"Sometimes we just check the place out." Tim smiled and pulled the hair away from his left ear so that he could scratch an itch by the dangling gold cross earring.

"And why is that?" Moyer asked.

"Lotsa times couples go there to park and make out. You know what I mean?"

Tim's smirk widened. "So we go see if we can catch them in the act. Hassle them a little."

"Hassle them?"

"Yeah, look in the windows, rock the car, stuff like that." Tim responded to the alarm on his brother's face by amending his story. "Understand, we didn't find nobody that night. Just the horse and buggy and the dead man."

"What did you do then? After you called 911?"

"We went home," Ryan said. "And then we saw it on TV the next morning."

"How did you happen to be driving on the old Philly Pike that night? Where were you going?"

Ryan started to answer, but Moyer stopped him and looked at Randy. "Why don't you tell us. You were driving. Right?"

Randy Miller cleared his throat and said in a croaky voice, "yes."

"Go ahead," Moyer urged.

"We were just cruising around. We were over at the bowling alley playing pinball machines and when we got tired of doing that, we just rode around for awhile before we decided to go home."

"Kind of a miserable night to be out driving around, wasn't it?"

"It wasn't so bad. There were a lot of people out."

"And why was that?"

"I think there was a basketball game over in Manheim that let out."

"How much beer did you have in the car?" Moyer asked.

"Beer?" Randy looked to the other boys for agreement. "We didn't have no beer."

"Drugs?"

"No drugs, neither."

"Just out cruising. Not looking for trouble or anything?"

"No, sir."

Moyer turned to Lapp. "You want to ask about the buggy?"

Lapp was ready. "How do you feel about the Amish?"

Ryan Holtzman shrugged. "What do you mean? I don't know. I don't feel nothing about the Amish."

"How about you?" Lapp asked Miller. "You were driving. How do you feel about their horses and buggies being out on the road?"

Miller shrugged. "I don't know. I don't feel nothing, neither."

"Do you think they hog the road?"

"I don't know. Yeah, sometimes. Sometimes it's hard to pass them."

"Does that make you mad?"

Miller's eyes shifted to the two brothers, asking for help.

"The reason I asked," Lapp continued, "is that the back wheel of the Amish man's buggy was bent. Like it was hit by a car bumper. The safety triangle on the back was bent too, like it had been rammed from behind. You got any idea how that might have happened?"

The three boys, shaking their freaky heads in unison, mumbled, "no."

"No idea, huh? None at all?"

"No," the three insisted.

Moyer leaned forward, anxious to get back into the fray.

He started with Randy Miller, the driver. "The car you were driving last night. Is it parked outside?"

"Yeah," Miller replied cautiously.

"And if we went down there and took a look at your front bumper do you think we'd find scrapes or traces of paint from the Amish man's reflector?"

"I don't think so." Randy Miller squirmed in his seat.

Moyer straightened up in his chair and turned up the intimidation skills. "Look, boys, boys. We're investigating a murder here. You were at the scene and that makes you prime suspects. I can place you under arrest and hold you for questioning for the next twelve hours. Tell us what happened out there last night. No more evasive bullshit. I want the whole story. Keep jacking us around and you're here until we get it. Tell us straight and you're out of here. Fair enough?"

Twisting deeper into their seats, the two older boys looked to sixteen year old Ryan Holtzman to do the talking.

"It was like he said," Ryan said softly, nodding toward Lapp. "The buggy was hogging the road and it kinda pissed us off, so we clipped him when we passed."

Lapp's face flushed with anger. "Clipped him enough to knock his wheel cockeyed?"

"I don't think we did that?" Ryan responded defensively.

Lapp countered. "I'd say you rammed him pretty good. And you don't think that caused any damage?" He glared at the three youths long enough to cause them to squirm.

Moyer, fearing Lapp was losing his cool, jumped in. "Whose idea was it clip him?"

The teens shrugged and again looked to Ryan Holtzman to answer. "I don't know. All of us, I guess. But we didn't run him off the road or nothing like that. I swear. I looked back and he was still following behind us."

"What time was that?"

"I don't know. 10 o'clock maybe."

"Where did you go from there?"

"We stopped off at the Turkey Hill store for some cigarettes and candy and talked with our friend who was working there and then came back down the road to go home."

"Which one?" Moyer asked.

"Huh?" Ryan asked, confused.

"Which Turkey Hill? There's Turkey Hills all over the place," Moyer demanded impatiently.

"Oh, yeah. The one on 340. Just past Smoketown. You know where it's at?"

"We know," Moyer said, then continued. "What's your friend's name?"

"Shawn Derr."

Lapp didn't wait for Moyer's approval before he asked, "you tell him you rammed an Amish buggy? You brag about it?"

"We mighta mentioned it," Ryan said with a guilty grin.

"Then what."

"When we left we wondered about the Amish man in his horse and buggy, so we were kind of looking for him. When we saw the lights on his buggy at the old gas station we pulled off to see. That's when we found him on the ground, blood all around and called you."

"I thought you told me you went there to harass neckers." Moyer asked.

"That too. We went back there for both." Ryan glared at the other two boys, signaling he was tired of being on the hot seat and giving all of the answers.

"Did you get out of the car?" Moyer asked.

"He did," Randy Miller said, nodding at Ryan.

"I just took a quick look. I felt like I was gonna puke," Ryan said, wrinkling his nose.

"He did puke," Randy said with disgust. "All over the floor of the front seat."

"Where did you go to call 911?" Moyer asked.

"The Turkey Hill."

"The same one?"

Randy nodded vigorously, yes.

"It scared the shit out of us," Tim Holtzman added.

"And that's it?" Moyer asked.

"That's all we know. Swear to God. I hope they catch the guy that done it," Ryan concluded.

Lapp and Moyer exchanged looks before Moyer said, "I want to thank you boys for reporting what you found and for coming in." Moyer pushed a yellow lined tablet and Scripto pen across the table at each of the boys. "Write down what you told me. Start with your names, addresses and phone numbers. After that, you're free to go."

Moyer rose from his chair and asked Miller. "What kind of car were you driving and where are you parked?"

Miller's eyes narrowed. He responded reluctantly, "in the driveway in front. A Red Mustang."

Moyer turned to Lapp. "I'll go grab some shots of their car and verify the damage. Hang in with these guys until they finish."

Lapp nodded. His earlier anger dissipated to amusement as the trio struggled to write their statements. Like unprepared students taking a test, their eyes shifted back and forth, attempting to cheat and copy from each other. Tim

Holtzman, the older brother, lifted his head and looked at Lapp. "How do you spell approximately?"

"Use the word about."

"Oh." Tim started to write but seemed puzzled over how to spell "about."

When they were finished, they pushed their tablets to Lapp, who scanned them quickly and said, "you're free to go."

Smiling with relief that their interview was over, the three boys scraped the linoleum floor with their chairs as they hurriedly rose and shuffled out of the interrogation room.

Moyer stood in the doorway and drained the last of his coffee from his cup. "That Mustang is a mess. Dents, rusted out fenders. You can see where they hit the buggy with the front bumper."

"You going to charge them?" Lapp asked.

"With what? Hit and run? Assault with a deadly weapon?"

Lapp shrugged. "For starters."

"I could, I suppose. What they did was wrong, but they didn't kill the poor man."

Moyer stepped to the table, grabbed the yellow tablet and scanned the information the teenagers had written down. "If those guys are any example, I'd say our education system is failing," he remarked after noting the spelling and sentence structure.

"I noticed." Lapp agreed.

"If it'll make you feel better, they're not off the hook. We'll run 'em through records. See what they come up with. We'll check out their Turkey Hill story. By the way, how did it go out there?"

Lapp's raised eyebrows said he didn't understand the question.

"With the widow. And the parents. You learn anything new?"

Lapp shook his head, no. "Not really. They don't seem to know anything."

"You believe that?"

"Not entirely."

"Good. Then keep at it. Somebody's got to break through. If not you, who?"

Chapter 6

John Lapp was directed to an empty desk and computer. In his report, he included as many details as he could recall of his meeting with Sallie and Eli, while being careful not to let his emotions interfere. Fifteen minutes later, he left a copy on Moyer's desk.

Feeling a bit uncomfortable over rubbing elbows with criminal investigators and being on the same floor as the barracks commander, he took the stairs down to the locker room.

Glad to be alone, Lapp pulled on his light grey long sleeved shirt with black epaulets on the shoulders and the elaborate insignia of Pennsylvania State Police Trooper on the upper sleeves. He cinched the black belt on his dark grey pants, and laced the black shoes. He tightened the black tie against his neck, grabbed the round black hat with black band from the top shelf of the locker and snapped shut the combination lock on the locker door. A quick once-over in a full-length mirror left him pleased with the result. Look sharp, be sharp.

Back in the interrogation room, Lapp was stirring powdered cream into the overcooked coffee in his Styrofoam cup when Moyer returned with two men trailing behind. Lapp recognized the first from his walnut-framed color portrait that hung in the barracks reception area. Captain Vernon Phillips, the barracks commander was a burly man with a ruddy square face and silver grey crew cut. He wore a tailored blue suit, white shirt and rep tie that established him as the boss.

Lapp, momentarily confused about protocol, snapped to attention and was about to raise his right hand in a salute, when Phillips said, "at ease, Trooper." The second man, tall, slim, and tanned in a police uniform with perfectly ironed pleats and black hair combed straight back, smiled sympathetically with Lapp's confusion. Moyer introduced him as Joe Handleman, from the Public Information Office in Harrisburg.

Handleman shook Lapp's hand, then returned to his fevered conversation with Moyer. "The press is all over us. There's reporters out there from CNN, the networks, the wire services, all of the newspapers from New York to Washington. They want to know what we know."

"My advice to you is go out there and do a little soft shoe, because as of now, we don't know squat," Moyer said in a tone that suggested he didn't much like Handleman.

"Well, you better come up with something," Handleman shot back. "The local stations want something for their noon news. We keep quiet and our bosses will hear about it in Harrisburg."

Phillips stepped in and calmly asked Moyer, "what can we give them?"

Moyer responded with respect to his boss. "Name, address, approximate age, apparent time and cause of death, sir. Not much more until we hear from the coroner and the crime lab."

Handleman pushed. "What time can we be ready? It's stopped raining for awhile. We can do it on the front steps."

Moyer grumbled, "let me make a couple of calls," and left the room, followed by Phillips, Handleman and Lapp, who, even in uniform, was feeling more and more like an extra thumb that didn't belong there.

At his desk, Moyer punched a pre-set button and waited for an answer. Lapp had never been into the investigators room before, a rectangle divided into a series of partitions along the walls and down the middle, each furnished with a metal desk, padded chair, file cabinet, desktop keyboard, monitor, multi-line telephone and two visitor's chairs.

The three men waited outside Moyer's cubicle while he barked a series of questions to the listener on the other end of the line.

"We'll get you something," Captain Phillips assured Handleman before turning to Lapp. "You were Amish?"

Lapp nodded and answered, "yes, sir."

"We appreciate your coming in to help. You knew the victim and his family?"

"Yes, sir."

"We'll find out who did this."

"Yes, sir." Lapp wondered if his humble responses were starting to sound stupid.

Moyer turned to his audience of three and grumbled, "I'm on hold."

Captain Phillips shrugged and said, "why don't we wait in my office?"

Lapp remained behind, sipping coffee, which he decided was too lousy to drink. Moyer muttered a series of uh-huhs, then finished with "anything else? You'll let me know." He turned to Lapp. "Have a seat while I try Bill Butler at the Crime Lab."

The deep horizontal lines in the detective's high forehead widened and narrowed as he questioned Butler. Put on hold, he held the mouthpiece away from his lips and said to Lapp, "We need a motive. Road rage might have gotten him to that old gas station, but it didn't get him killed. Something else got him killed. The Amish are going to have to kick in. There has to be a way." Moyer sighed. He raised his hand to stop Lapp from replying and concentrated on the phone receiver. "That's it, huh. Okay, let me know." He hung up the phone and rose from his chair. "Where did they go?"

"Captain Phillips office."

"Come on," Moyer said, leading the way down the hall. Lapp followed, feeling like a faithful dog.

Lapp remained in the doorway while Moyer seated himself on a couch facing Phillips and Handleman. "Here's everything so far. The victim was killed with two shotgun blasts, which we already knew because we found the two empty shells and the shotgun. The time of death has been established by a pocket watch that was stopped by shotgun pellets. 10:33 p.m." Moyer turned to Lapp and asked, "what time did those kids say they found the body?"

"Around 10:30."

"Jesus," Moyer exclaimed. "They must have just missed the killing."

A small, dowdy woman with short curly red hair, appeared next to Lapp and announced in a gravelly voice, "Bill Butler's on the phone. I'll transfer him over."

When the phone on Phillip's desk rang, Moyer jumped up from the couch and picked it up.

"Bill? What else you got?"

Moyer uttered another series of "uh-huhs," then hung up and stepped back. "They found some smeared prints on the stock of the shotgun, some cigarette butts, a readable tire track and some boot prints. That's about it."

Handleman shrugged. "Hey. What we got is what we got. It's good enough for now. I'm ready when you are."

"What about questions? Especially the real dumb ass ones?" Moyer asked.

"Like what?" Handleman asked, raising his eyebrows.

"Like this hate crime thing. I'm telling you, it's gonna come up. There's a minority involved."

"Do you think it was?" Phillips interjected.

"Who the hell knows?" Moyer shot back.

"Then say that. It works for me." Handleman patted Moyer on the back and coaxed, "Come on, Warren. You've done this before. If they get too bad, I'll cut them off. See you out there in two minutes." Handleman backed out of the room.

Moyer, his face shadowed with reluctance, said to no one in particular, "well let's go do it." He turned to Lapp, "you coming?"

"If it's all right with you, I'll watch from out in front," Lapp replied.

Moyer smiled. "Probably a good idea. We'll keep you in reserve. Our secret weapon."

They stopped at Moyer's cubicle where he grabbed his brown tweed sport coat, shrugged it on and pulled his tie tight to his neck. They made their way down the stairs and through a maze of hallways to the headquarters front entrance. Outside, Moyer joined Handleman at a lectern.

Lapp edged down the steps and stood to the side as the crowd of reporters and camera crews jostled for position.

The press conference was brief. Moyer confirmed the victim's name, address, age and that he was Amish. As expected, a persistent male reporter brought up the "hate crime angle" which Moyer brushed off with, "we have no indication that it was." His answer to "who discovered the body" was a terse, "some teenagers driving by saw the buggy lights. They are not being held." When a reporter persisted, asking for the teenagers names, Moyer responded, "I don't have them with me. They're juveniles. I couldn't give them to you anyway." His answers to the rest of the questions were mainly, "we don't know," and "it's too early in the investigation," or "we're working on it" and "no motive has been established."

Handleman acknowledged each question and answer with a smile and approving nod of his head.

Moyer continued, making his point directly to the TV cameras, "I'd like to hear from any and all citizens who may have been on Route 340, the old Philly Pike, last night any time after 10 p.m. and may have seen or heard anything at the old Sonoco station that might help with our investigation. Dial the Operator and ask to be connected." Then to the reporters, he added, "we thank you for coming today." Moyer ducked back into the barracks while Handleman again thanked the members of the press and announced he was always available to take their calls.

Lapp watched with curiosity as the TV reporters found areas on the steps where they made their short three or four sentence wrap-ups. When satisfied, they handed their logoed microphones back to the soundmen and drifted away.

Video cameras were lifted from their tripods and hustled back to their remote trucks and vans.

Lapp noted that the reporters were mostly young women, white, Asian, and African-American, all slim and beautiful. He received several broad smiles from them and decided to go back inside before any of the more zealous ones could accost him.

But he wasn't quite fast enough. A polite "excuse me" turned his head to see a willowy, young African-American woman in a tan raincoat with a hood pulled back to reveal her shiny shoulder-length black hair. The disposable pen in her right hand was poised over a steno pad.

"Do you have a second?"

Lapp shrugged. "Not really."

"Your name tag says, Lapp. That's an Amish name, isn't it?"

"Sometimes, not always."

"Obviously, you're not Amish," she said through purple-red lips and a flashing set of white teeth that went well with her light brown, oval face. "Were you ever?"

"A while back."

She relished his reluctance to talk. "You came out the door with Lieutenant Moyer. Are you on this case?"

Lapp hesitated. "I'm aware of it."

She smiled. "Okay, then, how about this? Did you know the victim?"

Lapp considered lying, then answered, "Yeah, I knew him. Who are you?"

"I'm sorry." She offered her hand and answered in a low, smooth unaccented voice that was made for TV. "I'm Lisa Robinson, a reporter for the Lancaster New Era."

"You're not going to put my name in the paper, are you?" he asked, feeling the length of her long fingers as he released her hand.

"Not if you don't want me to." The twinkle in her eyes said she was enjoying the conversation.

"Anything I say isn't official anyway."

"I'm not writing anything down, am I?" She reinforced the point by dropping her hand with the pad to her side.

Lapp shook his head, and put one foot up the next step before being stopped again.

"They'd be foolish not to use you, wouldn't they? Since you knew the victim."

"That's up to them. I'm a traffic patrol officer. I've got no homicide training."

"You can learn," she said, with a smile he was finding very hard to resist. He was certain she was flirting with him. Was it the uniform?

"Can I give you my card?" she asked. He noticed the maroon nail polish when she extended her right hand with a business card between her thumb and forefinger.

Lapp took the card and glanced at it before stuffing it into his front shirt pocket.

"Maybe at some point you could give me a call if anything comes up," she asked, dropping the cute for a more convincing tone.

"I think it's unlikely."

"You never know."

They exchanged smiles. Lapp took the steps two at a time and pushed through the headquarters door.

Chapter 7

At first light, about 6:45 in the morning, Rajah Patel pulled back the covers, slid out of bed and stepped into his corduroy slippers before pulling on a tattered woolen robe. He decided to fix his own tea and give his wife an extra half-hour of sleep. With the tea kettle plugged in and turned on to boil, he went back into the bedroom, buttoned up a multi-colored madras short-sleeved shirt, and stepped into a pair of brown corduroy trousers. He sat on the edge of a cane back chair to pull on white cotton socks and brown hush-puppy shoes. Back in the kitchen he poured the hot water over two bags of Darjeeling tea and while it steeped, he slipped into the office and turned the CLOSED sign dangling in the doorway to OPEN. He retrieved his tea-stained mug and carefully took the first sip. Satisfied that it was to his taste, he tossed the tea bags into the sink, grabbed a black leather jacket from the hook, shrugged it on, and stepped through the office door into the cool, grey, drizzly morning.

Walking past the long wing of two-story, Flamingo-pink motel units, he reached the wooden-rail fence that separated his property from a piece of grassy land that he had long coveted, and that, as of last night, was now his.

Patel was very pleased with himself for having acquired this extra five acre parcel. He got it at a good price. If the weather cooperated, he would have his Pennsylvania Dutch coffee shop open early next year. The parcel was large enough to allow for additional tour bus parking. He strolled back toward the office and offered a cheery "good morning" to a family of six, a grandmother, two parents in their thirties and three children ranging from the ages of three to twelve who were climbing into their Toyota SUV on their way to McDonald's, or the House of Pancakes for breakfast. Which is exactly why he needed to build the restaurant. Those people, and his other guests as well, were leaving instead of spending their breakfast money with him.

They would spend their lunch and dinner money elsewhere as well. After a day of stalking the Amish, they would come back to his motel, take a short rest, then go out to dinner someplace. In three or four months, Patel hoped to change that pattern.

The deal to acquire the five acres had happened faster than he had thought possible. It was only forty-five days ago that he first had the idea for the restaurant. When he found out the land was part of an Amish farm that extended like a thumb from the rest of his land, he thought he would never be able to buy it. Amish never sold their land.

But he never got anywhere by not trying. He let his interest in the land be known to Dave Gingrich, a Mennonite, who frequently performed carpentry work and skilled maintenance on his buildings. Gingrich had a wide network of customers and hired Amish workers for some of his jobs. Still, he was surprised to see the middle-aged, bearded Amish man climb out of his buggy and approach his office door. He introduced himself as Jacob Stoltzfus, the owner of the land that Patel had asked about. It was a hot September day and Jacob seemed pleased when Patel offered him a Coca-Cola and suggested they sit out by the swimming pool to talk. The Amish man took off his straw hat, pulled down his suspenders, and opened the top buttons of his shirt in order to enjoy the full benefit of the sun reflecting from the pool. The negotiations began in earnest and an agreement was reached within minutes. Both of them knew the land, with its valuable highway frontage, was worth $10,000 an acre or a total of $50,000. Patel would have the parcel surveyed and begin the permit and zoning process. He would also have a deed drawn and pay the transfer costs. They shook hands and the Amish man, seeming reluctant to leave, pulled up his suspenders and left.

Patel informed his wife, Bina, that he would take out a construction loan for the restaurant and paving of the parking lot, but he wanted to own the land outright. She volunteered to work the front desk while Patel went into their private quarters to begin the process of using the Indian finance plan to raise the money.

Rajah Patel had apprenticed for five years at two other Patel motels in Biloxi, Mississippi and Mobile, Alabama. After a two month nationwide search of motels that were for sale he found what he wanted. A Holiday Express Hotel in Lancaster County. When he asked, the family came up with the money. That was five years ago.

Now, it took just six phone calls to family members as far away as Florida to fund the purchase. He carefully presented his plan, and one by one, Patels from four states agreed to send money, anywhere from $5,000 (his minimum request) to $20,000, to the Farmer's Bank.

Five weeks later, with the $50,000 securely deposited and an assurance that there would be no objection from the County Planning Department to his motel expansion, he sent word through Dave Gingrich that he was ready to proceed. Jacob Stoltzfus arrived a day later and issued instructions that payment was to be in cash.

Withdrawing five-hundred $100 bills raised eyebrows on everyone's face from the bank president on down to the teller who handed him the white cotton bags of cash. Driving back to the motel, Patel had visions of armed highwaymen forcing him off the road and robbing him. He had no weapon of his own and had even considered buying one before taking possession of the money. The money was hidden in the office floor safe until last night when Jacob Stoltzfus arrived and they completed the transaction. With shades drawn in the crowded living area behind the office, the Amish man took the bundles of money from the white hemp bags and placed them in a gym bag he had brought with him. Patel assured him the bank had counted the money and cautioned that he had not recounted it. It was good enough for Jacob.

They shook hands and Patel watched as Jacob walked though the rain-reflected pools of light to his covered buggy, set the bag inside and climbed in. He jerked on the reins and disappeared into the traffic on Route 30.

Rajah Patel had barely re-entered the office door when his thoughts were jarred by an urgent call from his wife to come into their quarters. "It's on TV."

"What's on TV?"

Bina Patel, Rajah's wife, interrupted the brushing of her long, gray-streaked hair and pointed the brush at the small color television which was now showing a fast-speeding luxury car on a scenic highway. "The Amish man. Jacob Stoltzfus. It was on the news. The news says he was murdered last night."

Patel grasped the empty tea cup with both hands. "He was murdered? Are you sure, woman?"

"You must go to the police."

"If it is true, why should I? It is none of my concern."

Bina Patel resumed brushing her hair, which flowed over the front of her white linen, ankle-length gown. "When the police investigate, we will be drawn into it because Jacob was here last night and, furthermore, your exchange of cash money will become known."

Rajah Patel shook his head in anguish.

Lt. Moyer greeted John Lapp from behind the desk in his cubicle. "You're gonna love this. Captain Phillips just got a call from the head of the Convention and Visitor's Bureau. They're worried that the killing could affect their tourist business. He wants us to solve this murder fast so that he can assure the tour operators that this is an isolated incident and not some kind of a hate campaign against the Amish. Phillips told him we were on it 24/7, which we are anyway with any homicide. Can you believe that shit?"

"I'm glad they're so concerned," Lapp replied with mocking appreciation.

Moyer tapped his fingers on the desk. "Okay, let's get to work. We know most homicides are committed by people who know their victims. Mostly family members. I know that's not likely here, but we have to start somewhere. First off, we need to know where the victim was and what he was up to last night. That's where you'll have to step up to the plate."

"Sallie … the widow … claims she doesn't know. I'll start with his younger brother, Danny. He was at the Stoltzfus farm when I took Sallie over there. I didn't talk to him. I will now."

"Good. Start with him and anyone else you can think of. I'm finishing up a suicide case, and then I'll check out the story those teenagers gave us. We'll meet back here around five."

Lapp stepped back into the hallway and headed for the stairs. He flashed through Jacob's family tree. There was Eli, the father and Lydia, the mother. Then there was Mary, the oldest, who, by adding fifteen years to her age when he last knew her would be about thirty-six now. She was newly married at the time, but he couldn't remember to whom. There was Amos, thirty-four, who was slightly retarded and was still at home then, but had not been at the farm this morning. Jacob was the middle child. Then Katie, who would be thirty, Anna, twenty-seven, and Daniel, twenty-five. There may have been one or two more after he left. Amish women continued to have children into their late thirties and early forties.

Lapp placed his hat with the correct tip on his head and headed toward the motor pool.

Approaching his patrol car, he noticed an idling blue Toyota Sentra that had stopped next to the mechanics station. A dark-skinned man of medium height wearing brown trousers and a madras-plaid shirt that hung loosely over his thick waist, climbed out of the car, and, with a bewildered expression on his chubby face, waved to attract Lapp's attention. "Excuse me, please, sir," the man said, nervously using his hand to comb through his thick black hair, "I want to make a report about a terrible crime that has occurred."

Lapp walked closer and spoke softly to calm him. "I'll help you. You say you were the victim of a crime?"

"Oh, no, sir," the man said in a sing-song voice, "not to me, but to that Amish man who was killed last night. Jacob Stoltzfus was his name."

Lapp's jaw dropped. "You knew Jacob Stoltzfus?"

"Yes. Yes. My name is Rajah Patel. My motel, the Holiday Inn Express on Route 30, is next to his property."

"We appreciate your coming. Let's go inside where we can talk."

"My wife insisted. She said I must come forward. You must find the person who did this horrible thing."

Lapp ushered their way through the back door and started up the stairs. He turned to see that Patel appeared to have second thoughts.

"I hope this will not take too long," Patel said. "I have a tour bus coming in from New York and I must be there to greet them."

Lapp spoke quickly to overcome the Indian man's reluctance. "I'm sure it won't take long at all. We really do appreciate your coming forth like this."

"My wife said I must," Patel muttered again, and started up the bare wood steps.

Warren Moyer was on the telephone, using a polite tone of voice. "Yes, we do appreciate your call. I'm sorry, too, that you can't be of more help. If you think of anything that might help, please call." His tone edged closer to mockery. "Yes, we do need the help of concerned citizens. Thank you." He hung up the phone and acknowledged John Lapp and the strange, dark man standing in the doorway. "Lapp?"

"I met this man downstairs in the parking lot. He says he has some information regarding Jacob Stoltzfus."

Moyer, back in shirt sleeves and loose tie, jumped to his feet. "Come in." He pointed to the two padded chairs. "Please, have a seat."

"This is Lieutenant Moyer," Lapp said. "He's in charge of the investigation into Jacob Stoltzfus' death." He got around not remembering the witness's name by adding, "please, introduce yourself."

The Indian man sat down and, unsure about what to do with his hands, folded them into his lap. "My name is Rajah Patel," he began, his voice quivering with emotion. "I own and operate the Holiday Express Motel on Route 30 at the edge of the Stoltzfus farm. My wife had the TV on this morning and we saw that he had been murdered. This is such a horrible thing. And he was such a nice man."

"How well did you know Jacob Stoltzfus?" Moyer asked, first sitting back in his chair, then leaning forward and propping his elbows on the table to reinforce his interest.

"Well enough to buy five acres of his farm last night and pay him $50,000 in cash for it," Patel said, appreciating the surprised expressions of the two policemen.

"This happened last night?" Moyer asked.

"That's right. You see, I'm building a sit-down restaurant for my customers. It will be small but we have needed it for some time now."

"You needed five acres for that?" Moyer asked.

"Oh, no. I needed the land for more parking. Sometimes my lot gets full and my customers must park away from their rooms. I will also have space for tour buses."

"What time was this?"

"He came to the motel at 7:30. We completed our business in no more than ten minutes."

"And you say you paid in cash?"

"That was his wish."

"$50,000?"

"That is correct. In one hundred dollar bills. Five hundred of them," Patel said, impressed with the amount.

Moyer turned to Lapp. "Is that customary? Cash?"

"It used to be with the older generation. I thought it had changed."

"Did they kill him for the money?" Patel asked. "I would have preferred to pay by check or cashier's note, but he insisted on cash money."

"How did he carry it? The money?" Moyer asked.

"In a gym bag, I think they call it. About this big." Patel used his hands to indicate a rectangle of about eighteen inches long, six inches wide and twelve inches high. "He brought the bag with him for just that purpose."

"What color was this bag?"

"It was blue with a white stripe. I believe it had one of those athletic shoe marks on it. I don't know how else to describe it."

Moyer turned to Lapp. "What are some of those names? Adidas? What else?
Lapp added, "Reebok, Nike?"

Moyer turned back to Patel. "Was it any of those?"

"It may have been Nike. I'm not sure. I don't know these things," Patel said, throwing his hands into the air.

Moyer, worried that he might lose the witness, tried to calm him down. "That's all right. Don't worry about it. If you saw it again, do you think you could recognize it?"

"I would do my best."

"When you gave him the money was anyone else there?" Moyer asked.

"My wife. She was the only one."

"Anyone else know you were planning to pay Jacob the money last night?"

"No one," Patel said quickly, then paused to contemplate the question before adding, "the bank did, of course. They would know because they gave me the cash yesterday afternoon. They asked why I needed so much cash."

"And what did you tell them?" Moyer asked.

"Simply that I was buying some land. I didn't think it was any of their business."

"Which bank is that?"

"The Farmer's Trust. The branch on Highway 30. Just down the road in Paradise. It's all perfectly legal. I brought the deed to show you." Patel leaned forward, pulled the hastily folded paper from his back pocket and extended it to Moyer.

Moyer took the deed, glanced at it, and placed it on his desk. "We'll look it over and return it later." He turned to Lapp.

"Is there anything you want to ask?" Moyer asked Lapp.

Lapp had waited patiently to jump in. He moved next to Moyer's cluttered desk to give Patel a straight line of sight.

"I'm a little surprised that Jacob would sell any land. Most Amish farms are pretty small to farm profitably and here he is selling off some of it."

Patel responded defensively. "He came to me. I let it be known that I was interested, but it was he who came to me."

"How did he know you were looking to buy?"

"I thought I already told you this." Patel glanced at the watch on his left wrist. "I use a handyman, a Mennonite, named Dave Gingrich. I asked who owned the land next to mine and the next thing I know, the Amish man came to my door."

Moyer wrote the name on a desk pad. "Where can we find this man, Gingrich?" he asked Patel.

"Call me at my office. I will give you his address and phone number." Patel rose from the chair.

Lapp quickly stepped forward, not letting the Indian man go. "Did Jacob tell you why he wanted to sell?"

"I asked him that. He would only say he had a good use for the money."

"Nothing else?"

"I think he was playing with me, but he said that whenever he worked that piece of the land he felt like a monkey in a zoo." Patel smiled. "The tourists, including those who stay at my motel, would come into the field with their cameras. He said he should charge admission." He added, with a chuckle, "he was glad to be rid of it."

That sounded like something Jacob would say, Lapp thought as his eyes caught Patel staring at his black plastic name tag with white lettering.

"Lapp," Patel pondered aloud. "We have four Amish girls that clean for us. One of them is named Lapp. Her name is Mary. Are you related?"

"It's a common name," Lapp responded.

"They're very hard workers. Much better than the Puerto Ricans who like to stand around and chatter. You don't know Mary?"

"No." Lapp looked to Moyer to see if he had any more questions.

"Did Jacob have the money? When they found him?" Patel asked.

"That's police business now," Moyer responded. He concluded the meeting by rising and again offering his right hand to Patel. "Thank you for coming in. There's a good chance we'll want to talk with you some more. We'll call you first before we come by. Do you have a business card?"

"As you wish," Patel answered, pulling a card from his shirt pocket and handing it to Moyer. "I'm happy to be a good citizen." Then, "would you come in a regular car? I wouldn't want the neighbors or people driving by on our busy highway to think there was any trouble with the police at my motel."

"We'll try to accommodate," Moyer said, smiling.

"It's just that people talk. There's a lot of jealousy and competition among the motel owners."

"We understand," Moyer replied. "Could you do us a favor?"

"I told you everything I know," Patel responded.

"Would you take that desk over there," Moyer asked, pointing to an empty desk in the next cubicle, "and write down what you just told us."

"All of it?"

"As much as possible. Begin with his arrival last night and how you gave him the money."

"I am in a hurry, sir. I have a tour bus arriving."

"We'd appreciate it," Moyer said, nodding toward the desk.

Moyer and Lapp watched Patel begin to write on the yellow-lined paper as they stepped out into the hallway. "Well, well, well" Moyer said. "We've got ourselves a motive. No cash was recovered, there was no amount of money on his person, so whoever killed him made off with the fifty grand. When you question the victim's relatives …"

Lapp didn't let him finish. "I'll start with the widow."

Chapter 8

Sallie Stoltzfus set the peck-sized basket of Winesap apples on the sink counter and pulled a black handled paring knife from the drawer. She had promised fresh applesauce topped with powdered cinnamon for the children when they got home, but after coring the first apple, she set the knife down and retreated to the kitchen table where the family bible, a Martin Luther German translation, lay open. She had no heart for housework or anything else. Staring blankly at Jacob's empty chair at the head of the table, she had never imagined a life without him. They were husband and wife forever. They were promised to each other at their wedding. Now Jacob was gone.

Flipping aimlessly through the pages of the oversized bible, the words and verses refused to register. She searched for scripture that promised peace for the dead and comfort for the living. Nothing eased her grief. When the Seth Thomas clock on the wall struck four, she stood up, pulled an earthenware jug of homemade sarsaparilla out of the gas powered refrigerator, filled three clear plastic glasses and set them on the table. The children would be satisfied to have these as a treat instead of the applesauce that never got made.

Waiting at the kitchen screen door, she realized she had not thought of nor rehearsed the words she would use to explain their father's death. At the top of the lane, Samuel, as usual, was leading, urging the others on. David, the second son, was kicking stones, while little Lydia plodded and tagged along behind shouting in her tiny voice, "wait up, wait for me."

Sallie recoiled with alarm when a van, with its wiry antenna rising above, turned into the bottom of the lane. Following behind was a caravan of cars, vans and trucks. She pushed through the door and called to the children to hurry. Ignoring their questions, she gathered them one by one, and, like a mother hen protecting her chicks, ushered them inside.

The lead van pulled up next to the windmill. Sallie snapped the lock, pulled the curtains over the window and turned to her children.

"What do all those cars want?" Samuel asked as he threw his belted schoolbook on the table.

"They want to make pictures of us."

"What did we do?" Samuel asked, joining Sallie, David and Lydia in peeking through the door curtains.

Sallie was torn between sending the children upstairs, or telling them the truth. She pushed the children away from the door.

"Where's Papa? We'll get him to chase them away," Samuel said with conviction.

"No, he won't," Sallie answered too quickly. "Listen, children. I got some very bad news this morning." She took a deep breath but it was not enough to control the tremble in her voice. "You know how the bible teaches us that sometime during our life, mostly when you're very old, God decides it's time for you to come with him to heaven?"

With widened eyes, the children listened and questioned their mother's words.

"Last night he wanted a strong man. Your Papa has gone to be with God in heaven."

"What?" Samuel asked, while the other two exchanged questioning glances.

"Your Papa was killed. Last night. He didn't come home and I don't know why yet but today they came and told me he was."

"Who did?" The two younger children were content to have Samuel do their asking.

"The State Police."

"Those cars this morning? But how?" Samuel asked.

"They don't know yet," Sallie lied, knowing that their schoolmates would tell them soon enough.

Lydia cried out. "I want my Daddy! I don't want him to be dead."

Lydia's angered pain struck deep in Sallie's heart. She pulled the little girl's face to her apron.

"I hate God." David screamed in defiance.

"David. Lydia, that's enough. Papa's in a better place. We'll miss him and he'll miss us."

"He's in heaven already?' Lydia asked plaintively, looking up through tear-stained, blue eyes.

The commotion was building outside and Sallie knew the intruders would be at her door any minute. "He's with Jesus now."

"Wasn't he happy here with us?" Lydia persisted.

"Of course he was." She could hear the vehicles crushing the pea gravel outside.

Losing patience, she pushed the resisting children toward the stairs. "Geh auf" (go up)

"I want to say goodbye to him," Lydia cried.

"You will. He'll be here," she began, then corrected herself. "His body will be here tomorrow, but his soul is already in heaven. You can say goodbye then."

"I wish she'd stop brutzing." Samuel said, putting on a brave front and pushing his younger brother who also was crying softly. He turned back to his mother. "I'll stay here with you."

"We'll all go up." Sallie pushed the children up the first several stairs. Her eyes flared with anger at the knocking on the door, before mounting the stairs to join her children.

Chapter 9

John Lapp steered the patrol unit up the lane into a swarm of antennas and satellite dishes. The media circus had moved from the front entrance of the State Police barracks to the Stoltzfus farm. A half-dozen TV remote trucks, vans and stations wagons sporting call letters and logos lined the top of the lane and spilled over into the barnyard.

Lapp glided past them into a vacant space by the concrete base of the windmill. The squeak and grind of the turning blades above him were quickly drowned out by the stampede of reporters with their cameras and microphones that were thrust at him. His eyes swept through them and stopped at Lisa Robinson, a knowing smile on her face.

Lapp ignored the rapid-fire questions of "what can you tell us", "can you ask the family to talk to us", "do you have any suspects?" He lowered the din by raising his arms, and yelling, "please, please listen!" He was surprised when a hush swept through the swarm. Several microphones were shoved closer in anticipation of what he had to say.

"You're on private property here …" he started.

That brought out a chorus of moans.

"These people want to be left alone. You know that their religion does not allow them to be photographed and here you are trying to poke cameras into their faces. They have nothing to say to you right now and if you don't leave, you'll be arrested."

Lapp wasn't sure that he had the power to make good on that threat and when they refused to move, he wondered even more.

"You can stay down at the bottom of the lane, but you must vacate the premises immediately." To play it through, Lapp got back into his car, grabbed the microphone to his two-way radio and said loudly, "this is Unit 14 requesting backup. 10-4 at the Stoltzfus farm …"

When a male reporter with his nose next to the window announced, "he's calling for backup," and backed away, the others followed suit. Lapp suppressed a smile. He had not actually activated the radio.

Lapp stepped back outside of the patrol car, and with an authoritative pose of hands on hips, waited while satellite dishes were cranked down, doors slammed, engines roared to life, and tires crackled on the gravel as the press caravan receded down the lane.

Only one reporter hung back and that was Lisa Robinson. She walked toward him, raincoat off, wearing a blue outfit with the white blouse, blue blazer and short tight skirt, Lapp felt pleased rather than annoyed by her lack of obedience.

"You know," she said sweetly, "I still don't have anything, and I've got to turn my story in within the hour."

"You got what I got. I don't have anything either," Lapp said, facing her squarely.

"Seriously?" She asked, her brown eyes wider. "Nothing about the family? Nothing about the widow, children, simple facts? Something that would give some substance and human interest to my story?"

She was playing with him, but he wasn't playing along. "I'd like to help you, but now's not the right time. These people are grieving and I've come to help them if I can."

"You're not here to investigate? To ask questions? You're not here officially, even though you're in uniform?"

"I'm here as a family friend," he said firmly, and then added, "and to let them know how the investigation will proceed and what may be expected of them." His tone edged softer. "This sort of thing doesn't normally usually happen to them."

"So you do know them, then?"

"I knew them years ago," Lapp said, wondering why he was even talking to her.

"Then you can give me some background," she persisted.

Lapp shook his head firmly. "I can't do that."

"Can't or won't?"

"Both. I'd appreciate if you'd stop asking."

She dropped the pouting face and switched to a professional tone of voice. "If I'm pushing a little hard it's because it's my job."

"And my job is to go inside."

"Okay, I'm going," she said, stepping in the direction of the dark blue Ford Taurus. "Just promise me you won't forget me when you do have something."

"I'm sure you'll see that I don't." Lapp flashed a forgiving smile, then caught a glimpse of Sallie's face at the curtained window as he strode toward the kitchen door. She opened the squeaky aluminum storm door allowing Lapp to step inside. Her frightened face managed a smile which Lapp was happy to return.

"I'm sorry about all those people," he said, checking to see that all of the vehicles were gone.

"Thank you for making them go away. I just don't know what to make of all this," she said, unsteadily. She wiped the corners of her eyes with her black apron and turned back to him. "The children just got home. I just told them." She moved to the foot of the stairs and called, "Samuel, David, Lydia, you can come down now." Sallie's oldest boy and the little girl bounded noisily down the grey wood stairs. "Your drinks are ready," she said, pointing to the glasses of a dark, foamy liquid that Lapp guessed was root beer or sarsaparilla. The younger son quietly appeared at the bottom of the stairs and ran to his mother, burying his face in her black dress.

The little girl climbed onto the butt-worn wooden bench next to the long dining room table. Her eyes were glued to Lapp's uniform and badge. Lapp's smile was not returned.

The oldest boy stepped in front of Sallie and spread his arms to protect her. "Who are you?" he demanded.

"My name is John Lapp," he said, pointing to his name tag.

"Are you the State Police who said my Daddy was dead?" he challenged.

"That's enough, Samuel," Sallie interjected. "Johnny Lapp is our friend. Go have your sarsaparilla," she said, guiding him to the bench.

"Who do we have here?" Lapp asked.

Sallie stroked the clinging boy's hair and said, "this is David. He's eight. My shy boy." David, blond and fair, was a spitting image of Jacob as Lapp remembered him at that age. Sallie lifted David and sat him on the table bench. She moved behind the oldest boy, pulled the dusty black hat from his head and introduced him. "This is Samuel. He's ten. He's named after my father Samuel. Do you remember my father? He just died last year."

"I do remember and I'm sorry," Lapp replied, looking at the handsome boy, his face framed by straight brown hair, trimmed in the traditional Amish bowl-shape, and wearing a grey shirt, black pants and black suspenders. He refused to respond with a smile or nod of recognition.

"And here is Lydia. She's six. She just started school last month." Lydia's blonde hair was parted in the middle and braided with the braids tied around her head. "My Papa's dead," she gasped, holding back a cry.

"I know. I'm sorry," Lapp said quietly.

"I don't want him to be dead." She said defiantly, then began to sob. "Why does he have to be dead?"

Lapp, torn apart by the little girl's pain, swallowed back a cry of sympathy.

Sally bent down and pulled the little girl's head next to hers. "Remember what I told you? Papa's in a better place. We'll miss him and he'll miss us."

"He's in heaven," Lydia wailed. "I didn't say goodbye to him."

"You will. We will have a funeral for him. You can say goodbye then. Okay? Now go sit down and have your drink."

Lydia, using her hand to wipe her eyes and nose moved to the long table and asked, "can I write him a letter? I need paper."

"She doesn't even know how to write," Samuel grumbled.

"You can draw him a picture," Sallie suggested, suppressing a smile.

"I wish she'd stop her brutzing," Samuel grumbled, as he took a lined tablet from the schoolbooks on the table and pushed it, along with a pencil, to Lydia.

Lapp, caught up in the family's sorrow considered how he could question Sallie under these conditions ... He was relieved when Sallie said. "Samuel, I think you'd better go out now. Take David. It's time to fetch the cows."

Everyone in the room was distracted by the sound of a horse and wagon coming to a stop outside. Sallie moved to the door, peered through the curtains and opened it. "Cum rei", (come in) Sallie said, and ushered two Amish women into the kitchen. Both women wore traditional black dresses, bonnets and shawls. The stout, chubby-faced woman in her forties and the slender teen-aged girl stole shy glances at Lapp. Sallie did not introduce them. The mention of his name, "Johnny Lapp" set off a new round of secret stares. Condolences were offered in Pennsylvania Dutch, There was no touching or hugging. With black bonnets huddled together, duties were outlined and agreed upon with the nodding of heads, and mutterings of "ja, ja". Sallie led the women out of the kitchen to the front parlor. Lapp knew well the rituals, ceremonies and preparations for the Amish dead. The women would help Sallie with the moving of furniture to make room for the casket, and the setting up of chairs and benches. Everything would be ready when Kercher & Sons Mortuary, having embalmed Jacob's body, would bring him home, set him in place and open the upper hinged-end lid where he would be viewed from the waist up.

Lapp looked at his watch. 4:30. Samuel and David left through the kitchen door. Lydia, now calm, was involved with writing her ABC's. While waiting for Sallie, Lapp sat on a kitchen table bench across from Lydia and was still surprised at how modern her kitchen was. The walls were painted a cheerful light blue. Two calendars, one from Plasterer's Farm Supplies, featured a herd of cows, while the other, from Martin's Store, was a fall leaves landscape. The range and large white refrigerator were fueled by bottled gas lines fed from two large white propane tanks in the middle of the side lawn. Double stainless steel sinks and beautiful chrome faucets were surrounded by cupboards of walnut-stained wood. The rectangular kitchen table where Lydia worked was covered with a checked-print oilcloth and the floor was a brown squared-tile linoleum. Gas fed floor lamps extended from square boxes on rollers that held propane tanks like the one he used for his home barbeque and could be moved where light was required. A great improvement over the smoky, smelly kerosene lamps from his childhood that provided an odorous, yellow light that Lapp always found depressing. Sallie returned to the room. Her face was drawn, but there was no sign of tears. "Did you come to ask me more questions?" Sallie's tone was less friendly, more efficient now.

"There are a few things you might be able to help with. Maybe we shouldn't talk here," he said, nodding in Lydia's direction.

"We'll go outside. They brought Blackie home. I should look after him," Sallie said, leading the way to the door. "I asked the ladies in the parlor to watch Lydia."

The warm sun's rays played hide and seek with the white-pillow clouds as Sallie Stoltzfus and John Lapp strolled toward the barn. "He was still skittish when they brought him home," she said about Jacob's horse. "They kept the buggy. Why would they do that?"

"More forensic work. Clues to what happened."

"Oh."

"I don't think you want it back anyway. There are shotgun pellets embedded in the rear end. When the police return it, send it right away to a buggy shop and have the backend replaced."

"I understand."

They walked quietly for a minute before Lapp asked, "Do you know a man named Rajah Patel?"

Her eyes narrowed. "Patel? No. Should I?"

"He owns the Holiday Inn off the south end of your farm."

"Yes, I know the place, but I don't know him. Does Jake?"

"Jake went to the motel last night and signed over a deed for five acres of your farm at the corner next to the motel."

Sallie's mouth widened in surprise. "Jake did that? Last night?"

"Did you sign a deed for the lot?"

"No." She turned away to hide the redness that flooded her face. "He had no business doing that. This farm is barely big enough to support us now."

Lapp felt a small amount of perverse pleasure from Sallie's outburst against Jacob. He waited for her anger to settle before asking, "is the farm in joint ownership?"

"It should be. It was my Pop's farm before," Sallie said, but her face was uncertain.

"But you never signed anything?"

"No. Never."

Lapp made a mental note to check on the legality of the sale. "Patel paid him $50,000 for the land. What would Jacob want with that much cash?"

"I don't know." The snappiness in Sallie's voice told Lapp that she had a pretty good idea.

"Jacob left the motel with a bag filled with 500 one-hundred dollar bills. When his body was found there was no bag found anywhere. Not near him or in the buggy. So either he had already spent the money, hid it, or the person that killed him took it. That's why it's so important we find out what he wanted with that money."

Sallie turned her head so that Lapp could not see the tears that were pooling in the corners of her eyes. They walked another ten feet before Lapp gently grasped her arm and turned her to him.

"You need to tell me, Sallie. It's very important. Otherwise, we have nothing."

Sallie nodded her head but avoided his eyes. They entered the open door to the horse stables and stopped in front of Blackie's stall. The sweet smell of fresh alfalfa filled the air. The gelding stepped over and poked his head over the upper-half of the stall door. Sallie reached in and stroked his nose. When Lapp did the same thing, the horse snapped his head back, a conscious reaction to the strange hand and uniform.

Sallie's slender fingers outlined the white diamond on Blackie's muzzle. As if speaking to the horse she said softly, "Jake was never happy just being a farmer. Everything was horses. That's all he talked about and when I didn't get excited like he did, he'd get mad."

Her answer was no surprise to Lapp. Even as a sixteen year old, Jacob had the fastest and best-cared for horses. "You mean carriage horses?"

"No. Race horses. For horse racing."

"Thoroughbreds?"

"Trotting horses. Standard breds, he called them. Like Blackie here. He showed me once where he would build a track out in the field. Where he could train them and practice. I walked it with him. He knew it took a lot of land and we needed all the land we had for our crops." She shook her head and her voice cracked as she recalled the futility of it. "And then he wanted to build some new stables, too. And he talked about going to the horse sales and buying good breeding stock so that he could raise the horses and then sell them at a big profit." Her eyes asked Lapp if he understood.

He nodded.

"I let him talk," she continued, "because for awhile, anyway, he felt better when he did. I thought it was just talk."

"Would he have been allowed to do that?" Lapp asked …

Sallie glared. "You know the answer to that."

"Too worldly?"

"Almost for certain," she said, shaking her head.

"Did he ever talk about leaving the church?"

"You mean like you did?" She asked pointedly.

Lapp took the barb in stride and maintained an even tone. "Not as far as I did. Maybe become Mennonites. They would probably allow raising and breeding as long as he didn't gamble."

"If he left, he knew we couldn't go with him." Sallie looked into Lapp's dark brown eyes and said, "but back then, you knew that, too." She dropped her hand from Blackie's muzzle. "He seems fine now. I want to go back to the house. Lydia needs me."

Walking with determination, Sallie kept her eyes on the ground. "Jacob said the work here was too hard for such small rewards. But that's how it's supposed to be for us. It keeps us in our ways."

"I don't suppose he had any life insurance? To pay off the farm?"

"Why do you even ask such a question?"

"It's still forbidden?"

"Yes."

"And social security?"

"The same."

"There's one more thing I've been meaning to ask you. Those buffalo. Out in the cow pasture. They were quite a surprise."

Sallie stopped and turned to him. "That was another one of his ideas. He said they were going to be a big source of money. That one day everybody would be eating buffalo meat. We only got them six months ago."

"What about the church," Lapp wondered out loud. "Did anybody ever say anything."

"Not so far. But they were watching. I don't know what I'll do with them now."

When they arrived at the kitchen door, he asked for the names and addresses of family relatives whom he might talk to about Jacob. When she finished, he had filled two pages of his note book with names. "You know what they will think of me and my marriage when you ask about the money." Then she added, "some may not want to be bothered with you," she warned, and with no further words stepped into the kitchen.

As Lapp turned the ignition key of his car, an open horse-drawn buggy pulled up driven by a small, thin man, whom he recognized as Jacob's brother, Amos. It was followed by a team of draft horses hauling a large wagon with two young Amish men behind the reins. Help with the afternoon milking, feeding, cleaning and other daily farm chores had arrived.

The Amish system of self-reliance was kicking in.

Chapter 10

The images of Jacob Stoltzfus' tortured face and his pellet-shredded chest, combined with the deep emotional strains of seeing Sallie and her fatherless children were taking a toll on John Lapp.

There was a still a half-hour of daylight, enough to recreate the time frame from when Jacob received the $50,000 from Patel to the time his body was found at the old gas station. He started in the driveway of Patel's Holiday Inn. It was a typical budget motel. Two long wings, each two stories high, with the office, like a fulcrum, in the middle. A No Vacancy sign appeared on the reader board sign in front. Patel was doing well.

He set the odometer at 000 and drove north on Leacock Road 2.5 miles to the junction of Route 340. Turning left, he proceeded west on 340 to the driveway of the abandoned Sonoco station. The odometer read 5.2 miles.

Tired and depressed, Lapp climbed the stairs to the investigator's room. He was greeted by the two detectives he recognized from the crime scene. The bald, heavyset man in a checked sport coat that was stretched across his wide stomach introduced himself as Doug Martin. The tall man with springy piles of black curls on top of his head extended his fleshy hand and said, "Hal Eiseman."

Warren Moyer entered the room. "Let's go to the sweat box. There's more room."

Lapp followed the three investigators to the narrow, windowless interview room.

Moyer waved at everyone to sit down around the peeling walnut-veneer rectangular table. "Who wants to start?"

Eiseman looked at Martin. Taking his cue, Martin pulled two pages of a typed report from his side coat pocket. He squinted at the papers through puffy blood-shot eyes that looked like they hadn't been shut for 48 hours, cleared his throat and spoke with a hoarse, tobacco-scarred voice. "We canvassed a two-mile area around the crime scene. Basically came up empty. Nobody heard anything, nobody saw anything, everybody was sympathetic to our investigation, but were of no help. Nada."

"Pretty much what we expected." Moyer sighed.

Eiseman propped his elbows on the table, arched his bow-tied long neck and said, "I came up empty, too. Most everybody I talked to knew the victim. No one had any explanation for him being at that old gas station. I missed a few who were home that night but were off at their day jobs today. Even if I went back, I doubt we'd get much. By 10:30 all the farmers are already in bed."

Martin, making no attempt to disguise his boredom, used the file end of a nail clippers to dig beneath the nail of his middle finger. "One couple, who live about a half-mile up the road, thought they heard something, but decided it was the TV." He chuckled, "the wife bitched about her husband watching too many cop shows. When I left they were still going at it."

Moyer was not amused. He turned to Lapp. "How did you make out?"

Feeling nervous, like a rookie coming up to bat for the first time in the big leagues, Lapp took a quick breath and began, "I talked to the widow some more. She's still in shock." Lapp took a deep breath and continued, "basically, she knew nothing about selling the five acres. Jacob never told her, and she never signed off on it. I asked her if the farm was only in Jacob's name alone and she didn't even know."

"What about the money?" Moyer asked.

"She denied knowing about the money."

"You believe her?"

"Totally. When I asked her what he would do with $50,000 she said he would probably start a horse farm operation."

Lapp, annoyed that Martin was now noisily filing a nail, continued, "trotting horses, buggy horses, racing horses. The trouble is, the Amish would never approve of an operation like that."

"So why would he do it then?" Eiseman asked.

"I think he was ready to jump the fence." Lapp answered their quizzical faces with, "I think he was going to leave the Amish church. $50,000 in secret money is serious business."

Moyer nodded. "Keep after it. Talk to other family members." Moyer proceeded with his report. "Two callers responded to our plea for information. The first guy said he was on 340 and saw lights at the gas station around 10:30.

If those teenagers are telling the truth, that was probably their car lights. The other caller was an older woman who told me her life history before finally saying that she went by about 9:40 and said she saw what looked like a truck coming out of the driveway. I asked if she saw the buggy lights and she said, no. So that truck could have been there before the murder and have no connection whatsoever."

"Except, why would a truck be at an abandoned gas station on a rainy night?" Martin asked.

"Right." Moyer rose, grabbed his sport coat from the clothes tree peg, ready to call it a day. "I still need to check out the teen's story at the Turkey Hill."

"I can handle that," Lapp volunteered. "There's one other thing."

"What's that?" Moyer asked.

"I drove the route I'm pretty sure Jacob would have taken from the motel to the old Sonoco station. A total of 5.2 miles."

Lapp paused long enough to bask in their attention. "A good trotting horse can go as fast as 15 miles an hour. Considering the weather, I lowered the speed to 12 miles per hour. At 10 to 12 miles an hour, it would have taken Jacob 30 to 40 minutes to reach the gas station. He left the motel at 7:40. If he was killed at 10:30, that leaves an hour-and-a-half of time that is unaccounted for. Where was he?"

Moyer jumped in. "Not only where was he, but did he still have the money when he got there and was killed. I would bet that he did. Got any ideas?"

"No," Lapp responded. "But it's a new angle. I'll start with Jacob's brother, Daniel."

Moyer glanced at his watch as he stepped from behind his desk. "You still want to interview that Turkey Hill clerk? I can have one of these guys do it."

"I'll take it. It's only a few miles down the road from Daniel Stoltzfus' farm."

Martin snapped his clippers shut and rose. "Looks like we got us a regular Sherlock Holmes working with us."

Moyer and Eiseman smiled in agreement. Lapp took it as a back handed compliment.

Moyer turned back from the door and said, "we'll meet back here at 8 in the morning."

In the locker room, Lapp loosened the tie from his neck. He was never really comfortable in a uniform, not only because of the conformity, but because he liked the casual feel of a flannel shirt and khaki pants. He shrugged on his windbreaker and stepped through the rear door of the barracks.

Ten minutes later, he tightened his grip on the steering wheel in response to the loose gravel of the lane leading to the Stoltzfus farm.

Without electricity, Amish farms are dark and foreboding places at night. The rising moon, playing hide and seek with the thick cumulus clouds, provided brief periods of illumination over the harvested fields. A porch light and a dim glow from the house, probably the kitchen, indicated some activity there. Two pole lights beaming from the cow barn told Lapp that milking was still in progress.

He climbed out of his truck, surprised that his head lights had not raised a curious welcome. Fortunately, he knew his way around.

The high-pitched hum of the diesel engine that powered the lights and the equipment inside greeted him as he approached the rollup door of the cow barn.

Pulling open the galvanized metal door just far enough to slip inside, he stepped past the cooler, a four by six foot refrigerated concrete box which was run by a 12-volt battery, kept the milk at the legal temperature of 39 degrees. The acrid smell of constantly dropping manure attacked him as he crossed a three inch high concrete water barrier into the stable area.

Pairs of yard-long fluorescent tubes, strung out and mounted every ten feet on an overhead beam provided illumination for thirty black and white Holsteins.

Restrained by four foot long iron pipes on the sides and in front, the contented cows pulled hay from the floor trough and chewed at a leisurely pace.

Through the pumping sounds of milking machines, the curious eyes of the cows were the first to notice Lapp's appearance. Lapp unzipped his jacket for relief from the heat generated by the bovine creatures. Halfway down the line, Daniel, and his father, Eli, in black calf-high rubber boots, were forking hay into the trough. Two teenage milk maids in black with white aprons, were busily wiping the cow's teats with a disinfectant-soaked rag before inserting the milking machine suction cups.

All eyes turned to Lapp as he smiled and greeted Daniel. "I'm sorry to bother you, but some new information has turned up that I need to ask you about."

Daniel and Eli exchanged wary glances before Eli said, "you can talk with him if you want. I got nothing more to say."

"I can wait until you're finished milking," Lapp said.

Daniel pulled a battered straw hat from his head and said, "no. We're far enough along so that the girls can handle it now. If you think we must talk then

I guess we must." He stepped out from between two cows and led Lapp back down the wet concrete walkway to the cooling room.

Daniel grabbed a tin cup from a nail hook, dipped it into an open five-gallon ceramic jar and took a long drink. He wiped his mouth with the back of his hand and offered the cup to Lapp, who shook his head and muttered, "no thanks."

"How come if you're a state trooper, you never wear a uniform?" he asked.

"I do, most of the time."

"You come to tell us more about Jacob's death?" Daniel asked.

"Actually, some things have come up that raise more questions."

"A man dressed up in a brown suit came by this afternoon asking questions, wondering if we heard any gunshots last night."

Lapp wondered if it was Martin or Eiseman. "Did you?"

"No. We're asleep long before 10:30."

"There are two things I want to ask. First, Jacob was carrying $50,000 from selling five-acres of his land to the motel owner. Did you know that?"

Daniel responded evenly, without a note of surprise. "Sallie told me. I was just over there."

"Jake got the money at that Holiday Inn at 7:30. According to his pocket watch, he was killed at 10:30. Even if he ran the buggy fast, there's a three hour gap when he had to be some place, doing something. We need to find out where and what that was."

Daniel shook his head. "What does it matter any more?"

"It matters if we're going to catch whoever did this. If we solve this thing, then your lives can go back to normal. But until that time, you're under a microscope. The press and the curious, not to mention, God forbid, copycats, aren't going to let this go."

Daniel shrugged with resignation.

"We need to know about the money. What he wanted it for. Sallie said he talked about buying horses and starting a horse farm. You know anything about that?"

Daniel weighed his words before answering. "The last time Jake came over he asked Pap if he could borrow some money from us."

"When was that?"

"Maybe a month ago, I'm not too sure, now. He was never back since. We don't have money to loan out. Jake shoulda known that."

"Did he say what he wanted the money for? Did he talk to you about buying horses?"

"He did every once in a while. He talked about buffalo, too," Daniel said with a touch of irony.

"I saw them in his pasture."

A bitterness in Daniel's tone appeared. "He said there's a mixed breed of steer and buffalo, called beefalo. They're supposed to give better meat, so he wanted to buy a herd. Before that he talked about building a big chicken house so they could raise broilers. Like the "English" do, in cages, where they never set foot on the ground.

Then he heard the tobacco companies were coming around asking some of the farmers to grow a special strain for cigar wrappers." Daniel hesitated, then lowered his voice when Eli Stoltzfus stepped into the cooler room. Ignoring Lapp and directing his words at Daniel, he said, "we're pretty much done in there. I'm going back to see about the Mam. She was laying down before."

Eli passed by, eyes straight, refusing to acknowledge John Lapp. He stepped through the metal door to the outside. Lapp urged Daniel to continue. "What else."

"Nothing else." Daniel sighed with resignation. "Jake was always full of big ideas. He needed to do what the rest of us do. Work hard with what you got." He stepped to the water jar and drew another cup full of water. This time Lapp accepted the cup and savored the cool mineral-rich well water.

"I need to haul the cans out here to the cooler," Daniel said.

"You want some help?" Lapp volunteered.

"You think you're strong enough?"

Working to establish a friendly rapport, Lapp responded, "do I look weak?"

"No, you look okay. But I don't need no help."

Figuring he would probably slop milk all over his clothes anyway, Lapp switched subjects. "Does Amos still live at home?"

"Sure. He's never gonna leave."

"Can I talk to him?"

"He don't get home until 6. He makes weather vanes over at Smoker's Foundry. You should see them."

"I will. Is that the Quonset hut set back off Route 30?"

"That's the place."

Lapp realized he needed to get over to the Turkey Hill to question the clerk. "Will Amos be here tomorrow?"

"After noon. They work half-day on Saturday."

"How is Amos?"

"Amos? He's always the same. Special."

Lapp knew that meant Amos was still mentally "slow." Then, not sure why the question popped into his mind, he asked, "how was Sallie when you saw her?"

"She's all right. The kids seem all right, too, I guess. They'll make out okay."

Lapp thanked him and stepped outside into the cold evening. He took a minute to feel the long forgotten peace and stillness of a full moon over the fields and farm.

Choosing not to use his headlight's artificial beams, he coasted back down the lane.

Traffic on Route 340 through Bird-In-Hand and Smoketown was Friday night quiet. The Mennonite-operated Amish buggy rides and the semi-authentic shops and stores had all closed for the day.

The six parking spaces in front of the red-signed Turkey Hill Minit Market were all occupied. Fluorescent tubes lit the large glass display windows and the double stainless steel glassed doors of the rectangular building. Off to the left, a wooden pole hitching rail, built to accommodate Amish buggies, was unoccupied. When a Chevy Suburban backed out, Lapp pulled into his space.

Inside, Lapp waited while the clerk, a pimply-faced boy who looked to be barely sixteen, rang up the items and bagged the milk, bread, eggs and cinnamon buns for a hefty, short, middle-aged working wife. The only other customer in the store, an elderly man in a cracked black leather pilot's cap with the ear flaps pulled down, held a bag of potato chips in each hand trying to decide between the cheese-flavored or regular crinkled style. Lapp was amused by the variety of impulse items, everything from automobile deodorizers to jars of licorice sticks, that rimmed the counter. The clerk, with the sheep-shorn head and the ubiquitous double earrings in his left ear, responded with surprise to the badge held eye-high in Lapp's right hand.

"What's your name, son."

"Shawn Derr," he said, clearing his throat.

"You worked here Thursday night?"

"Last Thursday night? Yeah."

Lapp pulled out his note pad as a cheat sheet. "Do you know these guys? Tim Holtzman, Ryan Holtzman and Randy Miller."

"I know who they are, yeah. Why?"

"What time were they here?"

He thought for a moment. "10 o'clock maybe."

"What did they buy? Cigarettes? Beer?" Lapp asked the question, even though he knew that Pennsylvania was one of four states with archaic laws where beer could not be sold in convenience stores or any retail store, for that matter.

"I think they bought some chips and pretzels."

"Nothing to drink?"

"A six-pack of Coke, I believe."

"Cigarettes," Lapp added, accusingly.

"Not then, not here."

"They said they did." Lapp lied.

Derr shrugged. "They lied, then."

"Look," Lapp said, leaning in. "I just want a few simple answers. They had beer, I know that. Where did they get it?"

"Not here. Maybe next door."

That rang a bell. Lapp remembered that Hoffman's Tavern, the bar next door, had sold beer and liquor out the back door to Amish teens. He'd been there one time himself, and contributed some money. But right now it wasn't a priority.

"When those guys were here, did they brag about running an Amish man and his buggy off the road?"

"Not that I heard." Derr said, challenging Lapp to believe him.

"Who else was here," Lapp began, then rephrased his question. "Were there other customers here when those guys were?"

"Must have been. I'm busy all the time."

"Give me some names."

"I don't know their names. They come in here and buy stuff and they go."

"Try. That Amish man those kids ran off the road was murdered. Did you know that?"

"I saw it on the front page of the paper. Those guys didn't do it, did they?"

"We don't think so. We don't know."

Derr's eyes shifted to the old man, carrying the handles of his small basket, waiting to check out his purchases. He had decided to go with the cheese-flavored chips.

"Think. Give me some names," Lapp urged.

Anxious to get Lapp out of his hair, he thought a moment and said, "the guy that owns the bar next door. He was in here, I think. There was another guy, too, who I didn't know. He seemed to be hanging around by the magazines, reading, but not buying. We get guys like that."

"What was his name?"

"I don't know. He comes in every once in awhile, but …" he shrugged.

"What does he look like?"

"About your height. Good build. Usually needs a shave. Wears an orange baseball cap," Derr said, running out of words.

"What did he buy?"

"I think he bought a carton of cigarettes. Look, I got a customer," he said, responding to the man's sigh.

"Just one more minute," Lapp assured the man. "This is important."

The man shook his head impatiently.

Lapp continued, "what brand?"

"Marlboros. And he bought a couple gallons of water."

"That it?"

"That's all I remember."

Lapp wrote several notes and stuck the Scripto pencil and pad back into his shirt pocket. "Thanks. Here's my card. Call me if you think of anything else." Lapp started toward the door, then turned back. "Call me if you ever need someone to speak up for you. I appreciate your help."

Derr, unloading the man's store items, and ringing them up, said, with surprised enthusiasm, "thanks."

Lapp backed the truck away from the store and waited for traffic to pass before entering the road. He was hungry, exhausted, and not at all thrilled about going home to an empty house.

The house was dark and cold. He turned up the thermostat to 70 degrees and answered the blinking light by punching the PLAY/PAUSE button. It was Betsy. Her voice was flat, without emotion.

"Hi. I'm coming by tonight around 7:30 to pick up a few clothes. Just thought I'd let you know."

The machine told him that the call had come in at 5:06 p.m. A glance at the kitchen clock said it was 7:20. She'd be here any minute. Lapp pulled a chicken pie from the freezer, read the directions and stuck it in the microwave. He set the table, pulled out a Pepsi, popped the tab and took a long gulp.

With the growl of the automatic garage door opening, he felt a brief moment of satisfaction that Betsy wouldn't be able to pull her little Mazda Miata into the garage.

He had parked his truck in the middle.

Betsy came through the door that led from the garage into the kitchen, followed by a tall, heavyset woman who Lapp didn't know. Betsy opened the blue raincoat to reveal her white nurse's uniform and Red Cross shoes. He had not seen nor heard from her since last Saturday when they had met with the marriage counselor for the second of three sessions mandated by the court before a divorce decree could be issued.

"I thought you might not want to be here when I came," she said.

Lapp responded defensively, "why not. I still live here."

Thin, five-feet-three inches tall, her bottled-blonde hair, cut and permed in short, tight curls, Betsy was towered over by her friend, a large-boned woman with glowing red hair who stood close to six feet. Hefty, but not fat, she wore a brown, tweed coat-dress. "This is my friend, Leila Gordon. She's a gynecologist at the hospital."

Lapp nodded.

"I'm staying with Leila and her husband, Royce, while you look for a place."

It was a not so subtle way of reminding him that he had agreed to move out by the end of the month, which was less than two weeks away. "I'm supposed to go with Kathy on Sunday to look at places," he said, referring to Kathy Johnson, a realtor who lived three doors up the street and was married to a Sheriff's deputy. "But I'm on this murder case and I'm not sure I'll be able to keep my appointment."

Leila brightened. "We saw you on TV. Dorothy Sutton saw you on the evening news and everyone in the ward came in to watch. We loved the way you ordered those reporters off of the Amish farm."

"What are you doing on a murder case?" Betsy asked evenly.

He noticed she was wearing small hoop earrings. Except for her plain gold wedding band, which she still wore, and the gold Longines watch he had given her on their first anniversary, she had always claimed an aversion to jewelry. What's with the earrings? Were they a gift from the lover she claimed not to have?

"The victim was Amish. They want me to be a liaison with their community."

"That's right," Leila added with a syrupy tone that Lapp took to be sincere, not sarcastic. "Betsy told me you grew up Amish. And now you're a State Trooper investigating a murder."

"I owe it all it Betsy," Lapp said, trying to control the sarcastic irony. "She can explain it to you, if she already hasn't." Lapp was not about to go into the story about how Betsy's father, Joe Roblin, had been the one to suggest law enforcement as a way to support his daughter.

"I'll just grab a few things," Betsy said, disappearing up the stairs.

"I feel so sorry for those people. To have something like this happen," Leila droned. "Did you know the family?"

"I knew the victim and the family, yes. And it is a tragedy."

"I've treated a couple of Amish women. Minor problems after birth conducted by one of their midwives. They were so nice. Just like regular people."

The bell dinged on the microwave just in time to keep Lapp from saying, "did you think they were from Mars?"

Using an oven mitt, Lapp pulled out the pie and cursed when he saw it had bubbled over onto the microwave turntable.

Betsy came down the stairs hugging an armful of pantsuits, her standard off-duty wardrobe. He couldn't remember the last time she wore a dress over her boyish figure.

"Let me take those from you," Leila said. "I'll wait outside," she added as she went through the door into the garage.

"You bring your bodyguard with you?" Lapp asked.

"It doesn't help to be nasty," Betsy shot back.

"What does help?"

"I thought we were past all that? I thought we agreed to make this a friendly split."

"I was friendly," he said, pleading innocence.

"That thing is full of preservatives," Betsy said, nodding at the chicken pie. She had been a stickler for a healthy diet, which, with her gone, had been shot to hell.

"That's what I'm in to these days?"

"What's that supposed to mean?"

"Preservatives. Self-preservation."

Betsy did not return his sarcastic smile. "If you need more time to find a place, I guess I can wait another week or so. I'll see you tomorrow morning for our last counseling session."

"I have to cancel. I'm on this case full-time until we solve it."

"It's not going to help to put it off." The truce was fraying. Shots were being fired.

"I forgot about it. Call and cancel. Hopefully, we can go next week."

"We may get charged on such short notice."

Lapp shrugged. "It can't be helped."

"Will you at least have the courtesy to call and let me know one way or another about next week?"

"I'll do that."

"Fine," Betsy said, angrily. She grabbed the doorknob.

"Betsy?"

She turned back.

His tone was conciliatory. "I'll be there if I can. I'm ready to get it over with."

Betsy nodded and choked back a cry. "I'm sorry."

"Yeah. Me too."

He stared at the door and listened to the garage door close. He picked up the sticky, greasy chicken pie and dropped it into the waste basket. Then he popped another Pepsi, walked into the living room and sank into his leather covered chair.

Chapter 11

Lapp woke up feeling like he'd been through the wringer. The clock radio's digital numbers showed 6:30. The automatic thermostat had kicked in, but the room was still shivery cold.

He grabbed yesterday's clothing from the ladder back chair and pulled them over his boxer shorts and T-shirt sleepwear.

In the small, now warm bathroom, he stared in the mirror and stroked his stubbled beard. Sweeping the lathered whiskers away with skilled swipes of his safety razor, he imagined what he would look like as an Amish man with a full beard. Would it be bushy or stringy? Grey or snow white? Left untrimmed, Amish beards were not intended to be handsome or stylish. Instead of wedding rings, beards were the badges of married men. He fingered the back of his neck and played with imaginary hair that would have curled over his collar. In front, the bangs untrimmed, above his bushy eyebrows would be cut straight across the middle of his forehead.

Back in the bedroom, he stared at the rumpled Queen-sized bed. The sheets should have been changed a week ago. That had been one of Betsy's chores. The last one out of bed was in charge of straightening it up. They had maintained a strict division of household duties. She took care of the laundry. Except for drying the dishes at night and emptying the dishwasher, the indoor chores were her domain. That was their routine until Betsy began staying out late and leaving early in the morning. Nurses' duties. Labor union problems. Explanations he went along with. He never suspected that there was more to it until she asked for the divorce. And, although she continued to deny it, Lapp suspected a third party was involved. Most likely a doctor at the hospital.

He twisted and examined the gold band on the fourth finger of his left hand and decided to wait until their divorce was final before pulling it off.

Downstairs, he started the coffee pot percolating before stepping out the front door. The sparkling crystals of frost that covered his small front yard would soon dissolve. The sky was clear and blue. A beautiful fall morning. He lifted his face to feel the warm rays of the rising sun. The Maple trees that lined the cul-de-sac street had shed their shade. Leaves had been raked, burned, composted or collected and left in cans at the curb.

It was Saturday morning quiet. The usual parade of cars, SUVs, vans and trucks took weekend mornings off. He returned a wave to a Jeep Cherokee, whose middle aged male driver he knew by sight but not by name. In a few hours the street and sidewalks would come alive with the sights and sounds of mothers pushing strollers and the clatter of children riding "Big Wheels" or skateboards.

He pulled the rolled newspaper from the gaudy orange metal cylinder with the words "Intelligencer Journal" stenciled on it.

The headline blared, "Amish Farmer Murdered—Possible Hate Crime."

Retrieving yesterday's mail from the shiny aluminum box, he took a long look back at the white, two story square box house, with green shutters and trim. They had lived here in SunView Estates, an ostentatious name for a 60-unit tract of starter homes on the eastern edge of Lancaster city, for the past 6 years. The 1650 square foot houses were all cut from the same blueprints with alternating facades. Their house had a portico and front door entry to the right of the two car garage. The neighbor's house, with a garage six feet away from theirs, had its front entrance on the left, and so forth, down the cul-de-sac street. They were the second occupants. The original owners, a couple in their mid-thirties with three small children, had simply outgrown the 12-year old house. In fact, the neighborhood was still filled with young families and young children. John and Betsy Lapp, being childless, had little in common with their neighbors and kept pretty much to themselves.

Shivering from the cold, he ran up the sidewalk into the house.

Shuffling through the mail, he dropped two utility bills on the kitchen table.

Four solicitations for money from charities, a color wrapped sheet filled with ads, and a "winning" letter from Publishers Clearing House, were all dumped, unopened, into a white plastic waste basket.

He skimmed the major portion of the article that dominated the front page.

Except for sensationalizing the "hate crime" angle, there was no new information on the slaying of Jacob Stoltzfus. The story directed readers to the editorial section and an opinion piece, headed, "New Violence against the Amish."

He read the three-column editorial over a bowl of Cheerios and sliced bananas. It described the increasing incidence of violence against the Amish people, including the burning of six Amish barns in 1992 in central Pennsylvania. In addition to road accidents involving horses and buggies, there was the angry 24-year old carpenter in Monroe County, Wisconsin, who shot a 22-rifle at a horse and buggy carrying a young man and three school children, hitting the horse three times. The shooter continued his crime spree by forcing a 15-year old Amish girl into his car at gun point and driving to an isolated area where he used a hunting knife to cut the clothes from her body and rape her. Why? The young man stated it was in retaliation for the Amish buggies running his car off of the road. As in the case of the killing of Jacob Stoltzfus, the reaction of the Amish people was subdued. Speaking about the rape of the young girl, one Amish man who spoke anonymously said that they would work on forgiveness for the criminal but it would be hard.

The newspaper and the public were looking to the State Police and the courts to provide swift justice. And, to answer the question, why?

John Lapp vowed to do his best to answer that question.

At 7:45, John Lapp punched the code to the back door entrance, changed into his uniform and climbed the stairs to the detectives room. There, he exchanged morning waves with Eiseman and Martin both in their cubicles with phones held against their faces. Lapp took a seat in front of Moyer's empty desk and was soon daydreaming over how he got there.

It was Betsy's father, Joe Roblin, a retired police chief from the small town of Lititz, who first suggested that John Lapp become a policeman. It happened shortly after Betsy told her parents that she and Lapp planned to marry. When questioned about his career prospects, Lapp, already twenty-four and struggling financially through his second year at Millersville State College with an undeclared major, had little to offer.

Joe, after four years of military service, and fifteen years with the department, the last seven as chief, was set to retire. It left him, in his words, "sitting pretty." And Lapp could do the same with the Pennsylvania State Police. They required two years of college and some training. After reviewing the pros of steady work, good pension, something different every day, never boring, generally not dangerous, and the satisfaction of helping people, Lapp was amenable. The only cons he could think of were the uniform (but then he had dressed uniformly as an Amish for eighteen years), and an aversion to violence, which he was assured, was rare.

He was pulled from his daydream by the approaching footsteps of Lt. Warren Moyer. Juggling a steaming cup of coffee, he unzipped and shrugged off his padded blue Phillies baseball jacket and doffed the matching cap before settling behind his desk.

Moyer took a delicate sip and asked, "You had your morning coffee yet?"

"Yes sir. Before I left home."

"This stuff is hot. That's about all you can say for it. You get anything new?"

"I talked to Jacob's brother. He wasn't much help. He said Jacob was always full of big ideas."

Moyer drained his coffee and sat back. "Hopefully, we'll get some help from the forensics reports, fingerprints, footprints and other physical evidence found at the crime scene. We're also tracing the history of the shotgun. Who's next on your list?"

"Talk to a few more relatives, I guess." Lapp pulled his notebook from his pocket, flipped it open.

"Any of them benefit from the victim's death?"

Lapp scanned the list. "Not that I can see. The widow would inherit the farm. She can remarry, but I don't know if she will. There aren't too many eligible Amish bachelors. She'll need some male help, though. Maybe his brother, Amos. I used to know him."

"The brother?"

"Yeah. In school. Nearly twenty years ago. He was a little queer then."

Moyer cracked a wide smile. "A gay Amish man? I never heard of one of those."

Lapp quickly protested, "no, no, that's not what I meant at all, I meant he was a little strange. Mentally handicapped. A slow learner. Actually, the Amish use the word "gay" for someone who has left the church."

"Like you?" Moyer smirked.

"Yeah, almost like me. I never joined the church. I don't think the Amish even have a word for homosexuals. I've never heard one."

Moyer chuckled, "See? That's what we need you for. To interpret the Amish language from the English language."

"Anyway, getting back to Amos, he was a slow learner. Maybe even slightly retarded."

"I see. Is he married?"

"Not according to his brother."

"So? Is he queer?"

"From what I remember, more likely neuter. He works as a blacksmith," Lapp said consulting his notebook. "Daniel said he forges weather vanes in a Amish-owned business just off the main highway. They work a half-day on Saturday. It's just down the road."

"Want some company on this one?"

Lapp's face turned red. "I guess I haven't been doing all that well so far, have I?"

"It's always better when two go out on interviews. Helps to play good cop, bad cop." Moyer got out of his chair and yelled down the hallway. "Hey, Eiseman."

The tall, middle-aged detective with the bushy hair and eyebrows rose from his chair, hitched up his pants and lumbered toward Lapp and Moyer.

"How about going out with Lapp on this next interview?" Moyer asked.

"Later maybe. I just got a break on the LaTanya Johnson rape case. They're bringing in a woman who claims to have been a witness."

Moyer's interest perked up. "I want in on that one. Let's try Martin. Hey, Doug."

The short detective, with huge legs and thighs shaped like bowling pins, waddled into the cubicle. "You called?"

"You got time to go out with Lapp on an interview?"

Martin swiped his bald head with his hand. "Bad timing. I'm deep into the Kline arson case."

Lapp had read the newspaper accounts of the small wood-framed building that had been torched. The owner, Robert Kline, and his XXX-rated video store had been the subject of controversy in the little town of Bird-In-Hand. Kline died in the fire. Martin was the lead investigator.

"You better stick with it." Moyer turned to Lapp. "Busy people around here. Looks like you're on your own again."

"I'll do better," Lapp responded, glad he was going solo. "Knowing Amos, he would probably clam up at any sign of pressure, anyway."

"By the way, how you doing with your reports? Go heavy on details. You're not writing traffic tickets here."

"Got ya."

At 9:30, Lapp steered his patrol car into the oil-stained parking strip in front of a horizontally-set, tin-roofed Quonset hut. White smoke puffed from the three stovepipe chimneys that extended above the rounded roof. A wooden sign with the name, *Smoker's Ornamental Iron,* burned in script, hung by a chain over the windowed door. A small bell announced his entry.

A short, wiry, bearded Amish man in his thirties appeared from behind a beaded curtain and stepped up to the simple plywood counter. His curious brown eyes investigated Lapp's uniform and he cleared his throat before asking, "can I help you?"

"Are you Smoker?"

"Ja. Eli Smoker."

"I'm State Trooper John Lapp. I'm looking for Amos Stoltzfus. I understand he works here."

As Smoker shook Lapp's extended hand, his eyebrows rose in surprise at the Amish name, but did not pursue it. "Ja, he does. He's in the back. You want him to come up here?"

"I'll go back there, if that's okay."

"Ja, you can if you want to." He pointed to a narrow gate in the side of the counter that Lapp slipped through, then dipped his head between the parted beads to enter the foundry area.

The acrid smell of smoke, sparks and molten iron attacked his nostrils and grabbed his throat. He felt the heat immediately. Not a furnace blast, more like a radiant glove held against his face. A quick survey of the area revealed three work stations, spaced about ten feet apart, each with a tray of hot coals with smoke rising into the funneled exhaust pipes that extended down from the rounded corrugated roof.

The three smiths raised a cacophony of rhythmic tapping and pounding as they hammered the red-hot iron into various lengths, shapes and sizes. Lapp reviewed their faces twice before identifying Amos Stoltzfus. Of the other two, one was Amish, identified by his beard without the mustache. The other, a huge burly man with a blonde ponytail, definitely was not.

Feeling the suspicious eyes of all three smiths, Lapp turned to Eli Smoker and yelled above the noisy din, "I'd like to talk to Amos somewhere that is quiet. It's about his brother."

"I figured. You can go out in back. It's quiet there. I'll tell him."

Amos concentrated on his work, pounding on the red-hot form with a smith's blunt hammer, turning it repeatedly until he was satisfied with the shape. He dipped it in the water where it sizzled, steamed and cooled. Satisfied, he released the combed head of a crowing rooster from the tongs. Amos stared at Lapp as Smoker yelled Lapp's request into his ear. He pulled the asbestos gloves from his hands, lifted the sweat-soiled straw hat and scratched his thinning hair. He nodded to Smoker and backed away from his glowing coal fire pit. Lapp followed, past two small storage rooms, and out the back door where he was jolted by the cold, fresh air. Amos dropped the bib portion of the heavy asbestos apron that protected him from leaping sparks and embers and pulled a cigarette pack from the pocket of his smudged white shirt.

Amos lit up and stuck the pack back into his pocket. He was short, about five-foot-five, and, except for his sinewy arms, he was thinly gaunt. With his sharp nose and pointed chin, he bore no resemblance to his more handsome brother. His brown eyes flashed like those of a cornered animal. When Lapp offered his hand automatically, Amos recoiled with fear. He had forgotten. Amos had a phobia about being touched.

"It's me, Amos, Johnny Lapp. I'd like to ask you a few questions about Jacob."

"I knowed who you was," he replied through a breath of smoke. "I ain't seen you for a long time now, but I knowed your face. It ain't changed much. Even dressed up like that," he added, pointing at the uniform and badge and nodding his head, "I knowed it was you."

"You haven't changed much either, Amos. I'm sorry about your brother."

"Yeah, me too. I guess God musta wanted him," Amos said, nodding to reassure himself.

"Let's go over there." A gust of cold air suggested to Lapp that they should continue this interview from the protection of an open shed where two horses, one black and the other a roan, still harnessed to their buggies, noisily chewed on hay from a steel feeder trough.

They escaped the wind by standing next to an older box buggy with a branch scratched roof. "When did you last see your brother?" Lapp asked.

Amos opened his mouth to speak and then suddenly slammed it shut. "I don't know no more."

"I think you know, Amos. It's all right to tell me."

Amos squinched his eyes and arranged his thoughts before answering. "Maybe it was a few weeks ago, but I ain't too sure."

"You didn't see him very often then?"

"No, not so often. Sometimes he was over to our farm, but not so often."

"The last time he was over, did you talk to him?"

"He didn't come to see me. He was over to see our Mam and Pap."

"But you got along all right, you and Jacob?"

Amos nervously shuffled his feet before answering. "Sure, why not?"

"Did Jacob ever tell you he was going to sell a corner of his land? A piece over by the motel. You know the place I'm talking about?"

The question caught his interest. "You mean that Holiday Inn motel over there?"

"That's right. Did he ever tell you he was going to sell some land to the motel."

"No. He never said nothing like that. He wouldn't do nothing like that."

"He got $50,000 for it."

Amos shook his head. "He did?" A long strand of cigarette ashes fell to the ground.

"We believe he had the money with him last night when he was killed."

"He did?"

"We think he was killed for the money."

"How did he have it?"

"You mean, how did he carry it?"

"I guess."

"In a gym bag. Why do you ask?"

"It just wondered me." Amos turned his head to end the subject.

"What would Jacob do with that kind of money?" Lapp asked. "Amos?"

After ten seconds of staring at the ground, Amos turned back to Lapp. "I don't know. That wonders me, too. Maybe Sallie knows. You oughta ask her."

"Did you see Jake with that bag last night?"

"I told you already once that I didn't see him."

"Then why do you act like you did? Are you lying to me?"

Amos shook his head in denial. "No, I ain't lying. That's for sure."

"Where were you last Thursday night, Amos?"

"When?"

"Two nights ago at about ten o'clock."

"I musta been in bed. I'm in bed by that time. You oughta know that." His head bobbed like a dashboard toy.

"And you never got up during the night?"

"I think I mighta gone to the outhouse once. Some nights I hafta get up already."

"But you never left the farm?"

"At night? When it's dark out? Where would I go?"

"Maybe you were out courting. It's the season for that, isn't it?" Lapp teased, suddenly trying a different tactic.

Amos blushed. "Ach, no, I don't have no girl friend. You oughta know that."

"Why would I know that?"

"Cause I'm a fraidy cat, just like I always was.

"Can you think of anybody who Jacob didn't get along with?"

Amos eyes turned upward, giving serious consideration to a serious question. "No, nobody that I know of." Amos took a long last puff from the butt that was smoked down to the brown filter.

If Amos wasn't lying he was holding something back. Lapp couldn't come up with a question to tap it. "We can go back inside now."

"Okay ." Amos led the way to the rear door of the Quonset hut.

"I may want to talk to you again."

"Don't come here if you do."

"Why is that?"

"I won't be here no more. I'll be over at Jake's place now. Taking care of his farm for awhile. They know that already."

"Are you glad you'll be farming again?"

"I don't know. I guess." Amos tossed his cigarette butt to the ground and entered the back door. Lapp quickly reached for it, swiped it against the siding knocking off the burned end and thrust it into his pocket.

Amos was back at his foundry post when Lapp came through the door and noticed the crowing cock weather vane on a table next to him. It was still in an unpolished state, but was a beautiful work of art. Lapp pointed and yelled over the din of the other ironworkers, "Did you make that, Amos?"

"That's one of the ones I do," Amos shouted back.

"It's beautiful."

Amos turned his head away from the compliment. To accept it would demonstrate pride.

Lapp examined the rooster with its wavy comb and noticed that the eyes were open wide and the beak seemed to be protesting rather than crowing. He put it down and asked, "Amos, are you on any medication?"

"What?"

"Do you take pills every day?"

Amos nodded vigorously, like a patient assuring a doctor. "Every day. Every morning and every night, too. Like I'm supposed to."

"What are they supposed to do for you?"

"I'm not sure, exactly. I chust know I'm supposed to take them."

"Who's your doctor?"

"Dr. Diehl."

"Where's his office?"

"Over in Intercourse. It's not far." Then, "I guess you know that."

Lapp sat in his patrol car and debated his next move. During his training, he had only one class in interrogation. It had not been enough to help him find out if Amos was lying or holding something back.

Consulting his notebook with the list of Jacob's relatives, he didn't see any names that stood out as providers of information. Curiously, his thoughts turned to Lisa Robinson. If his memory was correct, there was a New Era newspaper rack in front of the Nike shoe outlet, a couple of blocks down on Route 30.

Jacob's death was still front page news. And beneath the photo of his covered body, at the top of the story was Lisa Robinson's byline. The story was brief. Three columns wide and eight inches deep. Just the basic facts from the press conference.

He wondered why, with the amount of attention she had paid to him, his name was not mentioned. He concluded it was probably better, politically, that he wasn't. Or, maybe she intended to keep him as her own private source.

Chapter 12

When John Lapp returned to the barracks and stood in front of Warren Moyer's desk he was totally unprepared for what was coming.

"There you are. I been waiting for you." Moyer's words came through a poker-face that Lapp had not seen before. "We got some interesting new developments in the Stoltzfus case." He reached beside the filing cabinet behind his desk and stood up, holding a double barreled shotgun. With one hand on the polished walnut stock and the other mid-way down the black barrels, he thrust it at Lapp. "Here."

Lapp matched his hands to Moyer's and took the shotgun.

"Look familiar?" He didn't wait for Lapp to respond. "That's our murder weapon. The one we recovered at the crime scene." Moyer lifted a piece of paper from his desk and held it up for Lapp to see. "We had one of our cadets checking the stores that sell shotguns. This is what she came up with. A bill of sale for that very shotgun. It was purchased on July 17 of this year at Sears. By guess who?"

Lapp shrugged his ignorance.

"By one Amos Stoltzfus. What do you think about that?"

Lapp failed to disguise the shock that jolted through his body. While gathering his thoughts, he examined the shotgun by rotating it in his hands and feeling the fine grain in the walnut stock. "I don't know what to say. I talked with Amos this morning and he never said a word about it."

"He say anything at all?" Moyer took back the shotgun, and leaned it, stock down, against the filing cabinet.

"Not much. He claims he knew nothing about Jacob selling land or having money. He said he rarely saw his brother. Which doesn't surprise me. When I knew them, Jacob was constantly teasing and tormenting his poor brother."

Moyer's eyes widened. "Maybe Amos decided it was time to get even."

"Amos wouldn't have the stomach for murder. He'd be afraid."

"Then explain the shotgun?" Moyer persisted.

Lapp shrugged. "Maybe he bought it for rabbit hunting. Amish hunt game for food. They also shoot predators like rats, fox, raccoon, that go after their chickens."

"How did he respond to your questions? Was he nervous? Defensive?"

"He was Amos. Nervous? Yeah. A little. He was born nervous." Lapp said, still debating how Amos could have been the owner of the murder weapon.

"You get anything out of him at all?"

"Yeah. He said he's quitting the foundry and moving to Jacob's place to help with the farm."

"Isn't that nice," Moyer said mockingly. "Maybe he'll marry the widow and raise her kids while he's at it."

Lapp was angered by the allegation. It was ludicrous. "He knows that's not going to happen. He's doing it out of duty to his brother's family. It's the Amish way."

"That it?"

Lapp decided to keep Amos' interest in the gym bag to himself. "I did get this," Lapp said, reaching into his pocket and pulling out the little brown envelope containing the cigarette with the brown filter and handed it to Moyer. "It's probably coincidence, but he smokes the same brand of cigarette that were lying around the crime scene."

Moyer smiled as he opened the envelope and examined it. "I'll have it sent over to the crime lab. Getting a little more interesting, isn't it?" He picked up another piece of paper from his desk and raised it for Lapp to see. "This came in from the lab. Another match. The boot prints at the site? A Wolverine high-top."

"I know the style. They're kind of a Wellington boot. I still own a pair. Anybody that works in cow shit or mud owns a pair."

"One, two, three," Moyer offered. "Gun, boots and butts. All a match. I say we bring in Amos Stoltzfus and have a little talk with him. What do you say?"

Lapp countered, "If Amos was the killer, why would he leave a new shotgun that can be traced to him, drop a trail of cigarette butts and be so careless with his boot prints?"

"You said yourself he's retarded."

"No, not retarded. Slow, maybe, but not stupid."

"Well," Moyer cracked. "Stupid is as stupid does. Isn't that what they say? It's enough for me. I'll have him picked up."

"Are you charging him?"

"There's a damn good chance"

"What would happen if you waited a day?"

"Why would I do that?"

"The funeral is tomorrow. It will be devastating to the Amish for something like this to come out during a time of mourning."

"Well, Johnny, my boy," Moyer said as he rose from the chair and grabbed his coat from the rack, "I'd like to accommodate you, and I'd like to accommodate them. But the heat is on. You say he's at Jacob's farm?"

"That's what he told me."

"Then you can come with me or not. It's up to you."

Lapp didn't hesitate. He would try to make it easier on Sallie by being there, although he wasn't quite sure how. "I'll come."

Chapter 13

Sallie Stoltzfus stared at Jacob's colorless face and, with her index finger replaced a hair that had strayed in the bushy beard she had so lovingly combed and stroked. His body looked uncomfortably low in the bottom of a rough pine coffin that had been built by Stubby Beiler and her brother, David, in the barn workshop using Jacob's tools. She had watched them plane the top boards, and hammer them together. The banging of each nail pierced her heart. Jacob's body was dressed in a cotton white shirt and white muslin pants that she had stitched on her treadle machine.

The cuffs were sewn by hand. She had draped the inside of the coffin with a white sheet, but removed it after being told by a Bishop's wife that it was not allowed. "We come into this earth plain, and we leave it that way."

It was dinner time on Friday when she received word that Jacob's body had been released by the police and taken to Behney's Funeral Home to be embalmed. On Saturday morning, he was delivered in a hearse to the farm. The hearse driver, a man in his fifties and his young helper, both dressed in black suits, white shirts and black bow ties, carried the sheet covered body on a litter into the house where it was transferred to a portable bed that had been set up in the parlor. The driver of the hearse watched Sallie lift the sheet from Jacob's head before warning her that when she dressed the body it would be wise not to remove the wrappings around his middle. They had done their best to patch him up but he had been severely damaged in that area. His chest and stomach area would be best left undisturbed.

Feeling weary, Sallie pulled over a straight back walnut chair, folded her hands in her lap and continued to contemplate this man who had been her husband.

The weather had been sunny and cool on the November morning of their wedding twelve years ago. Their courtship began within weeks from the time they had been baptized and committed their lives to the church and Jesus Christ. Jacob reassured Sallie that his "rumspringa", a year-long period of "running around", where Jacob and other boys, sometimes joined by girls, hung out in "gangs", drove cars, dressed "English", drank, and even experimented with drugs, while family and church members looked the other way, was out of his system.

He was ready to join the church and settle down.

Their commitment was a well-known secret that became a reality on the day Jacob followed the tradition of informing his favorite church deacon of their intentions.

The deacon, in turn, "published" the wedding on a church bulletin board.

From that time until the wedding, two weeks later, Jacob followed the Amish custom of staying as a guest at Sallie's house, where he was on his best behavior, gaining compliments from Sallie's parents and siblings for his sincerity and hard work.

Written letters of invitation were sent to friends and family households. In the days approaching the wedding, the Yoder household bustled with activity. Sallie remembered her mother's frayed nerves, and sometimes sharp tongue that cut her father, her brothers and sisters, and even Sallie herself when things did not suit her.

Sallie stared at Jacob's wax like cheeks and lips and remembered how he had been playful and happy, constantly teasing Sallie about forgetting the words during the ceremony. On the wedding morning, his mother told her how Jacob breezed through the kitchen, mingling and laughing with the dozen cooks and helpers, the leaves of a celery heart protruding from his lips before being sucked in, chewed and swallowed.

Then he danced to the sideboard and broke off a piece of brown crust from a pumpkin pie and pronounced it perfect, pleasing the cooks no end.

Upstairs, with her mother in attendance, Sallie smoothed her new black dress. It was no different from her regular Sunday clothes, but she remembered being extremely pleased and happy.

Then it was nine o'clock and the singing had begun. Sallie and Jacob sat shoulder to shoulder on a front bench and listened to the minister's hour-long sermon. Before the next sermon began, Jacob whispered into Sallie's ear, "I got to go," jumped up and left for a few minutes. The service continued with accounts of events from the Bible: Adam and Eve; the wickedness of mankind before the Flood; Noah's warning not to marry non-believers; the plight of the adulterous Solomon; and, finally, how Tobias obeyed his father's instructions to marry a wife from his own tribe despite overwhelming circumstances.

Sallie remembered glancing at Jacob, noticing his restlessness, the sweat on his brow, even though the room was not warm. She also remembered receiving reassuring nods from Moses, Sarah and Lizzie Lapp, Johnny's father and sisters, and wondering where he was and hoping he was as happy today as she was.

The minister reached out, inviting them to step forward. Jacob squeezed her hand and they rose together. The minister laid his hands on theirs and put them through their vows of confidence, fidelity, and promises. When he asked Sallie if she promised to care for her husband until "the dear God will separate you from each other," she proclaimed, enthusiastically, "yes!"

The minister pronounced them man and wife.

It was during the handshakes and congratulations after the wedding that a feeling that Sallie had not felt for months, swept through her: that she was his prize from a game he had played and won. In the days after, while they traveled from farm to farm visiting relatives and helping with the reduced winter farming chores, he bragged about Sallie's beauty and what a lucky man he was to have claimed her. She was embarrassed and heard the grumbling among friends and relatives that Jacob Stoltzfus was too full of pride for his own good.

In early January, they set up housekeeping in her parent's house. Over the next year, they agreed to buy the farm from her parents who moved into a retirement house along Route 896.

Sallie soon realized that Jacob was not prepared for the overwhelming tasks of running the farm. Even working side by side with him during the planting and harvesting seasons, it was not enough. Family members helped, and hired hands were taken on during the times when they could afford it.

During the first years of their marriage, they were happiest when a new child entered their lives. He could point to them as being beautiful, bright, and a well-deserved gift from God. Something to once again raise his pride.

That too, wore off. He lost interest in having more children. Sallie wanted more and had tried to entice him in subtle ways by standing behind him and messaging his shoulders, or in bed, placing her hand on his hip. But he did not often respond. And, most recently, not at all.

Then, over a year ago now, she had found one of his handkerchiefs soiled with, she was almost sure, his semen. Was he abusing himself or was the handkerchief used to catch the semen before it could burst inside another woman?

Sallie lowered her head, placed her hands over her eyes, and massaged her temples with her fingertips. Had she brought this on? Had she been a bad wife? She had prayed for God's help. She had studied her bible every night, seeking guidance.

"Mam?"

Sallie raised her eyes to see her oldest son in the doorway. "Yes, Samuel?"

"Aunt Sarah says she needs help with the clothesline. She says the wet clothes are too heavy and the wind's too strong."

Sallie smiled thinking of how her busy-body aunt had insisted that the washing couldn't wait until Monday, the usual "Washentag". "Tell her I'm coming."

She rose and stared at her husband's face. So innocent now. So peacefully at rest.

She joined Samuel at the door.

Chapter 14

While John Lapp drove the marked patrol car and worried about the effect of their visit on Sallie, Amos, and the entire Amish community, Warren Moyer sat in the passenger seat and decided to be chatty.

"I'm as surprised as you are that things turned out the way they did. Especially the shotgun. That boy's got some explaining to do."

"You never know with Amos," Lapp said. "What he'll say or won't say."

They rode in silence for a couple of minutes before Moyer asked, "you got a family?"

"A wife. She's a nurse at Lancaster General. No kids." He decided to not reveal his impending divorce. As far as he knew, no one at the barracks knew about it and he wanted to keep it that way for awhile. He wasn't ready to get "fixed up" with dates by his fellow troopers. "How about you?" Lapp asked.

"Married twenty-three years," Moyer said proudly. "Three kids."

"That's great."

"Two girls. Twenty-one and nineteen. The oldest a senior at F&M and the other one is a Sophomore at Albright College over in Reading. My boy Sean's a senior in high school. He's got a soccer scholarship to Millersville."

"That's where I went for two years. It's a good school."

"You didn't finish?"

"No. I got married. Amish schooling ends at fourteen. Because of that, I was twenty-two before I got my high school degree. After two years at Millersville, it was time to make a living."

"I'd like to hear the whole story sometime. From what I've heard, it's not easy doing what you did."

Lapp could feel Moyer staring at the side of his face. "It got easier after the first year."

"What about your Amish family? You ever see any of them?"

"Not really. My mother died when I was a child. I haven't seen my father in 15 years. I have two sisters—the oldest practically raised me—and dozens of aunts, uncles and cousins. We live in separate worlds."

"Ever think about going back?"

Lapp shook his head. "Never did."

"You a confirmed trooper?"

Lapp smiled. "For the most part, yeah. I'm pretty even tempered. You need that in my job. The day-to-day patrolling gets a little boring. I hate the court appearances where they try and beat the violation. Especially when they have a lawyer with them. You waste a half-day sitting in court and some judge lets the offender off." He shrugged, "I guess it goes with the territory."

"I'm with you. For eight long years. Put in for detective first chance I got."

"How long you been in altogether?"

"Going on twenty-five years, if you count the credit I got for two years as an MP in Viet Nam. I was one of those guys who came back and couldn't figure out what to do with his life. I was lucky I connected here."

They rode in silence for the next mile before Moyer said, "by the way, I checked out your personnel file. Good performance reports. Not to mention the sixteen complimentary letters versus two complaints. That's a hell of a ratio. Normally a guy gets nothing but complaints. Seems to me you're in the right place, too."

Lapp smiled. "Most days, anyway."

Moyer stared out the passenger side and said wistfully, "It's beautiful out here. The open fields, the big white puffy clouds, the cold wind. My time of year. Someday I might have time to enjoy it."

Lapp nodded. His mind had moved ahead to the Stoltzfus farm.

Moyer mused out loud, "hunting season starts in a couple of days. That'll bring at least one accidental shooting. Somebody getting killed or maimed. You a hunter?"

"I never was." Lapp turned the patrol car up the lane. The cows and "bee-falo" were nowhere to be seen.

Moyer got back to business. "Well, we'll soon find out what your friend Amos went hunting for."

Coming to a stop, they were greeted by a barking dog, a medium-sized, black mix with a white diamond on his forehead. Sallie propped up a heavy clothesline with a notched wooden board, and stepped forward, squinting through the rays of the sun in order to identify her visitors.

Lapp scanned the two long lines of clothes flapping and flying like flags. Some were Jacob's. Most were children's shirts, pants and dresses along with Sallie's white underwear and black stockings.

The dog looked to be more bark than bite as they climbed out of the patrol car.

Sallie's sharp "Queenie! Ruick!" at the dog shut him up and set him off on a round of sniffing at the visitor's legs. "The neighbors thought we should have a watchdog. I'm not so sure," she said, her face weary and drawn.

"I'll bet the kids like having a dog," Lapp offered.

"They would except she runs away from them and chases the cats," she said, her cheeks blazing red from the cold.

The fresh, clean smell of wet clothes brought back Lapp's childhood memories of running between the lines and dodging the clothes that slapped at his face.

Moyer nodded to Lapp to begin the conversation. "Sallie. We're here to talk to Amos."

Still no smile. "Amos? What do you want with him?"

"We think Amos knows more about what Jacob was doing the night he was killed," Lapp said diplomatically. "He's not telling us everything."

"Ach, what would he know," Sallie scoffed.

"It can't be helped, Sallie. Now please tell me where he is. In the barn?"

"He said he was going to shoot some rats over at the corn crib."

"He has a gun?" Moyer asked.

"What kind of gun does he have?" Lapp asked.

"An old 22 rifle. He said it was better than using poison or traps that might kill the cats or, now, the dog." Sallie face suddenly changed, reflecting the alarmed exchange between Moyer and Lapp. "I thought it was all right. The children are at the neighbors," she added.

"What kind of 22? How many bullets does it hold?" Lapp asked.

"It's just a single shot. It belonged to Jake. I can get him for you."

"How many bullets did he take with him?"

"I think he took the box."

"Have you heard any shots yet?"

"No. I guess he hasn't seen any rats."

Moyer stepped next to Lapp. "Great. Now our main suspect is somewhere out here armed with a rifle. We're both armed, but I'm thinking of calling in some backup, just in case."

"Can we wait and see?" Lapp asked.

Sallie interrupted. "I'll find him." Her eyes were drawn to Lapp's black holster and side arm. "You stay here. I'll fetch him."

"We'll go with you," Moyer insisted.

They walked along a grass path that sparkled from the wetness of the melted morning frost.

"The corn crib is past the barn, behind the pig pens," Sallie said, pointing them out.

As they passed the muddy sty, not a oink or snort was uttered by the laid out, sleeping hogs that Lapp had slopped three days ago. Sallie turned the corner and yelled out, "Amos?"

They saw the heavy-wired, wood slatted corn crib, filled to the 10-foot high brim with golden ears of field corn, but no sign of Amos.

Sallie did a 360 degree spin. "I don't know where he is."

Moyer muttered to Lapp, "he heard us coming. He's probably in the next county by now."

"I don't think he would run," Lapp reasoned. "But he could be anywhere. There are a hundred hiding places on a farm."

"Amos. Wo bisht du? Where are you?" Sallie called again. She stepped back to Lapp and Moyer. "I don't know where he is. I'll find him." Sallie's determined footsteps led back toward the barn.

"You think it's a good idea for us to go hunting for a man with a rifle? He could pick us off from anywhere."

"He won't shoot us. He might hide, but he won't shoot us," Lapp said with conviction.

"Tell that to his brother," Moyer shot back.

They followed the sounds of Sallie's voice as she continued to call out impatiently, "Amos! Where are you?"

Sallie, wiping the moisture from her brow with the back of her hand, met Moyer and Lapp in front of the barn.

"I don't know where he is," she said again, her voice wrought with frustration.

The crack of the rifle shot froze them in their tracks. Lapp's first reaction was to protect Sallie. Moyer reached beneath his coat jacket and pulled a 9mm Beretta from a shoulder holster. The cackle of frightened chickens drew their attention toward the hen house.

At the sight of the handgun, Sallie cried, "no", and sprinted past the rectangular shingled house and turned the corner, out of sight.

Amos called out, "don't come back here."

"I'd use that sidearm, trooper," Moyer said as he raised his weapon and jerked his head at Lapp to crouch low and move cautiously forward.

Sallie reappeared from the corner of the henhouse holding the 22 rifle in her right hand. Raising it up in a signal of truce, she said, with relief, "It's all right. He shot a fox."

"What?" Moyer said with disbelief and lowered the Beretta.

Lapp exhaled a sigh of relief, smiled and holstered his sidearm. Moyer did the same, and, with the outstretched palm of his right hand, beckoned for the rifle. When she handed it to him, Moyer pulled back the bolt and expelled the spent cartridge. Sallie led them around the chicken house where Amos, amid a small blizzard of chicken feathers, sat on his haunches and stroked the small body of a red fox. He lurched to his feet and fear crossed his face when he saw the uniformed John Lapp and the strange sport-jacketed man with him.

Lapp's eyes moved from the small bullet hole in the fox's whiskered head and held up his hands in peace. "It's okay, Amos," Lapp reassured. "This is Lieutenant Moyer. He's with the State Police. We came to ask you some questions."

"It was killing our chickens," he whined like a child explaining a misdeed.

"I know Amos," Sallie said, moving closer to defend him.

Moyer stepped forward. "Amos! Do you own a Remington 12-gauge double barrel shotgun?"

Amos looked at Sallie who nodded her approval to answer. "No."

"Amos," Lapp admonished. "It's okay to tell him. Amos?"

"I did once. But it's not there no more. Somebody took it," Amos said in response to Sallie's puzzled face.

"Where was it taken from?"

"Beside the back door at the foundry. I kept it there in the corner. I didn't want to bring it home."

Lapp searched his memory for the location and remembered two push brooms set between the studs of an unfinished wall by the door. He could imagine a shotgun propped there. "Did you tell anyone your gun was missing?"

"No."

"Why not?"

Amos shrugged, childishly. "I don't know."

"Why did you buy the gun?" Lapp asked.

"I was gonna go hunting with it. For rabbits and pheasants. They're good eating."

"Why didn't you keep it at home?"

"They might not of let me keep it."

"Who was that?"

"My Pap. And my brother, Daniel. He coulda taken it away from me. Sallie knows."

Moyer jumped in. "When did you buy it?"

"In the summer sometime. I'm not too sure."

"Where did you buy it?"

Again, Amos paused before answering. "Sears, I guess. I like to go there and look at stuff. Yeah, Sears. That's where."

"Did you ever hunt with it?" Lapp asked.

"No, I never did. I tried it out once out in the woods, but it had such a kick, I didn't like it no how."

"When did you know it was missing?" Lapp continued.

"A few weeks, now. I thought somebody mighta taken it to go hunting. I thought whoever took it would bring it back. Nobody ever asked me for it."

Moyer spoke softly, but firmly. "Amos, I think you already know this. That shotgun was used to kill your brother."

Sallie gasped audibly. A flush of anger raced through Lapp's head. Moyer's bluntness and his lack of concern for Sallie's feelings were either an interrogation trick Lapp wasn't aware of or else he was a plain old asshole.

When the words were finally processed, Amos shook his head. "Nay. Nay net. Is net so."

When she was able to speak, Sallie asked, plaintively, "Johnny, is it really so?"

"I'm sorry."

She snapped her head back in angry denial.

"You'll need to come with us to the barracks," Moyer stepped toward Amos.

"Where's that?" Amos backed away. "Johnny? I can't go no place. Sallie won't let me. She needs me here now."

Sallie stepped next to Lapp and, with eyes blazing, went face to face with him. "Johnny, this can't be so. If it was his gun, then somebody took it. Don't you believe him?"

Lapp shook his head. "If he's telling the truth, we'll find out."

"Let's go," Moyer ordered.

Lapp turned and led the way back toward the car.

"Something's wrong here. You know it, too." Sallie insisted, dogging Lapp's heels.

A loud screech rang out. Lapp and Sallie turned to see Amos running toward Sallie, with Moyer standing behind, dumfounded.

"What the hell," Moyer protested, shaking his hand like he'd been burned. "I tried to help him along and he screamed bloody murder."

"I forgot to tell you. Amos doesn't like being touched. It scares him. He's always been that way. From a boy on up."

"Jesus Christ! What next?" Moyer pulled out a much needed cigarette and lit it.

Amos followed six steps behind Lapp and Sallie until they reached the clotheslines. Their voices competed with the chorus of wet clothes flapping in the brisk, cold wind behind them.

Lapp turned to Sallie. "I must do my job now. He has to come with us. And he won't come willingly unless you say it's okay."

"Ach, how can I do that? It's like I'm sending an innocent lamb to slaughter. You must look out for him."

"I promise you I will."

"You must do it for me. And for Amos. And for all the Amish. You'll talk to him and then bring him home?"

"That's what I'm hoping. I don't know for sure. They might keep him over-night."

Wanting to hide from his words, Sallie placed her hands briefly over her eyes, then asked, "The funeral's tomorrow. Can't this wait till after?"

"I'm sorry. I already tried. They won't wait. He has to come with us now."

Sallie shook her head in disbelief. Her glistening eyes bored into his. "Johnny Lapp, you must watch out for him."

"I will, Sallie. I will."

"I mean it," she warned.

She pushed away the flapping legs of blue bib overalls and walked over to Amos. As she spoke, a cloud of fear crossed Amos' face and he shrank back. In a childish tantrum he stamped his feet and cried, "nay. Ich muss net."

Moyer exchanged an impatient glance at Lapp, then dropped his cigarette and ground it into the dirt. His body relaxed when Amos, head bowed and walking like a condemned man, approached Lapp.

"You can ride in the back, Amos."

Lapp held the passenger side door as Amos climbed in. "Put on your seatbelt," he counseled before stepping into the passenger seat. Moyer, still disgusted, climbed behind the wheel.

In the side view mirror, Lapp caught a last glance of Sallie standing among the waves of laundry.

Down the lane, the staring "beefalo" were back, still out of place in the herd of dairy cows. But no more so than John Lapp, caught between the law and the certainty that Amos Stoltzfus could not have killed his brother.

Chapter 15

"Shit. Hopefully, they're not in back." The words flew from Moyer's mouth when he saw the TV remote van that was parked in the circular driveway by the front door of the barracks.

Taking a right on Oakview Street, Moyer raced through the rear parking lot and stopped by the employee entrance. Lapp jumped out, opened the unit's back door and reached in to grab Amos' arm. Amos shrank back. Lapp raised his hands in surrender. "Let's go, Amos. Come on. You need to hurry."

Confused, Amos slid out of the back seat and waited anxiously for Lapp to punch in the security code, open the door and point him inside.

Lapp led the way, turning sideways to make sure that the wide-eyed and frightened Amish man was following. In the "sweat box", Lapp pointed to a metal chair behind the long table. "Would you like some water, Amos?" Lapp asked as he filled a cone-shaped paper cup. Amos stared straight ahead and refused to answer. Lapp drained his cup and filled another, extending it again to the bewildered man with long hair that was parted in the middle and reached to the center of his ears. "You sure?"

Amos shook his head.

Warren Moyer entered the room carrying a black ceramic coffee cup. "Let's get started. You like some coffee, Amos?"

Amos did not respond. Moyer turned to Lapp. "Do they drink coffee?"

"Sometimes. I guess it depends."

Moyer extended his hospitality. "How about a soft drink? Water?"

Amos remained stone-faced.

Moyer sat down and grabbed a lined tablet and pencil from the center of the table. He stared at Amos, and began.

"You have to understand something, Amos. We're here to help you. Trooper Lapp and me we understand that sometimes things go wrong between brothers. Maybe you didn't intend to shoot him. Maybe the gun went off by accident. Those things happen sometimes. And if that's the case with you, we can help you explain it." Amos lowered his eyes to the table and picked at his earlobe with the fingers of his left hand.

Moyer turned to Lapp. "If he's not gonna talk, tell him in Pennsylvania Dutch we're going to lock him up until he does."

Knowing full well that Amos understood the threat, Lapp responded, "it won't make any difference."

"Then we'll lock him up. I'm not screwing around all day ..." Both men turned in response to a knock on the door. A bushy male head popped in. "Warren, got a minute? That report on the armed robbery case just came in and we'd like your take on it."

Moyer pushed back his chair. "No problem. This isn't going anywhere so far."

Before closing the door behind him, Moyer spoke out of the side of his mouth. "See what you can get out of him."

John Lapp leaned across the table at Amos and immediately noticed his squinched up face. "What's the matter, Amos?"

"I gotta go," he cried out.

Lapp started to say, go where, then realized what Amos was saying. "You have to go to the toilet?"

"Bad."

Lapp wasn't sure about the procedure for taking a suspect to the toilet, but couldn't ignore the poor man's discomfort. "Okay. Come on."

Lapp led the shuffling Amish man down the hallway until they came to a door with the Men/Women sign on it.

Inside, Lapp pointed to a stall that Amos quickly entered. When Amos latched the door from inside, Lapp questioned whether he should allow Amos to be alone in there. He could hear a stream of urine splashing so he knew Amos hadn't been lying. Then things got quiet.

"You okay in there, Amos?"

"Yeah. Okay."

"Hurry up then."

He heard the toilet flush and then waited as he imagined Amos buttoning up the fly on his pants.

Amos came out and walked directly toward the door.

"Wash your hands, Amos. And use soap."

Amos stared at the unfamiliar wall-hung soap dispenser. Lapp pointed to the button on the dispenser and ran water into the sink. Amos got the idea and washed his hands.

Lapp was glad to be back in the interrogation room.

Amos took his seat and heaved a sigh of relief.

Lapp sat on the opposite side and asked, "you want to smoke, Amos? It's okay to smoke in here."

Amos' stiff wax-figure pose melted. He reached beneath his coat, pulled a pack of cigarettes with a book of matches stuck in the cellophane wrap from his pant waist and lit up.

Lapp set a black plastic ashtray in front of him. "Amos. You're going to have to answer some questions."

"I'm not talking to that guy. I'm glad that guy's gone."

"Yeah, well that guy's coming back. And when he does, you need to talk. If you don't, you'll be arrested and put in jail."

Amos sighed a cloud of white smoke and tapped the white ashes into the ashtray.

"Why didn't you tell me about the shotgun?"

"I guess I forgot. I never used it no how."

"You better start remembering things that can help you. You hear me, Amos? You need to tell the truth."

If the black clothed man with brown dirt on his sleeves was concerned over Lapp's threat he didn't show it. "If I'm going to help you, you're going to have to do more to help yourself."

The cigarette, inhaled in deep pulls, had an anesthetic effect. So much so, that Amos did not react when Warren Moyer re-entered the room, closed the door behind him, and took a chair at the left end of the table.

"How's it going?" Moyer asked Lapp.

"I think he's better."

"You read him his rights yet?"

"No."

Moyer faced Amos and spoke quickly. "You have a right to remain silent. If you give up that right, anything you say can be used against you in a court of law."

If Moyer's intention was to slip those words past Amos, it worked. Amos' face was completely blank.

Moyer propped his arms on the table and leaned in. "Tell me about you and your brother. Did you get along?"

Amos did not respond. Maybe he understood his rights after all. He stubbed the cigarette butt into the ashtray. His hand shook nervously. "We got along good."

"When was the last time you saw him?"

"Not for a long time. Sometimes he comes over to see our Mam."

"Did he say anything about selling some land for $50,000?"

"I never talked to him. I just saw him. I was down by the barn."

"So you knew nothing about the land or the money?"

"Not until Johnny told me."

Surprised, Moyer turned to Lapp. "When was that?"

"This morning. At the foundry. I asked him about it." Lapp explained.

Moyer turned back to Amos. "How come you're working at the foundry and not farming," Moyer asked Amos.

"There's no farm for me. Jacob got one. And Daniel got Mam and Paps."

"Daniel the other brother?" Moyer asked Lapp.

Lapp interjected, "The youngest gets the family farm. Jacob was the first to be married and the farm Sallie grew up on was available."

"Jake didn't like farming." Amos added.

Sensing a lead, Moyer rose from his chair and circled behind Amos. "Is that right? You like farming, don't you, Amos?"

"Yeah, I like it. I like making those wanes, too," pronouncing his "v's" like "w's".

"The weathervanes I was telling you about," Lapp added.

"Jacob often said I should be the one that was farming. Cause I liked it. He didn't," Amos said, nodding his head with assurance. "He said so a lotta times. He said he was gonna have some papers written up that would give the farm over to me. I would work and pay for it."

"Wait a minute!" Lapp's voice rose. "Are you telling me that Jacob was going to give you the farm that belonged to Sallie's parents?"

"He said so, yeah."

"When was this?" Lapp pressed.

"He said it first a year ago, maybe. He just never got around to it, I guess."

Moyer moved next to Amos and talked down to him. "You get tired of waiting?"

"For what?"

Lapp read Moyer's frustrated expression. Was Amos jerking them around? Moyer stayed with his line of questioning. "For the farm he said he was going to give you."

"No. When things like that are ready to happen, they happen."

"If he gave the farm to you, what was he going to do?"

"I don't know. He didn't say nothing."

Lapp interpreted the answer to mean the Amish man's thought process had never gone that far. Or, knowing that Jacob had always teased him, he had not believed the offer. "Did Sallie know about this?"

Amos thought for a moment. "She never said nothing."

"So he broke his promise to you, didn't he," Moyer leaned down and spoke directly into Amos' face. "Did that make you mad?"

Amos hesitated, then shrugged. "No."

"But now that he's dead you get to go back to his farm. Do you get his family, too?"

Lapp started, "I don't think he thinks …"

Moyer's blazing eyes cut Lapp off. He turned back to Amos. "Well? Am I right? With Jacob gone, you get what you want. Right?"

Amos' head shrank into his shoulders.

"Answer my question," Moyer demanded.

Amos stared at the table.

"Great," Moyer muttered. He stepped back to his chair, picked up his coffee cup and drained the contents.

After a good thirty seconds of silent frustration, Lapp leaned across the table and said, "Amos, the gas station backs up to your farm. So you must go over there sometimes. Amos. You have to answer our questions. Did you go over to the gas station sometimes?"

"Yeah, sometimes," Amos mumbled.

"When did you go there? In the daytime or at night."

The question sparked a brain synapse. Amos raised his eyes. "Sometimes in the daytime. To smoke a cigarette. Before I go home for the milking and supper."

Lapp looked at Moyer. An approving nod told him to continue.

"What time is that?"

"Around four-thirty, I guess. When I get off work."

"Why did you smoke there?"

Amos looked at Lapp as though he should already know the answer. "They get after me at home. You shouldn't smoke around a farm. It ain't good."

"You did that almost every day, right?"

"Yeah."

"You'd pull your buggy up there? Did you get out and walk around?"

"Yeah, I often did that. I like to look at those numbers on the gas pumps. The ones that kept track of the gas."

Lapp looked at Moyer as if to say, that explains the cigarette butts and the boot prints.

"Where's the money, Amos?" Moyer asked in a friendly voice that was calculated to avoid Amos clamming up again.

"Money?"

"Jacob had $50,000 in cash with him when he was killed. What did you do with it?"

"I didn't do nothing with it."

"Come on, Amos. You knew about the money, didn't you?"

"Not until Johnny told me."

Moyer was distracted by Hal Eiseman, who again stuck his head in. "Sorry to disturb you, Captain Ellison's on the phone. You might want to take it."

"Yeah, okay."

As Moyer stepped toward the door, Amos asked Lapp, "can you bring me back to Sallie's now?"

"I think you'd better get yourself a lawyer," Moyer said, turning back.

Amos squinched his face.

"The Amish don't use lawyers," Lapp said.

"We're not through with him. In the meantime, get him into the lab for prints. He's going into the system." Moyer left the room.

"Can I go home now, Johnny?" Amos pleaded.

"Not just yet. Do you know any lawyers, Amos?"

"Just the one who was supposed to draw up the papers for the farm."

"Do you remember his name?"

Amos responded quickly, proud of his memory. "His name was Lentz. Yeah, Lentz," he reassured himself.

"What was his first name?"

"I don't know no more."

"Amos, wait here. Have another cigarette. I'll see if I can find this man, Lentz."

Lapp was through the door before Amos could object.

In the detective's room, Moyer was on the phone, mostly listening. Lapp approached Hal Eiseman. "By any chance do we keep a list of lawyers?"

"Not as such," he answered while reaching beneath his desk and pulling out a battered volume of Yellow Pages. "Try this."

"Thanks." Lapp plopped into a chair and paged through the attorneys until he found the name of Walter Lentz. "Is there a phone I can use?"

The detective waved his arm toward a row of empty desks. "Take your pick."

His call was put through to Walter Lentz who confirmed that, yes, he knew Jacob and Amos Stoltzfus. He was shocked to hear of Jacob's death. Yes, Jacob had been in his office about a year ago to draw up an agreement to transfer a part ownership of the farm. He was supposed to have it signed, notarized and returned but never did. Lentz also informed Lapp that he would not act as Amos' lawyer because he did not do criminal work, but he would call him back with some names.

Lapp returned to Moyer's desk and waited for him to hang up the phone. When he did, Lapp relayed his conversation with Walter Lentz. "Amos told the truth."

"That just confirms a motive. The gun, the footprints, the cigarette butts and he wanted the farm. He admitted it," Moyer concluded. "A thousand to one, his fingerprints match the ones on the shotgun. I'm going to seek an arraignment. We'll hold him over."

"You're charging him?"

"That's exactly what I'm doing." Moyer's eyes bored a hole in Lapp's face. "You questioning my judgment?"

Lapp quickly backed down. "No. No."

Moyer started for the door. Lapp grabbed his arm. "I know I asked before, but is there any way you could hold off just a day so that he can attend Jacob's funeral. It's tomorrow. I'm sure Sallie will take responsibility for him, and if not, I will."

Moyer's reaction told Lapp he had crossed the line. "You know what Lapp? I think we got our man. I had a call from your Sergeant asking how long I was going to keep you. Now that we've made an arrest, there's not much else you can do around here."

Moyer's sudden dismissal angered Lapp. He took a deep breath to retain his composure. "When are you going public with the arrest?"

"That's up to Captain Phillips and Handleman. Since it's the weekend, they'll probably issue a statement today and hold a conference on Monday."

"It's going to be very hard on the Amish."

"Yeah, well, we're not in the business of protecting religions or an outdated way of life. We're here to learn the truth about a murder and to apply justice."

You're not doing either, Lapp thought as he turned and walked out.

Without asking for Moyer's permission, Lapp returned to the interrogation room and found Amos blinking at him through a cloud of cigarette smoke.

"Amos. Listen carefully to what I have to tell you."

The stern tone in Lapp's voice got the Amish man's attention.

"A man in a white coat is going to come and take you to a room where he's going to put ink on your fingers and copy your prints." Lapp softened his tone. "You understand what I'm saying."

"A man's going to come and take me to a place where he's going to look at my fingerprints," Amos responded.

"That's right. Then sometime today you'll be taken in a police van to a big castle building," Lapp counseled, referring to the facade of the Lancaster County jail. "When you get there, they're going to take your picture."

Amos opened his mouth in protest, but Lapp cut him off.

"It's not a regular picture like the tourists take. It's only for the police. It's something the law says they have to do, so I want you to do what they tell you to."

"Can I go to Sallie's then?"

"No. Sallie will come to see you. You'll have to stay in the castle place. You're under arrest. The police think you killed Jake and until you help us prove that you didn't. You'll have to stay there."

Amos turned his head away, like a child ignoring a scolding.

"I'll make sure Sallie comes to see you. Maybe your Papa, too."

Amos refused to look at Lapp as he closed the door behind him. Sallie was right. He was like a lamb being led to slaughter.

The bile in John Lapp's stomach was so sour and he could taste it in his throat. He found an empty desk and computer where he spent the next half hour writing up Amos' detainment, interrogation and subsequent arrest.

Glad to be outside, he sucked in the cold fresh air. Before he could escape in his patrol car, Lisa Robinson was next to him, keeping pace stride for stride. He was in no mood to talk to her.

"I understand you brought Amos Stoltzfus in as a suspect in his brother's murder. Has he been arrested?" Then, "can you confirm that?"

Lapp stopped and they faced off.

"Hang around. There'll be a statement sometime this afternoon, I'm sure," he said before setting the pace again toward his car. She ran, high heels clacking, to keep up with him.

Her voice rose with excitement. "So it's true then. They've arrested him. Do you believe they have the right man? What about the $50,000 that the victim had when he was killed? Has it been recovered?"

Where in hell is she getting all this information, he wondered. He opened the car door to his patrol car, preparing to climb inside. "I can't comment. I'm going back to traffic patrol. You'll have to pick on someone else."

"I'm just trying to get the truth … and the story," she added with a disappointed pout.

It didn't work this time. Lapp revved up his engine and said, "Aren't we all?"

Chapter 16

Someone would have to tell Sallie that Amos wasn't coming home. Lapp didn't look forward to the task, but, like it or not, it was up to him.

Sallie was wrestling dry clothes from the plastic-coated lines, folding them into a wicker laundry basket, and looking up at the ominous black clouds gathering overhead.

Jacob Stoltzfus' body, dressed in white shirt, coat and pants was lying in a wooden coffin in the parlor of the house. Lapp was there to tell his widow that the police had arrested his brother, Amos, for his murder. He got out of the patrol car and ignored the annoying dog that barked and sniffed at his legs. When Sallie saw that Amos was not with him, the color left her face.

He kept it simple. Amos was being held over. Later today, he would be transferred to the Lancaster County jail. He should get a lawyer. If not, his case would be turned over to a Public Defender. He would be held until a judge could decide on bail. Sallie listened, shook her head, then turned abruptly back to her clotheslines.

Talking to her turned back, he called out, "Sallie, I've been assigned back to traffic patrol."

She wheeled around and snapped, "who will help us, then?"

"I'll do everything I can to keep up with the case. I'll talk to his lawyer. I'll help with his defense."

Sallie picked up a full basket of clean clothes, and walked toward the house.

Lapp felt a strong urge to spring to her side, grab the basket from her hands, and assure her that he believed Amos was innocent and that things would turn out all right. Instead, he turned and drove back down the lane of the Stoltzfus farm. His throat was dry and his heart ached, overwhelmed by a sense of hopelessness.

Hungry, Lapp stuffed his sorrows with a forbidden meal. Seated in the patrol car in the shadow of the Golden Arches, he removed the wrappings from a Quarter Pounder, large fries and poked a straw through the lid of his vanilla milk shake. It was a thousand calories that he couldn't wait to enjoy. The crumbs that landed on his black police belt reminded him that he had loosened it by another notch this morning.

His waist size didn't really matter. What mattered was what he could do to help Amos Stoltzfus who sat, bewildered, in a holding cell.

He reported back to the barracks for a patrol assignment. His sergeant, Harry Johnson, a tall, muscular African-American man with a shiny shaved head that fit perfectly with his precisely creased uniform and spit-shined shoes, reacted with surprise at Lapp's appearance. When told that Moyer said he was wanted back on duty, Johnson shrugged and said, "that's news to me." He flipped through the duty rosters and said, "we're pretty well set for today. There's only about three hours of normal duty left. You got any comp time coming from homicide?"

"Actually I do. About a day and a half's worth," Lapp replied.

"When you want to take it? You're off on Sunday, anyway."

"Can I let you know?"

"I'll go ahead and schedule you on Monday's roster. Give me at least 24 hours when you plan to take that comp time."

"I'll do that. Thanks, sarge."

Lapp changed into his civilian clothes and headed for his truck. There was still enough daylight to revisit the scene of the crime.

A couple of large drops of rain from a layer of black clouds muddied his windshield as he pulled the Ford beneath the canopy that covered the faded yellow Sonoco pumps.

The yellow tape had been removed. A few pink traces of blood were still visible between the cracks of the broken concrete.

Putting his hands around his eyes like binoculars, Lapp peered through the dirty square glass panes on the upper half of the padlocked pull-up garage door. The cement floor of the two empty service bays was splattered with grey and black oil spots. Old newspapers were scattered here and there. Otherwise, it had been stripped. The same was true of the adjoining small office. No furniture, just the frayed end of a telephone cord.

The west side of the rust-stained stuccoed building carried two lines of red spray paint—one that said, "FUCK YOU" in big block letters, and beneath it, a shaky, "*the same to you.*" Around the back, a small driveway circled the garage building. Behind that was a clump of woods that, Lapp guessed, was part of the Stoltzfus farm. His eyes scoured the ground for anything unusual and found two discarded yellowed condoms. This was a good place to hide.

He followed a path into the woods, made up mostly of bare-limbed elm and locust trees, some twenty feet high, along with a couple of white birch, all native, spread by the wind and nursed by the rain. There were clumps of Scotch and soft-needled White pines that had grown too large to be Christmas trees. Lapp brushed past a patch of raspberry vines, as well as vines with red leaves that looked suspiciously like poison oak. The eight inch round trunk of a white birch tree had been stripped of its bark. Next to the tree was a large limestone rock and at its base was a pile of at least two dozen cigarette butts. Amos said he came here to smoke. He sat in his buggy and sometimes would walk around the gas pumps. That was in daylight. What about at night? The teens had said they came here to harass the lovers who parked here. Was this a place where Amos came to smoke and maybe spy on the lovers in their cars, and imagine what they were doing behind the steamed up windows?

Another path split off deeper into a jumble of trees and brush. The ground was wet and pitted with small puddles, but Lapp found no visible footprints, nor any animal spores or tracks, for that matter. He scrambled through the brush for another hundred feet and came to the edge of a field that had already been plowed, disked and probably planted with winter wheat. Straight ahead was a clear view of the barn and silver silos of the Stoltzfus farm.

Lapp returned to the large rock and the cigarette butts. There was little doubt. This was Amos' place to sit, smoke, think, wait and watch.

He completed his circle of the gas station and garage, looking east to a still-green pasture, enclosed by barbed wire fence.

The threatening rain had not delivered. But the approaching darkness brought colder air, and Lapp was glad to be back in his truck, heading for home.

The house was dark, reminding him to reset the timer for the floor lamp by the front picture window. He turned up the thermostat and switched on the kitchen light. Coming home to an empty kitchen was not all that unusual. As a strong advocate for nurse's rights, Betsy had been heavily involved in the ongoing union contract talks with the hospital that kept her out late at least two nights a week. She usually left a post-it note with meal instructions stuck on the refrigerator door. Now it was up to him to plan ahead, get in a stock of TV dinners, or go out to eat.

Deciding he was not hungry, he plopped down in his lounge chair, hit the ON button on the TV remote and watched a local weather reporter stand in front of a national weather map and talk about the 100 degree temperatures in Death Valley. It would be another 20 minutes before the local news headlines at 6 o'clock. He pushed the MUTE button and quickly dozed off.

A consistent knocking on the door startled him. According to the VCR clock, it was 5:55 p.m. A quick glance out of the front window revealed a horse and buggy parked beneath a street light.

He switched on the porch light, braced himself with a deep breath and opened the door.

It took a moment for the faces of the two elderly Amish men to register through the glass storm door. One was Eli Stoltzfus, father of Jacob and Amos. The other was his own father, Moses Lapp.

"Johnny?"

"Ja, Papa." The shock wave that bolted through his body was quickly grounded as he pushed the storm door latch and opened it, inviting them inside.

"Herr Stoltzfus. Cum rei".

Although the weather was dry, the two men automatically wiped their black work shoes on the WELCOME mat before stepping inside. Both wore broad rimmed black hats, and wool mutzi overcoats against the cold. "We don't want to bother you …" his father began in English, examining the face and figure of his son, a boy of nineteen, rail thin and 30 pounds lighter when he last saw him.

Lapp stared at his father and wondered, should he shake the hand of a man he had not seen nor talked to in fifteen years? A man he had feared? A man who had lost self-esteem when his son left for the outside world? His face was redder, and through the wire frame eyeglasses, his blue eyes seemed more watery than he remembered. His white beard curved at a curious right angle from his chin. A stray piece of straw clung to his father's shoulder. He resisted the temptation to brush it off. The harsh face that Moses Lapp had always displayed toward his son had sagged and softened.

The two Amish men pulled their hats from their heads and Moses repeated, "we don't like to bother you," he said while trying to control his curiosity. He didn't want to know about his son. He didn't want to be here.

"No, it's all right, Papa," Lapp said before turning to Eli Stoltzfus. "I wanted to tell you again how sorry I am about Jacob."

Eli nodded his appreciation.

As Lapp examined these two men from his past, they took the opportunity to scan the room. His father's eyes settled on a framed photo of Lapp and Betsy perched on the lamp table.

Lapp broke the silence. "My wife's not home. She's a nurse at Lancaster General. She works late some nights," he added, thinking that was all they needed to know.

"You have children?" Eli asked.

"No. No children yet."

Eli's eyes were glued to the muted TV.

Lapp picked up the remote control to turn off the TV, but was stopped by an "up next" teaser that flashed on the screen. "They'll be talking about Amos soon," he said, pointing at the screen.

"Amos did not kill his brother," Eli Stoltzfus said in a burst of protest. "Where do they come up with these things? To say that he would shoot and kill his own brother is such foolishness. I can't believe it. Then they come to our farm this afternoon, tear up Amos room, looking for 'ich weiss net was', scared the missus and asked me a bunch of dumb questions."

Lapp suppressed a smile. Searching an Amish bedroom, especially male, with its sparse furnishings, would take all of two minutes. "How many men were there?"

"Three all together."

"In uniform?"

"Two were. One was in a regular brown suit."

Lapp figured it was either Doug Martin or Hal Eiseman with a couple of troopers he recruited.

Eli's pitch and anger rose. "And then they went into the barn. They didn't know where to start. This fella kept asking questions like where would Amos be and what would he do in the barn. Finally, I just left them there," he grumbled in frustration.

Lapp turned away from Eli, unable to control a smile at the thought of the lawmen searching the hayloft, stables, corncrib and manure piles.

"Where is Amos? Why didn't he come home?" Eli demanded to know.

"By now he's been transferred to the Lancaster County Jail." Lapp answered.

"He's in jail?" Eli asked incredulously.

"For now, at least."

"Why do they say these things about Amos?" Moses asked his son.

"They have evidence against him."

"What evidence? What did they make him say? He's not all there. He can't help that."

Eli folded his arms defiantly.

Lapp's father interjected. "Did you see this evidence? Do you believe Amos did such a thing?"

"He owned the shotgun that was used to kill Jacob," Lapp said.

"Ach, what would Amos want with a shotgun? He couldn't shoot nothing," Eli argued.

"He said he was going to hunt for rabbits and pheasants." Lapp decided it would not be wise to tell how Amos had killed a fox with a single shot to the head.

"Who did he say this to? Did they make him say it?" Eli demanded.

"He told me himself. He told me at Sallie's. And they have a receipt from Sears. Amos bought the gun." The news report was about to begin. Lapp pointed to the screen and to the sofa. "Would you like to sit down?"

"We do not watch television." Moses Lapp protested.

"I think you should make an exception here. It will explain the situation better than I can."

Both men remained standing as Lapp undid the mute button and raised the volume. A young Asian female reporter stood on the State Police barracks steps and read a statement outlining the charges and evidence.

The Amish men shook their heads, denying what they were seeing and hearing.

The shotgun, the matching fingerprints found on it, the missing $50,000, the cigarette butts, the footprints and a possible motive that Amos had been promised Jacob's farm. The reporter concluded with, "the arrest of Amos Stoltzfus for the death of his brother, has come as a shocking surprise." She responded to the in-studio anchor's question, "is the suspect eligible for bail," with "there's been no word on that so far. A press conference has been sched-uled for Monday which may shed some more light on this sad story." The authoritative silver-haired male anchor in the studio turned to his female co-anchor and closed with, "a shocking development that is sure to have a major impact on the Amish community."

They had seen enough. Lapp hit the OFF button. "Did you know any of this?" he asked Eli Stoltzfus.

"Nothing about what they said. Sallie told me about the foolishness of the $50,000. And they haven't found this money? What would Amos want with money? He's happy the way he is."

"Do you know where Amos was last Thursday night at 9:30 or 10:00 o'clock?"

Eli answered, "where he always was. At home in bed. That's what gets me. How can they say he did this when he was home in bed?"

"What time does Amos get home from work at night?"

"Around 5, usually."

"And what does he do when he gets home?"

"The same as always," Eli began impatiently. "He takes care of his horse, helps finish up the milking, then we have supper."

"And after that?"

"He sits in the kitchen by the stove. He has a little table there where he keeps some wooden farm animals that he plays with. He listens while I read the Bible and at 8:30 we go to bed."

"Everybody went to bed at 8:30?" Lapp asked.

"Same as always."

"And the next morning? What time did you see him?"

"5 o'clock." Eli lost his patience. "Why do you ask these questions? You know how we live."

"I need to hear it from you."

Eli continued, grudgingly, "we do the milking and feeding, and have breakfast. Amos goes off to work at the foundry."

"Did he seem or act any different on Friday morning?"

Eli thought for a moment. "No. Amos is always the same."

Lapp pondered the at-home, in-bed alibi. Amos had not been seen after 8:30. The gas station where Jacob was killed was only a quarter-mile or so away from the house. No conclusive proof either way that he had or had not left his bed.

Moses Lapp took a step forward and, avoiding his son's eyes, said, "you must help us, Johnny. Amos is innocent. Don't you think he is?"

"Yes, I think he is innocent. But I don't know what I can do."

"You must tell them what you think," Moses interjected. "They will listen to you."

"Papa. I'm a patrolman. I mostly hand out traffic tickets, investigate accidents, and help people who have car trouble. They aren't going to listen to me unless I give them hard evidence to prove that Amos is innocent."

"What will happen to Amos," Eli groaned. "He must be so scared."

"They'll hold him over, assign a lawyer, probably a Public Defender, to represent him. The District Attorney will ask a judge to hold an arraignment hearing. The Public Defender will probably ask for bail, but in a murder case, it probably won't be granted. Besides, you wouldn't pay it anyway. What it means is they'll keep him in jail while they build a case against him."

"But he didn't do nothing," Eli protested.

Moses Lapp put his hand on Eli's shoulder to comfort him, then turned to Lapp.

"Will you help us, Johnny? For Amos?"

"Papa, I'm no longer on the case. I'm back on patrol. Anything I do would be unofficial."

"Then you must do it however you can," Moses said. "We will be thankful. Come, Eli, we will go now and pray. God will show us the way."

With his hand still on Eli's shoulder, Moses turned him toward the door.

Lapp was bemused by his father's humbleness. It was a side he had rarely seen. As a church Bishop, Moses Lapp was self-righteous as a man, and a tyrant as a father. He must have prayed long and hard before coming here tonight. In the eyes of the Amish, his father had to shoulder the blame for his son's defection. Not because he had been too severe, but because he had not been strict enough. And although John Lapp was not officially shunned, and, at least early on had contact with his sisters, particularly Lizzie, he had seen his father only once since walking down the lane to his new life. Knowing that it must have been very difficult for him to come here, Lapp made an offer.

"I think Jake was killed for the money. The $50,000. And I think Jake must have told someone what he planned to do with it. Talk to all the relations. If you can bring me any information, I'll check it out. It's the only way I can think of to help Amos."

"We will go now, but first we must go outside and talk," Moses Lapp said opening the door, then the storm door and guiding Eli Stoltzfus ahead of him. "Can you wait a minute for us?"

"I can wait."

The two old Amish men stood beard to beard on the front porch, speaking in muffled Pennsylvania Dutch. The overhead porch light illuminated the white puffs of breath from their animated conversation.

Moses Lapp pulled the latch on the storm door and jerked his head, asking his son to come to the door.

Lapp stepped onto the porch.

"We cannot talk to the relations about what you asked until after the funeral tomorrow," Eli Stoltzfus said. "We come back to the house at twelve o'clock. If it is not too much trouble, you could come out and eat with us. Afterwards, we men will talk."

Lapp hesitated until the plea in Eli's dark eyes convinced him. "I will come."

The two Amish men nodded their thanks and walked down the sidewalk to their buggy. Lapp waited on the porch until the reins were snapped and a "giddap" set the horse on their journey home.

Lapp stood by the door and pondered what he had just agreed to do. He would not attend Jacob's funeral. That was a private ceremony for family and friends. The dinner after, lunch really, was more open. Although it was rare, close "English" friends were sometimes invited. He was neither a relative nor a close friend. How would he be received?

Still not hungry, he pulled a Rolling Rock beer from the refrigerator and settled into his easy chair. The network news was on Channel 8. He idly surfed through the 40-odd cable channels of programming before settling on Turner Classic Movies, and a favorite movie, *Battleground*. The battle worn American soldiers, led by a hobbling James Whitmore marched down a road singing, "cadence count", as the music rose in a final flourish. It was still only 7:30 when he clicked off the TV and went upstairs.

The Amish wanted his help. They were able to accept and forgive the fact that Jacob Stoltzfus was murdered. But they couldn't accept the possibility that his own brother did it. He thought about Jacob lying in his coffin. He thought about Amos, alone and frightened in a jail cell. and he pictured Sallie. Sallie, even with friends and relatives buzzing about, preparing for the funeral, feeling empty and alone. Her children, still young, facing life without a father. And, finally, he thought of his own situation. Separated, soon to be divorced, and also alone. People, like pieces in a puzzle that had been pulled apart. How would they ever fit together?

Chapter 17

Sallie Stoltzfus said good night to Samuel, David and Lydia, all snug in their beds, although Lydia whimpered that she was cold, even under the heavy quilts. Samuel cried out for her to shut up and Sallie admonished them to all be quiet and "go to sleep."

When the children had settled down, she carried the kerosene lamp down the stairs into the kitchen, and threw an extra shawl over her shoulders rather than adding another shovelful of coal to the stove. She was glad to be alone. Daniel's wife, Lydia and her teen-aged daughter Annie, had been the last to leave. Tomorrow, before daylight, the house would again be buzzing with men and boys setting up the tables and benches. Sallie's mother would direct the dozen or so women and girls busily preparing the after-funeral dinner.

Queenie, the dog who slept on the kitchen door stoop, began a series of small grumps that grew into a barrage of barking loud enough to rouse the kids from their beds. In the nearly full moonlight, she was relieved to see that it was a horse and buggy coming up the lane not some motor vehicle belonging to a TV or newspaper reporter. She watched the tall Amish figure climb out of the buggy and recognized Eli Stoltzfus. She felt a hand on her bottom and turned to see Samuel in his long woolen underwear, shivering and asking, "Who is it?"

"Grossdawdy Eli. Go back to bed."

Samuel peered past her to confirm her words. Satisfied, he turned back and climbed the stairs.

Sallie stepped aside as a stern-faced Eli entered the kitchen. "Cum rie," she said, her face filled with curiosity over his unexpected visit.

"We just come from seeing Johnny Lapp," Eli said in a tone that indicated he would say what he had to say and then be gone.

"Who went?"

"Me and Moses Lapp."

"Johnny's Pop?"

"Yeah. It took some doing on his part. It took some on my part, too. We asked him to help us with Amos."

"Where was this?"

"We went to his house," he answered impatiently.

Sallie immediately wondered about Johnny's house. What it looked like. Was his wife there? Questions she couldn't ask.

"This business with Jacob is one thing. He's in heaven already. But we can't let Amos suffer. We asked Johnny Lapp to help us get Amos out of jail. He doesn't belong there no how."

"What did he say?" Sallie asked.

"He said he would do what he could. But the only way was to find the real killer and to do that he had to ask us more questions. Which is not something we want. We don't want to talk about this. But it seems there's no way around it. So we asked him to come to dinner after the funeral. He's not one of us, so we don't want him at the funeral, but Moses thought we should tell you anyway."

Sallie reacted slowly, torn over what John Lapp's continued presence in her life should be. "I'm glad you told me."

Eli Stoltzfus stepped toward the door, and shook his head in worry. "I don't know where this is gonna all go. I don't like none of it. Johnny's an outsider. He turned his back on us. But we gotta help Amos, and we don't know where else to go."

"He may not be one of us, but he knows us and he said he wants to help."

Eli raised his eyebrows. "When was this?"

"When he came to tell me Amos had been arrested."

Eli grumbled, then was through the door, back in his buggy and snapping the reins at his horse to take him down the lane.

Sallie closed the door and, feeling weary, dropped onto the bench of the kitchen table. Yes, she thought, Johnny's an outsider. He has a different life. But, as much as the Amish do not want outside help, she felt warm and secure in his presence and confident that he would help Amos.

She pictured Johnny dressed in his plaid flannel shirt and cord pants. She preferred him that way. Except for the black leather pistol belt and the protruding handle of his gun, she was not intimidated by the starched blue State Police uniform. When in her presence, he politely took off his round hat with the chinstrap and carried it in his hands until he went back outside. Fringes of grey around the edges of his short curly brown hair had made him more handsome with age. The expressions on his clean-shaven face were easier to understand. Amish men's beards are not attractive and weren't meant to be. They were a safeguard against a handsome face that might turn a woman's head and distract from her duty to her own man.

Yes, Johnny Lapp is an outsider. But one she felt comfortable with.

Chapter 18

Lapp woke from a fitful night of tossing and turning, aggravated by Amos' arrest and conflicted by the unexpected appearance at his front door of his father and Eli Stoltzfus asking for his help. None of the scenarios that ran through his mind was enough to get Amos released. The only way to do that would be to find the real killer.

He found a cool spot for his ear on the down pillow, pulled the covers over his head and slept solidly until nine o'clock.

The morning newspaper carried a large front-page photo of the Stoltzfus farm taken at a distance from the bottom of the lane. Below the photo was a 3 column wide, 6 inches deep story of Amos' arrest. Lapp glanced at the story but didn't have the heart to read it.

The last of Betsy's homemade granola was gone, so he settled for a breakfast of Cheerios, sliced bananas, and 1% milk. The farmer's breakfast he coveted was still too much trouble to prepare. He brewed himself a particularly good cup of percolated coffee this morning and savored the aroma while looking through the glass storm door into his back yard. A silver-white frost covered the faded lawn, flower and vegetable beds. According to the thermometer nailed to the outside door frame, it was 42 degrees. The sky was partly cloudy. Possible snow flurries were in last night's forecast.

He picked up the phone and called his neighbor and real estate agent, Kathy Johnson, to tell her he had to cancel their appointment. She quickly described two houses with large lots, trees and garden space still below his $300,000 purchase ceiling that met his qualifications. He promised to reschedule.

Back upstairs in the bedroom, he stripped the three-week old sheets from his bed, and made it up with new ones. In his small walk-in closet, he decided against his black suit, and instead chose his only other option: a brown tweed jacket and gabardine slacks, white shirt, autumn leaves brown tie, brown Oxfords.

From his house on the east side of the city of Lancaster, there was no easy, direct way to get to Jacob's and Sallie's farm without going through the highly commercial and touristy Route 30. Cars with license plates from New York, New Jersey, Ohio, Virginia and Maryland, equaled the Pennsylvania plates that were lined up facing restaurants and diners with local names like Smoker's Family Restaurant, the GoodnPlenty, Miller's Bakery, Bounty Fare, and Zook's Diner. They competed with national chains like McDonald's, Jack In The Box, and Burger King, all advertising breakfast specials from 99 cents to $2.99.

The windows and entrances of faux Amish and Pennsylvania Dutch craft shops, outlet stores, motels and antique stores were decorated with corn shock scarecrows, gigantic orange pumpkins carved into Jack O Lanterns, black crepe paper and bed sheet ghosts. Halloween was less than two weeks away.

He turned up the volume to his favorite oldies radio station when the song, "Love Will Keep Us Together" came on. During his last days as an Amish teen, that song, and other favorites of the day, had provided a temporary escape from his structured life.

By the age of 14, he had finished the eighth grade and ended his formal schooling. But, unlike his fellow Amish school graduates, he was not ready to give up his education. Sojourns off the farm, for work, errands, or social visits, were opportunities to find books or magazines that held the power of information and a knowledge of the outside world.

The only book permitted in his home was the Bible. Some families received the "Die Botschaft" (the Message), a local Amish newspaper that carried "approved" news, but not the Lapp family. To Moses Lapp, besides the basic schooling of English and Arithmetic, the scriptures carried all of the wisdom needed to live an Amish life.

For almost two years, until he was betrayed by Hec Martin, the hired man that worked full-time for the family, a small battery powered portable radio was his link to the outside world. During that time, he was an avid fan of the Philadelphia Phillies baseball team, knew the names of all the players, kept a notebook with team statistics and delighted in the Phillies winning the World Series.

He also treasured the music on his radio. Particularly songs of love and happiness, songs that made his feet and fingers tap along with rhythm. The Carpenters, Captain and Tennille, the Bee Gees, Bette Midler, Christopher Cross.

Songs, with words of love, that expressed the feelings he wanted to share with Sallie.

But when he played them for her, she refused to listen. She admonished him to reject the influence of worldly music.

During those four years of secrecy, he kept up with the news of the nation and the world: President Reagan's inauguration and his attempted assassination; John Lennon's murder; the overseas wars in Iraq and Iran and in Israel and Lebanon; the astronauts traveling in outer space.

And Three Mile Island. He was astounded that the Amish could ignore the radiation released at Three-Mile Island which was only 35 miles from their homes in Lancaster County. 144,000 nearby residents of Middletown, near Harrisburg, had been evacuated. Lapp concluded that if the Amish had been ordered to leave their farms they would have refused.

From age fifteen to eighteen, he secretly met with other young Amish men who had plans to leave the church, mostly before, some after they had become church members. He learned, first-hand, of the difficulties of leaving and pressures to return.

Those who were successful in leaving had become Mennonites.

John Lapp made his first visit to the Mennonite Information Center, located just off Route 30, when he was eighteen. Although it provided area information, brochures and tours for the tourists, the Center's primary purpose, through books, films, educational materials and personal contact, was to introduce the public to their conservative religious beliefs. While "plain" in many ways, their more liberal interpretations of the Bible, primarily the disagreement over "shunning" and their approved use of most modern conveniences, separated them from the Amish.

During his next six visits to the Center, he became friends with Benjamin Hostetler, a sympathetic man with a full white beard, who reminded him of a picture he had once seen of a jolly man named "Santa Claus." Benjamin was a teacher at the Mennonite High School in Lancaster who also worked as a greeter and counselor at the Center on weekends and school vacations. When Lapp was serious about leaving the Amish and would not be convinced otherwise, Benjamin Hostetler became an active facilitator, paving the way for his schooling and employment.

Approaching a block of decorated stores, Lapp saw an open spot at the curb and ducked his truck into a space in front of a store that John Lapp knew well. It had been his employment and home from the time he left the Amish until he started college four years later.

A wooden red and white sign, with the words, THE HAPPY HEN, arched over a simple outline of a nesting chicken, was mounted over the heavy-glass front door. A small one by four piece of wood hanging inside the door said, "Open 11 a.m.—4 p.m.", but he knew that the owner, Rufus Martin, was already there baking the famous chicken pies that would be boxed, ready for the dinner table, and sold by the end of the day. A Mennonite, Rufus had special permission from the church to work on Sundays.

A bell attached to the unlocked door announced Lapp's entrance. A short, stout, chubby-cheeked man with a clipped grey beard and mustache and a perennial smile, pushed through the swinging doors from the kitchen. The mouth-watering aroma of the baking pastry accompanied him.

"Johnny Lapp! Cum rei! I haven't seen you for awhile, now."

Lapp stepped into the narrow service area. A six foot counter extended across the entire room. At the head of the counter was an ancient cash register. Three butt-worn wooden stools with low backs stood in front of the counter for customers awaiting their pies. The Happy Hen was strictly a take-out operation and had been for as long as he could remember. There were no menus posted on the wall behind the counter. Rufus Martin sold one dish and one dish only. A 9-inch round, three-inch deep pie, enough to feed three or four people, served in an aluminum, returnable pie tin. Requests for side dishes like cole slaw, chow-chow, or shoe peg corn went unfilled. Rufus' response was, "I sell chicken pies. I'm not a restaurant."

"It's not so long. Two weeks, maybe. Wie bischt?" Lapp spoke loudly, knowing that Rufus, at the age of 72 was hard of hearing.

"You're all dressed up? You going to a funeral?" His blue eyes sparkled behind the wire-rimmed glasses.

"As a matter of fact, I am. For Jacob Stoltzfus."

Rufus raised his eyebrows in surprise. "Jacob's funeral you're going to?"

"Have you been following the reports of Jacob's murder? Well, I've been helping with the investigation. At least I was until yesterday. After they arrested his brother Amos, they don't think they need me any more."

"I heard about that." Rufus said with amazement. "Would Amos do such a thing?"

"Of course not. But some of the evidence points to him. The Amish don't care if they catch Jacob's killer or not, but they do care about Amos."

"I should hope so," Rufus responded.

"Last night, my Pop, who I hadn't seen in nearly fifteen years and Eli Stoltzfus, showed up at my door."

"They came to your house?"

"They asked me to help Amos. I told them I had to know what Jacob was up to on the night he was killed."

"What do you mean, up to?"

"I mean what was he going to do with the $50,000 he had on him."

"I saw that in the newspaper. I wondered about that, too."

"That's why Papa and Eli invited me to talk with the "freindschaft" after the funeral today at the farm."

Rufus Martin pointed to a stool. "Sit down. The first "butt boi" is coming out of the oven."

Lapp climbed on the stool and thought about the chicken pot pie with the thick square "butt boi" noodles, large pieces of white and dark meat chicken, peas, potatoes and carrots in a thick chicken gravy and topped with a flaky, lard pastry. "I'm having dinner at the farm. I'll be by one day soon to have one."

"How about some coffee then?"

"I can handle that."

"Black?" Rufus filled and set two brown mugs, with chicken beaks on the handles, on the counter. He wiped his hands on the grey-striped apron that he wore everyday except to church on Sunday and sat down next to Lapp.

"So you ain't seen your Pop since he came here to rescue you?" Rufus asked.

"Not a day since."

"I remember how you stood up to them that day."

With a fresh haircut and a new blue denim shirt and khaki pants, Lapp was brought to the Happy Hen by Benjamin Hostettler, his counselor at the Mennonite Center. Rufus became his employer, landlord, and more importantly, a kind and understanding mentor.

In the kitchen, Rufus prepared the chickens, cutting, cooking, and filling the pie tins, while Lapp helped by peeling and cutting fresh potatoes and carrots, opened the commercial-sized cans of peas, and washed the tins and pans.

Less than a week after his arrival, a hired van carrying his father, his two sisters and two Amish ministers had arrived at the shop.

He was prepared for their visit. In fact he would have been disappointed if they had not come. It would have meant he wasn't worth saving.

Even though John Lapp had no intention of returning, he led them through the kitchen into the alley in back. His father's face was angry and embarrassed from having lost a son.

The first minister spoke calmly and explained that Lapp could come back and confess and that all would be forgiven. He claimed to understand the temptations of the outside world, but their way was the only true way to eternal salvation.

When Lapp, nervously defensive, tried to explain that he wanted an education and a less structured life, his words were met with scowls, a shaking of heads, and was told he was totally wrong. His sister, Sarah, whose eyes were red from crying, urged him to return for awhile and give it another chance. He could wait a year or two more before deciding on whether or not to join the church. When neither side was willing to give in, the second minister threatened Lapp with a life in hell and eternal damnation. Lapp told them to go. Lizzie, his oldest sister, in a last ditch effort to conciliate, asked Lapp if he was going to be a good Mennonite. Knowing that an affirmative answer would appease, he replied, "yes." As the rescue party left, his father turned back and said, quietly, "you can always come home."

Lapp replied "you can always come here too, to see me."

Then they were gone.

Rufus Martin's voice broke the memory. "You did good that day. You stood up to them. And, you didn't get mad, which don't do nobody no good."

Lapp nodded. "You helped me more than I can ever say."

"You were a very bright boy who deserved the chance to do whatever it was you wanted to do. You fooled me good, though, when you became a State Trooper," Rufus said, smiling broadly and slapping Lapp across the back. "That, I never would a thought."

"Me neither at the time," Lapp mused.

"As I recall, soon after that time you had another visitor. I thought at the time, now he's a goner."

Lapp took a sip of coffee and vividly remembered that Saturday, two weeks after the rescue van. He was up to his elbows in soap suds washing pot pie tins when Rufus, with a twinkle in his eyes, announced that he had a visitor waiting at the counter in front. When Lapp groaned that he did not want to face another rescue attempt, Rufus teased, "this one's different."

That's when he knew it was her. His heart was pounding as he broke through the swinging doors.

"Johnny! I found you!" Her eyes sparkled and her smile lit up the room.

Lapp caught his breath. "Wie bischt, Sallie?"

"Ich bin gut, und du?"

"Good. I'm good. I was working," Lapp stuttered, wiping his hands on his grey striped apron.

"Can you get a little time off?" she asked, turning to Rufus who stood by watching with amusement. "My buggy's out in front."

"I don't know. I …"

"Of course, he can," Rufus said. "He just works a little harder when he gets back, that's all."

"Okay. I will," Lapp said excitedly, pulling off the apron and tossing it on the counter.

In the open spring wagon, Sallie pulled on the reins guiding the chestnut trotting horse out into the traffic on Route 30. The horse found a rhythmic pace and the buggy wheels rolled noisily on the concrete road. An Amish girl, and an "English" boy in an open buggy attracted curious smiles from pedestrians and drivers along the road. "People are going to wonder when they see us," Lapp said.

"Maybe they think I'm one of those buggies for hire and you're a rich customer," she giggled. "That would be pretty funny."

Lapp was exhilarated to have Sallie at his side, exchanging smiles. The sun reflected from the light brown bangs of hair that reached out from beneath her white net bonnet. His eyes followed her short-sleeved grey dress with a black apron down to her light brown cotton stockings and brown laced shoes. Lapp was pleased. She had dressed up for him.

Sallie took the first side road she could find, and pulled into a bed of fallen yellow maple leaves beneath the giant tree above.

"You look all different," Sallie said, assessing his short haircut which was parted on the left side in an Ivy League style.

Lapp wiped his sweaty palms on his pants and blurted out, "you look the same."

"Well, why wouldn't I? It's only been a few weeks since I seen you. My life hasn't changed at all."

"Not like mine has, huh?"

"Do you like your job?"

"It's okay. I work after school and on Saturdays."

"You go to school already? Where?"

"Lancaster Mennonite High School. I can take a bus there."

"What grade?"

"They put me in tenth."

"Since I'm not there to beat you out I bet you're the best speller in your class already."

"No. I'm not the best. I'm just the oldest. Most of the others in my class are only fifteen years old. I'm almost nineteen. It feels funny sometimes."

"What do you study?"

"English, math, science, social studies, Bible class, stuff like that. Then we have gym, too. They have this nice big gym. I'm not too bad at shooting basketballs."

"Do you have a girl friend, already," Sallie asked, only half-kidding.

Lapp blushed, "ach, no. I told you they're just little kids."

"What about the 12th graders?"

"They don't have anything to do with me."

"Are the girls pretty? They don't have to dress like me. You can see more of them."

Lapp's face reddened even more. "I guess some aren't too bad."

Sallie's face fell. She blurted out, "I wish you'd never went."

Lapp's heart jumped. He took a deep breath. Not sure of how to handle her outburst, he stayed on the subject of school. "They tell me if I work hard they'll skip me ahead so I can graduate in two years instead of three."

"And then what will you do?" Sallie asked, her eyes lifting back to his.

"I don't know. I still have some time to find out."

"You were always such a good farmer."

"Yeah, I know, but …" Lapp shrugged.

"You talk different already, too. You're not as Dutchy."

"It's something I'm working on." Lapp was surprised she noticed since he felt like he had fallen back into the sing-song Pennsylvania Dutch accent.

"Where do you live?"

"Behind the kitchen, there at the pie shop. Rufus, the owner, fixed up a place for me."

"Do you have a TV already?"

"No, but I can play my radio without hiding."

"And are you happy?"

"Yeah. Pretty much. It wasn't easy."

"I know it wasn't. One day I see you at my baptism, and the next day I find out you're gone."

"I wanted to tell you," Lapp said, lowering his eyes.

"I wasn't so surprised."

"I'd been thinking about it for a long time."

"I know you had. I'm just sad it happened. Are you happy?"

"Ja, yeah, I think I will be. There's too much in the world. I had to be a part of it."

"I saw your Papa and sisters at church. They seem okay. I didn't talk to them."

"I'm sure the elders blame my Daadi for my leaving. For not keeping me in the church. For not knowing that I might go."

Sallie nodded. "They always do that when somebody goes."

"How's Jacob?"

"You haven't seen him?"

"No, why?"

"He said he was going to see you and talk to you. He said he could make you come back."

"He hasn't seen me. And he couldn't anyway."

Sallie stared into his eyes and said, solemnly, "I guess I can't either, huh?"

Lapp shook his head, no.

"I didn't come here to do that. I just wanted to see you. Because I liked you so much."

Lapp squirmed in the seat, feeling awkward about expressing his feelings.

"I liked you too, Sallie, more than I can tell you."

"I often wondered if you left because of me."

"I left when I knew you would never leave the church and I could never stay. That's when it was time to go."

Sallie leaned toward him, but they did not touch. "You can come back, Johnny. You can admit you were wrong. Everybody wants you back."

"And then what?"

"Then we can see how it goes with us."

"And what about Jacob?"

"What about him?" She asked softly.

"Aren't you supposed to marry him?"

Sallie's jaw dropped with surprise. "Where did you get that idea?"

"You're not?"

"Not that I know of. Do you know something I don't know? Who told you that?"

Lapp's turned red with embarrassment. Jacob had told him that. He had told him that they had kissed and that she agreed to marry him.

Sallie persisted. "Well, I'm still waiting to know."

'I …" Lapp stuttered. "I don't know. I just thought with me gone … I know you like him."

"I do. He's funny and he's reckless. You were always more serious. Can't I like both?"

Lapp surprised himself by blurting out, "if I came back, would you marry me?"

Sallie's cheeks blushed apple red. "I can't say now. You can't ask me something like that now. I know we could be happy, but I don't know if you can live Amish. You said yourself you couldn't. How would it work?"

While they stared at each other and choked back their emotions, a yellow maple leaf drifted down, through the shards of sunlight that pierced the tree and landed on top of Sallie's bonnet. Lapp reached over and tenderly plucked it from her head. He held it out to her.

Sallie's eyes studied the leaf and her eyes glistened with tears. "Oh, Johnny."

Lapp choked out the words, "I know."

"We can't settle nothing, can we."

"I guess not," John Lapp said.

Sallie guided the chestnut horse back onto the road. They rode quietly exchanging shy, almost embarrassed smiles.

"So now you're going to see her at her husband's funeral," Rufus Martin observed. "It's funny how things happen, ain't it?"

It is funny, Lapp thought angrily. That son-of-a-bitch Jacob lied to me and I fell for it.

Chapter 19

Back in his truck, rolling down Route 30, John Lapp passed Dutch Wonderland, a local amusement park. Lapp fondly remembered the yearly August visits when he, Jacob, and Stubby Beiler paid their admissions and stashed their straw hats and black coats in a cube locker. They laughed and screamed and their round-headed haircuts blew in the rush of air as the Sky Princess Rollercoaster dipped and soared above the far reaches of the park. Closed for the winter, the track, which extended over the front entrance of the park, was eerily silent.

He checked his watch. 11:15 a.m. The two-hour funeral service in the Stoltzfus house was over. The coffin had been placed in the back of a spring wagon and the procession of buggies, had, by now, reached the cemetery. John Lapp did not have to attend the funeral in person to know the customs and order of the service. He remembered, with dread, those he had attended as a boy and teenager. When he was twelve, his grandfather, who lived in the "grossdawdy haus", an attached wing to the house on his farm, had died after a lingering illness. His body lay in an open casket in the front parlor and Lapp peeked bravely at the lifeless body.

He pictured Sallie's children viewing their father's body. Without being there, he knew Jacob had been dressed all in white by Sallie and Jacob's sisters, his long hair and stringy beard stroked and combed with love by Sallie. When the preparation of the body was complete, and before the invited mourners arrived for the services, the children had been brought in to say goodbye to their Papa. Through quiet sobs, they whispered their goodbyes, so that their voices would not disturb his eternal peace. Lapp's heart was with the children and all of the mourners who took comfort in the Amish beliefs of immortality and life after death.

There were no flowers or ornamentation of any kind around the casket.

After the family said their goodbyes, the doors were opened. Relatives and friends found chairs and benches that took up every inch of space in the parlor and kitchen.

At the stroke of nine the men removed their hats in perfect unison. The minister's sermon was filled with biblical quotes reinforcing their beliefs. God had spoken. He had called Jacob home. Jacob would be missed but God needs good men, too.

The second minister spoke of Jacob as a good family man and praised him. He admonished the mourners to live righteously, since it is never known when "their time" would come. "Be ready to meet death when it comes. Don't put it off!"

The two-hour service concluded with a minister reciting the words of a hymn. There was no singing. The mourners filed past the coffin for a final viewing of Jacob's body before the lid was closed.

Another brief service was held at the cemetery. Two stout poles supported the coffin before it was lowered into the ground by four men holding long felt straps. The loud thumps of shoveled gravel hitting the coffin were like shots to the heart of the mourners. When the grave was half-filled there was a brief pause for the minister to again recite a hymn. The family members, followed by other mourners, returned to their buggies while the grave was filled and mounded.

The procession, at least twenty buggies strong, began the journey back to the farm.

At 11:40, Lapp was stopped by two poles that spanned the entrance to the Stoltzfus farm lane. The makeshift gate was their way of keeping the media, tourists and the generally curious away.

He leaned through the window to be recognized by the four young men who served as gatekeepers. They hurriedly moved the poles allowing Lapp to proceed up the lane. Through his rear-view mirror he could see them gossiping over who he was, and why he was there.

From past experience, he knew where the horses and buggies would be parked, so he drove next to the pig shed where his truck would be less conspicuous.

He turned off the engine but kept the radio on, tapping his hands on the steering wheel, not to the music on the radio, but to calm his nerves. He worried about how many people he would remember, and how they would receive him.

In less than ten minutes the horses and buggies began to arrive. A squad of teenaged boys grabbed the horse's halters and held them steady, while Sallie, her children and the women stepped out and went straight to the house. The men climbed out and the boys walked the horses to the barn where they were unhitched, fed and watered.

Lapp left the truck and strolled toward the mourners. The men, gathered in small groups, spoke in Pennsylvania Dutch, their words no longer about the dead, but of the weather and how it would affect the day's and week's work activities. They knew why he was there and nodded polite greetings. Children stared with curiosity at the brown-suited "English" stranger, while the few women, those not too shy, smiled graciously.

He turned when he heard a voice say, "all you need now is some black clothes and a beard and you'd be right at home." Even though he had not seen her for at least six years, he recognized the voice of his sister, Lizzie.

"Wie bisht, Lizzie?" He smiled broadly.

"Ich bin gut. It's good to see you. It's been so long now," Lizzie said with a warmth that bridged their cultural and religious gaps. A pink-faced infant child, wrapped in a blue knit blanket was cradled in her left arm. "You're looking good. I was so happy when I heard you were coming today."

Even though it was against Amish custom, he wrapped his arms around Lizzie and the baby. She happily returned his hug.

"I'm happy to see you, too," Lapp responded. When their mother died giving birth to a baby boy who also died, Lizzie took over. She was eleven, John Lapp was not yet two. Their sister, Sarah was six. Lizzie ruled the roost. Lapp had no memory of her, but was told that Lizzie resembled their mother, short, a little over five feet tall, slender, with an oval face that was always smiling, talking and cheerful. "It's too bad it took something like this to get us together again. Thanks for coming. It wasn't easy for Papa to ask."

"How did he find out where I lived?"

"He asked me," she replied with a twinkle in her eye.

"And how did you know?"

"I looked you up in the phone book. There's a booth at the end of our lane."

They smiled over the incongruity of being able to use a phone as long as it was not in or too near to the house.

"How's Sarah?" He asked, referring to his other sister.

"Why don't you ask her yourself?" Lizzie waved at a group of three women and wagged a finger at one of them to come over.

"Did she ever marry?"

"No. I doubt she ever will. She takes care of Papa. Just like always."

Lapp mentally figured their ages. If he was 35, then Sarah would be 38 and Lizzie, 46. As she drew near, a shy smile broke across her red, chapped face.

He greeted her in the same way, with, "Sarah, wie bischt?"

"Gut. Und du?" She was nearly as tall as Lapp, but a foot wider across.

"Gut." There was an awkward pause. Lapp turned to the baby in Lizzie's arm.

"And who is this?"

"This is Aaron," she said proudly, pulling the blanket away from his face. He's three months old, and getting heavy." Sarah reached out to take the baby, but Lizzie instead held him out for Lapp to take. "You hold him."

Lapp shrugged and took the baby by the waist before settling him into a cradle formed by his left arm.

"They feel good, don't they? How many kids do you have?"

"None yet."

"What are you waiting for," she scolded. "You probably don't know it, but after four girls, I had two boys. I was a grandma before this last one came along. He'll be the last. John wanted boys and now he has two," Lizzie said, referring to her husband, John Gingrich. "He can't wait for them to be old enough to help with the farm work. Girls are just as good and work just as hard, but you know how it is, he wanted boys."

"How old are they now? I remember Ruth and Rebecca ..."

"Ruthie is twenty-five. She's married to Dan Yoder. They live over in Lebanon County. She has two kids of her own. Rebecca is twenty-two. She married Eli King, and has a little boy ... Katie is eighteen. She's still at home and so is Annie who is fourteen. Then I had Jacob who is eight and now this one. He was a little surprise," she giggled. "But a very good one."

As if responding to his name, little Aaron's chestnut eyes opened so that Lapp could see they matched Lizzie's. Lapp rocked him from side to side to calm the whimper that threatened to become a real cry.

"My wife is a nurse at Lancaster General," Lapp explained. "That keeps her pretty busy right now. We hope to have kids though, someday."

"I feel awful bad for Sallie. Have you talked to her?"

"Twice," he began, but was cut short by Aaron's wailing which had risen to full pitch. "Here, maybe Sarah should take him." He held the baby out for Sarah to take. She happily accepted.

Sarah cooed to the baby. His crying stopped in mid-sob. Lapp was convinced that Sarah had hoped for marriage and children of her own and his anger rose toward their father who, evidenced by her raw, calloused hands and weathered face, used Sarah as a servant and had taken away all hope of having her own family.

"It won't be easy for Sallie," Lizzie said. "First she loses Jacob, and now this business with Amos …"

"I'm here to help. Not as a State Trooper, but as a friend."

"You'll do what you can. I know that much," Lizzie said as she took Aaron back into her arms. She turned back to her brother and asked, straight-faced, "I want to ask you something. What was it like seeing Sallie after all these years?"

Sarah's face blushed at the question, but Lizzie held tough. "Didn't you ever wonder?"

Lapp stared at the ground before facing Lizzie. "I did at first, but not for a long time, now."

"She was worth staying for," Lizzie admonished.

Lapp shrugged his shoulder. "Maybe. There were a lot of things against it."

"I still say it's too bad," Lizzie persisted.

Lapp nodded, shrugged and smiled.

A female voice called, announced, "es ist zeit fur esse, I think it's time to eat."

John Lapp and his sisters joined the small groups of Amish, men, women and children, moving in waves to the kitchen.

Sallie Stoltzfus stood by the door, with Samuel on her left and David and Lydia on her right, welcoming the guests as they stepped into the kitchen. John Lapp was greeted with a shy wave from little Lydia which he returned with a broad smile. His eyes met Sallie's as he stepped through the doorway. "Johnny, you're at the children's table. You understand," she said, meaning that as a non-church member, he could not sit with church adults.

"That's okay," he replied. "That will be fine."

The rows of benches used for the funeral service were now divided by long communal tables pre-set with stainless steel tableware, celery hearts in half-filled water glasses, sticks of butter next to stacks of white bread on plates, and jars of jelly and apple butter. A dozen Amish women, young and old, tall and short, thin and hefty, brought out platters of ham, fried chicken, bowls of mashed potatoes, corn cut from the cob and soaked in butter, chow-chow, pickled beets and sweet pickles. Pitchers of ice water and red Kool-Aid were the beverage options.

Lapp took a spot with the Stoltzfus children, across from his only ally, little Lydia. The boys, aged six to twelve, weren't sure how to react to him and avoided his glances. The girls, all cute and pretty in their black bonnets, were more accepting. They whispered to each other and giggled when he smiled at them.

The room grew quiet as all eyes turned to Eli Stoltzfus. He lowered his head for the silent prayer. Thirty seconds later, heads popped up and platters of food were passed.

As with any Amish meal, breakfast, dinner, or supper, the table was for eating, not for talking. Lapp ate heartily, drank his Cherry Kool-Aid and forgot about the abundance of fat, salt and sugar in the meal. It was finished off with apple dumplings with vanilla ice cream and a slice of shoo-fly pie.

When the children had finished, their heads again turned toward Eli, hoping to get his attention and to encourage him to begin the silent prayer that would conclude the meal. After many long, agonizing minutes, Eli complied. When he lifted his head and opened his eyes, the children took their cue, slid off the benches and quietly drifted away from the table.

Next, the men and women rose and left the room. Lapp remained at the table waiting patiently for his instructions. When the room was nearly empty, Daniel Stoltzfus, Jacob's younger brother approached. "When you're done, the men are meeting at the barn."

Daniel Stoltzfus and John Lapp walked up the grassy rise that led to the wide open barn doors on the upper level. The barn floor had been swept clean. Dusty cobwebs swayed eerily from the rafters and support beams. Four long benches had been set up facing the barn doors. The front row was occupied by the oldest men, several of whom leaned on their canes to prop up their bodies. The younger Amish men occupied the rear. There were no women or children present.

The Amish men, dressed against the cold in their black Mutzi or "frock coats" ended their conversations as John Lapp, in his brown suit, feeling almost as though he had been called upon to confess some transgression or grievous wrongdoing before a religious tribunal, stood in front and faced them. His eyes found his father sitting at the far right end of the front bench staring straight ahead, indicating to his peers that his son was not forgiven for leaving church and family.

"Thank you for coming, Johnny," Eli Stoltzfus said, rising from his seat on the front bench. "Maybe it wasn't so easy for you to do this but it's not so easy for us to do this either."

"I said I would help if I can. Jacob was my friend once," Lapp responded, while his eyes wandered among the twenty or so men, recognizing about half by sight if not by name.

"Amos would never kill nobody." Eli raised his voice. "And now he's in jail where he don't belong, no how."

"I know he wouldn't," Lapp agreed. "But in order to free Amos, we have to find the real killer."

"Then we must help him if we can," Eli proclaimed, before slowly sitting back down. Lapp caught his father nodding in agreement.

"I want to know something before this thing goes too far." The speaker was a buzzard-headed old man with a scraggly beard. Lapp remembered the man as a strict fundamentalist Bishop named Levi Miller.

Levi surveyed the group to see that he had their full attention. Leaning on his cane, he struggled to his feet. "I want to know something. I want to know why we are trusting this man to help us."

"He was one of us," Eli countered.

Levi snapped, "I know what he was. I want to know what he is now. And I want to know when this mess with the all these cameras poking at us and people bothering us with stupid questions every where we go is going to stop?" Levi punctuated his words by jabbing his cane into the planked floor.

All eyes turned to John Lapp to respond. "The press and the curiosity seekers will be around as long as it takes to solve Jacob's murder. And as long as Amos is held responsible."

Levi's voice resembled the quacking of an angry duck. "I say we should just let it rest. We don't need him poking around, or anyone else for that matter."

"Ach, Levi, what about Amos? We can't just leave him in jail," Eli protested.

"Well, how is he going to help, then?"

Lapp took his cue. "First you must know that I'm here as a friend. I am not a homicide detective. I'm a patrol officer. If I can learn anything that can help Amos, I will take it to my superiors."

The men's nodding heads signified their understanding. Lapp was about to continue when he noticed that the men were now looking past him to the barn doors. He turned to see Sallie Stoltzfus, dressed in black cape and bonnet, her face barely showing, backlit against the outside.

Sallie spoke before Lapp or any of the men had a chance. "If you're going to talk about my husband, then I should hear what you have to say."

A voice rose over the mumbling of the gathered assembly. It was Sallie's father, Joseph Yoder, rising from his seat in the second row. "Sallie," he said in an angry voice, "you must not be here. This is men's business."

Sallie glared defiantly at the men. "I've always been a good wife and should know what you say, good or bad."

John Lapp, worrying that the men would hold back because of Sallie's presence, was about to ask her to trust him, but was stopped by the stubborn expression on her face.

Levi Miller, leaning on his cane and walking like his feet were stuck in a muddy pig sty, plodded toward the barn door. "I warned you about this foolishness. If she wants to stay, then we'll go."

Three older men in the front row started out as did four others behind them.

Lapp, worried that he had come there for nothing spread his arms to stop them. His voice rose to a shout. "If you don't want to help Amos, if you want to see Amos be sent to prison for the murder of his brother, then go ahead." Lapp stepped dramatically aside. The men, confused over who to believe and obey, stopped and listened. "I'm trying to help Amos and I can't unless you help me. How else can I say it?" Lapp argued.

The grumbling echoed through the barn, but those remaining returned to their seats. Sallie, her hands hidden beneath the cape, stepped to the side of the front bench and waited for Lapp to continue.

The rebellion temporarily quelled, Lapp began, "you must tell me what you know about Jacob," Lapp began. "Where did he go when he went out at night, particularly that night. Who his friends were, particularly "English" friends. You must tell me if he was in trouble with the church for anything. Did he go places in cars or trucks. Anything that might give me something to investigate."

The men looked at one another to see who would speak. Lapp was not surprised by their silence. He knew it was difficult for them to repeat rumors or even say anything negative about members of their community.

"Does anyone know why Jacob sold his land? Or why he wanted the $50,000?"

The men shook their heads, no.

"What about his interests in horses? I understand he would go over to Hanover to look at horses. Do any of you know who he went to see? The name of the farm?"

The Amish men shook their heads, no.

"Daniel?" What about you? You're his brother."

"I just know he went over there sometimes. We all knew that. He talked about wanting to raise and train horses."

"For what? Racing?"

A low rumble of disapproval rolled through the Amish men. Daniel Stoltzfus was not about to go any further with this.

Lapp eyes scanned the rows of men waiting for someone else to speak up. He glanced back at Sallie. Her expression of defiance hadn't changed. "I guess I've wasted your time and mine coming out here." Lapp turned toward the open barn doors. Sallie had also turned to walk out with him.

"I know something." A handsome man in his thirties with his hat tipped back stood up, glanced first at Sallie, then at his father, before speaking. "I'm Danny Yoder. Sallie's brother. Maybe you remember me?"

They turned back. Lapp said, "sure, Danny, I remember you." He remembered him as a tow-headed boy who tormented them when he and Sallie wanted to be alone.

"Sometimes at night, Jake used to go to Hoffman's Tavern, next to the Turkey Hill over on 340," he said in a nervous, regretful voice.

All eyes turned toward Sallie. Lapp was pleased that she did not glare her brother down.

Every Amish man who was in his thirties or younger had been there. Located next to the Turkey Hill convenience store, Hoffman's was notorious for selling beer and whiskey out the back door to Amish teenagers during "rumspringa". It was a way of getting liquor without going to the State Stores where an ID would be required. Plus, they'd be seen going in and out of the front door.

"Did he go there often?" Lapp asked.

"Pretty often, I think. He didn't stay long. He told me that a couple of drinks helped to calm his nerves."

There was some general mumbling among the Amish men, wondering, but not voicing out loud, what Jacob had to be nervous about.

Still no reaction from Sallie.

Lapp did not embarrass Danny by asking if he had been to Hoffman's with Jacob. "What about other places. Did he go to any other bars?"

"Not that I know of," Danny assured the others.

"I'll check it out. If Jacob was at Hoffman's that night it would explain the time lag between when he left the motel with the money and the time he was found at the gas station."

It was a fresh lead. He waited for more but it was not forthcoming. Before ending the meeting he took one more stab. "What about Amos? Other than family members, did any of you see Amos the night that Jacob was killed.? That was last Thursday night."

Still more shaking of heads. Sallie abruptly turned and disappeared through the barn doors.

Lapp was glad to see her go. Maybe others would open up. He asked again, "think about it. It could make a difference. What about Amos? Did any of you see Amos on Thursday night or know anything that might help him?"

Eli Stoltzfus stood up, his eyes, begging for a response. When there was none, Eli turned to Lapp. "Amos was backward around people. He didn't talk much to nobody. Not even after church. When people talked to him, he just shook his head a lot. You had to pull things out of him. Johnny, you have to make him talk."

"On Friday, the day after, how did Amos seem? Did he act any different?" Lapp aimed the question first at Eli, then at Daniel. Who told Amos that Jacob was dead."

"He said he heard it at work," Daniel Stoltzfus said.

"He didn't come right home when he heard it?"

"No. Same time as always."

"Did he say anything to you about it? Daniel? Eli? Any of you?"

They shook their heads. Lapp wanted to dig deeper, but was happy to have the Hoffman's bar lead. "Okay. You know where to find me if you think of anything else. I'll do what I can."

The men nodded their appreciation, rose and filed past him and through the barn doors. Lapp held fast, hoping that someone who didn't want to talk in front of the others would express themselves privately.

Eli Stoltzfus and Moses Lapp stepped next to John Lapp, nodded their heads in thanks, and walked away.

"Don't you know me no more?"

Lapp remembered the voice before acknowledging the short, broad shouldered man wearing a broad grin behind the heavy brown and white whiskers. "Stubby Beiler?"

"It's been a long time, huh?"

Elam "Stubby" Beiler got his nickname from his five-foot, four-inch height and the stubbed middle finger of his right hand that had been chewed up below the knuckle in a meat grinder accident when he was ten years old.

"This is an awful business, ain't it?"

"I hope I can help."

"Is that what you're doing?" Stubby said, moving closer so they could not be overheard.

Lapp, surprised by the question and sudden change of attitude, answered, "that's why I came."

"I'm chust worried that with all of this noseying around, pretty soon it's Jacob Stoltzfus who's gonna be blamed for his own killing."

"What do you mean?"

Stubby's blue eyes narrowed. "I mean we both know Jake wasn't perfect. Never was. You keep snooping round and the next thing you know you're gonna find stuff that should be left alone. He's dead. What went on before is done. Leave it that way."

Lapp was dumbfounded. "What about Amos? You think he killed his brother?"

"Amos didn't do nothing. Sooner or later, you people will figure that out. I ain't worried about Amos."

"What should I do, Stubby? His Pop asked me to help. My Pop asked, too. You want me to just go away?"

"I ain't saying nothing else. You said yourself, it's not your job to be here. Chust listen to me. Let it go before it hurts Sallie." Then Stubby abruptly ran off to catch up with the last of the Amish boarding their carriages.

Stunned by Stubby's warning, Lapp climbed into his truck.

He glanced at the kitchen door hoping for a final glimpse of Sallie. As he followed the procession of buggies down the lane, Lizzie's words rang in his ears. "She would have been worth staying for."

Chapter 20

Lapp spent the last hour of daylight at home in his back yard gleaning his garden of a couple scraggly cabbages, two stalks of celery and a half-dozen eight-inch carrots. The meeting with the Amish men earlier today brought mixed emotions.

He smiled, thinking of how Sallie stood up to the men, but was puzzled by Stubby Beiler's dire warning. What was he afraid of? If he continued to probe Jake's death, what would he find that could hurt Sallie?

He raked up enough fallen red Maple leaves to add a six-inch layer into his black molded plastic composter. Poking and prodding with his pitchfork, he turned the decaying green scraps, grass and leaves revealing a rich, black, sweet-smelling loam filled with balls of earthworms doing their job for Mother Nature. When he moved to a new house, the composter was coming with him.

He did not expect to be hungry after his Amish noon meal, but his stomach told him differently. At five o'clock he popped a low salt frozen meatloaf into the oven, and cut up and sliced some of his cabbage, celery and carrot harvest. He added some head lettuce into a bowl which he stuck in the refrigerator until his main course was ready. The local five-thirty TV newscast carried a short piece on Amos' arrest, but there were no new details. The story had taken a Sunday break, but would surely become headline news again on Monday.

After supper, he spent the next two hours switching on and off the lights in every room of the house, including the garage, conducting an inventory of what he would take with him and what he would leave behind. Except for his clothes, the golf clubs and fishing rods he rarely used, and some basic tools from the garage, Betsy was welcome to the rest. At least until he moved. New surroundings might demand additional negotiations and confiscations.

She wanted him out. He was ready to go. But he concluded that he was not about to take an interim apartment for her convenience. When he found a house, he would move. Not before.

By eight o'clock, he was itching to follow up on Jake's activities on the night of the murder. His preppy outfit of blue jeans, checked shirt covered by a Millersville State sweatshirt and a pair of old Nike's was deemed appropriate for nighttime detective work. Attempting to recreate Jacob's timeline, he steered his truck along Route 30, past the police barracks, and through the tourist area, before pulling into the parking lot of Patel's Holiday Inn Express. Checking the odometer, he took the back roads that Jacob would most likely have taken, which were also the most direct way to Bird-In-Hand, then a left turn on 340 to the Turkey Hill convenience store and the bright neon TAVERN sign next door. The distance from motel to tavern was just under four miles. Adjusting for the bad weather that night, it could have taken less than twenty minutes to get there by horse and buggy.

Instead of another grungy teenager, this time the clerk behind the counter of the Turkey Hill was a heavyset, middle-aged woman with a full head of blonde curly hair. She wore a white blouse and blue checkerboard apron over tight blue jeans. Approaching her, he noticed a couple of teenaged girls down one of the aisles, who, by their glances at the counter, were serious shoplifting candidates.

Lapp presented his badge to the cheery-faced woman.

"Yes, sir. How can I help you?"

"Were you working here last Thursday night?"

She responded quickly. "No, sir. I only work weekends. Saturday and Sunday nights."

Lapp saw her eyes glance toward the security mirrors set up at the end of each aisle, keeping tabs on the girls.

She returned her focus to Lapp. "I'm sorry. Is there any way I can help?"

"Did an Amish man named Stoltzfus ever come in here while you were working?"

"There's Amish men in here every once in awhile, but I don't know none of their names." Then, the light bulb went on. "Say, is he the one that was killed by his brother?"

"He's the one that was killed, yes. His brother may have been involved."

"It's the damndest thing, you know that? Who would've figured?" Her eyes shifted to the stringy blonde-haired teenagers wearing letter jackets approaching the counter, holding out two Hershey candy bars. "Excuse me," she said, looking past Lapp's right shoulder.

He stepped aside.

"What about them combs you got inside your belt, honey? You planning on paying for those?"

"I didn't get those here," the first girl protested.

"That little white bar code sticker says you did."

"I bought these at Wal-Mart, didn't I?" The first blonde asked the second.

"If that's true, they won't scan. Can I give them a try?"

The embarrassed, red-faced girls were an easy bust. "Maybe we made a mistake," the spokesgirl said. "Here." She laid three large blue combs on the counter.

"That's easily corrected." The clerk swiped the combs and said, 'that'll be $6.23.

The girls pooled their money, laid out $6.25 and got two pennies back. Their eyes avoided Lapp as they hurried out the door.

Lapp congratulated her. "Good eye. Nice work."

"Aw, I can handle them kind. I don't like busting them like that. But it's wrong to steal."

"I hope the Turkey Hill people appreciate what a good employee they have with you." Lapp smiled.

"They don't," she said curtly. "But that's another story. You were asking about the Amish. On my shifts, we get Amish teenagers out on dates or running around that come in here."

"How do they behave?" Lapp asked.

"Funny you should ask. You have this picture of these pious people in their black outfits. The boys get a little mouthy, showing off in front of their girlfriends. Even the girls sometimes can be sassy." She was on a roll, so Lapp let her continue. "They come in for candy, soft drinks, snacks, stuff like that. Sometimes they drink coffee to sober up. I've even caught a couple shoplifting. I think they do it on a dare more than anything. At least, they're quick to admit it, not like those girls."

"Where are they getting the alcohol? Next door?"

"That would be my guess." She added quickly, "I don't mean to insinuate it's just the Amish kids that come in here half looped. I get customers, young and old alike, who come in here that had a few too many." The clerk swiped the beading sweat from her forehead. "It gets warm behind the counter, sometimes."

Lapp pulled two black licorice twists from a jar on the counter and stuck one in his mouth. He fished out a quarter and dropped it on the counter. "I appreciate your time. Keep up the good work."

"You, too," she shouted after him.

Hoffman's Tavern was situated in an old, two-story brick building that, thirty years ago, had been a roadside residence. The front double-sashed windows, equally spaced on each side of the entrance, were collages of red, white, green and blue neon signs advertising Budweiser, Rolling Rock and Samuel Adams. The upstairs windows were covered by white lace curtains, suggesting that somebody lived up there.

He swallowed the last of his licorice twist before pushing through the solid wooden door. Finding his bearings in the dimly lit room, he approached the ten-foot bar, with low-back stools lined in front, a brass foot rail and a huge mirror that reflected about a hundred different bottles and brands of spirits and liquor behind. The room was shadowed by a cloudy haze of cigarette smoke. The floor was black and white checked linoleum, easy to mop, he presumed. The primary sources of the dim lighting were three old lantern glass chandeliers that were grey with dirt and smoke. A first class operation, it wasn't.

None of the red naugahyde bar stools was occupied, so Lapp claimed one in front of the beer taps. He was tempted to grab a handful of red-shelled peanuts from a blue plastic bowl, but resisted when he speculated over the unwashed hands that had already dipped into that bowl. It was his observation that men in this part of the country frequently neglected to wash their hands after using the urinal.

He twisted around to survey the four wooden booths lined along the outside wall. One booth was occupied by two couples in their sixties wearing denim pants and white sweatshirts. The only thing that separated the men from the women were the team logos on their baseball caps. They swigged from tall neck beer bottles and their heads tilted, eyes shifted, and mouths wagged with minor curiosity over this stranger who had invaded their inner sanctum.

In the other occupied booth, a woman in her thirties in a red vinyl raincoat sat snuggled next to a man of the same age with long sideburns and a tan cowboy hat propped on his head. They were too busy nursing their mixed drinks and stealing long passionate kisses to pay any attention to Lapp.

The song, "Don't That Make My Brown Eyes Blue", played on a Wurlitzer chrome-plated console juke box with red and green neon tubes racing up and down the front and sides.

Local dives like this were a vanishing breed. Today's drinkers and fun seekers went to chains like TGI Friday or Robbie's Roadhouse, drank tequila and imported beers, ate good food, watched sports on TV and shopped for bed partners all at the same time.

The far end of the room featured a lineup of arcade games. An All-Star Bowling Game, Major League Baseball pinball machine and two Star Wars arcade games flashed and pinged but failed to attract any customer's coins.

Four small tables, each with four low round-backed chairs, were placed in the middle of the room. All were empty. Sunday was obviously a slow night.

The bartender, a slender man in his forties, with a pencil-thin mustache and long black hair slicked straight back, seemed in no hurry to serve him so he got up and took a padded chair at a table that would give him a more strategic view of the entire room. Thirty seconds later, the waitress, a fleshy blonde with large breasts that threatened to pop the quarter-sized white buttons on her skimpy pink blouse asked, "what can I getcha?"

Lapp had to think for a moment. He was not a drinker. Savoring the candy taste in his mouth, he asked, "What goes good with licorice?"

"What?" She asked. She looked to be fortyish and had a pretty face except for the overdone lavender eye shadow that conflicted with, rather than enhanced, her blue eyes.

"Isn't there a liquor that has licorice flavor?"

"Yeah. It's called anise," she said, amused by the question.

"I'll have that. Thanks."

Lapp watched her walk away and wondered if Jacob might have been attracted to her. Except for the hint of cellulite on her visible thighs, she wasn't bad looking in her short black skirt and pink flat shoes. She was totally different from Sallie but, who knows, that may have appealed to him.

When the waitress arrived with his drink which, to his surprise, was clear liquid served in a thin necked glass, he asked, "could I ask you a couple of questions?"

"What about," she asked, standing over him and causing him to crane his neck past her ample breasts to see her face.

"Could you sit down? I'll get a stiff neck like this."

She was not amused. "Sorry. I can't fraternize with customers." She took two steps back, allowing him a better view.

"A friend of mine, Jacob Stoltzfus, used to come in here on a regular basis."

"You're a friend of his?" she asked.

"We grew up together."

"You're an Amish man?" Her accent was not dutchy, more Philadelphia or Baltimore.

"Was once. I was shocked to find out he had been killed."

"You weren't the only one."

"Was he in here Thursday? The night he was killed?"

She pretended to think about it. "He might have been. I'm not sure. If you left the Amish, what do you do now?"

"I'm with the State Police."

The answer surprised her. "As a civilian?"

"No. I'm a trooper," he said casually. "Off-duty."

"Humm." Her eyes narrowed. "Are you investigating his death?"

"Not officially. I'm just trying to help out. I went to his funeral today. A couple of Amish men say they saw his buggy next door on the night he was killed. Does that refresh your memory?"

She glanced nervously at the bar. "I have to get back to work. You okay with that one or do you want another?" It was an evasive question since he hadn't even touched the drink.

"No. I'm okay."

He sipped the sweet liquor and felt the heat as it went down. Not bad, though. Like drinking candy with a burn.

At the bar, the waitress and the bartender had their heads together sharing their opinions of him. Lapp drained the last sip from his tiny glass and held it up for them to see. In half a minute, the waitress replaced his empty glass with a full one.

"Just a couple of questions?" Lapp asked, half pleading with a smile.

The front door opened and another couple in their sixties, slipping off their matching light blue windbreakers as they came in, exchanged greetings with the occupants in the booths. "As you can see, we're getting busy," she said, openly annoyed with him.

"When's a good time to come back?'

"I don't know. Why don't you ask the boss?"

"Good idea."

The waitress moved over to the booths and Lapp carried his drink to the bar.

The bartender gave him a sideways glance.

"Did your waitress tell you about me?" Lapp asked.

The sleeves on his white shirt were rolled up to display his muscular arms and biceps. He ignored the question and pulled a pitcher of light, foamy beer.

Lapp extended his hand. "My name's John Lapp."

"John Hoffman," he replied, reaching his wet hand across to take Lapp's.

"Lloyd's son?"

"That's right. Did you know him?"

"Yeah, he used to serve us out the back door when we were teenagers. You know how Amish kids are."

"We don't serve teenagers."

"That's not what I hear," Lapp said, figuring a little threat might get his attention.

"So what do you wanna know?"

"Just a few details on Jacob Stoltzfus' visit here last Thursday night. Things like what time he got here, what he did here, what time he left. Stuff like that."

"This is not the best time." Hoffman grabbed a bar towel and wiped down what appeared to be a perfectly clean counter top. Either he was a compulsive cleaner or Lapp's presence was making him nervous.

"I can come back. If you want I'll wear my uniform and make it an official visit. Or, maybe you'd rather come over the barracks to be interviewed."

"I'd like to see some ID."

"I'm old enough to drink."

Hoffman was not amused. "You know what I mean."

Lapp complied.

"What do you want to know?" Hoffman growled, throwing down the towel.

"Let's start with how often Jacob came here."

"Three or four times a week, maybe."

"What time did he get here that night?"

"About seven, I'd say. I was kinda surprised to see him. It was a miserable night to be out in a horse and buggy."

"How long did he stay?"

"Not too long. Maybe an hour."

"Is that how long he usually stayed?"

"Yeah. That's about right." Hoffman's eyes searched the room, hoping the waitress or a customer would demand his services and interrupt the interview.

Lapp persisted.

"What did he do. What did he drink?"

"Seven and seven. Or sometimes rum and coke."

"Seven and seven. Seagrams 7 and Seven Up?" Lapp smiled. It was the drink of choice among Amish kids when he was growing up. "How many did he have that night?"

"Two, maybe three."

"The usual amount?"

"Yeah. I'd say so."

"Where did he sit?" Lapp asked, twisting his body toward the tables and booths.

"The booth that's furthest back. Next to the toilet sign. That's where he always sat."

"Did anyone join him?"

"Not usually."

"So he never met anyone here?" Lapp asked.

"Not that night. Not recently, either. For awhile there, another Amish man would come in."

"How long ago?"

"Two-three months? Hell, I don't know." Hoffman did try to hide his anger over being questioned.

"Can you describe the other Amish man?"

"Short, husky, big head, big beard."

"How short?"

"Five-three, five-four."

Stubby Beiler. Not much doubt about it. "How often did he come in?"

"A couple times, maybe. That was all. Most of the time he sat alone back there."

"He sat there and drank by himself?"

"Mostly. He'd play the bowling machine. And sometimes the pinball machine."

"So he sat over there and your waitress ... what's her name?"

"Donna."

"Donna what?"

"Donna Trautman."

"Donna served him. Did she ever sit down with him?"

"Not that I can remember. She's not supposed to."

"Did Jacob talk to anyone Thursday night?"

"No one. I think he made customers a little uncomfortable. I mean, they didn't quite know what to make of him."

"So mostly he came here, sat alone and drank. Why would he do that?"

Hoffman shrugged. "Because he couldn't do it at home is my guess."

"Were any of these customers here that night?"

"Probably. I think the Steinmetz's were. They're in the middle booth," Hoffman said pointing. "They're here almost every night."

Lapp pulled a notebook and Scripto pencil from his breast pocket. "Steinmetz. First names?"

"Bill. Bill and Betty."

"Anybody else?"

"Thursday night?" He thinks then says, "yeah, the Boyers. They're in the next booth. Kenny and Pat," he added so that Lapp could write it down.

"What about that couple that just came in."

"The Bichers? No. I don't think so. Not on Thursday."

"And the lovebirds?" Lapp asked referring to the kissing couple still going at it in the end booth.

"They're not regulars. Never saw them before tonight."

"Anybody else? How about here at the bar?"

"Yeah. Roy was here. Roy Brubaker. He was here, left for a while, then came back."

Lapp's curiosity perked up. "Who's Roy Brubaker?"

"He owns the gas station and garage a couple of miles down the road toward Intercourse. It's an ESSO station."

Lapp wrote it down. "They were all here when Jacob left? Including Roy?"

"That's how I remember it."

"Who was the first to leave after that?"

Hoffman pondered the question, then responded, "Roy, probably. He left for about half an hour, then came back."

"What time was that?"

"About 9:30. He was back shortly after 10:00."

"How do you know that?"

"The ten o'clock news had just started. We watched it for the 76'ers score and the weather."

"Anything else you can remember about Jacob?"

"He almost always used that pay phone over there," Hoffman said, jerking his chin in that direction.

"Any idea who he was calling?"

"No idea."

Who would Jacob call? Was he betting on the horse races at Penn National? Or maybe at the Meadowlands in New Jersey? "He used the phone every time he came in?" Lapp asked.

"Damn near. I didn't exactly keep an eye on him. I didn't even know his name until it was on TV."

Donna pushed herself up next to Lapp and said to Hoffman. "Order. Refills for the Boyers and their friends."

Hoffman jumped to it.

"You get what you wanted?" she asked Lapp.

"He was very helpful. Now maybe you could too if you tried a little harder."

"I told you I'm busy."

"While you're waiting, tell me, did you like Jacob?"

"He was okay. Pleasant to serve. He was nice enough. We never talked much."

"Was he a good tipper?"

"Average. Maybe a couple of bucks."

Hoffman set four full highball glasses on her tray. "If you don't mind, I'll take care of my customers," Donna snapped.

"Don't let me stop you," Lapp shot back.

Two heavyset bruisers wearing black studded motorcycle jackets blasted through the door and took stools at the far end of the bar. While Hoffman was occupied with them, Lapp drifted over to the pay telephone and scanned the wall behind it searching for telephone numbers. Nothing. It was clean. He picked up the receiver and examined it. It looked new, barely used. Then his eyes turned to the cigarette machine. Amos' brand of cigarette was available in two slots.

Back at the bar, Lapp pulled out a ten dollar bill and asked Hoffman for the tab. Six dollars. Then he pushed the four one-dollar bills he was given as change back at Hoffman.

"Give them to Donna."

"You get everything you want?" Hoffman asked.

"For now. Keep an eye out for underage kids. Amish or not."

Hoffman did not return Lapp's smile. "I'll do that."

Chapter 21

Lapp pulled into the driveway and appreciated the light from the living room lamp that served as a welcoming beacon.

He pulled off his sweatshirt and was drawn to the blinking light on the telephone answering machine.

The first message had been recorded at 8:20 p.m. It was Betsy. The marriage counselor was already booked all day next Saturday, so she scheduled their session for 7:30 Friday night. She saw that they had made an arrest in the Amish case so he should have time to make this appointment. She left a number where she could be reached and asked him to confirm.

The second call was from his father-in-law, Joe Roblin.

"Hey, Johnny. Joe here. Remember when I told you, in homicide cases, always look at family members first? Just the same," he continued, "it's a hell of a shame, though. Call me back and let me know how it went down and your part in it." There was a long pause, before he added, "listen. I know we said it before, but Mary and I don't want this divorce to stand in the way of our being friends. Don't disappear on us. Okay? You know our number."

Lapp erased the messages.

He found a yellow-lined, legal sized tablet, sat down at the kitchen table, and wrote out a narrative of his visit to Hoffman's Tavern. Stubby Beiler's warning in the barn and his appearances in the bar reinforced that whatever Jacob was up to, Stubby had been a part of it. Getting it out of Stubby would be a challenge. Two pages later, he was pleased with the result. Since the interviews were unofficial, he would keep them as a memo of record.

Dead tired, Lapp flopped down in his Barcalounger and surfed through the thirty or so cable channels before settling on the Fox channel which was showing a repeat of the always entertaining program, *Cops*. When the 10 o'clock news came on, he hit the Mute button, kept one eye on the TV and browsed through a *Time Magazine.* But his thoughts were really on Jacob, Hoffman's Tavern, Stubby's warning, and as always, they led to, and ended with, Sallie.

On Monday morning, he got to the barracks at 8:00 a.m. dressed out, stood muster, and received his patrol assignment.

He warmed up his patrol car for a good minute before driving off. The weather was overcast again, with a chance of rain. The temperature was in the mid-forties, held steady by the cloud cover. There was little chance of snow.

He debated about requesting a permanent shift change. While the day shift was easy, mostly traffic related, it was also boring. The night shifts were apt to include domestic disputes, burglary, and sometimes mayhem. But for today, he was patrolling Route 222, a four-lane divided north-south road that was popular with tourists who moved back and forth between the charms of the Amish in Lancaster and the bargains at the Reading area Outlet Malls. He tended to give more warnings than tickets to tourists.

It was a different story with the locals. The road was ripe with temptation. Large open stretches where drivers ignored the 35 mph speed limit. The limit was too low and Lapp usually allowed a 10 mph grace. But those clocked over 45 mph were pulled over. Some days it was businessmen, who excused their speeding because they were in a hurry to get to meetings or to catch a commuter plane from the small Lancaster Municipal Airport.

Other days it was mostly housewives in station wagons or those big SUV's and vans who were late for doctors or dentists appointments or for meetings with school counselors. If there were small children in their vehicles, Lapp made sure their car seats were properly installed and the kids safely secured.

He handed out three citations before lunchtime. Today, he sucked up two croissant sandwiches and a medium Sprite at Jack In The Box. At a pay phone, he dug out a piece of paper from his shirt pocket with the phone numbers of Bill Steinmetz and Kenny Boyer, numbers that he had copied from the phone book at home. He was in luck. The ladies of the houses answered.

After he identified himself, both ladies confirmed they were at Hoffman's Bar that night and were very cooperative in making appointments to see them. The Steinmetz's were set for 3:30 p.m. The Boyer's for an hour later.

Lapp spent the next two hours hoping he would not be called to any accidents that would tie up his time. He issued a ticket to an elderly woman in an old Studebaker who blatantly rolled through a stop sign. Otherwise, things were blissfully quiet.

At the precise time, he pulled into the pea gravel driveway next to the Steinmetz residence. Six feet of sidewalk and four concrete steps led to the front porch of the freshly painted, two-story white frame house. He was greeted at the front door by a perky, rail-thin woman in a mustard-colored pantsuit who introduced herself as Betty Steinmetz. He followed her swirls of reddish hair into a small living room that was dominated by a large 35 inch big screen TV. Oprah was standing in the audience soliciting comments from a lineup of women guests seated on the stage.

A chunky man, wearing a flannel shirt under blue bib overalls and grey work stockings, hit the "off" button on the TV remote. He said, "Bill Steinmetz" as he struggled to rise from the black vinyl recliner. Taking the man's hand, Lapp guessed that Bill and Betty were in their late 60's or early 70's.

Lapp's eyes were attracted to the innocent looking ten-point buck mounted over one end of the couch and the snarling fangs of a mounted black bear over the other. In the center, on a small plaque was a mounted "Jackalope" a joke that was appealing enough for them to hang. The only thing missing was the flopping, "singing" bass fish that was constantly being advertised on TV.

Betty invited Lapp to join her on the flaking tan leather sofa. Bill, the big game hunter, aimed his rear end at the center of the recliner and plopped back down.

Bill Steinmetz spoke first. "Betty says your name is Lapp. That's an Amish name, isn't it?"

Lapp was getting a little tired of hearing that, but answered amiably, "I was born Amish. I left fifteen years ago."

"I heard a lot leave. I never knew how many, though," Bill wondered aloud.

"I understand it's around twenty per-cent," Lapp answered.

"It's too bad there aren't enough farms to go around. We sold our 90-acre farm to some Mennonites. They're taking good care of it. Truck farmers. Have a little roadside stand in the summer, too. They seem to be doing all right. Nice people. The Amish are nice people, too. The ones I knew were, anyway."

Betty Steinmetz smiled approvingly and turned to Lapp. "I guess you're investigating the death of Jacob Stoltzfus."

"That's right. You saw him the night he was killed, I believe."

Bill piped in. "They arrested his brother, I hear. Saw it on TV. Hard to believe. Sounds like they got the goods on him, though."

"There's a good deal of evidence," Lapp agreed.

"It seems such a shame," Betty said, rubbing her hands on her thighs. "We never paid much attention to him, you understand. We didn't talk to him and he never talked to us, either. He just sat in that back booth by himself for an hour or so, then around nine o'clock he went home. We're regulars there on Thursday and Friday nights. Sometimes Saturdays, too, but we never saw him on Saturdays, did we, Bill?"

"He probably couldn't get out on Saturdays," Bill offered with a knowing chuckle.

Lapp smiled at Bill's humor and asked, "did you notice anything different about him that night? Was he drinking more? Did you overhear anything he might have said?"

Betty shook her head, no. "Not really. Like I said, the only person he ever talked to was Donna, the waitress. I noticed she sat down with him two or three times that night, more than usual, I'd say. I even said to Bill how they seemed a little cozy that night. Didn't I, Bill?"

"That's right," Bill confirmed.

"Did he appear drunk?" Lapp asked.

"Not that night. But I've seen him drunk, all right."

Lapp leaned forward. "when was that?"

"Oh, maybe six months ago. One night he was in there playing those noisy machines ... sometimes the noise gets so loud you can hardly talk in there ... a couple of guys, I think they're plasterers or something, they were covered with white paint or plaster, were playing pinball games with him and whoever lost would buy a round. In the end they got him pretty drunk. Remember, Betty? They weren't regulars."

"I do. I was ready to say something about it to Johnny Hoffman."

"When those guys left, that Amish man could barely walk straight. Way too drunk to drive a horse and buggy, that's for sure," Bill added.

"How old would you say those plasterers were?" Lapp asked.

"In their thirties," Bill responded. "about his age. It's hard to tell an Amish man's age behind all those whiskers."

"You were saying, when those guys left ..."

"Yeah, anyway, when those guys left, Donna sat Jacob in a booth and gave him some coffee. Then she came over to our booth and asked me if I'd give him a ride home. I said I would if he could tell me where he lived, but I wondered what to do about the horse and buggy that he parked at the Turkey Hill, next door."

"I suggested he get another Amish man to take him home," Betty added.

"That's right, I remember. Someone said he had a brother who worked at the foundry which stayed open late Fridays. Donna called over there then she came back to me and asked if I would take my truck and go over there and fetch him. I said I would. And I did."

"Do you remember who knew he had a brother at the foundry?"

"Do you remember, Betty?"

"I'm trying to think who else was there that night," Betty said, closing her eyes to raise a better picture. "You know I think it was Roy Brubaker who said he had a brother," she added with a nod of certainty.

Bill brightened up. "That's right. That's who it was."

"Then you picked up Amos?" Lapp asked.

"That's right. The same fella they say killed Jacob. Strange looking bird, I thought. Never said two words the whole time."

"While Bill was gone, I kept watching him. Jacob. We never knew his name, of course, until we saw it in the papers. He put his arms on the table and fell asleep," Betty said. "When we got back there, Amos, you said his name was Amos, woke him up. That Amish man was mad as a swarm of bees. Pushed that guy away and yelled at him in Pennsylvania Dutch. I can understand some Dutch but I didn't get much of what they were saying. I know he wasn't swearing at him. I know all the swear words," Bill added with an odd sense of pride.

"What happened then?"

"I helped him get Jacob out the door and he said he'd take him and that's the last I saw of them that night."

"Last Friday night? Was Jacob drunk when he left?"

"He didn't seem like it," Bill said.

"He was happy though," Betty chimed in.

"Why was that?" Lapp wondered.

"He smiled and tipped his hat to me," she beamed with a touch of pride. "He's never done that before."

"What time did he leave?"

Betty and Bill's faces pondered the question before Betty answered. "Close to 9:30, I'd say. We were getting ready to go home ourselves. We thought our friends, the Shoemachers, might still show up, but they didn't."

"So we left," Bill said, finishing the thought.

"And the next day we saw it on TV. It must be rough on the family. On all the Amish, really," Betty added.

Bill summarized with, "and then to have one of their own having done it, you just don't know what to make of the world anymore."

Lapp figured there was no more to be learned here. He thanked them for their time, gave Betty one of his cards and motioned to Bill, who was struggling to get out of his chair, to stay put.

Betty walked him to the door.

His next stop was less than two miles away. Pat and Kenny Boyer lived in a green vinyl-sided double house, common in the area, with a wide porch that spanned two front doors, separated by a freshly painted ornamental iron rail.

A woman in her late forties, with short mousy brown hair and wearing an ankle-length flowered housecoat, was busily sweeping the leaves and spiny pods that had fallen from the chestnut tree that towered overhead. Her eyes, through tortoise-shelled glasses, widened at the sight of Lapp's trooper uniform as he came up the front steps.

"Is this the Boyer's?" he asked, pointing to the front door on the left.

She nodded and answered, "yes".

Lapp knocked on the front door and it was quickly answered by Pat Boyer, a short blond woman in her fifties with balloon shaped breasts bulging from the top of her scoop neck print blouse.

"Mrs. Boyer," Lapp asked?

"Yes. Please come in." As she ushered Lapp through the door, she snapped at her neighbor, "he's here to ask some questions about a man we know. It has nothing to do with us," she added quickly to squelch any gossip.

Lapp found himself in a small living room filled with frou-frous, knick-knacks, and souvenir photos from Disney World, Opryland, Niagara Falls and Branson, Missouri. He was greeted by Kenny Boyer, a husky man in his late fifties, early sixties, with big arms and hands that extended from the rolled up sleeves of his red checked flannel shirt. Boyer gripped a bottle of Rolling Rock in one hand and a lit cigarette in the other.

"I always have a cold one when I get home. Can I get you one?" Boyer asked.

"No, thanks."

"Can't drink on duty, huh."

"That's right."

"Sit over here." Kenny pointed Lapp toward a blanket-covered overstuffed chair with stained doily-covered arms, while he took the brown corduroy recliner for himself.

Pat sat on the matching sofa and crossed her legs exposing more of her overstuffed thighs from beneath her short denim skirt than Lapp cared to see. She immediately lit up a cigarette.

Lapp figured they could smoke if they wanted. It was their house. He unzipped his uniform jacket and pulled it off. Like the Steinmetz's living room, the Boyer house was overheated. One of the first things he remembered when he became "English" was how overheated their houses were due to the coal and oil furnaces which, when turned on for the winter, made temperatures hard to regulate.

"You were at Hoffman's Tavern last Thursday night, the night Jacob Stoltzfus was murdered. And what I'm trying to find out is if you may have seen or heard anything that might be useful in our investigation of his movements that night."

"Well, we were there, that's for sure," Kenny said. "And, yeah, we saw him."

"He came in all the time," Pat Boyer said through lips heavy with red lipstick.

"Did he do anything unusual that night?"

They looked at each other and shrugged.

"He was feeling pretty good, I'd say, wouldn't you, Patty?"

"He didn't usually smile or laugh a lot, but he did that night," she said with a rough throaty voice that told Lapp if she didn't already have cancer from smoking, she was on a fast track. "They had their heads together pretty much the whole time he was there."

"Who?" Lapp asked.

"Him and Donna. The waitress," Pat replied.

"You're right. Even more so than usual," Kenny added.

"It's like they was sharing some big secret."

"Any idea what it was?"

"I think it had to do with money." Kenny noticed Lapp's increased attention, encouraging him to continue. "He was putting money down on the table every time Donna brought him a drink and insisting she take it. Of course, I had no idea he was carrying $50,000. At least that's what the TV and the newspaper said he had."

"I think Donna knew it, though. Giggling about it like it was their little secret." Pat added.

"So Donna liked Jacob?" Lapp asked.

"I don't know if she liked him. Maybe she was playing up to him for tips," Kenny offered.

"I wouldn't put it past her," Pat agreed with a snippy tone.

"Are you friends with Donna?" Lapp asked, looking first at Pat, then at Kenny.

Pat shrugged. "Yeah, we get along."

"Have you known her long?" Lapp asked.

"What would you say, Kenny, two years?"

"I think she started there about two years ago. We'd been going there on a regular basis before Johnny hired her." Kenny lit up another cigarette and blew out a long stream of smoke that swept down and tickled Lapp's throat.

"Did she ever say anything about Jacob?" he asked Pat, figuring if there was gossip to be had he'd get it from her. "Did he come to the tavern because of Donna?"

Pat smashed her cigarette into the ashtray and immediately used a red Zippo lighter to light up another. "Do you mean, did they have a thing going?"

Lapp shrugged innocence.

"I doubt it. They may have wanted to but it would have been pretty hard with Roy Brubaker always hanging around. He probably figured it was all right for her to flirt with him as long as he bought drinks and left big tips."

"She goes with Roy?" Lapp asked.

"For at least the last six months," Pat said. "They're thick as thieves."

Lapp flushed with joy. A possible motive. Jealousy. A glance through the lace window curtains told him he'd better get going if he was going to call on Roy Brubaker before dark.

He thanked the Boyers. Their faces fell over his sudden decision to depart. But he had bigger fish to fry. He left his card, shrugged on his jacket, and jumped back into the patrol car.

Fifteen minutes later he saw the large, illuminated EXXON sign mounted on two high poles. Below it, stuck in a patch of weeds, on a 4x4 pole, was a Good Neighbor Realty sign with a strip across that said "SOLD" . It looked like Roy Brubaker was planning a lifestyle change.

A single row of two double gas pumps lined the front of the station office. A Pennsylvania State keystone-shaped plaque, "Official Inspection Station" was nailed above the door and two racks of Quaker State Motor Oil stood like guards at the office entrance.

A double service bay with the doors rolled up was filled with back to back vehicles. Roy appeared to have a prosperous business. Why was he selling?

At the edge of the property, thirty feet off to the right of the garage, a large, silver Airstream house trailer stood, surrounded by weeds, indicating that, although it was still on wheels, it had not been moved for some time. A beat up Dodge pickup was parked facing the trailer's side entrance.

Lapp drove past the pumps, parked and approached a teenager who sat in a webbed lawn chair next to a brightly lit Coca-Cola vending machine. Long blond curls spilled from beneath his black MTV cap. His face was immersed in an Auto Trader newspaper.

Lapp announced, "I'm looking for Roy Brubaker."

The youth, unfazed by the trooper uniform, pointed to the open service bay. "In there."

An old Chevrolet rested five feet off the ground on a hydraulic lift. A bent-over man in dirty blue coveralls wielding a large wrench was waging war on the front suspension system.

"Roy Brubaker?"

"Yeah. Just a minute," he barked. "Goddamn thing," he muttered as the wrench slipped off the nut he was tightening. "Shit!" He reset the wrench, grimaced, groaned, and jerked with all of his strength until the nut turned.

The bays were a mess. An uncoiled air hose snaked through oil and water on the floor. Two work benches were piled high with tools. Racks of new, wrapped tires ran along the back wall.

Roy ducked from beneath the hoisted Chevy and was startled by the uniform.

"What can I do for you?" he asked, pulling an oily rag from the rear pocket of his coveralls to wipe his hands.

Roy looked to be in his forties, about six feet tall, with broad shoulders and a husky build. Edges of grey hair extended from beneath his orange Fram Filters cap. His angular, stern face, which carried a couple of days worth of stubble, seemed adverse to smiling. "Grease Monkey" may be a popular word for mechanics, but Roy was more like a "grease gorilla."

"I'm going around talking to people who were at Hoffman's Tavern last Thursday night. The night Jacob Stoltzfus was killed."

Roy made a ritual of pulling a cigarette from a pack that was the same brand that Amos smoked. He lit up using a flip-top chrome lighter.

"Yeah, I was there," he said, blowing out a line of white smoke.

"So I understand. We're trying to figure out his movements after he left the bar."

"I saw him there, if that's what you're asking. But I never talked to him. Not that night or any night."

"You didn't like him?"

Roy shrugged. "I had nothing to say to him. Or him to me. I think if he wants to be an Amish man, then he should act like one and not hang around a bar."

"Donna seemed to like him."

"Yeah?" He recovered from the surprise question. "That's her business. It's her job to serve him."

"And that didn't bother you?

"Bother me? Why the hell should it bother me?"

"I'm told you two go together."

"Yeah, we go out. It's no big deal. There's nothing serious about it."

"So you weren't jealous?"

"Over an Amish man?" Roy laughed and spit on the floor. "If I was gonna be jealous there's a whole lot of others would come ahead of him."

Before Lapp could ask another question, Roy injected, "who told you that stuff about me and Donna? I bet it was Pat Boyer. She's the one's jealous because I won't give her a hump. But I won't because I like her old man. Otherwise, why the hell not?"

Cocky bastard, aren't you, Lapp thought, before changing the line of questioning. "I see your place has been sold."

"Saw the sign, huh? Yep, it's sold. Time to move on."

Lapp waved his hand at the smoke. "The smoke is getting to me. Would you mind?"

Roy shrugged and stuffed the butt into an overflowing quart sized motor oil can filled with sand.

"What do you plan to do?"

"I'm going west," Roy announced. "California, probably. Maybe Nevada."

"I'm told you left the tavern for about a half hour that night."

"I did? Yeah, I guess I did. I left my diagnostic machine on and I came back here to turn it off. That probably took a half-hour."

"Had Jacob left before that?"

"I don't have a clue. It wasn't my day to watch him." Roy was pleased with himself for the glib remark.

"So there's nothing you can think of that would help me."

"Not a damn thing. Now if you don't mind I got more work to do on this heap."

Lapp reached into his wallet and pulled out a five dollar bill. "I could use a coke for my ride home and I don't have any change for the machine. I wonder if you could change this."

"You don't have to buy one, I'll get you one."

"I can't do that. We can't take anything."

"Bullshit." Roy called out, "hey Robbie. Get your ass in here." Then to Lapp, "I'll have the kid get it for you."

Lapp's plan to get Roy away from him so that he could grab a cigarette butt from the can was temporarily foiled. His eyes focused on the rack of new tires.

"You got a P235/75R15 for a '95 Ford Ranger? I need two front ones."

"I've got some Firestones that are on sale. You want me to look?"

"If you don't mind."

Robbie arrived with a can of Coke. He popped the tab, gave it to Lapp, then headed for the pumps to serve a customer. Roy disappeared into the office.

Lapp pulled out his handkerchief, grabbed up a couple of the longer butts, wrapped them up and stuffed them into his side pocket.

"You're in luck", Roy said, returning to the bay. "I've got two. They're $94.80 each. With tax they come to $218.90."

"Good. How long you gonna be here?" Lapp asked, sipping from the can.

"Maybe another three to five days. Then, that's it. I'm gone."

Roy followed Lapp as they walked past the pumps to the patrol car and said, 'I see they already arrested his brother for killing him. You don't think you got the right guy?"

"Looks like it. I've been asked to check out every angle. You understand, just doing my job. I find it hard to believe another Amish could have done it. They're not violent people."

"Let me tell you, nothing surprises me anymore. With the way the world's going, the Amish are getting to be as bad as everybody else."

With that piece of wisdom, Lapp drove away, hoping to come back, not to buy tires, but with a reason to nail Roy Brubaker.

Chapter 22

It was past 7:00 a.m. when Lapp, dressed and ready for breakfast, stumbled down the stairs to grab the ringing telephone. Only the barracks or Betsy would call this early.

"John Lapp?"

He recognized her voice immediately. "Yes?"

"The State Trooper Lapp?"

"Yes. How did you find me?" he asked Lisa Robinson.

"You know who this is?" She asked with a low pleased-with-herself tone.

"I recognized your voice. How did you find me?"

"You're in the book. You and one other John Lapp. The other one wasn't you."

"Why are you calling?"

"I'm at the county jail. Amos Stoltzfus is refusing to take any food or water."

"He's on a hunger strike?" Lapp's voice rose.

"For now anyway. I went to his arraignment yesterday. I thought I'd see you there."

"I told you, I'm no longer on the case."

Her voice turned more serious. "Well, I think you should be. I heard the charges and some of the evidence, and there are holes you can drive a truck through."

"You got any other suspects?"

"No. Do you?"

Yeah, I do, Lapp thought, but I'm not going to tell you or anyone else right now. "I'm no longer involved."

"'I think you will be. Gloria Ebersole, the public defender assigned to his case, says he refuses to answer any questions and won't defend himself. And now he won't take any food or water. Somebody has got to help that poor man."

"That somebody is me?" He could picture her expressive face as it changed from a brilliant, white-toothed smile, to pouty lips to blazing eyes of confrontation.

"You know anyone better?"

"Why are you telling me this?"

"Because I don't think the story of Jacob Stoltzfus' murder has been told yet. And when it is, I want to be the one to tell it. Are you coming over to see Amos or not?"

"I'll have to get permission from my duty officer. I'm supposed to be on the road handing out tickets."

"Then get his permission."

"Are you going to be there?"

"I may and I may not. I've got another story to cover today. If I'm not, I'll catch up with you."

"I'm sure you will," he said, placing the receiver back into the cradle.

His duty sergeant, Harry Johnson, frowned impatiently as Lapp explained his request for a half day of comp time. It was reluctantly granted with the proviso that since two other patrolmen had called in sick that he be on his beat no later than noon.

It took two tries, with long waits in between, to finally reach Gloria Ebersole at the county jail. She confirmed that Amos was still not taking any food or water.

"Does the family know?" he asked.

"Not yet. I can't find anybody to drive out there and I'm tied up in court."

"I'll do it," Lapp said, and hung up, cursing the fact that the Amish had no telephones. He got into his patrol car and drove to the Eli Stoltzfus farm.

Fortunately, Eli was easily found, sitting on a bench in the barn, mending some harness. His initial refusal to accompany Lapp to the jail was reversed when Lapp suggested they get Sallie to come with them.

Sallie appeared in the kitchen doorway as they drove up. When she heard why they were there she grabbed a black shawl and climbed into the back seat.

On the way, Lapp continually glanced back at Sallie through the heavy wire screen that separated the front seats from the back. At the farm, he almost asked Eli to allow Sallie to sit in front. But it would have been an insult, since in buggies and cars, the Amish men always sat up front and the women in back.

Still it hurt Lapp to see Sallie separated by a heavy steel screen meant to keep criminals at bay.

The anxiety on Eli and Sallie's faces increased as the patrol car approached a pretentious-looking castle-like building at 625 East King Street. Constructed of tan sandstone blocks, the Lancaster County Jail featured two Roman towers and an arch with a faux grilled door in the center. Lapp parked and led Eli and Sallie to the real entrance, a glass double-door affair at the East end.

Inside, two middle-aged African-American women, seated in single plastic chairs that were attached on pedestals to the tiled floor, buzzed with curiosity over the Amish man and woman who had been brought in by a State Trooper.

Lapp approached the chunky uniformed guard at the security desk. She responded to his request by picking up the phone and calling inside. Lapp directed Eli and Sallie to take seats, but almost immediately the door to the interior opened and his name was called. A slim, blonde woman, thirtyish, tall, about five-nine, wearing a white blouse with a big silk bow and a short, navy blue skirt and blue pumps approached with an extended right hand. "I'm Gloria Ebersole."

"John Lapp." He pointed to Eli and Sallie who remained seated. "This is Amos' father, Eli Stoltzfus and Sallie Stoltzfus, widow of the deceased."

"I'm pleased to meet all of you," Gloria said, flashing a warm smile. "Let's go see what we can do with Amos. He won't help me at all."

She led them to the security check. Lapp smiled as Eli and Sallie tried to curb their nervousness over the large, heavy-set African-American guard who swiped their clothes with a metal detector.

"I need to see a picture ID," the guard said gruffly.

Sallie and Eli were stumped by the request.

Lapp jumped in. "They don't carry picture ID's. They don't have their pictures taken."

"Has to be a government issued ID with a picture on it. Driver's license," the guard insisted.

Lapp persisted. "They do not have driver's licenses."

Gloria spoke up. "Walter. Please. I'll vouch for them."

The fat-cheeked guard eyed Lapp and his guests with suspicion, then pointed them toward a three foot square table. "They need to sign in. That includes you, Trooper."

"Thank you," Lapp and Gloria said in a duet.

Lapp signed first, followed by Sallie, then Eli.

Gloria led the way down a hallway and into a waiting room.

There, she pointed to three folding chairs behind a long veneered walnut table facing an interior door. "He won't eat or drink and he won't talk to me or answer any of my questions. I'll be right back."

Lapp pulled Gloria off to the side. "You have a second?"

"Sure."

"I wondered what you thought of the evidence?"

"Tell you the truth, I just got the case and have barely cracked the file," Gloria responded. "From what I can see, owning the shotgun is the most damaging. Let's put it this way. We've got work to do."

"I know what you mean," Lapp agreed.

The public defender went through the interior door and Lapp sat next to Sallie.

Glances were exchanged, but no words were spoken. Sallie's face sagged with exhaustion and sadness. Eli Stoltzfus' eyes were closed and his lips moved slightly in prayer.

Gloria Ebersole reappeared. Amos Stoltzfus, in prison blues, followed a few steps behind. His head drooped to his chest and his hair and beard were scraggly and dirty. Gloria stood at the end of the table and pointed for Amos to take the single chair across from his visitors. He sat down, eyes glued to the table.

"Amos, look who's here to see you," Gloria said in a cheery tone normally used on a child.

Lapp looked to Eli to speak, which he did in Pennsylvania Dutch. "Amos, des is net gut. Du muss esse."

Amos refused to look up.

Sallie spoke in English. "Amos, you must listen to your Daadi."

Amos raised his head, and through watery eyes stared first at Sallie, then Eli and finally at Lapp.

"We're here to help you," Lapp said while sweeping the room with his hand to include the three of them as well as Gloria Ebersole. "But we can't if you don't let us."

Amos responded by lowering his eyes to the table. "Amos," Lapp said more forcefully. "Vorstei?"

Lapp, Sallie, Eli and Gloria exchanged glances on who would speak.

"Will you at least eat and keep up your strength? Otherwise, you will get very sick and you could die. It would be suicide," Lapp said, looking to Eli to pick up the point he was making.

"Such a thing is verboten. The Bible forbids it," his father said with a stern tone.

Amos refused to respond. Sallie again tried to reach him. "Your Daadi is right, Amos. This is not the way. The police are wrong. Time will prove it so."

Amos lifted his head and aimed his eyes at Lapp. "And what about you? You're the police. Do you think I killed my brother?"

Lapp folded his hands on the table and leaned in. "No, I don't, Amos. I know you. I don't think you could kill anyone. We must prove to them that you didn't do it. That's why you must help Miss Ebersole here so she can put up a strong argument for you."

Amos lowered his head and mumbled, "if they want to punish someone for Jacob's death, then it should be me."

"Ach, don't talk so dumb," Eli admonished.

"No, wait." Lapp raised his hand. "Why do you say that, Amos?"

"I coulda been a better brother. I shoulda tried harder to keep him straight." He continued, glaring at Lapp. "You took the easy way out. My brother couldn't do that."

Eli straightened up, offended by Amos' words that suggested Jacob would even consider leaving the church. His eyes asked Sallie for confirmation. She turned away.

Lapp jumped in. "That's right, Amos. I left. But that's what you're doing, isn't it? Taking the easy way out? If you die because you won't eat, or if you don't help Miss Ebersole defend you then who will suffer for it? Your Mam. Your Daadi. And Sallie. All your relations. All of the Amish even. They're the ones that will suffer."

"Listen to him, Amos," Sallie urged.

Amos lowered his eyes and retreated into silence. 'I'm ready to go back inside."

"These are his pills," Eli said, holding out a plastic cylinder.

Gloria Ebersole took it and read the label. "I'll have them checked in."

"Don't give up on us, Amos, and we won't give up on you," Lapp urged. "Vorstei?"

Gloria Ebersole held the door open for Amos to pass through where he was met by a uniformed jailer.

Lapp, Sallie and Eli rose from their seats. "We will make him listen," Eli vowed. "If not today, then tomorrow. As long as it takes."

"I think your coming here helped," Gloria said. "I'll see if I can get him some light food. Something that won't upset his stomach." All three offered their thanks before leaving the interview room.

In the reception area, Lapp resisted a strong urge to place his arm around Sallie's shoulder to comfort her. Then, to his surprise, Sallie touched his arm and raised her eyes to meet his. "Thank you for what you are doing for us."

"What will happen now?" Eli asked.

"We keep working," Lapp said, glancing at this watch. Ten-fifteen. An hour and forty-five minutes before he must report back on duty. "Can you get a ride home? It would save me time."

Eli asked, "can we get, what do they call it, a taxi cab?"

"You can but it will be expensive."

"Then we will pay."

They said their goodbyes. Lapp asked the desk guard for a phone and was pointed to one behind the desk. First, he ordered a taxi cab. Then he placed a call to Donna Troutman. She answered and, after some hesitation, agreed to see him.

Fortunately for Lapp, her Rohrerstown address was less than ten minutes away from the county jail. The large yellow house was divided into four apartments, with two up and two down. Donna Troutman lived in one of the downstairs units.

The smell of baking reached his nostrils even before she opened the door.

He couldn't tell from her tone of voice on the telephone if her agreement to meet him was voluntary or made under duress. Her smiling invitation for him to step inside eased his concern.

"You really are a Trooper after all," she said.

She looked less of a floozy in her blue jeans and a man's light blue denim shirt with the sleeves rolled up. Her blonde hair was tied and knotted in the back. Her face showed only modest makeup. Pink lipstick, but not the heavy eye shadow she wore at the tavern.

"You didn't believe me?"

She shrugged, "I guess I did. I didn't mean to be difficult but I was pretty upset about Jacob. The boss said you were okay. I guess he answered your questions."

"He helped some."

"I'll try to be a little more helpful, too. Want to sit down?"

Lapp pulled the cap from his head. "Sure." A quick look around the small living room revealed a small seventeen inch TV with a Nintendo joystick on the floor in front of it. A computer sat on a desk beneath a window. Team photos of boy's soccer and baseball teams sat on side tables by the brown chintz-covered couch. The bell on the oven timer caught their attention.

"You know what, if you don't mind, could we talk in the kitchen?"

"No problem," Lapp responded, following her through the door.

Donna slipped on an oven mitt, pulled out a tray of cookies, placed them on the the counter to cool and shoved a second tray into the oven.

"It's my day to bring refreshments for my boy's soccer game. We might as well sit here at the kitchen table." Lapp sat on a red corduroy chair at a rectangular table with a formica top. "Can I get you anything? Coffee, tea, a soft drink? How about a cookie when they cool?"

"No thanks. I don't have a lot of time."

"They're chocolate chip." Donna teased as she sat across the table from Lapp. "How are Jacob's wife and children doing?"

"They're doing okay."

"What's his wife like?"

Lapp was surprised at the question and was not sure how to answer it. "She's nice. Pretty. A good mother to the kids."

Donna's hands wrestled, trying to calm her emotions. "How many did he have?"

"Three. Two boys and a girl."

"Amish usually have more, don't they? How old?"

"Not always. Boys ten and eight, girl six."

Her uneasiness remained evident as she picked at the chipped edges of her red fingernail polish. "I'm so sorry about what happened to him. What will they do without him?"

"They'll be fine, eventually. The Amish look after their own. They have a strong support system."

"We could use some support around here sometimes."

"There's no Mr. Troutman?"

"There is, someplace." The crow's feet around her eyes did not detract from an innate beauty that had seen some hard times.

"They never see him?"

"Not Ryan's daddy. He's ten. Jimmy's twelve. I had Jimmy out of wedlock. His daddy provides a little support. If he didn't, I couldn't make it. Working in a bar doesn't pay enough to raise two kids."

Lapp decided to move on. "Tell me about that night? What did Jacob have to drink?"

"His usual. Seven and Seven and a cherry with a stem. When his drink was finished, he raised his face toward the ceiling, dropped the cherry into his mouth, bit it off the stem and then grinned at me until I noticed. It was his signal that he was ready for another."

"How many did he usually have?"

"Two. Once in awhile, three. When he was ready to go, he would stand up, square away his hat and leave. Never waved or said goodbye. He'd just leave until the next time."

"Did he tell you that he had $50,000 with him that night?"

"No, I saw it in the newspaper."

"He never told you?"

"No. Why should he?"

"You said he was feeling pretty good."

"Yeah, he was feeling his oats. He was a damn nice man. He had a really nice smile. Take away that beard and fix up his teeth a little, and even with those wire rim glasses, he'd be handsome. I know some of the others weren't thrilled having him around, didn't like him coming around. But he never bothered nobody."

"You think he came to see you?"

Donna smiled. "I wouldn't go that far. I think he came to kick back and get a taste of our way of life."

"Did he tell you why he was feeling so good?"

"He said he was celebrating. He was buying into a horse farm."

"Did he say where?"

"No, he said it almost in passing. I didn't ask."

"And he never mentioned that he had a bag of money with him?"

Donna shifted her buttocks in the chair. The questions were getting uncomfortable. "No. Why would he? But now that I think about it, he had a blue gym bag."

"So now you believe he had the money?" Lapp asked.

"Like I say, he had a bag. I didn't know what was inside of it. It never crossed my mind he could by carrying money. Jesus," she added bewildered, and repeated the words emphatically, "Fifty thousand cash."

"What time did Jacob leave that night?" Lapp asked.

Donna thought about it. "Around nine, nine-thirty, maybe a little later than usual."

"After he left, did you tell anyone what he told you?"

"No, why would I?" She shot back, offended by his tone.

"Not John Hoffman?"

"No."

"What about Roy Brubaker? Did you tell him?"

"Not that I can remember. Why?"

"Is Roy the jealous type?"

"Why are you asking me about Roy?"

"I've interviewed several people in the tavern that night and that seems to be a consensus opinion."

"Roy had no reason to be jealous."

"That doesn't mean he wasn't, does it? Think about it. It's important. Did you tell Roy what Jacob told you?"

Donna hesitated, working to keep her story straight. "Yeah, I guess maybe the part about buying a horse farm came out. But nothing about the money. I didn't know nothing about the money."

"I've been told that when Jacob left, Roy left soon after."

Donna thought it over, then said, "not right after. He said he forgot to turn off his diagnostic machine. It wasn't the first time, either."

"How long was he gone?"

"A half-hour or so. Are you saying you suspect Roy?"

"I'm just asking questions. Trying to put together a time line of who came and left and what time. When Roy came back, how did he act?"

Donna shrugged. "Same as always."

"No different than when he left?"

"Not that I noticed."

"Was he happy, sad, nervous?" Lapp fired the question.

Donna straightened up. "I didn't notice. I was busy."

"Roy came back to take you home?"

"No. He left before we closed up."

"Did you go to his trailer that night?"

"That's none of your business. But the answer is no."

"Roy just sold his garage. You knew that?"

"Yeah, I knew that. He hated it."

"What's he going to do now?"

"I don't know. He says he's looking at some things."

"Do they include you?" Lapp asked.

Donna shrugged. "I don't know and I don't much care," she said, but her tone betrayed her.

"Have you talked about it?"

"Not really. What are you picking on Roy for? I thought they already arrested Jacob's brother. They must have enough evidence against him," Donna said.

"Someone wanted that $50,000 bad enough to kill for it. Someone familiar with Jacob's movements and someone who knew Amos. I'll keep looking until I find him."

The timer on the oven interrupted the frosty silence that had fallen between them. Donna rose from the kitchen chair and asked, "you want some cookies to keep up your strength?"

Chapter 23

Lapp reported back to the barracks, a half-hour before he was due back on patrol. He pulled a pink phone message slip from his pigeonhole box next to the communications center.

It was from Lisa Robinson and contained her cell phone number and the word, "important". He acknowledged a wave from Latisha Jones, the young African-American woman dispatcher who always had a toothy smile waiting for him. She pulled the headset from her braided cornrows and walked toward him with a message in her outstretched hand. When he reached out to take it, she playfully pulled it back.

"Warren Moyer wants to see you. Just got off the phone," she announced.

"What about?"

"He didn't sound too happy," she teased.

"Thanks a lot." Lapp mocked. His smile and a flirty, "thanks," sent her wiggling back to the ringing switchboard.

In the detective's room, Moyer was busily tapping away on his computer keyboard. When he turned to acknowledge him, Lapp's initial urge to snap to attention was eased by Moyer's greeting.

"Lapp. Good morning. I guess it's still morning. Want some coffee?"

"Actually, I would," Lapp responded.

"You know where it is. Help yourself."

At the coffee counter, with his back to Moyer, Lapp braced himself for a chewing out. He burned his lips on the first sip of the steaming-hot black coffee and sat down facing Moyer's desk.

"I hear you've been doing some undercover work," Moyer said, poker-faced.

Lapp responded cautiously. "I'm not sure what you mean."

"My spies tell me you've been over at the jail, in uniform, talking to my suspect. Since you're off the case, you think that's wise?"

"Amos is on a hunger strike. I took the widow and his father there to convince him to eat."

"Yeah, I heard about that." Then, "if you don't mind my asking, what else have you been up to?"

Lapp hesitated a moment, then decided to come clean. "I was invited to Jacob's farm to meet with the Amish men after his funeral. They feel Amos is innocent and asked me to help them prove it. Of course I told them anything I did would be done off-duty and unofficial."

With eyebrows raised, Moyer asked, "you get anything out of them?"

"I found out what Jacob was doing the night of the murder." "And?"

"He was at Hoffman's Tavern over on 340 from about 8:00 to 9:30."

Moyer leaned in, confirming his interest. "I assume you followed it up."

"I talked to the owner, barmaid and most of the patrons that were there that night."

"Any suspects among them?"

"One maybe. Trouble is, he has an alibi. He was in the tavern at the time Jacob was killed."

"Anything else?"

"Jacob told the barmaid he was buying a horse ranch. He also was carrying the blue gym bag, the one Patel said carried the money."

"So you think we should follow up this horse ranch thing?"

Lapp shrugged. "That's not up to me."

Moyer rose, stretched to his full height and straightened his rep tie around his blue oxford shirt collar. "I know the case against the brother is no slam dunk," he confessed. "We acted quickly based on the evidence we had. We could follow up on what you told me, but we all got other cases. I'm close to making an arrest in the Kreider arson case. So when I heard you were still working on the case … unofficially … and, since you've gotten in with the victim's family it makes sense to see what else you can find out. That work for you?"

Lapp subdued his enthusiasm. "It works fine. Thanks for your confidence."

Moyer waved him off. "Don't get carried away. Just remember one thing. If you find that Amos is hiding something or something turns up that confirms his guilt, it's your duty to report it. Don't make me or the department look bad."

"Of course not, sir."

"Then get out of here. I've already cleared it with the boss, your captain and your sergeant."

Lapp dumped his coffee into the sink, found an unoccupied desk and phone, fished out his notes and called Lisa Robinson back on her cell phone number.

He reached her immediately. She suggested they meet at the Dutch Treat Diner on Route 30 in half-an-hour. He used the time to write up a report, official this time, of his visit to the jail and his session with Donna Trautman.

A twenty-foot tall wood carved Amish man in a bright blue shirt with white suspenders that was an insult to any self-respecting member of the religion stood next to the entrance of the Dutch Treat Diner. The owners were "English" from New Jersey. Even the most commercially oriented Mennonite would not do that to a fellow Anabaptist.

The vehicles in the small parking lot in front of the 50's style, stainless-steel diner had equal numbers of Pennsylvania and out-of-state license plates. The Paul Bunyan-sized totem-pole was doing its job.

There was nothing Pennsylvania Dutch about the interior, either. Unchanged since it opened in the mid 1950's, the tables and counter tops were covered with red formica. Small, chrome juke boxes with flip-through selections and red push buttons were located by each booth and spaced every four feet on the counter. A mirrored back wall reflected customers, waitresses, coffee urns and pie cases alike.

The booths were full. He found Lisa Robinson, in a white blouse, blue blazer and a short blue skirt that was riding up to mid-thigh, waiting at the counter.

"Thanks for coming," she said with that flashing smile that he found ever more appealing, not to mention intriguing. "I think I've got something that's worth following up."

"You mean you didn't invite me here for lunch?" Lapp joked.

"You want to eat? Let's do it. Pull up a stool," she said, pointing to the empty seat beside her.

Lapp enjoyed the way she handed him a menu, waited about ten seconds, asked if he was ready to order, then called the bustling, plaid-aproned waitress.

"Margie, I know you're busy, but we're ready to order." She ordered a salad plate with oil and vinegar dressing and a diet Coke. Lapp followed with the Fried Chicken platter that came with bread filling, brown gravy, corn, coleslaw and a Coke. When the waitress picked up their menus, Lisa said, "Margie, I'm going to tell Trooper Lapp here what you told me. Is that okay?"

"If it helps I'll be happy," she replied, cracking a wad of gum in her mouth.

Lisa Robinson spoke with a confidential tone. "Did you know your victim, Jacob, was planning to buy into a horse ranch over in Hanover?"

"I know he had talked about it. I was about to get on it."

Disappointment washed across her face. Now sorry that he had burst her surprise bubble, he decided a compliment would help. "You continue to surprise me with the things you find out."

It worked. "Well here's what I know and you don't," she teased, leaning into his right ear to cut through the noisy din. "Margie was working the night shift when Jacob was killed. Two men sat in that booth over there until eleven o'clock that night waiting for him. He never showed up." Then she added, "for obvious reasons."

Their conversation stopped briefly while Margie set their Cokes in front of them.

"How does Margie know that?"

"Because they asked if she knew where they could find a Jacob Stoltzfus who lived on Route 30, and she was sorry, but she couldn't help them. The older guy wearing a yellow checked sport coat, was particularly irritated. When they left at eleven he gave Margie his card." She reached into her blazer jacket pocket and handed Lapp a business card. He read, "Chestnut Hill Farms—Racing Stock", along with an address in Hanover and a phone number.

Lapp smiled broadly, "this certainly saves me from going through the process of elimination."

"I could have gone over and talked to them myself, researching my story. But I decided to call you. What now?"

"I'll check it out."

Lisa Robinson squeezed his forearm and asked with a tone that was mockingly seductive. "Are we a team?"

Lapp laughed. "Up to a point, I suppose."

"All I'm asking for is the story. First." She added, hopefully, "agreed?"

"It's not up to me. But I'll do what I can."

"You're sure now?" She teased.

"Like I said …" It was time to change the subject. "Tell me something?"

"What's that?"

Their eyes met and held until Lapp broke away. "How did you get to where you are. Did you grow up around here?" he asked.

"I'm from Richmond, Virginia. My father was a high school principal and my mother was a teacher. Education was priority one in my family."

Lapp mused, "just the opposite of me. I had to quit school after the eighth grade."

"That's too bad."

"You probably know the story. The Amish think advanced education is worldly. It opens the minds to too many alternatives."

"That's why you left?"

"That's the main reason, yes. Where did you go to college?"

Lisa wiped a few strands of long black hair that had strayed across her right cheek. "American University in Washington, D.C. They have a good journalism program. From there I worked at a small paper in Leesburg, Virginia, and I've been here in Lancaster for the past three years."

Lapp did some simple arithmetic and concluded her age to be late-twenties. "You like it here?"

"I do," she answered with conviction. "People are very nice and I'm learning a lot. Now it's your turn. How does an Amish farm boy become a Pennsylvania State Trooper?"

"Short answer. Graduated from Mennonite High School at twenty-two … Then went to Millersville for two years, got married and needed a job."

"Any children?"

"Not yet. My wife's a nurse at Lancaster General. Very serious about her career." He could have continued by saying he was in the process of a divorce, but asked instead," you're not married?"

"Not yet. Someday maybe. I was pinned to a fraternity boy at American. He was a big time basketball player. I came to my senses. But yeah," she said, taking a deep breath, "I want it all. Right now, career first, family later."

They sat quietly for a few moments amid the hub-bub of the busy restaurant before Lapp asked, "how come you're not a TV reporter? You're better looking, more personable, and smarter that most of what I see now."

"I've had offers. Nothing great. Mostly from smaller markets like Norfolk, Virginia. And Wilkes-Barre called the other day. Anyway I probably will do TV some day. But first I want to be a journalist. A good one. Someone who writes and reports. Not just another talking head. And," she added, "thanks for the compliment."

The heat building between them was interrupted when Margie the waitress arrived with plates balanced in each hand.

The differences in their meals brought mutual smiles and chuckles.

"Now that's a man's meal," Lisa said surveying his filled-to-the-rim plate.

"And that's what I used to feed my rabbits. I'm willing to share."

"This will do me just right," Lisa Robinson said, raising her fork. "Now I want details. How does an Amish farm boy get to be a Pennsylvania State Trooper?"

When the check came, Lapp offered to pay, but Lisa insisted they "go dutch" at the Dutch Treat.

Lapp walked her to her car. They shook hands before she climbed into her Ford Taurus and drove away.

Feeling lingering amounts of admiration and sexual attraction for her, Lapp went back inside the diner, found a pay phone by the rest rooms and punched in the number for Chestnut Hill Farms. He identified himself as a State Trooper and talked to a man named Bill Sterner who confirmed that he knew Jacob Stoltzfus and, yes, he would meet with Lapp at his farm.

Lapp radioed dispatch with his location and said he was going to Hanover to do a follow-up investigation. Latisha gave him a 10-4.

Lapp worked his patrol car into the heavily traveled Route 30, the main road between Lancaster and York and beyond that, Gettysburg. The three, sometimes four-lane highway had been under constant reconstruction for as long as he could remember. Long distance eighteen wheel trailer trucks, mixed with local and tourist vehicular traffic clogged the construction zones. Troop J patrolled these zones. Stop and start traffic patterns contributed to excess speeds in open sections that quickly came to a screeching halt. An accident or two-a-day in this stretch was not uncommon. So far, Lapp had cheerfully avoided this tour of duty.

Growing up in Lancaster County and now living in Lancaster City, Lapp was aware that the city's population of 56,000 had remained fairly stable, while the County, on the other hand, was growing by leaps and bounds, with a steadily rising population of 500,000 living in 60 small municipalities.

Continuing west along Route 30, Lapp shook his head and sighed with resignation over the housing developments, large manufacturing plants and warehouses, that, like black clouds, crept across a beautiful countryside of wide open fields and large farms. Crop land was being lost on a daily basis to the point where only 5% of jobs were still in agriculture.

Sometimes tourists would flag him down to ask directions, with questions on where to find the Amish. He took pride in being able to tell them that, even with the slow drift away from farming, Lancaster County, with its 4500 farms, ranked first in the U.S. for total non-irrigated agriculture receipts. It also ranked first in total farms preserved due to the 18,000-strong Amish population.

Lapp swung onto the Route 30 bypass at York, and continued west to Abbotstown, turning south on Route 194, a two-lane road into Hanover.

Hanover, the home of Dan Patch and other legendary trotters, is fourteen miles southwest of York, 15 miles east of Gettysburg and only a few miles from the Maryland border.

After working his way through the old part of town, the two lane road became country-scenic again. Two miles down the road he found a modest white sign with black letters that announced, Chestnut Hill Farms. The short lane to the house and barn was bordered on both sides by white board fences. An oval racing track which he guessed was a half-mile around, was off to the left. To the right a dozen horses grazed in the green pasture.

He passed a carousel for cooling down horses and stopped next to a stack of trotter hacks pushed together like grocery carts.

A short, thin man in his forties wearing a Levi jacket appeared from the barn carrying a long pitchfork. When he saw Lapp he jabbed the fork into the ground, wiped his hands on his pants and came over to greet him.

"I'm Bill Sterner. The one you talked to on the phone. Let me get my partner. He's up in the office." Sterner stepped away and yelled loudly. "Woody! Hey, Woody."

A jowly man with a totally bald head wearing khaki pants and a dark blue sweater with a Polo logo on it lumbered toward them.

"I'm Bill Harwood," he said, offering his hand. "Everybody calls me Woody," he said with an Okie twang. "Billy tells me you want to ask us about that Amish man that was killed."

"That's right. I understand he was interested in buying into your farm."

"More than interested, I'd say. We had us an agreement."

"On paper?" Lapp asked.

"Better than that. An Amish man's word is his honor."

Lapp had never heard it expressed that way before, but it was surely true.

"That Amish man, he sure loved horses," Woody continued. "He'd come by here and watch Billy train our horses and sometimes he'd pitch in. He followed Billy around like some little kid."

"Asked a lot of questions," Billy chirped in.

"He bought one of our best horses for his buggy," Woody boasted.

"How did he pay for the horse?" Lapp asked.

"How did he pay? In hard cash. Right Billy?"

"Twenty-two one hundred dollar bills. You don't forget something like that."

"Where did you meet Jacob?" Lapp asked.

"He showed up for one of our sales. We get Amish men all the time, especially the younger ones. They like fast horses for their buggies. I hear they like to race each other." Woody did the talking and Billy did the nodding in agreement.

"How often did Jacob come over here?"

"Maybe five or six times over the last six months."

"Did he come alone?"

"Mostly. Two, maybe three times he brought a friend. They talked Dutch, but you could tell they were talking about being partners."

"What did the other Amish man look like?"

"Short, stocky, beard, you know."

Lapp thought, Stubby again. At Hoffman's, now here at the horse farm, where else?

Woody continued, "then one day he asked if he could buy us out, and we said hold on. Takes a lot of money to buy us out. This is a prime place we got here. When we told him how much, he wanted to buy in. Yep. He wanted a piece of all this," Woody said, waving his arm around the expanse of the property.

"And that night, the night he was killed, you were to close the deal?"

"Like I said, more than close. We had ourselves a firm deal. Papers drawn up and everything. Last Thursday night at the Dutch Treat diner. That's where he said he'd meet us."

"What time?"

"9:30," Woody answered.

"Why so late?"

"We had a couple horses running in the third and fourth at Penn National. We thought we had a winner."

"And we shoulda, too," Billy added.

"I blame the third race on the driver. He got himself boxed in and that was it, folks. It was all over. When Billy here was driving that never woulda happened. That's the last time that guy is ever hacking for us."

"What time did you get to the Dutch Treat?"

"What time was it, Billy? Nine? Nine-fifteen? We filled ourselves up with coffee while we waited."

"And when he didn't show up? What did you think?"

"We didn't know right what to think. At first it mighta been the weather, which was pretty shitty, but when he didn't show up after two hours we didn't know what the hell to think." Woody said, shaking his head. "I asked the wait-ress if she knew Jacob and where he lived. She said there were probably a half-dozen Jacob Stoltzfuses in the area. We described what he looked like. She said they all look like that. I said his address was Leacock Road. That didn't help neither. Then the next day we heard about him on the TV. And that was that."

"What was your deal? What was Jacob getting for his $50,000?"

"The farm is worth 1.2 million. We have $200,000 in equity—and a million dollar mortgage. He was getting 25% of our equity."

"And what were you getting?" Lapp asked. "Did you need a partner?"

"You can imagine that daily operating expenses here can be pretty high. That $50,000 would have got us through the winter to the Spring Sale. Then we would have been ahead of the game."

"You said you had a partnership agreement all drawn up."

"That's right," Woody said, with Billy nodding in agreement.

"Can I see it?"

"Yeah, I guess so. It's in the office."

"How did you expect to be paid?"

"What do you mean?"

"The method of payment."

"Cashier's check, probably."

"Not cash? You didn't ask for cash?"

"We don't take credit cards," Billy chuckled.

Woody ignored the stupid comment. "No way. We saw on the TV that he was carrying cash. I take it they never found the money?"

"Not yet."

"Well, I hope they do. If the money is recovered, you think the widow might honor the bill of sale? She was all excited about it too, you know."

John Lapp was jolted by Woody's remark. "Why do you say that? How do you know that?"

"She stood right there and said so."

"Wait a minute. Let me get this straight. You're saying Jacob brought his wife here to see this place?"

"Sure as shootin'. They was all giggly and happy. Brought their baby with them. Cute little girl. Her big head was all happy and smiley. She had short arms and legs. I think she might be a dwarf."

Lapp felt like he had been blindsided with a two by four.

"Think she might be interested?" Woody persisted.

"What did she look like, his wife?"

"What would you say, Billy? Plain looking. A little over five foot tall, maybe. Big busted, big hipped, slim waist. Hard to tell with all those clothing they wear. You could tell that Jacob was crazy about her."

"Did he ever say her name?"

"Not that I can remember. What about you, Billy?"

Billy narrowed his eyes as he thought, and then spit out, "Annie. I think one time he called her Annie."

"You know, I think you're right," Woody confirmed. "I think he did call her that."

"When were they here?"

"Together? It was just that one time. Two, three weeks ago, maybe, as best I can recollect … You don't think she'd be interested? Kinda in his memory?"

Lapp was firm. "Take my advice. Don't pursue it. You hear what I'm saying?"

"Yeah, I guess we do," Woody said reluctantly, while Billy nodded. "Maybe we can find that other guy. The short one. I know he was interested, too. Don't know where we'd find him, though," he added, talking mostly to himself.

Lapp knew exactly where Stubby Beiler was, but he wasn't about to tell them. He concluded the interview by thanking them for their cooperation.

Woody and Billy nodded their disappointment over the lost deal. Lapp thanked God that Jacob had failed to hook up with these clowns. He would have lost his religion and his money as well.

"One more question," Lapp interjected. "How did Jake get here. He didn't come all this way in a horse and buggy."

"You got that right," Woody replied. "He always came in a white van. A Dodge, I believe."

"What about the driver? Did you ever meet him" Lapp asked, hoping he could find him and question him.

"Never did. Did you, Billy?"

"No. Jake would get dropped off and then the guy would leave for an hour or so, then come back to pick him up."

"This same driver brought his wife, too?"

"Same guy every time," Woody confirmed.

"No lettering on the van? Anything to help me find it?"

"Nope, plain white."

"Can you give me any idea what the driver looked like?"

"We just saw him at a distance, didn't we, Billy. He wore a baseball cap. From the way he sat, he looked to be medium height. Didn't wear glasses like

Jake did. No beard. Wasn't Amish. That's for sure. We're not much help are we?"

Lapp knew that the Amish generally used Mennonite drivers for motorized, long-distance transportation. Mennonites usually drove black vehicles. Some still painted their chrome trim and bumpers black. Searching for a white Dodge van with no other particulars would require time and detective work. But first there was a more important question that needed answering.

Who the hell is Annie?

Chapter 24

John Lapp, his mind bursting with questions about Jacob, Stubby and the mysterious Annie, steered the patrol unit across the Susquehanna River bridge at Columbia before getting stuck in a construction zone five miles west of Lancaster.

Locally, there must be a couple of hundred Amish women with the name of Annie. Where to start? Stubby would know, but would he tell? Based on his warning at Sallie's barn, it was highly unlikely. He retrieved a small spiral notebook from his shirt pocket and scanned the names of Jacob's relatives. Not one Annie was listed. What now?

Sallie's brother, Danny Yoder had come forth with information about Hoffman's Bar at the barn meeting after the funeral. He felt comfortable trying Danny again.

Thirty minutes later, Lapp escaped Route 30 by swinging on to Route 340. At Bird-In-Hand, he turned north on Orchard Road. A road sign, with the outline of a black cow crossing the road on a yellow background, preceded the Yoder farm. What had once been a small lane between the barn and sheds on one side and the house on the other, had, over the years, been widened to accommodate a two lane paved road that went right down the middle of the property.

The orange glow of a setting sun lit the way as Lapp edged the patrol car's right tire into a puddle of water next to Danny Yoder's barn. Pulling his jacket collar up to defend against the cold air, he followed the roar of a gasoline engine to the edge of the corn field. Danny Yoder lowered the lever on a strange-looking horizontal contraption with two tires in the front and an iron balance arm in the center. The engine in the rear propelled a piston into a hydraulic cylinder with a steel splitting wedge on the end. Danny set a log into the trough, pulled the lever and the 6-inch diameter, 18 inch log was cut like butter. Neat piles of what looked like dried oak were piled on either side of the log splitter.

Who says the Amish don't use labor-saving devices.

Lapp yelled his arrival through the roaring din, "Danny?"

Yoder was startled by the appearance of the man in a trooper uniform. "Johnny?"

"Danny, I need to ask you a few questions," Lapp yelled. "Can you turn that thing off for a minute?"

Lapp followed Sallie's brother as he backed ten feet away and pulled a plastic-gel earplug from his right ear. "I can't turn it off because it's hard to start up again. I don't know why that is, but it always gives me trouble."

"I didn't want to bother Sallie with this. She's seen enough of me these last few days."

Danny nodded his understanding.

"First, do you know who Jake used as a taxi service when he needed to go some distance. Someone he might have used regularly?"

Danny Yoder fiddled with the end of his beard as he reviewed the question. "I think maybe he used Ezra Martin. He's there on 340 in Smoketown. He has a sign out in front. Ezra Martin Transportation.

"Does he have a white Dodge van?"

"Not that I know of. He uses a black Ford van and a black panel truck. I never seen no white van."

"You think Jake used him, though?"

"Once in awhile, maybe. I've used him once or twice myself. He's cheap. And he's reliable. Why were you wondering that?"

Even idling, the sound level of the gas engine on the log splitter was annoying the hell out of him. Lapp kept his voice at a high level. "I found out Jake made several trips to a horse farm in Hanover. They said he came in a white van. I wonder who drove him?"

"It wonders me, too," Danny mused.

That was the warm up question, Lapp thought. Time to cut to the chase. "I was wondering something else. Is there a register of names of people who came to Jake's funeral?"

Yoder shook his head. "No, we don't do nothing like that. Didn't you know that no more?"

"In my time, no, but I thought things might have changed. Then let me ask you this, did anyone named Annie come to the funeral?"

"Annie? I suppose so. There must have been some Annies."

"Someone about my age?"

Danny pondered the question, then answered, "Not that I can think of."

"How about someone named Annie who was invited but didn't come?"

"The only ones who didn't come that I remember were Moses …" A light bulb went on as he said the name, "and Annie King. They sent word that Annie was sick. You musta knowed her. Annie Fisher. She's about your age."

Lapp remembered her all right. Annie Fisher. The answer to every Amish male fantasy come to life in secret sessions in the hayloft during teen parties known as "singings". And Moses King, timid and quiet, was the least likely one to end up with her.

"Where do they live?"

"Off of Eastbrook Road. The 896. It's the first farm after Segrist Road."

Lapp knew where it was.

"Why are you asking about Annie King?" Yoder asked.

"Her name came up. Nothing to worry about."

"I gotta get back to my logs now. Besides wasting gas, it's getting dark."

"I'll let you get back to work. Thanks, Danny."

Lapp had a slight headache as he got back into the patrol car. He blamed the noise, but he was also annoyed at the thought of Jacob cheating on Sallie. Seventeen years ago at a singing Jacob told him he was sneaking away to the barn for a smoke. Lapp was happy to see him go because he could have Sallie all to himself for awhile.

A half hour later when Jacob returned, he pulled Lapp aside and, his face red with excitement, said he had been with Annie Fisher in the hayloft and he touched her everywhere. And she touched him, too, through his pants.

That was it. Somehow, Annie and Jacob had rekindled their desires and she was the one Jacob presented as his wife to Billy and Woody over in Hanover.

Twenty minutes later, the mailbox at the end of the lane helped Lapp find the King farm. The real surprise was that the farm was only a few hundred yards from Hoffman's Tavern. How convenient for secret trysts.

Except for the dim yellow lights coming from what was probably the kitchen of the two-story frame house, it was pitch dark. As Lapp pulled up, a barking black border collie mix patrolled through the headlights of the patrol car.

The dog's wagging tail convinced him that it was safe to get out. Using his 4-cell flashlight, he approached the kitchen door. Before he could knock, a growling voice asked, "what do you want?"

Startled, Lapp gasped and turned the flashlight into the face of a thin man wearing wire-rim spectacles with flecks of straw in his beard and on his black work coat.

Lapp turned the beam of light on himself. "Moses. It's me. Johnny Lapp. Do you remember me?"

"Ya. What do you want?"

"I came to talk to Annie."

Moses eyed the uniform and badge. "As a policeman? What do you want Annie for?"

"I have a few questions to ask her."

"She can't talk," Moses said sharply.

"Why not?"

"She sick. She has bad nerves."

"I'm sorry to hear that," Lapp said. "What brought it on?"

"You know already, or else you wouldn't be here."

"I need to talk to her. I won't take long."

Moses King pulled the glasses from his face and studied them in his hands. When he put them back on his face, he had come to a decision. "It's probably best you get it over with."

"Thank you, Moses."

"Wait here." "I'll send the kids upstairs and go talk to her."

Moses closed the door behind him, but Lapp could still hear the questions coming in English from at least three children who sounded to be between the ages of six and ten. Their questions were all shouted down in Pennsylvania Dutch. Then it was quiet. Lapp petted the wooly black dog who had climbed up his leg with his front paws.

The door opened. Moses ordered, "blieb" (stay) to the dog and ushered Lapp into the kitchen. It was lit by three propane-fed standing lamps. The linoleum floor, oil cloth covered table, plain pine cupboards, zinc sink and coal burning cook stove were more like Lapp remembered as a child. Not nearly as modern as those in Sallie's kitchen. The smell of cooked turnips permeated the room.

"She's in the parlor."

Moses led the way into the dark room where a small figure holding a blanketed bundle sat in a rocking chair. He reached into the box beneath the floor lamp, turned on the propane tank and struck a match. The light bulb warmed up slowly. Then it was bright enough to see Annie King's face framed by a black bonnet. Lapp stepped closer. "Annie? It's Johnny Lapp."

"What do you want?" She snapped at Lapp, then glared at Moses, who took the hint that he was not invited to stay. He left, leaving the kitchen door slightly ajar. The room, heated by a kerosene console parlor stove, was stifling hot.

Lapp doffed his round hat. "I'm investigating Jacob Stoltzfus' death," he said quietly.

Annie pulled the blanket away from the baby's face. Lapp stepped closer and recognized the infant's dwarfish features. She responded in a low voice. "What does it matter. He's dead anyhow."

"It matters that we find out who killed him. Since you were seeing him, you might know if he had any enemies."

"Jake had no enemies. Everybody liked Jake."

"How long had you been seeing Jake?"

Annie's sullen face matched the intensity with which she rocked back and forth.

"I don't need to tell you nothing."

"It's my job to find out who killed him."

"I told you. It don't matter no more."

"Won't you feel better if we punished his killer? The one who took him away from you?"

The rocking slowed and she stroked the baby's face. "We saw each other for over a year now. One time when he came to Hoffman's I was working in the field next to it and we saw each other." The baby gurgled and stirred. Annie shifted her from one fleshy breast to the other. "He would come to the field after supper and I would meet him. He wasn't happy with Sallie and I wasn't happy with Moses. We wanted each other."

Lapp pictured Jacob and Annie grappling through layers of clothes in the field with its cover of corn, wheat, possibly tobacco, to satisfy their lust. He pitied the result. "The baby?"

She ran her finger tenderly across the baby's cheek. "It could be Jake's I guess. We don't know for sure. We're first cousins," she said, alluding to what had been a history of birth defects because of intermarriage. "There's a better chance that she might be different."

"You were planning to buy the horse farm and live together?"

Annie interpreted Lapp's tone and question to be so outrageous that it needed to be defended. "Jake wanted me and I wanted him. I almost had him back. Now ich hab nix."

"What did you have before, Annie?"

"We had each other."

"But you're both married to others. There's no divorce in the church. What were you going to do?"

"We hadn't figured it all out yet. He was ready to leave Sallie. He said so."

"Annie, you must have known everyone would be against you."

She shrugged. "It didn't matter. Moses didn't do nothing about it."

"Moses knew about the two of you?" Lapp asked, surprised.

"Yeah, he found out."

"When was that? How long ago?"

"A few months ago now, I guess. When he saw the baby."

"Do you think Moses could have been mad enough to kill him?"

Moses' voice proceeded his entrance back into the room. "I could have, but I didn't. Are you finished here?"

Moses King led the way back to Lapp's truck. "How long you been a policeman?"

"It's been going on nine years now."

"And it's your job to find who killed people?"

"No. Not usually. I'm a traffic officer most of the time. I'm sorry about having to come out here and bring all this up."

"It's better you than someone else. I made my bed with Annie. I should've known better. When Jake decided to marry Sallie ... that was after you left, ain't?"

"It was."

"Once Jake was taken, I gave in to Annie in the hayloft one night and I've been paying for it ever since. She told me we had to get married. I was ready and I never expected to have such a woman like Annie for a wife."

"Do you think she'll try to tell Sallie?"

"Ich glaub net. It was all such foolishness. Even if they'd gone to live over in Hanover, Jake would have soon found out what she was really like. They would have come back, but not before wrecking two families and shaming the church."

"I have to ask, Moses. Where were you the night Jake was killed?"

"I was home, in the kitchen, reading the bible. Just like I do every night. The children can testify to that."

Lapp knew that wouldn't be necessary.

Chapter 25

The next morning, Lapp sat on his back porch steps. The business with Jacob and Annie haunted him. When he left the Amish he had cleared the way for Jacob to court and win Sallie. In all likelihood, Annie, having lost Jacob, and, with some sort of distorted revenge, trapped Moses. Then Annie got him back. Or thought she did.

Would Jacob really have left Sallie?

The cold from the cement step seeped through the blanket and his denim pants. He rose and grabbed the latch on the storm door to go inside. Instead, he hesitated. The loneliness he felt in the kitchen, in all the rooms in house, was sad and depressing. It was almost as if Betsy had died. He rationalized their breakup by searching for the reasons they had married in the first place. What did he and Betsy ever have in common? Their immaturity? He was 26, she was 22 when they married.

He had always been quick to fall in love. His second love, after Sallie, was Nancy Gingrich. They were in the 10th grade at the Lancaster Mennonite School, but because of his lost school years, he was twenty-one and she was only sixteen. Dating was carefully chaperoned, both by adults and by fellow students. Although there was touching, controlled kissing and restrained hugging among couples, there was rarely any sex. There were exceptions of course, but not John Lapp and Nancy Gingrich.

Nancy was the prettiest and brightest girl in school. She called him, "her older man".

But as was the case with Sallie, her commitment to a strict religious life was too much for Lapp to accept. In their senior year, with graduation approaching, Lapp was pressured by teachers, ministers, and particularly by Nancy, to go on a mission.

While the adventure of service in a foreign land was appealing, the religious aspects were not. Lapp procrastinated on his decision to a point where Nancy lost face in the eyes of her peers. When she announced he was not "serious" and she no longer wanted to see him, he was deeply hurt. But, before long, he concluded it was for the best. There were worlds to be explored right here in Lancaster County.

Lapp continued to work at the Happy Hen, and was promoted to counter-man and cashier. He also bought his first car, a 1979 Dodge Dart. It was a rusted wreck, but his Mennonite friends kept it running. His main objective was to continue his education. He lived sparsely in the rear of the restaurant and attended the Mennonite Church, but with little fervor. He applied for and received student loans and grants, which, combined with his earnings and good grades got him into Millersville University, a four-year school less than ten miles from the restaurant. There, as a 23-year old Freshman, he took basic classes of English literature, American history and Social Sciences. Oddly enough, as a born pacificist, he was drawn to the classes on law and order and the legal system.

It was in a Sociology class that he met Betsy Roblin, who was completing a two-year course in nursing. She was the aggressive one. She picked him. She was his first sexual experience. Her father, Joe, suggested a career with the Pennsylvania State Police.

Now, nine years later, they had one more counseling session before they stood before the judge who would dissolve their marriage.

What now? Getting fixed up by his fellow troopers? Personals ads in the newspapers? On-line dating services? Lisa Robinson? Now there was a pleasant thought. He was attracted by her beauty, her manner, her sexiness, and, yes, the fact that she was African-American also was attractive for him to contem-plate. She seemed to like him. Flirted with him. The gold band on the fourth finger of his left hand said he was married. She seemed to be available. When his ring was gone and he found enough nerve to ask her out, how would she react? Was she simply a fantasy?

Then there was Sallie. She was still beautiful and had all of the loving attributes she had fifteen years ago. But nothing had changed. She was still unattainable, out of reach. He imagined an idyllic return to a life on the farm. He missed the power of the land and the rewards it provided. He was young and strong and knew how to farm the Amish way, using hard labor in place of modern machinery. But could his love for Sallie, and her children, too, be enough to overcome the unyielding demands of the church? And, if he decided he could go back, would she have him? A divorced man. How would he even begin to find out?

Now that Warren Moyer had more or less made him a free-lance detective, he debated whether to work in plainclothes. He decided that the uniform demanded more attention and respect.

He was dressing out when the phone rang in the barracks locker room. "This is Lapp."

"This is Gloria Ebersole from the public defender's office. Good. I'm glad I found you."

"How's Amos?

"That's what I'm calling about. He's taking food and water, so that's good. But he's still not cooperating or helping me put a defense together. He said he would only talk to you."

"Will it help his case?"

"At this point, it certainly won't hurt," Gloria said with an audible sigh.

"Get him ready. I'll be over in 15 minutes."

"He'll be waiting."

When Lapp arrived at the jail he was informed that Gloria Ebersole had been called away to court, but arrangements had been made for him to see Amos.

It was less than a minute before Amos stepped into the interview room and took a seat across from Lapp. His face sagged and his shaggy hair and stringy dirty beard indicated a lack of personal hygiene.

"How are you doing, Amos?

"Okay," he shrugged. "When can I have my own stuff back? I don't like these." Amos pulled first at the dark blue cotton prison uniform shirt, then at his pants.

"We're trying to get you out of here. But your lawyer tells me you're not helping her."

Amos' chin dropped to his chest. Lapp was in no mood for stalling. It was time for answers. "Amos? Look at me," he snapped.

The bedraggled man's head snapped up.

"Listen to me. I'm sick and tired of this. You're not telling me everything you know. I'm fed up. We're done fooling around." Amos shrank back from the attack.

"Now I'm going to tell you what I think. You say you used to go to the gas station and smoke after work. I think you used to go there other times, too. You know why? I found your hiding place in the woods." Lapp leaned across the table until he was inches from Amos' face. "You were there the night Jacob was killed, weren't you?" Amos turned away. "Amos? Look at me. Don't look at my badge and uniform. This is Johnny Lapp you're talking to. From a long time ago. When we were kids"

Lapp backed away and sat down. Amos' eyes welled up and tears rolled down Amos' cheeks. He whimpered, "it's my fault that Jake was killed."

Lapp softened his tone. "Why was that Amos? What did you do?"

"I didn't do nothing about it. I didn't know what to do so I didn't do nothing," Amos cried, choking out the words. "It happened so fast. I never expected nothing like that to happen."

Lapp waited while Amos wiped the tears from his cheeks and eyes with his prison shirt sleeve.

"I was right. You were there that night."

"Ja. I used to go there a lot. Almost every night."

"After everybody had gone to bed?"

"Ja."

"What were you doing there?"

"Smoking."

"What else, Amos?" Lapp pressed, but not too hard, fearing Amos might clam up at any time. "Why did you go there?"

"To watch."

"Watch what?"

"The kids, the teenagers. They would park their machines back there behind the garage."

"You watched them?"

The cheeks on Amos' face turned red. "Sometimes you could see what they were doing. I liked to watch that. I could hear them, too."

Lapp pitied the poor, sex-deprived voyeur. "You were there the night Jake was killed?"

"I was ready to go home. When it rains, their windows get all steamed up and I can't see nothing anyway. Can't hear nothing, either."

Lapp gave Amos lots of time to piece together his thoughts before asking, "Then what?"

"I heard a horse and buggy come in and I couldn't figure out why one would be there."

"Did you come out from your hiding place?"

Amos shook his head vigorously. "I didn't want nobody to know I was there."

"Then what happened?"

"I snuck into the building. I can squeeze through the back door. It was chained shut, but I can squeeze through. That's when I seen it was Jacob."

"What was he doing?"

"He was pulling at the wheel on his buggy. Like it was broke."

"Why didn't you come out?"

"He woulda laughed at me."

"Laughed at you? Why?"

"Because he would guess why I was there. He'd make me tell. I couldn't come out."

"And then what?"

"Then it wasn't long before this truck pulled up. I ducked my head down, out of the lights." The intensity of his words poured out. "And when I looked up again this guy was pointing a shotgun at Jake and yelling at Jake to give him a bag he had in his buggy and Jake went and got the bag and dropped the bag on the ground ... and then the shotgun went off, first once ..." Amos squinched his eyes and pressed his hands over his ears. "Then another time."

"What did you do?"

"I must of made a noise because I heard him yell, who's there?"

"He knew you were there?"

"He didn't know it was me."

"What did you do then?"

"I was scared. I ran back to where my rock is. I listened until the truck drove away. After awhile I came around to the pumps and petted Blackie to quiet him down. It took awhile before I could go over to look at Jake. It was raining on him. I could see his guts ..." Amos covered his face with his hands and whimpered.

"What did you do then, Amos?" Lapp asked quietly, the words working around the lump in his throat.

Amos wiped the tears from his eyes. "I couldn't do nothing for him. I couldn't help him no how." Amos dropped his head in shame.

"Amos, look at me. Did you see the man's face? The man with the shotgun?"

"He was wearing a hankie over his face. And he had on a black raincoat. The hankie dropped from his face and that's when he shot Jake."

"Did you recognize him?"

Amos shook his head, no.

"If you saw him again, would you know him?"

"It was dark."

"Did he have a beard or a mustache?"

"I don't think so."

"How big was he? How tall?"

Amos thought about it. "Bigger than you, maybe a little. He was bigger around than you."

"What else?"

"He was wearing one of those caps, like everybody wears."

"Was there a name on the cap?"

"I don't know."

"What color was it?"

"Brown or orange, I think. I think Jake musta knowed him."

"Why's that?" Lapp asked with surprise.

"Cause he said he wouldn't tell nobody."

"Who did?"

"Jake."

"Tell nobody what?"

"I don't know. That's when he shot him."

Lapp's pulse quickened. Jake knew his killer. "What about his truck? Did you see his truck?"

"Ja, I saw it. It was old."

"Was it a big truck? A pickup?"

"It wasn't too big."

"What color was it?"

"I think it was black."

Lapp, frustrated, wanted to shout, come on Amos, give me something to go on. "Did it have an emblem, letters, on the front of the hood, like Ford or Chevy?"

"I didn't see none. It was pretty noisy."

"What was?"

"The engine. It made a lot of squeaky noises. I think the fan belt needed fixing."

How would he know that, Lapp wondered, before remembering that the Amish frequently used a system of belts powered by gas motors to run saws and power tools in their shops.

"Would you recognize it if you ever saw it again?"

"The truck? I don't know. Maybe."

Lapp concluded that Amos, even if he was called to testify, would be a weak witness. "Why didn't you tell us this when we brought you in to the police station. If you had, you might not even be here."

"It don't matter."

"We need to tell your lawyer about this. It explains a lot of things."

Amos jumped from his chair. "No! You can't do that, Johnny. You hafta promise. I only told you. Nobody else. I won't tell'em nothing."

Holding his hands chest high in surrender, Lapp said, "okay, Amos. I won't say anything. Not yet anyway."

"I won't tell nobody else what I told you. Nobody."

"Promise me something, okay?"

"I guess." Amos agreed reluctantly.

"You must eat and take your medicine. Do you have enough?"

Amos nodded. "I want to go now."

"Okay, Amos." Lapp walked to the interior door and waved for the guard. Amos lowered his head and left the room. Lapp stayed a moment, digesting what he had just been told. He now had an eyewitness to Jacob's murder, but how could he use him? Would anyone else believe what Amos had revealed? Would his lawyer? Most likely. Would the State Police? Probably not. At least not yet.

He checked his watch. 12:30. He would tell Sallie that Amos was eating again. He would not tell her that Amos had witnessed her husband's murder. And, she would never, ever, know about Jake and Annie King.

Chapter 26

Even with sunglasses protecting his eyes, John Lapp squinted and blinked into the brilliant sun and bright blue sky. It was a perfect October day.

Driving up the lane to the house, the sight of hundreds of mallard ducks pecking and gleaning the harvested corn field brought back a vision from his childhood. He was ten years old when he carried a small bag of husked corn to feed the wild ducks. Throwing the seed into the wind, he laughed at the ducks as they clamored and pecked them up. The ducks took flight when his father appeared behind him and screamed his name. He had seen and felt his father's anger many times before, but never as intense as on that day. Shelled corn was for the pigs and chickens. Feeding wild ducks could change their migratory patterns, which was going against God and nature. Lapp's fear that he had gone against God frightened him for weeks until he reasoned that God had already put the ducks in their field before he began feeding them. He wanted to tell his father this, but was afraid to challenge him. His challenges to Moses Lapp would come later.

The buffalo, or "beefalo", he wasn't sure which, grazing near the fence, like brown bookends to the black and white dairy cows, curiously followed his arrival. Lapp stopped and left the patrol car for a closer look. Placing his hands between the barbs on the fence, he listened to the grunting sounds of the humpbacked, horned creatures. The male, his long beard dangling from his chin, was curious about the creature in the blue uniform with the reflecting glasses over his eyes. The bull ambled toward the fence. His brown eyes and hanging tongue suggested a handout was in order. The female, with a stump of grass dangling from her teeth, stepped next to the male. Had Jake tamed them? He reached through the fence to touch the shaggy brown face. The male jolted back and projected his curved horns. Lapp got the message.

Pulling into his usual parking spot, the ever-present watch dog went through his barking and sniffing routine before Sallie, standing at the kitchen door, yelled at him to shut up. She stepped out into the sunshine where her cap glistened like a white halo over the back of her head.

He left his hat and glasses on the passenger seat and stepped out to meet her.

"I hope you're bringing some good news for a change." Her smile was missing but her tone was friendly.

"I am. Amos is eating again," he announced happily.

She beamed. "That is good news. Cum rei. Can you have some dinner? I'm warming up some ham. The 'friendschaft' brought so much, I won't have to do any cooking for a week."

"I can only stay a few minutes." Lapp followed her into the kitchen. He dropped his plan to ask Sallie about the van service Jacob used. He knew about the horse farm and he knew about the "wife" who had come there with him. That was enough for now.

Sallie stepped to a blue wooden cupboard giving Lapp the opportunity to appreciate her firm figure and the slim ankles visible from below her long black dress. How could Jacob even think about Annie Fisher when he had Sallie?

She set a stainless steel knife, fork and spoon, a white china dinner plate and a filled clear plastic water glass in the first position to the left of the head of the table. The one reserved normally for the youngest son. Amish family members always ate in the same places. The father at the head, the wife to his immediate right, the oldest son at the opposite end, the daughters on the mother's right and the sons to the father's left.

Sallie waved her hand at his place setting and Lapp sat down.

A warm feeling rushed through him. He felt at home, like he could belong here, as he swallowed the cold water and watched Sallie set down serving dishes and platters of fried ham, mashed potatoes and buttered white corn she had canned.

She sat on the bench across from him. "You said Amos is eating?" Sallie asked.

"I saw him just an hour ago."

"How does he look?"

"Pretty bad. He could stand a good washing up."

Sallie smiled her approval and asked, "shall we give thanks?"

Lapp lowered his eyes, then glanced at Sallie's closed eyes and solemn face. Was her silent prayer a thank you for the food on the table? Was she praying for

Jacob and her children? Was she thankful for his presence and his desire to help Amos? Lapp lowered his eyes again and waited for Sallie to whisper. "Amen".

Her expression brightened. "Let's eat."

They served themselves from the platters and ate hungrily, occasionally smiling at each other, but remaining silent. Sallie's high cheekbones had regained their rosy patina, and her face showed no sign of the recent sadness she had endured.

Within ten minutes the last of the gravy on their plates had been wiped clean with slices of soft white bread. "Do you want some more water? I have some 7-Up."

"More water is good."

She returned with a glass of water and a whole molasses pie. When the pie was served, they could talk. "Is he taking his medicine again?"

Lapp swallowed the first bite of the super sweet pie with the molasses filling and brown crust. "I forgot to ask. I guess he must be."

There was a long pause before Sallie looked at Lapp and said, "I hope I didn't make it hard for you yesterday in the barn with all the men."

"No, not at all."

"I think if they have something to say about Jacob then I should hear it, too. They probably think I'm a bad wife anyway."

"Why would they say that?" Lapp asked.

"Because he was mad all the time. They weren't here to hear about how he was wasting his life. They weren't around then."

Lapp had to ask. "Did you know Jacob went to Hoffman's Bar like they said?"

"He would go off after supper for an hour or two. Whatever he was doing seemed to relieve the pressure. He never said where he went," she said, shaking her head with regret.

"And you never wondered?"

"Of course I did. I asked him about it. But all that did was make him mad again. And when he was mad he wasn't nice to the kids or to me either."

The thought of Jacob mistreating Sallie or the kids made his stomach turn. He kept his voice on an even keel. "Did he ever hit you? Or the children?"

"Ach, no. He never did nothing like that. I was never afraid of him like some women are of their husbands. After awhile it seemed that when he came home from being out he was calmed down and was a nicer person. He never came home drunk except for that one night Amos brought him home. That night he chased poor Amos out of the house, and yelled at me, saying he was sick of the farm and everything on it. He was always saying dumb things like he wasn't good enough for me and the children. He should just go away. I told him he was wrong, but he didn't want to listen."

Lapp waited for more.

After a long pause she raised her eyes . "There's nothing else. Where is this place, Hoffman's?"

Lapp drained his water glass. "It's over on 340. Our gang used to go there during "rumspringa". They would sell us beer and whiskey out the back. How far back was Jake going out at night?"

"He first started maybe a year or two ago. Sometimes he would go for a couple of months, then not at all for a while. But here toward the last, he went lots of times. Was he there that night?"

Lapp nodded. "Yes, he was. A barmaid who served him three drinks that night said he was in a happy mood. It turns out he was meeting some men to buy a 25% interest in their horse farm over by Hanover."

Sallie did not seem surprised by Lapp's words. "Jacob bought Sandy, a three year old filly at a place over by Hanover."

"It was the same place. They said Jacob was real good with horses. He would have been a good trainer."

Lapp scraped his fork across the small plate and snagged the remaining crumbs of the lard-based crust. "You're not eating your pie."

"I guess I'm not hungry anymore."

Lapp tried to force the vision of Jacob and Annie pretending to be husband and wife out of his head. Again, he vowed silently that Sallie would never know.

"He wanted more than a strict Amish life. Now it's too late. I got what I wanted. I'm still Amish. But I lost a husband over it."

Lapp responded in a low husky voice. "You're not to blame."

Sallie asked, "more pie?"

Lapp patted his stomach. "No thanks." Lapp picked up his plate and followed Salllie to the kitchen sink.

She turned. They were face to face. Their eyes met and he felt an urge to wrap her in his arms. She stood fast, not turning away as he had expected. It seemed like an eternity before he backed away, afraid that if he touched her it would be all over. She would be insulted, he would be embarrassed, and what existed as a relationship between them would be severed. He asked, "can I help you with anything?"

"You know better than that," she laughed with relief, and he was sure she blushed, confirming that she had felt something, too. "Men don't help in the kitchen. You know that. Go sit."

Lapp sat back down, poured more water from the pitcher into his glass, took a big gulp, and waited until Sallie was again sitting across the table from him. She smiled, indicating she was comfortable with him, then spoke with some hesitation.

"We've done all this talking about me and our life here, but I've often wondered about you. You just disappeared from us. You didn't have to stay away. We would have welcomed you here."

"I don't know why I didn't," Lapp replied. "I guess that part of my life was over and it's better not to look back."

"Are you still happy that you left? Have things turned out like you thought?"

Lapp responded softly, staring self consciously at his hands folded on the table in front of him. "Most of it, yes, not all, I guess. When I left I had no idea where I was going. I wanted to be educated. I knew that. I wanted to enjoy the life I knew was out there. One thing's for sure. I never thought I'd be here as a policeman."

"And your wife? What about her?"

The debate that ran through his mind whether to tell her about his divorce was quickly resolved. "Betsy is a nurse at Lancaster Hospital. I'd like to have kids. Betsy wants to wait. Her job is important to her."

"You should have kids. You'd be a good father," Sallie said warmly. After a pause, she added, "I thought I'd have more kids. It's pretty clear that at our age when the kids stop coming, things aren't going any too good."

Lapp was taken aback by her admission and nodded his understanding.

"Well, you have an important job, now. And that's good. And you're trying to help Amos. That's good, too."

"I want to help."

"Did you become a Mennonite then?"

"For a little while, I did. Then I married a Lutheran."

"Jake wanted us to become Mennonites. That way, he'd be free to have his horse business. It's hard to stay Amish sometimes, but it's who I am. It's who you were. It's who I wished you had stayed." Sallie reflected upon her words, then surprised him with what was really preying on her mind. "This woman at the bar? This barmaid?"

"You mean Donna?"

"Yes, if that's her name. Do you think he liked her?"

Lapp knew that the term "liked" in their culture meant "loved". "No. Not that way. I think she served him because that was her job. She told me he was polite and that they talked a little. He mainly went there to hide his drinking. Not to see her."

"Do you think he could have gone with her?"

Lapp's jaw dropped at her question. He quickly responded. "No. I'm sure it was nothing like that."

While Sallie was nodding in agreement, Lapp wondered what brought up a suspicion that Jacob had been unfaithful. Which of course he had been, with Annie King.

"I'd like to see her sometime."

"Who?"

"The woman at the bar."

"I guess I could arrange that. But there's really no reason."

Sallie suddenly jumped up from the table and announced, "I have something to show you."

Before he could ask what, she ran up the stairs. The sudden silence in the room was interrupted only by the loud ticking of a grandfather clock that sat at the bottom of the stairs. When the clock struck one and then a ding for the half-hour.

One-thirty already? His watch said it was only one o'clock. Then it struck him. Why had it taken him so long to remember? Amish set their clocks one-half hour ahead in order to stay out of sync with the rest of the world. That would hold true for Jacob's pocket watch. Which meant that he was killed at 10 o'clock, not 10:30.

And that opened a whole new world of possibilities.

Chapter 27

Lapp stood by the kitchen door, anxiously awaiting her return, his head filled with the discovery of the time differential of when Jacob was thought to have died and when he actually was killed. Sallie bounced down the stairs wearing a big smile and carrying a black leather bound book that looked like a hymnal.

"I want to show you something," she said, standing shoulder to shoulder with him. She opened the book and revealed a perfect red maple leaf that was pressed to the page. "You gave this to me. Do you remember?"

Lapp, surprised, asked, "I did?"

"It fell on my head and you handed it to me. You still don't remember?"

A broad smile broke across Lapp's face. "Of course I do now."

"I came to see you at the chicken pie place, we went for a ride in my buggy and parked under that maple tree in front of the schoolhouse."

"I remember like it was yesterday."

"I tried to get you to come home. But it didn't work," she added ruefully.

"I can't believe you still have it."

"I had forgotten about it, then today I remembered." Sallie was pleased with herself and Lapp was pleased that she felt that way. She thrust the book toward him.

"Maybe you should have it."

Lapp hesitated and wondered what he would do with it, and also wondered if there were any hidden meanings in her offering. "You know what, Sallie? It would be better if you kept it for me. It could get lost or destroyed while I'm on duty. I'm still on duty."

The answer seemed to please her and she pulled the book back, closed it, and held it to her chest.

"And now, I've got to go," Lapp said apologetically. "You've been very kind and a big help to me. I've overstayed my visit. I'll be back, hopefully with more good news."

Sallie smiled her appreciation and then Lapp was out the door, past the sleeping dog, back into his patrol car, moving down the lane and looking for the buffalo, who, along with the cows, had moved toward the barn.

Sallie Stoltzfus watched from the kitchen door until the patrol car disappeared down the lane. Her hands stroked the back of the kitchen table chair where John Lapp had sat, then pressed her left hand to her heart. The moment of closeness by the sink had sent a rush of desire through her body that she had not experienced in a long time. If John Lapp had touched her she would not have resisted. If he had taken her into his arms she would have welcomed him. And if he had kissed her she would have returned his kiss. Shaking her head in disbelief, she sucked in air, trying to calm her overwhelming desire for affection. Was it the Devil at work, leading her into temptation? Or was she simply a woman who had suffered and needed a strong man to love and comfort her. She would pray to God and ask His guidance so that she would be better prepared for her next meeting with John Lapp.

Lapp accelerated the patrol car to 65 miles per hour on the country road, radioed his position and headed for Roy Brubaker's garage.

A brand new metallic red Ford Extracab 4x4 truck was backed up against the silver Airstream trailer. It looked like Brubaker was planning to hitch up and leave.

The station office had a "closed" sign in the window and the rolling garage doors to the service bays were shut and padlocked. He parked next to the new truck, knocked on the rusted metal side door of the trailer and waited for a response. There were some banging noises from inside before Roy appeared in the doorway. He was clean-shaven and his hair was slicked back to cover a bald path. His blue western shirt with white piping, dark blue denims and bolo tie were so new Lapp expected to see the sales tags still on them.

"Sorry to bother you. But I've got a few questions that I forgot to ask before," Lapp said in his most official sounding voice.

"Like what," Roy grumbled. The good-sized spare tire Roy carried around his waist was exaggerated by the silver and turquoise belt buckle that beamed at Lapp.

Roy stepped down to the ground and stood face to face in a direct challenge. "Make it quick. I got alot of things to do." He took a step back and used the index finger on his right hand to tap the grey ash from his burning cigarette.

"I'll do my best," Lapp said, ignoring Roy's 'hot shit' attitude. "Soon after Jacob left the bar, you left too. And then you came back about thirty minutes later."

"Yeah, I thought I already told you that. I left my diagnostic machine burning in my shop. I needed to turn it off."

"Yeah, you did. It's what … ten minutes from here to Hoffman's?"

"Something like that."

"But you were gone a half hour. Isn't that what you said?"

Wrestling with his temper, Roy swiped his palm across his pomade-glazed hair to flatten it down. "I took care of a few other things while I was here. What are you getting at?"

"These are just routine questions."

"They seem more than routine to me. If you're accusing me of having something to do with that Amish man's death, you're pissing on the wrong tree. I saw on TV that he was killed at 10:30. I was in the bar at 10:30. Got all kinds of witnesses who can testify to that. Now if you're satisfied …"

"Do you know Amos Stoltzfus?"

"Should I?"

"Is that a yes or a no?"

"I might know who he is."

"So you think you might?" Lapp added a tinge of sarcasm to his tone.

"Yeah, if he's the one that works at the foundry. I was over there having some welding done."

"So then you do know Amos."

"Did I ever meet him? No. Did I ever talk to him? No. Like I told you before. I don't have nothing to say to the Amish. And they got nothing to say to me. They stick to themselves, which is fine with me."

"When's the last time you were over there?" Lapp asked.

"Where? The foundry? I don't know. Two, three weeks ago. What the hell does it matter?"

Lapp shrugged. He was satisfied. Roy could have stolen Amos' shotgun. His tone shifted to friendly. "I see you got yourself a new truck. You come in to some money?"

"Yeah. I sold my garage. It's locked up and ready for the next sucker. What do you care, anyway?"

Lapp strolled around the truck and pretended to admire it.

"So when and where are you off to?"

"Las Vegas, Nevada. My mother and stepfather live there."

"You taking Donna and her kids."

Roy, a little annoyed at the question replied, "Nope. Just me. Free as a bird."

Not if I can help it, Lapp thought.

Roy used the toe of his new black hand-engraved boot to grind the cigarette butt into the ground. "Now if you don't mind, I got a date to keep."

"I can see that," Lapp mused as he disappeared for a moment behind the silver trailer. Moments later, he reappeared. "I see that the license plate on the trailer has expired. I wouldn't drive away with an expired license. The fine is a hefty one."

"You're shitting me, right?"

"Nope. Expired months ago."

"Shit. I never even thought about it. What time does the DMV close?"

"4 o'clock," Lapp lied, knowing it was five.

Roy looked at his watch. "Shit. What time they open?"

"Nine, I think."

"I'll take care of it."

Lapp nodded. "Good idea. Then he added, "good luck."

"Same to you," Roy growled before walking around the back of the trailer to verify what he already knew to be true. The license on the trailer had expired last June. Watching the patrol car pull away, Roy muttered, "I wonder what that'll cost?"

Chapter 28

One good thing about being a traffic officer with the State Police is that you know the people at the Department of Motor Vehicles.

Lapp found an Atlantic Bell blue-hooded phone shelter in the parking lot of a Turkey Hill store. Fortunately, there was a full set of phone books that had, oddly enough, not been stolen or vandalized. His finger quickly found the number for the Department of Motor Vehicles.

Unfortunately, he got an answering machine that said all lines were busy. He was gradually losing his patience when a human voice answered. Lapp identified himself, asked for his friend, Joe Staley, and was told the line was busy, and promptly put on hold.

Finally, Joe answered with a friendly, "halloo".

"Joe. This is Johnny Lapp. I need a favor."

Joe Staley was a roly-poly little man with a shape and smile like Frosty the Snowman. But instead of a voice like Jackie Vernon he sounded more like Jackie Gleason. "Johnny. How the hell are you? It's been awhile."

"Listen, I need a favor."

"What do you need, buddy?"

"Tomorrow morning a guy named Roy Brubaker will be coming in, probably when you open, to renew a tag for an Airstream trailer. You got to stall him."

"How am I gonna do that? We'll have four windows working."

"Spread the word."

"Why? What's the deal?"

"If he gets the tag he's out of here. And, depending which way he goes, he's out of the state in anywhere from 30 minutes if he goes south into Maryland or a couple of hours if he heads west.

"Who is this guy?"

"A murder suspect and I need more time to build my case."

"I might be able to stall him for a half-hour at most. That won't help much."

"It's better than nothing. Do what you can."

"You got it, buddy."

Lapp hung up. He remembered the SOLD sign at the garage was Good Neighbor Realty and the agent's name was Ray Butler. But he had not written down the phone number. He paged through the Yellow Pages again and found listings for three offices. He dialed the one closest to the garage. A receptionist answered.

"Do you have an agent named Ray Butler there?" Lapp asked.

The young female voice on the other said, "yes, Ray Butler works out of this office."

"May I speak to him?"

"I believe he's with a client right now. Could I have him return your call?"

"Tell him this is Trooper John Lapp of the Pennsylvania State Police and my call is an emergency."

"Oh, dear," the girl said. "I'll go get him."

Lapp listened to Fats Domino sing, 'I'm Walkin' and two minutes of commercials for a tire store and a fitness gym before Butler got on the phone. Lapp re-identified himself. "I understand you handled the sale of an EXXON service station for a Roy Brubaker."

"That's correct. Is there a problem?" Butler asked.

"Possibly. I need to know the net proceeds of the sale."

"I can get you that if you'll hold on." Then as an afterthought he asked, "how do I know you're state police?"

"I'll come over there if I have to, but I'm trying to save time. The figures are available to the public. What difference does it make?"

"Okay. Okay."

Lapp was again put on hold and forced to listen to Pat Boone sing, "Friendly Persuasion."

Butler came back on and Lapp could hear him shuffling through a file of papers. "Let's see," he muttered. "List price $95,000. Possible toxic waste problems, urgency to sell, accepted a sales price of $65,000, after fees and commissions, he netted $55,000.

Lapp's heart sank. There went his theory that Brubaker was desperate for money. "He walked out of there with fifty-five thousand dollars?"

"Now I didn't say that. I said that's what it sold for. He had some liens against the property. Take away a first and second mortgage, an equipment loan, closing costs, he walked out the door with forty-eight hundred."

Lapp muttered, "now that's more like it."

"I'm sorry? Was there anything else?" Butler asked.

"That's it for now. Thanks."

Lapp ran back to his patrol car. Two more stops to make and time was running out.

He wheeled the patrol car past the giant marquee sign, "Austin Ford", followed the sign post for New Trucks, and parked beneath a "Super Sale" banner.

Pushing through the glass doors into the showroom, the uniformed trooper caught the attention of the four salesmen and the female secretary.

A short, chubby man in his fifties, wearing a white short-sleeved shirt, solid blue tie, and a nametag that said, "Muster" got up and asked, "can I help you, officer?"

"I hope so." Instead of speaking only to Muster, he raised his voice so that everyone in the office could hear him. "A man named Roy Brubaker bought a truck here yesterday and I'd like to talk to the salesman who sold it to him."

Lapp's eyes swept the men behind their desks waiting for a response. A thin man, fortyish, with a crew cut, rose and walked toward him. "That would be me, sir. Is there a problem?" The name tag on his brown tweed jacket identified him as "Hartman".

"Could you get a copy of the invoice? I'd like to see it."

Hartman waited for an approving nod from Muster. "Certainly. I can get it from the accounting office. It'll only take a minute."

"Thank you, I'll wait." Then he called out to Hartman, "where's his old truck?"

"I believe it's already gone out of here."

"Someone bought it?"

"No," he chuckled, "it was put with the wrecks that are hauled out to be dismantled for parts. I'll be right back."

"And you're sure its gone?"

"Pretty sure. They picked up late yesterday. But, I'll check." Hartman made a hasty exit from the showroom floor.

"Thanks." Lapp said. That takes care of getting a photo to show to Amos. Unless the truck was still in one piece at the wrecking yard, there was nothing to identify.

To kill time while he waited, Lapp strolled over to a large, fire-engine red F150 model and peered inside at the shiny black leather interior. The bottom line on the suggested invoice pasted to the side window was $29,900.

His interest was enough to set the blood rushing through salesman Muster's veins. "We can make you a good deal right now. You interested?"

"I'm interested, but I can't afford it. My truck will have to last me a couple more years."

"We've got easy credit and some fantastic leasing plans," Muster said, hopefully. With a nod to Lapp's uniform, he added, "I'm sure you'd have no trouble qualifying. No trouble at all."

"I'm pretty much a cash and carry guy." He felt a flush of relief when he saw Hartman re-enter the showroom. Lapp moved forward to meet him and directed him to a more private corner behind a blue Ranger model.

Lapp scanned the legal sales contract from top to bottom. Brubaker had paid, with tax and license, $29,425.47 for the truck, less a trade-in of $3,000 on his old truck, leaving a balance of $26,425.47

"You gave him $3,000 for his old truck? I thought you said it was junk?"

"Well, yes, it is," Hartman agreed. "It wasn't worth anything near that. It's something we do to make the customer feel good. We make it up on the other end."

Lapp was not surprised. He handed the invoice back to Hartman and asked, "how did he pay for it? Check?"

"No, cash. In hundreds."

Lapp perked up. Cash? He had a pretty good idea where Brubaker got it. "Didn't you wonder about that?"

"What's that?"

"That he paid in cash."

"It happens every once in a while. Some farmers still pay cash."

"What about Brubaker? Would you have expected him to pay in cash?"

Hartman shrugged. "I was just happy to make the sale."

"You didn't ask him about the cash?"

"No."

"How did he carry it?"

"In a Foodtown grocery sack. I thought it was a little weird."

"Where's the cash now?" Lapp asked, wondering, no hoping, that when the bank issued the cash to Patel, they had kept some serial numbers.

"We took it to the bank."

"Which one?"

"The Farmer's Bank in Intercourse."

The same bank that had issued the cash in the first place. But at this hour it would already be closed.

"Is there something wrong with the sale?" Hartman asked.

"No. It seems to be in order," Lapp said, noting the relief on Hartman's face. Lapp turned to leave, then asked, "can you make me a copy of that?"

At 4:30, when he pulled into the motor pool at the barracks, he prayed silently, "Moyer. Be there. Please."

He fumbled with his seat belt and when he was released, ran into the building, took the steps two at a time, and entered the detectives room. No Moyer. Hal Eiseman, sitting at the adjacent desk was on the phone, but gave him a welcoming smile. When he hung up, he said, "you looking for Moyer? He's taking a couple hours off. Went to see his kid play in a big soccer game."

Lapp fretted over what to do, then asked, "where's the game?"

"Lancaster Catholic High School."

"I really need to talk to him. Do you think he'll mind?"

"If they're winning and Sean's got his goals, no. If not, yes."

Lapp took a deep breath. "I guess I'll take my chances. Do you know where the school is?"

"It's not far from here—about 4-5 miles. It's easy. Turn right out of here onto Route 30, go west to New Holland Ave., which becomes the New Holland Pike. I think there are signs to the school. Take you about 10 minutes."

"Thanks." Eiseman was right. 10 minutes later, he pulled into the parking lot and took the only available space in the "Faculty Only" section.

He followed the cheering to an open athletic field with a set of bleachers on each side.

The four-foot circular logo of a helmeted Crusader with a lance and shield on a charging horse was mounted in the center of the scoreboard which read:

LCHS 0

ELCO 0

Lapp scanned the wooden bleachers and quickly understood the term "soccer moms", made popular by politicians and the press. Women in their 30's and 40's, dressed in blue jeans and colorful logo and letter jackets cheered and moaned with every referee's whistle on the field. A group of uniformed girl students in white oxford cloth blouses covered with grey sweaters and red kilted skirts were less enthusiastic about the game. Their neatly coiffed gossiping heads were pieced together like a puzzle. Between giggles, their sideward glances at the smattering of boy students in white shirts, ties, grey pants and blue jackets in attendance were mostly ignored.

Warren Moyer was not among the few scattered men in the stands.

"Pass it to the wing!"

He recognized Moyer's excited voice even before he spotted him stalking the sideline like a caged circus lion.

Lapp approached slowly, his eyes torn between Moyer and the action on the field.

"Lapp. What are you doing here?

"I'm sorry to bother you here, but some things have come up...."

Moyer, dressed in his black raincoat as a precaution against the dark black clouds overhead used a white handkerchief to wipe the beaded sweat on his forehead. "Can't it wait, for Christ's sake. This is a big game."

"I wouldn't be here, if I didn't think ..."

"It's the last game of the regular season and Sean needs one lousy goal to break a school record."

Lapp said sheepishly, "I know sir, I only need a minute."

"That's Sean. Number 2 in the purple and gold." Moyer stepped away and yelled, "Get it back in the middle. Come on. Get it to Sean."

Lapp was drawn into the action as Moyer's son took control of the ball in the center of the field and with short, controlled kicks, dribbled the ball toward the opponents goal.

"What the hell! Did you see that? Number 23, that skinny little shit in the blue and white, deliberately tripped him. That's a penalty."

Sean Moyer was on the ground, writhing and twisting with pain. The coach, a husky 40-year old in a Crusader cap and leather jacket ran on to the field. He and several members of the team surrounded the injured player.

"Come on, Sean. Shake it off," Moyer yelled. To Lapp, he said, "he'll get a penalty kick. A clean shot at the goal. That's all he needs." Moyer turned his attention back on to the field and saw that Sean was being propped up by two players. Satisfied that his son would be all right, he turned back to Lapp. "So what is it?"

Lapp talked fast. "First of all, the time of death was not 10:30. It was 10 o'clock. Amish set their watches a half-hour ahead of time to stay out of step with the rest of the world. I don't know why I didn't think of it sooner, but I didn't." He emphasized his memory lapse by slapping his forehead with the heel of his right hand.

Moyer clapped his hands and Lapp followed suit, joining the applause coming from the bleachers on both sides as Sean tried to walk off the tenderness in his right ankle.

Lapp worried that he wasn't getting through to Moyer. "Remember how I told you Jacob went to Hoffman's Tavern the night he was killed? One of the people in the bar was Roy Brubaker who runs … ran an EXXON station and garage on the highway. He left the bar right after Jacob did and he had an alibi. He was in the bar at 10:30, the time of the murder according to Jacob's pocket watch. But he wasn't in the bar at 10 when the murder really took place. So he no longer has an alibi."

Moyer's attention was again drawn to the field. "I wonder who'll take the penalty kick?"

"Here." Lapp pulled a baggie from his jacket and held it in front of Moyer's face. "This is one of Brubaker's cigarette butts. Same brand as Amos. Same brand found at the murder scene."

Moyer looked up at the dark clouds and muttered, "they'd better get going out there or it's gonna come down in buckets and this field'll be a mudbath."

Lapp was angered by Moyer's non-responsive attitude to what he was being told. "Brubaker admitted he has been to the foundry where Amos kept his shotgun."

"He told you that?" Moyer's eyebrows rose.

Lapp, relieved, finally had his attention. "I told you he ran a garage. Well, he just sold it. He netted a big forty-eight hundred dollars. That's hundred, not thousand. Then …" Lapp pulled out the invoice copy to the truck and held it up for Moyer to see.

Moyer pulled his reading glasses from his inside shirt pocket and took the paper. His eyes dropped and rose, reading, but still following the action on the field at the same time.

"Then yesterday, he paid, in cash, $26,000 for a new truck. Carried the money into the dealership in a grocery sack."

Moyer pulled his reading glasses from his face and watched his son join his teammates about 20 feet from the goal. The goalie, a tall, lanky young man, got into position and shook his arms to relieve the tension. The remainder of the blue and white-shirted ELCO players moved behind the line of the ball. "Sean's gonna take the penalty kick."

Except for a solo female voice that shouted out, "come on Sean," the bleachers and sidelines were silent.

Sean Moyer, one of the smaller players on the field, hobbled toward the ball, stepped back, and lined up his kick. The goal keeper, waved his long, loose arms like a gorilla.

Sean Moyer stumbled slightly before the ball left his foot. The ball soared toward the left end of the goal net, but it had no velocity and was easily grabbed by the goal keeper. The near stands quietly moaned, while a cheer went up from the small group of ELCO supporters in the opposite bleachers.

Moyer's face dropped to the ground in disappointment. "That kid crippled him. The coach should have had someone else take the shot."

Sean Moyer's disappointment was salved by pats of condolence from his team members as the goal keeper tossed the ball to a teammate and play continued. They moved past Lapp and Moyer threatening the LCHS goal.

Lapp said, "I'm sorry."

"Yeah, well, these things happen. Sometimes I forget it's only a game."

Moyer clapped his hands and yelled out, "it's okay, we still got time." He turned to Lapp, ready to listen.

Lapp took his cue. "Like I was telling you, Brubaker paid $26,000 for a new truck, in cash. He's got that truck hooked to the trailer he lives in by the garage and is planning on leaving first thing in the morning. The only thing that's keeping him here is expired license tags on the trailer. I called the DMV and asked a buddy of mine to delay Brubaker as long as possible when he goes over there in the morning. Once he gets them he's gone. How can we stop him?"

"We can't." Moyer said bluntly.

"If we could search his trailer we'd find the gym bag and the rest of the money. We need a search warrant. It's that simple."

"Slow down. You're getting ahead of yourself. Your boy's in jail because of the evidence that he was there that night and killed his brother."

"Hey, Warren." The Crusader's coach toed the sideline and from twenty feet away, asked, "you want me to take him out."

"Don't ask me, ask Sean." Moyer yelled back and shook his head in disgust.

"You're right," Lapp said. "Amos was there that night."

"So now you're agreeing with me?"

"Amos told me he was there."

"He admitted it?"

"This morning at the jail. He went to the gas station almost every night because the horny teenagers would park behind the garage. He watched them make out. He got off on it. He was hiding inside the empty office of the gas station. He saw the killer drive up in his truck, aim the shotgun at Jacob and kill him."

"Then why the hell didn't he tell us this? Moyer snapped, frustrated by the game and over this new development.

"He feels guilty that he didn't stop it. Plus, he won't admit to watching the kids in their cars. You have to remember, Amos is a frightened, slightly retarded man."

Moyer countered. "And that explains the footprints?"

"After the killer left, Amos stood over Jacob's body and saw that he was dead and there was nothing he could do about it, so he went home to bed."

"Just like that? His brother's laying there dead and he goes home to bed? Jesus!" Moyer's attention flipped back to the game. The Crusaders again had control of the ball. "Pass it to the left wing. He's open. Take a shot!" He turned to Lapp and muttered, "you'd think by the end of the season they'd know what to do. I blame the coaches. I'm sorry. You were telling me about Amos."

"I know it's weird. Running away like that. But he had a reason." Lapp waited until he was sure he had Moyer's full attention. "Amos said the killer yelled out, who's there?"

"Can Amos identify the killer?"

"He says not. It was too dark."

The long blast of the referee's whistle ending the game drew their attention to the field. "Too bad," Moyer lamented. "They should've won. They had plenty of chances. What about the truck?"

"Brubaker traded it in for his new truck. According to the dealer it's been sold to junk yard for parts."

"And you think the rest of the money is in Roy Brubaker's trailer?"

"I'm positive."

"We need a search warrant. Let me talk to the boss." Moyer smiled. "You've been a busy boy." He waved to a woman in a heavy wool coat and a uniformed teen-ager standing in the bleachers. "My wife and daughter. You got time to meet them?"

"I'd better get back to the barracks."

"Maybe some other time. I got to talk to Sean. Then I'll be back, too." The cell-phone in Moyer's jacket rang twice before he picked it up. "Moyer. Yeah. Yeah, okay. Right." He flipped the shiny metal cover over the keypad. "Well, this oughta make you happy."

"What?"

"That was the DA's office. Your boy Amos is being released to the custody of his family. The judge has decided he's not a flight risk."

Lapp's heart beat faster. He was happy for Amos, Sallie, in fact, all of the Amish.

Moyer's eyes turned skyward in reaction to big drops of rain that stained his jacket. "It's gonna come down in buckets any minute now."

Lapp was aware of the rain, but it would take a hundred year flood to keep him from telling Sallie that Amos was coming home.

Chapter 29

It had been quite a day for Roy Brubaker. Lapp's visit left him in a very pissy mood. He was sorry he had even answered the knock on the door.

Then, again, maybe it was a good thing he'd talked with that nosy cop. So damn cocky telling me my time alibi is questionable. So what? He thought, "they still got nothing on me and I'm sure as hell going to keep it that way." In the morning he would shut off the electricity at the box, disconnect the wires and do the same for the telephone. The tires on the trailer were pumped up to the right pressure and ready to go. By 10 o'clock he'd be out of there.

In the afternoon, Brubaker left the trailer briefly, making sure it was locked up tight, to pick up an extra tank of bottled gas at Nissley's. He stopped at the auto supply store and bought a trailer hitch that would bear the weight of the Airstream. Back at the garage, he opened a service bay door and, fifteen minutes later, smiled with satisfaction when the round silver ball was properly mounted and ready to roll.

Now, back in his cocoon-like living space with plenty of propane, he shoved a Swanson's TV chicken dinner into the oven, popped the cap from a Rolling Rock and sat back to enjoy the six o'clock news.

He was only half-watching when an Asian woman, with the name "Lisa Kim" superimposed across the bottom of the screen, reported from the front steps of the County Jail. The State Police apparently have new information regarding the murder of Jacob Stoltzfus. Amos Stolzfus, the victim's brother, who is being held in County Jail as the prime suspect, will be released sometime tomorrow. According to the District Attorney's office, Judge Harry Swanger has ordered that Mr. Stoltzfus be released to the custody of his family. He is not considered a flight risk.

Phil Simms, the news anchorman with grey hair sprayed into a pompadour, asked the reporter if she had any information on why the case seemed to be taking a different direction. Lisa Kim replied that neither the State Police nor the District Attorney's office had much to say, but it appears there may be some new information which could cast some doubt on Mr. Stoltzfus' guilt. His Public Defender, Gloria Ebersole, confirmed that the suspect had undergone a lie detector test. Simms thanked the reporter before going live to Betty Hammond, a pretty, blonde reporter standing at the entrance of the People's Place, an Amish and Tourist Information Center in Intercourse. She reported that she had been soliciting comment from the Amish community but was sorry to say that she had been unsuccessful in getting anyone to come on camera. Off camera, both the Amish and Mennonites claim to have no knowledge of the situation.

"Son of a bitch," Roy Brubaker's temper rose from simmer to boil. He screamed out loud, "what do they mean they have new information? Son of a fucking bitch!" He cocked his right arm and threw the empty beer bottle with full force against the wall. "I knew somebody was out there and it's my own fucking, stupid fault for not hunting him down. It was that half-moron brother."

The phone rang. Roy jumped from his chair, stepped to the refrigerator to grab another Rolling Rock, popped the cap, took a long swallow, then picked up the receiver on the fifth ring. "Yeah," he shouted angrily.

"What's the hell's the matter with you?" It was Donna.

Searching for words, he sputtered that the TV wasn't working right, reception was lousy and it was pissing him off. She was calling from Hoffman's. She'd be off work between 10:00 and 10:30 and would be over, noting it had been almost a week since they'd been together. He hadn't even been by the bar to see her. She purred that she was looking forward to a good time. Brubaker thought, but didn't say, that normally he would be too. The sex was great. Best he'd ever had. He called her honey and said he'd miss her, but he needed to get to bed early because he had to be up early in the morning.

She asked, "what for?"

"What for what?"

"Why do you have to be up early?"

"Do I have to explain everything to you?" He shot back. "How about tomorrow night?"

Donna's disappointment turned whiny. "Is something wrong?"

"No, nothing's wrong."

"Then why not tonight?" She persisted. "The boys are at a friend's house overnight."

"I got shit to do, that's all." Brubaker tried hard to curb his impatience. He cut off her question of "you're not tired of me, are you," by arguing that everything was fine. "Come over tomorrow night. Bye." He replaced the receiver in the phone cradle and thought maybe Donna was just a loose end he'd leave dangling. He smiled when he pictured her showing up to find an empty cement pad and find him and the trailer gone.

All the time he was talking to Donna he was haunted by the TV news reporter's words.

He sat down in his chair, clicked off the TV, lit up a cigarette to go with his beer and began to think it through. A simple little robbery. That's all it was supposed to be. If he hadn't recognized me I never would have had to kill him. Here I was, free and clear, and now where am I? I got to think this out. Think clearly. If Amos saw me there that night he didn't recognize me or else they'd be breaking down my door and hauling my ass off to jail. So what am I so worried about? I'll get the license renewal for the trailer in the morning and be out of here for good.

The oven timer dinged that his dinner was ready. He pulled out the TV dinner and burned his fingers pulling off the aluminum foil. Sucking on the burn, he dropped into his recliner, turned off the floor lamp and put the brain cells back to work.

Except for the glow from his cigarette his face was dark. What about his truck? If Amos saw him, he also saw his truck. It may have been more recognizable than he was. It's at the Ford dealer, but it could still be traced to him. He'll go by there in the morning. Maybe he could buy it back, drive it to one of the abandoned limestone quarries that were common in the area, and sink it in fifty feet of water.

Brubaker concluded that Amos passed the lie detector test and they believed his story. Otherwise, why would they let him go?

That nosy cop, Lapp, made a point of saying his alibi of being at Hoffman's at 10:30 no longer worked . He'll keep noseying around, too. Brubaker reasoned, hell, even if he left town, they could still track him down. Something's gotta be done. But what?

Thirty minutes later, Brubaker picked up the phone and punched the keypad. When Donna answered, he apologized for being an asshole earlier. He wanted her to come over. He smiled when she said she'll be there about 11:00. He'd be waiting. He hung up and said out loud, "Donna, baby, you're gonna make yourself useful one more time."

Chapter 30

John Lapp was still at the barracks, changing from his uniform to street clothes when he got the call from Gloria Ebersole. She confirmed Moyer's words. Amos would be released as soon as someone from his family claimed him. Lapp congratulated her. "How did you do it?"

"I presented my defense, such as it is, to Judge Swanger and since he trusts and is sympathetic to the Amish, he agreed. Now back to you Trooper Lapp. The Stoltzfus' have no phone, and no one in my office is interested in driving out to the farm at night, not to mention working overtime, so I'm tossing it into your lap. I'm counting on you to notify the Stoltzfus family and make the arrangements for his pickup. He'll be ready about 9:00 a.m., I would guess."

"Consider it done," Lapp said, elated over being chosen to be the bearer of good news.

Since he had just been there earlier that day, Sallie's initial reaction to seeing his truck lights rumbling up the lane, the barking dog, and recognizing his figure as he approached the kitchen door, her greeting was cautiously optimistic. But when he announced the news her face beamed with delight. The children, at her side, jumped with joy. Even ten-year old Samuel, still wary of his presence, smiled broadly.

"Amos can be released in the morning to your custody," Lapp said. "He will be confined to the farm. Is there anyone with a car who could drive you to the jail?"

"I'll ask my neighbor, John Miller. He has a car."

Remembering that she had no telephone, Lapp offered, "can I drive you over there?"

"No, I can walk. It'll feel good to walk."

Sallie barely heard Lapp's admonition that Amos had not been cleared of any previous charges. He would certainly be called for more questioning, and he still might go to trial, although that seemed less likely now.

"Will you be at the jail in the morning?" Sallie asked.

"You know I will if I can. I have to report for duty first."

Sallie squeezed his arm. "Thank you, Johnny."

John Lapp left the farm flushed with the warmth of Sallie's touch ...

A piercing, fast-talking male announcer's voice pitching a truck close-out sale at Austin Ford poured out of the clock radio on the nightstand next to John Lapp's head. He reached out and tapped the button to shut if off and blinked at the LED to check the time. 6:00 a.m. sharp.

Lapp showered, shaved and pulled on his flannel shirt, khaki pants and boots, then went downstairs to start the coffee. The thermostat had just kicked in for the day so the house was still freezing. Shrugging on his overcoat, he ran out the front door and retrieved the morning newspaper from its cylinder by the curb.

By the time he fixed his Cheerios with banana slices, the coffee was ready. Between bites he scanned the front section of the paper. No longer headline news, the story about Amos being released to the custody of his family was relegated to page five. The warmth that rushed through his veins had nothing to do with the strong coffee he was sipping. It was the memory of his visit to Sallie and her children last night.

He was clearing his breakfast dishes from the table when Lisa Robinson called.

"Do you know what time Amos will be released? Are you going to be there?"

He was pleased to hear her voice. "9 o'clock, I expect. I hope to be there, but I've got to report to the barracks first."

"Do you have anything you can tell me about his release? The new information the police have discovered? Anything about the lie detector test? Did they hypnotize him? Did he take and pass a polygraph test?"

"You know more than I do. Frankly, I'd be surprised if he'd agree to take a polygraph. Maybe Gloria Ebersole talked him into it." Lapp said. Then reflecting out loud, "it's funny. She didn't mention it to me last night as one of the reasons the judge granted bail."

"You think he was hypnotized?"

"I don't know." In fact, Lapp thought, it would be a good idea to probe the recesses of Amos' brain and pull out suppressed facts about Jacob's murder.

She broke the phone conversation gap with a sugary tone . "When Amos goes home today, could you do me a favor?"

Lapp answered warily, "what's that?"

"I think it would help Amos' case if the public had a better understanding of what it's like to be accused of your brother's death. And also what the widow has had to endure."

"What are you suggesting?" He asked, even though he knew the answer.

"An interview with Amos and the widow."

Lapp temper flared. "I can't believe you'd even ask."

Her voice rose in defense. "I'm a reporter. Think about it. There's an important story here. It could help Amos build public sentiment."

"I don't think he needs your help."

"It would be a positive story," she insisted. "It would provide an insight into how a tragedy can affect an entire community."

She was right. Jacob's death did affect the entire community. But she was wrong to think the Amish wanted that effect known. "You forgot to mention that the story could run nationally. Put you in the big leagues."

"That's totally unfair," Lisa protested.

Lapp pounded the words home. "Forget it. It's not going to happen."

There was a long silence. Both parties had had their say. "John?" Her tone was conciliatory.

Lapp responded in kind. "What?"

"I'll see you at the jail. Nine o'clock."

"I expect to be there."

Seconds after he hung up the phone with the reporter, it rang again. He was sorry he picked it up. It was his sergeant, telling him to report for duty as part of a motorcade for the Governor of Pennsylvania who was coming to Lancaster. Lapp reminded the sergeant that he was back working for Warren Moyer.

"Not today, you're not," the sergeant shot back. "We're shorthanded. This morning your ass is mine. Report immediately, as ordered."

The dial tone in his ear ended the conversation.

Chapter 31

Streaks of daylight slid through the high, narrow bare windows above Roy Brubaker's bed. The digital clock said 7:15. He had not overslept as he had feared. He reviewed his plans for the day before slipping out from beneath the warm sheets and heavy comforter. Naked and shivering, he ran to the bathroom, emptied his bladder in a strong, noisy stream, then pulled on his jockey shorts, tee shirt, wool plaid shirt, black levis, and black boots. Donna Trautman, naked beneath the sheets, opened her eyes when she heard the rattle of her car keys.

"What are you doing?" She groaned.

Roy closed the snap on her purse. "Borrowing your car keys."

"What for? Where you going at this hour? Is something wrong with your new truck?"

"Nothing's wrong with it. It hasn't been licensed properly. I want to be at the Motor Vehicles Office when they open."

"Why so early?"

He grabbed a pair of binoculars from the small bookcase and started toward the door.

"What are those for?" Donna asked.

"There's a pair of eagles that like to hang around on those trees in back. I'm gonna have a look. Go back to sleep." He grabbed his black raincoat, unlocked the door and went outside.

At 7:45, Roy Brubaker was cruising King Street, first east and then back west, surveying the two asphalt-paved parking lots that straddled a wide strip of green grass in front of the faux castle facade of the Lancaster County Jail. The lots were empty except for a TV remote truck with Channel 8 on the side, and two station wagons that he figured were also media. He wasn't the only one waiting for the release of Amos Stoltzfus.

He parked on King Street, directly across from the entrance to the parking lots and settled in to wait.

The good thing about Donna's old Ford station wagon was that it was anonymous. The bad thing was that the heater and defroster didn't work worth a shit. He had cleaned the frosty windows with a plastic scraper, but the wiper blades just smeared the watery residue. It was fucking freezing. The black raincoat he wore was unlined, as were the black leather gloves. He should have stopped at Dunkin Donuts for a couple of glazed twists and a large carton of hot coffee.

His new truck was at home because the metallic red color shouted for attention. He loved that truck. When he first saw it on the showroom floor it spoke to him. They were meant for each other.

The low black clouds overhead began to shed a light, steady drizzle. Roy was sick of the weather and just about everything else in this town.

The black Chevy sedan with the bumpers and trim painted black caught his attention as it pulled into the East parking lot and stopped two spaces away from the double glass doors of the jail entrance.

An Amish woman, dressed in black from head to toe, got out of the passenger side. She was joined by the driver, a man dressed in a blue parka and a hunting cap with flaps that covered his ears. They reacted with alarm to the husky male TV cameraman and two female reporters, one with a microphone, the other with poised pen and writing pad, racing toward them. The Amish woman's escort grabbed her arm and they quickly disappeared behind the jail's double doors. Reassuring himself that there were no cops in sight, particularly his nemesis, Lapp, Brubaker pondered what to do about the TV people. He concluded if his plan was going to work he had to take some risks.

Deliberately wearing the same black raincoat and Fram filter cap he had worn that fateful night, Brubaker stepped out of Donna's station wagon, waited for the traffic to clear, and crossed the street. With confident strides, he approached the glass doors. One of the female reporters, holding a blue umbrella shivered from the cold. Next to her, a chubby man in a yellow slicker set his video camera down and lit up a cigarette.

A pretty black woman, pushed through the glass doors from inside, and reported, "they're not in the reception area any more. They're inside, somewhere."

Brubaker was torn between talking to or ignoring the reporters who were probably wondering why he was there. They would certainly be able to recognize him if ever called upon to do so, so he decided to chat it up. As he reached for the pull on the glass door, he asked, 'what's going on? Why are you guys here?"

A young blonde in a grey wool pants suit, looking pretty much like all TV reporters did these days, responded, "just doing a story. They're releasing the Amish man who was accused of killing his brother."

Brubaker eyed the beautiful black woman in a hooded black raincoat . She was holding what looked like one of those new digital cameras. Lewd thoughts entered his mind. Probably lots more like her once he got to Las Vegas.

He turned his attention back to the blonde. "Is that right?" Brubaker said with an innocent tone. "I saw it on TV. I guess they think now he didn't do it. Maybe I'll get to see him. I'm picking up a buddy of mine who's getting out first thing this morning. I hope it don't take too long, I ain't got all day." Brubaker added a phony smile to his acting job before entering the reception area.

Inside, his eyes scanned the walls and ceiling and counted three security cameras. This plan better work, Brubaker thought, because his face was now part of a permanent record. He sat down in a plastic seat that was molded to fit a person's ass and was attached to three more in the row. He glanced across the room at the heavy-set, short-haired, middle-aged woman in a brown uniform who sat on a stool behind the security desk. He caught her staring in his direction and responded by calling out to her, "I'm waiting to pick up a buddy. He's supposed to be released this morning."

Brubaker hissed a quiet sigh of relief when the guard went back to writing something in what looked like a log or journal. When she picked up the phone his heart stopped. Was she calling a guard from inside to confront him? He was dead meat if she did. Long minutes went by and no one came out. He yawned loudly and dropped his chin to his chest, pretending to doze.

Fifteen minutes later, he glanced through the glass doors to survey the activity that was building outside. The crowd of TV reporters and cameramen had swelled to at least ten people. But, Brubaker figured, as long as they stay outside, they won't screw up his plan.

Brubaker checked his watch. It was close to 8:30. Still no action from behind the security desk and door. It would be just his luck if they had sneaked Amos out a back door so that he wouldn't have to face the cameras.

His concern was short-lived. A burly black guard who must have weighed 250 pounds and stood well over six feet tall came through the security door, followed by Amos Stoltzfus, the Amish woman and the man in the blue parka. Brubaker stood up and thought "here goes everything".

Putting on the face of a curious spectator, Brubaker quickly stepped toward the glass doors. The black guard threw his arm out to keep Brubaker back. But Brubaker got what he had come for. The Amish man's eyes widened and his bearded face froze with fright when he saw Brubaker's raincoat, cap and face.

The guard led the way through the double doors, but Amos grabbed another quick look at the intruder's grinning, smirky face. Holding his broad brimmed black hat across his face, Amos was led through the gauntlet of bright lights and barking reporters.

Brubaker slipped through the door and walked quickly toward the street. The cameras and reporters were now focused on the back seat of the black Chevy sedan which was edging its way through the mob toward the street. Except for the black reporter who caught his eye as he left, no one paid any attention to a man in a black raincoat and orange Fram Cap making a hasty departure.

Roy Brubaker's body shook with excitement. Or was it fear?

When the black Chevy turned left on King Street, Roy waited for a station wagon with the letters WGAL on the side, to pass. Already aimed in the right direction, he swung the Ford station wagon onto the street and joined the procession. They continued east on King Street before bearing to the right on Route 340. As he had hoped, they were leading him to the Stoltzfus farm.

The Chevy turned up a long farm lane which was immediately closed by two young Amish men hauling two long poles. The radio station vehicle pulled off to the side and Brubaker slowed to 10 mph in order to take in as much as possible.

For the next ten minutes Roy Brubaker, with the nearly rubber-less wiper blades noisily scraping the rain away, cruised back and forth observing the growing media crowd. At the top of a rise two hundred yards down the road, he got out of the station wagon, and, using his Bushnell 10x 50 power binoculars, surveyed the farm house, barn and buildings. A couple of hunters in orange fluorescent caps and vests in a corn field next to the road were surprised by a cock pheasant that crowed in distress as it flew away. They raised their shotguns and fired. Three shots and the bird fell like a rock from the sky.

It was the first day of hunting season.

Chapter 32

The Governor of Pennsylvania made the trip from Harrisburg in a black limousine with American and Commonwealth flags flying, accompanied by State Police escorts in front and back. When they arrived at the Lancaster barracks, two local blue and whites, one in front and one in back enlarged the escort by 100 per cent. Lapp, shoes shined, uniform pressed and all spiffed up at the wheel of his newly washed and polished patrol car, brought up the rear.

The trip to the new regional U.S. Post Office in Southwestern Lancaster city was less than 15 miles and Lapp was annoyed by the waste of time and manpower. Most of their time was spent standing around in a small cluster of police and limo drivers trying to keep warm, while the Governor, along with six other government officials sat on folding chairs on the broad front steps, and, one by one, made short speeches at the podium. The event was lightly attended, fifty people at the most. Lapp spotted one TV camera and reporter, one radio newsman with a palm-sized tape recorder and a couple of newspaper reporters. Lisa Robinson, was not among them.

Lapp fiddled with his white dress gloves and fidgeted, waiting for the ceremony to end.

Roy Brubaker studied the Stoltzfus farm. For thirty minutes, he memorized the lay of the land, the location of the house, barn and other out buildings. It was so peaceful out here, he hated to leave. According to his trusty Timex watch, it was still only nine o'clock when he unlocked the door and entered his trailer. Donna Trautman was awake but still in his bed. He tossed her car keys next to her purse on the kitchen table, pulled off his raincoat and Orange cap and replaced them with a padded Dallas Cowboys jacket and logo cap.

"Shouldn't you be getting home?"

Donna responded sleepily, "yeah, I should." She smiled seductively and patted the opposite side of the bed. "Unless you give me a good reason to stay."

"You know I'd like that, doll, but I got too many things going today."

"Like what?"

"Like none of your business." He leaned over, kissed her, and pulled away
before she could drag him into her arms.

Much as he was tempted to climb back into the warm bed and Donna's
open arms, Roy Brubaker had other business to attend to.

They were just dropping the chain across the driveway of Austin Ford when
Roy drove in. Inside the showroom, Ed Hartman beamed while Roy gushed
over how much he loved his new truck. He asked if he could retrieve an item
left between the seats of his old one and pretended to be disappointed when
told that the truck had been sent to the salvage yard. By now it was flat as a
pancake.

"It was just an old snapshot. Sentimental value, was all." Roy said.

Roy Brubaker was one big, hulking bundle of joy as he climbed back into
his truck. One less thing to worry about.

Roy's joy dissipated thirty minutes later while standing in line at the
Department of Motor Vehicles. He was next in line when they closed his window and he was directed to another line. Getting a simple, goddamn license
tag sticker, which should have taken fifteen minutes took over an hour.

But then he was back in the cab of his truck again, bouncing up and down
to the song, "Mustang Sally", and howling "Ride, Sally ride." The song blasted
from the side and rear speakers as he thought about the ride Donna had given
him last night. He was going to miss her. But what the hell. Vegas was full of
women like her, even younger and prettier.

It was nearly noon by the time John Lapp got back to the barracks. He ran
upstairs to the criminal investigator's section to see if Moyer had secured the
search warrant.

Hal Eiseman was at his desk reading the newspaper. "Moyer's out with the
Sheriff's Department picking up a suspect in the Bradley arson case."

"What about my search warrant? Lapp asked.

The curly haired detective responded, "I have no idea."

"Did he say when he'd be back?"

"No idea," Eiseman repeated, before changing the subject. "So they released
the Amish brother? What's that all about?"

Lapp ignored the question. "I'll use Moyer's phone."

"Help yourself."

Lapp dialed Joe Staley at the DMV. Joe informed him that Brubaker had been in at 9:30 a.m., was stalled as requested, bitched about how long it took and was out of there about 10:15 a.m. "We did what we could," Staley explained.

Lapp chuckled at Brubaker's annoyance, if nothing else. "I appreciate it, Joe. I'm on my way out to his place to see if he's still there. Thanks again."

Halfway out the door, Lapp decided he would be less conspicuous in street clothes. Brubaker would be more likely to dodge a patrol car than a four year old truck.

He was pushing through the back door when Sadie called him back to the phone. It was Moses King.

His voice was shaky and nervous. "Annie took the baby and left in a buggy about twenty minutes ago. I'm not sure, but I think maybe she's going to Jake's place. She acted funny at breakfast. She said Sallie needs to know that Jake was going to be hers. I wish she'd stop talking about it. She even says it in front of the kids."

Lapp thanked Moses for calling, ran out the door, jumped into his truck and raced toward the Stoltzfus farm. When he arrived, less than ten minutes later, everything was peaceful and quiet. He removed the long pole barrier to the side and proceeded slowly up the lane until he had a full view of the house. No sign of a buggy parked outside. Exhaling a sigh of relief, he maneuvered the truck in a series of back and forth turns until he was heading back down the lane. He hoped that Sallie had not seen his truck.

A horse, with mane flattened in the wind, feet flying and pulling a clattering Amish buggy came into sight.

Shiny with white lather and drool, the thin brown horse pulled the box-like black buggy up the lane until it was blocked by the truck. Lapp stepped into the glare of Annie King's angry face. The bundled baby was in her lap.

"Now she's got you to watch her, too," Annie snarled. "Everybody looks out for her. Even Moses. That's how you got here ain't it. Nobody caring nothing about me or my baby."

"Moses does care. We all do. Annie. This is wrong. Leave Sallie alone."

"I just want her to see Jake's baby. Don't you think she should?"

"Why do you want more people to be hurt? What was going to happen or not happen with you and Jake is over. He's dead. Let his memory rest in peace. His friends and neighbors spoke well of him. Do you want to spoil all that?"

"I chust want her to know." Annie choked back a sob, and tears appeared in the corner of her eyes. "To know that I had him."

Lapp waited and watched until some of the anger had drained from her face. He placed his hand on her arm to calm her but she jerked away.

"Annie, listen to me. You and Moses are the only ones who know. Leave it that way."

"You think nobody else knows? Stubby Beiler knows, too. Maybe more."

"What good would it do if Sallie knew? Would she hate you? Is that what you want from her?" Lapp asked.

Annie King shrugged her shoulders and brushed back the hair from the deformed child's sleeping face.

"She wouldn't hate you. She would forgive you. And then what would you have?"

"If you'd stayed Amish, Johnny Lapp, you would have married Sallie and I would have had Jake," she snarled angrily.

"I know you think that. But it had nothing to do with me. Sallie picked Jake and he picked her. And you picked Moses King. He's a good man, Annie. You can tell that by the way he's taking care of you."

Annie King began to rock and hush the stirring baby.

Lapp continued his plea. "It'll take time to get over this. I know that. I can help you find a doctor who deals with these kinds of problems."

Still no response, but a natural pallor had returned to her face. Tears streaked her cheeks.

"Annie? Go home to Moses. Put this behind you. I'll come over with the names of some doctors. Talk it over with Moses, and you decide what you want to do." He nodded at the baby. "You can't be a good mother to this little girl or your other children until you let it go. Verstei?"

Annie took a long time to digest his words. Then she nodded, yes. She tugged on the reins and the horse backed the buggy onto the road. Lapp sighed with relief as he watched her move down the road. There was no activity up at the farmhouse so he concluded they had not been seen.

Taking a series of parallel roads where he could catch occasional glimpses of the buggy, he saw Annie home.

Chapter 33

Roy Brubaker was starving when he ordered two Big Macs, a large fries, and the largest cup of Coca-Cola they sold at McDonalds. He ate too fast, but two large belches helped relieve his gassy stomach. It was 1:30 now. He was still on schedule.

Heading into Lancaster, he liked the way he sat high in the seat and could look down on cars and smaller trucks on the road around him. He also liked the oversized side and rear view mirrors, which he continually checked to see if he was being followed. If anyone was, they were doing a damn good job of hiding.

The flashing warning light for his unfastened seat belts was annoying and he decided he would try to find a way to disconnect it. He had never worn a seat belt before, and he wasn't about to start now, especially with this powerful new truck wrapped around him.

He pushed through the heavy glass doors of the Big 5 Sporting Goods Store to do some shopping.

First, he bought himself a hunting license and received a booklet on the rules and regulations for small game hunting. Twenty bucks for that. Then he fixed himself up with a hunting wardrobe. Green camouflage pants and shirt. Florescent orange vest and cap. Another $120 bucks. Good thing he had filled his pockets with hundred dollar bills.

Next, he handled and inspected some shotguns. Double barrel, side by side, over and under. The cheapest one was a Remington 12 gauge. What the hell, he wasn't planning to use it, but bought a box of shells, just in case. Next, he searched through a large selection of rope before settling on a 20-foot length of mixed filament that should do the job. He added the largest battery-powered lamp he could find to his shopping cart. Finally, he browsed through a series of hunting knives with price tags up to two-hundred dollars before settling on a

Special Forces Survival knife with a seven inch stainless steel blade, cheesy black plastic handle and case for $24.95. If needed, it was enough knife to do the job.

Before checking out, he pulled three ski masks with chris-crossing patterns from a shelf and carried them to a full-length mirror to try them on. They were uncomfortable and scratchy. The hell with it. There was no reason to hide his face. A dead man can't testify, anyway.

Chapter 34

John Lapp steered his Ford Ranger past the gas pumps and stopped next to Roy Brubaker's trailer. For someone who was in such a hurry to get out of town it appeared he was still here. But where? Hoffman's? It was probably open on Saturday afternoons for football games on TV and maybe hockey, which was popular in these parts. He could drive by and look for Roy's flashy red truck. Another idea might be to go by Donna Trautman's house. Does she know he's leaving? Maybe she had a picture of Roy with his old truck that Amos could identify. It was probably too much to ask for.

Still upset over the lack of a search warrant, he was sorely tempted to shut off the engine, go around the back of the silver Airstream, smash in the window and climb inside. He also knew, even if he found the gym bag and the money, that it would be inadmissible in court. He could put out an APB on Brubaker and his vehicle. But without legal cause, he'd be asking for a reprimand.

Roy Brubaker, cruising down Route 30, sang, "A hunting we will go, a hunting we will go, heigh ho, the merry-o, a hunting we will go." He had second thoughts about going home to change. He pulled into a Texaco station, filled the truck with gas, and borrowed the key to the rest room. Being careful to avoid the wet, possibly piss—slick floor, he changed into his hunting shirt, pants, vest, and cap before returning the key to the teen-aged girl behind the counter with a verbal thanks and a cute wink.

Then, he was off again.

He drove past the lane to the Stoltzfus farm and saw the pole with the No Trespassing sign that blocked its entrance. That didn't bother him. He had no intention of driving right up there. He continued on to the patch of woods where, just as had done previously, he pulled out his binoculars to scope out the activity there. Too many Amish would spoil his plan. He smiled at the distant laughter of three children who were chasing each other around the windmill that stood near the farmhouse. They would be inside having supper by the time he got there.

Ten minutes later, he pulled up next to a big black dumpster at the far end of the Dairy Queen parking lot. It was 4:30 and he figured he had a half an hour of daylight for hunting rabbits and pheasants. The empty cornfield next to the Holiday Inn ran up to the Stoltzfus barn. No signs were posted against hunting. He grabbed the shotgun from behind the front seats, cradled it over his arm and waited for the traffic on Route 30 to clear before proceeding to a single barbed wire strand that separated the field from the road.

John Lapp slowed and stopped his truck in front of Hoffman's Bar. No sign of Roy's red truck. Inside, the bar stools were occupied by eight men of various ages and sizes. All but two wore orange fluorescent hunting vests. The tables and booths were unoccupied and there was no sign of Donna. Lapp approached John Hoffman and was told that Donna's shift started at 6:00. An hour-and-a-half from now.

At Donna Troutman's duplex, a red-haired boy of twelve, chewing on a soft pretzel that was smeared with mustard, answered the door. Lapp asked to see his mother and when asked who he was, said, "tell her John Lapp is here."

The boy didn't have to repeat his words because Donna appeared at the door. Her hair was turban wrapped in a pink towel and her curious expression said she wasn't particularly glad to see him.

"I have a few questions to ask you. It won't take long."

Donna backed away as Lapp pulled open the storm door, stepped inside and was met by the loud blaring of an MTV music video. "Randy, turn that damn thing down or better yet turn it off for a few minutes. Why don't you go out back and take the wash off the line like you're supposed to before it gets dark."

"Who's he anyway?" Randy asked.

"A friend. Do what I tell you."

Randy, his shoe laces untied and dragging on the rug, grumbled and shuffled out of the room.

"I'm trying to find Roy," Lapp said. "He's not at his trailer. Any idea where he might be?"

"I have no notion. Why? You still after him for that Amish man?" She reached for a pack of cigarettes, tapped one out, put it between her lips and lit it with a red Zippo lighter. She hadn't smoked on his last visit. Maybe she had a reason to start.

"I'm not after him. I just want to make sure he doesn't leave town."

"Why would he do that?" She turned her head to keep the smoke from blowing in his direction.

"Didn't he tell you? He's hitching up his trailer and moving west. He said something about Las Vegas."

"He's just shittin' you. He never said nothing about that to me."

"I got the impression he didn't want you to know."

"When did you hear this?"

"Yesterday. He was all hitched up and ready to go, but I saw his license tag on the trailer had expired and that if he drove off with it and got caught, he'd be in for a hefty fine. He seemed very upset about the delay."

Donna's face flashed from surprise to anger. "I still think he's yanking your chain."

"I hope you're right. But what I really need from you now is a picture."

"Of Roy?"

"Of Roy and his truck. His old truck. The one he traded in for that expensive, flashy new model. You ever stop to think about where he got the money for it?"

"He sold his garage."

"That's right and you know how much he cleared after mortgages and liens?" Lapp didn't wait for her to answer. "Forty-eight hundred dollars. You know how much that truck cost? Twenty-eight thousand dollars. Now where do you think he got the money?"

Donna's face pinched tight with shock.

Lapp pressed on, "if you have a picture of Roy's old truck it would help."

"What's his old truck got to do with anything?" Even though it was only half gone, she stubbed the cigarette out in a grey plastic ashtray and immediately lit another.

"There was a witness to Jacob's murder. He can't identify the killer, but he says he can identify the truck he was driving."

Donna moved to the lamp table next to the easy chair and pulled out the drawer. While she dealt through a handful of photos, she asked, "why don't you just go to the Ford dealer and take a picture, or better yet, what do you call it, confiscate it."

"Because it was sent to the junk yard and has been crushed."

Donna held up a picture and extended to Lapp. "This is the best I got."

Lapp took the four x six inch photo and smiled. There it was. Roy and a boy, probably Donna's other son, in glorious color standing next to the truck.

"Roy didn't really kill Jacob, did he? He couldn't be that stupid."

"There's a lot of evidence that says he did."

"But he was in the bar at the time Jacob was killed. That's already been established."

"Jacob's watch was set a half-hour ahead because the Amish want to be out of step with the rest of the world. Roy's alibi is shot. This picture may be the rope I need to hang him."

Donna plopped down in the chair and choked, "holy shit!"

The boy came through the kitchen arch back into the living room and saw his mother slapping her forehead with the open palm of her hand as if that would knock out the guilt she was feeling.

"Mom?" He turned to Lapp. "What have you done to my Mom?"

"Nothing, son. She's just had some bad news. I'll be going now." Lapp pushed through the glass storm door and, walking down the steps, examined the photo at eye level, and said out loud, "You're dead meat, Roy."

Chapter 35

With the falling sun at his back, Roy Brubaker walked the stubbled corn and hayfields on the western side of the Stoltzfus farm, keeping a legal distance for hunters from the house and barn. He never fired a shot, never saw any game except for Amos whom he spotted walking from the house to the barn to begin his evening chores. Amos shaded his eyes and stared in his direction for a few moments, but turned away, unable to recognize the hunter from that distance.

Back in the cab of his truck with the V-8 engine running, he welcomed the hot air streaming from the heater vents. The shotgun had been safely tucked behind the front seats. In another fifteen minutes it would be dark.

John Lapp was feeling sky-high hoping that Amos could identify both Roy and the truck. But first, he had to see that Roy didn't skip town. In order to do that he had to find him. He drove by the garage and trailer. No sign of the truck or of Roy. A call to Moyer told him their search warrant was sitting on a judge's desk waiting for the next adjournment.

He tried Hoffman's bar again. No truck in the parking lot. Inside, John Hoffman's answer to, "have you seen Roy," was still no. "But there was a pretty colored woman here looking for you."

"How long ago?"

"Twenty, thirty minutes. She's a reporter. Left her card. Wants you to call her."

He dealt her card onto the bar. Lapp picked it up. "You can use the phone behind the bar."

"Thanks." He reached her on her cell phone.

"Where are you?" She asked urgently.

"Hoffman's."

"Stay there. I have something to show you. I'll be there in fifteen minutes ... or less."

Roy figured that death by hanging was the perfect way to get rid of Amos. It would look like suicide. The Amish would be so ashamed of a suicide, they'd refuse to cooperate with the police and the police would finally accept the suicide as Amos' admission of guilt over his brother's death. Signed and sealed. Case closed.

At 5:15 p.m., he tore the plastic wrapping from his package of rope, and pulled out a three-foot length. Pressing the electric seat control button, he pushed the front seat back as far as it would go in order to use his legs as a table. Taking the rope, he formed a 12-inch diameter loop, brought the end up another 12 inches, dropped down to the loop again and began to wrap. Two or three turns would probably do the trick, but he wanted it to look like a real hangman's noose, so he finished off with nine wraps, one for every life Amos was going to wish he had. It wasn't as easy as he had expected and he cursed when he had to start over. He should have practiced at home. Testing the noose by sliding the full end down, Roy congratulated himself. It would do the job.

Now, how to carry it. He unzipped his camouflage pants and pushed the loop end down the front, then tucked the bundle end into his belt. It was practical, comfortable, and, when he closed his bulky jacket, impossible to see.

Another time check. 5:30. Milking would be finishing up. It was time to go. He pulled the seven-inch Smith & Wesson .40 semi-automatic handgun from the glove compartment. He'd kept this baby hidden beneath the counter in the gas station office in case anybody tried to rob him. He checked the 10 rounds in the clip and the safety, then tucked it into his belt. Leaving his truck, he pressed the automatic key lock, and crossed the road.

His boots crushed the corn stalk stubble as he cut across the slightly mounded rows.

Choosing to forgo the use of his battery-powered lamp, he made his way slowly across the field. The soil was sticky wet but not muddy. The quarter-moon that was expected had not yet made an appearance, but the dimly glowing yellow lights coming from the farmhouse served as a beacon. The air was cold but, thankfully, there was no rain. He held out his left hand and admired the tight fitting leather kid gloves that had been added to his wardrobe at the last minute. There would be no rope burns wearing these babies.

A barking dog stopped Brubaker in his tracks. By not moving, he hoped the dog would stop. But instead, the barking became more incessant, causing a woman's voice to yell, "Queenie! Ruick!" Suddenly, the dog, a small collie, was next to him, jumping against his legs and barking. Brubaker smiled because he had expected a dog and was prepared. He pulled off his left glove, reached into his jacket side pocket and pulled out a bag of McDonald's French fries. He spread them on the ground in a six-foot arc like chicken feed, making the dog sniff out each one. That should take care of the dog for awhile. He picked up his pace toward the cow barn. If Amos was alone inside, as expected, it would be almost be too perfect.

Lapp was finishing his draft Lowenbrau at the bar and trying to decide if he should have another when Donna arrived for work. Their eyes met but she turned away before he could speak. Standing at the far end of the bar, she busily wiped down a tray full of salt and pepper shakers and spoke to John Hoffman in a low voice. Lapp assumed that what she had to say was not complimentary.

He slid off his bar stool and strolled toward Donna. "Have you heard from Roy?"

"No, have you?" Donna snapped back before walking away. Hoffman shrugged, indicating he couldn't explain her attitude, then nodded toward the door, "you got company."

Lapp met Lisa Robinson halfway, took her by the elbow of her long black wool coat and guided her to an empty booth. They slid in on opposite sides.

"I was at the jail when Amos was released," she said urgently. "Where were you?" Her lowered voice was just above a whisper.

Lapp responded with a similar tone. "I got called in for special duty directing traffic for the Governor over at the new post office," Lapp grumbled.

"You should have been at the jail." She propped her elbows on the table and leaned in with her head.

Lapp responded with a similar pose. "I wanted to be. But I couldn't help it. By the way, Amos is at home and he's fine."

"I'm glad to hear it. He wasn't looking so good when he left the jail."

"I'm not surprised."

"What I wanted to tell you was there was this weird guy hanging around who claimed he was there to meet a buddy who was being released. He went into the waiting room and stayed there. When Amos left, the guy left too, in a hurry. I took a picture of him."

Lapp noticed that both Hoffman, from behind the bar, and Donna, next to a table she was serving, were watching intently.

Lisa Robinson pulled a large black leather handbag from her shoulder, reached inside and pulled out a manila folder. "Do you know him?" She dropped a 5x7 color print on the table.

Lapp's face dropped.

Lisa responded to his alarm. "You know that guy? Who is he?"

He continued to stare at the picture as he said the name, "Roy Brubaker."

She reacted to the startled expression on his face. "What's the matter? Who's Roy Brubaker?"

John Lapp shoved the picture back at Lisa and slid out of the booth. He mumbled, "Roy has figured it out. Damn it, I should have thought further ahead." Before Lisa could slide out of the booth, Lapp was halfway through the outside door.

She caught him as he climbed into his truck. "Tell me. Who is he? What's going on?"

"He's our killer. And now he's stalking Amos."

"Take me with you."

"I can't do that. It's against regulations." Lapp said, surprised she would even ask.

"You're not on official duty," she protested.

"All the more reason," Lapp shot back.

The engine roared to life. She grabbed the door handle, keeping him from closing it.

"This is my story."

Lapp ripped the door from her hand and pulled it shut.

"Thanks a lot," Lisa Robinson said even though Lapp couldn't hear her. Seeing her frustration, he rolled down the window. "You know where the Exxon station is on 340? That's Roy Brubaker's garage. His silver Airstream house trailer is next to it. I'm convinced that's where the money is. And that's where this whole thing will eventually end up. Then you'll have your story." He threw the automatic gears into drive, ripped away, and immediately regretted having told her about Roy's garage. Was it her reward for tipping him off about Roy? If so, he prayed it wouldn't backfire.

Roy Brubaker figured the hum of the propane generator that provided the light for the milking area was just loud enough to cover any noisy missteps he might make as he edged up to the high, narrow paned glass windows. Peering inside, it was just as he had hoped. Amos, looking to him like a little bearded worm, was pushing a broom through the stray straw on the floor into a neat pile. And, right above Amos was another part of the plan. A perfect hand-hewn, 8 x 8 inch open wood beam.

Amos leaned the broom against the wall, and, ready to leave the barn, took out a cigarette and lit it. He used the same match to light a kerosene lantern. When the flame was high enough to provide the necessary light, he hit a latch switch that slowed the hum of the generator. The overhead lights began to fade.

Brubaker waited as Amos stepped though the side door then greeted him by pressing the handgun to his left temple.

"That's a gun you feel, Amos," he snarled with a gruff tone. "A gun that can blow your brains out if you make any noise. Now let's go back inside where it's nice and warm."

Amos shrieked with fear.

Brubaker shoved Amos back inside and slammed the door. "Give me that lantern. We need to talk about what you saw that night at the gas station. You saw me there, didn't you?" Roy held the lantern to the side of his face, giving it a devilish glow.

Amos Stoltzfus trembled with fear. He stuttered, "I didn't see nothing. I didn't know who it was."

Roy poked the lantern at Amos' face. "You're lying Amos. You're not supposed to lie. It's against your religion."

"I'm not lying," Amos repeated in a pleading voice.

"You gave yourself away this morning at the jail. You recognized me. You knew it was me."

Amos shook his head violently in denial.

Roy shoved Amos into the feed storage room next to the stalls. Through the door-less arch, the black and white cows chewed and crunched noisily on the fresh hay.

"Nice cozy place you got here, Amos."

Brubaker set the lantern on the cement floor.

"You see that bale of hay over there? Pull it over here," Brubaker ordered as he stood directly beneath the overhead beam. Amos, confused, stood frozen.

"What are you, dim?" Roy poked the gun against Amos' chest and repeated the order. "I guess you are dim."

Amos grabbed the straw bale by the twine strings, and, grunting from the weight, pulled it to Roy's feet.

The yellow light from the floor lantern beamed up and created an eerie halo over the two men. "Sit down on the hay, Amos. Put your hands behind your back." Roy's hand pushed Amos down. He pulled the pre-cut three-foot length of clothesline from his pocket. He set the gun down, grabbed Amos' arms, first one, then the other, twisted them behind him and wrapped his wrists. You don't commit suicide with your hands tied, so Brubaker was careful not to tie it too tight so as to leave marks after the rope was removed. Brubaker pulled his hunting knife from the sheath laced through his belt and cut off the excess line.

"You like my new knife?"

Amos jerked his head away.

Brubaker taunted, "It's called a Special Forces knife, the kind they use on sneak attacks. If you don't behave and do what I tell you, I can cut your throat like you were a lamb being slaughtered. You know all about butchering, don't you? You butcher your own meat. Your sheep, your hogs, your chickens. Don't you?"

Brubaker resheathed his knife. He pulled the rope from his pants waist, unraveled the length, tossed the loose end over the low beam and tied it loosely to a railroad spike imbedded in the rough-hewn support post.

"You are one ugly little man. You know that, Amos? But I'm not going to shoot you or cut you, Amos. We're going to have a little necktie party." Brubaker sneered as he opened the noose. "It's your fault, anyway, isn't it Amos? If I had known you were there at the gas station, I would have chickened out and your brother would be alive today. You know that don't you, Amos?"

Amos' eyes rose and studied the words from his attacker's lips. His rigid face slowly nodded, yes. Brubaker couldn't tell if he believed him or was nodding out of stupidity. Either way, it didn't matter. "And since you did nothing to save your brother, you're guilty of his death and don't deserve to live. Ain't that so?"

Amos eyes widened as the noose was dangled and swung like a pendulum in front of him. He jumped to his feet and tried to run, but Brubaker's strong hand shoved him back down on the bale.

"So I'm going to help you," Brubaker continued in his child lecturing voice. "So that you won't feel guilty anymore. You'll be with your brother in Heaven. Isn't that where you want to go?"

Brubaker slipped the rope over Amos' head and yanked the noose tight around his neck.

"Stand up on that bale, Amos."

Amos frantically shook his head.

The heat generated by the cows in their stalls plus his rising agitation caused Brubaker to break into a sweat. "Do what I say, Amos. Or I'll just shoot you."

Shaking his head like an angry child, Amos refused to budge.

"Do it," Brubaker screamed, "you fucking little bastard." He grabbed Amos by the arm and yanked him to his feet. "Get up there like I told you."

Amos shouted, "Nay!"

"Shut your mouth, Amos. You hear? All right then. We'll do this the hard way."

Roy loosened the end from the coat spike and pulled the rope until it was taut. Then he yanked with all his might and lifted Amos by the neck until his feet were off the ground before retying the end to the spike.

Amos tried to yell, but his windpipe was being shut off. His feet flailed in the air.

A calling, inquisitive voice interrupted.

"Amos. Supper is getting cold." Sallie, carrying a kerosene lantern entered the grain room and immediately saw Amos dangling. Her single scream of horror reverberated throughout the dairy.

John Lapp blasted through the pole that extended across the entrance to the lane. With rear wheels spinning, he sped up the lane, pulled his truck up to the house, jumped out and ran to the kitchen door. He knocked before bursting into the room. The children, at the kitchen table with their open books in front of them, jumped up and the little girl shrieked.

"Don't be afraid. Where's your Momma? I must talk to her."

The children responded quickly, almost in unison. "She's at the barn telling Amos to come eat his supper."

Lapp collected his bearings and ran toward the barn.

"Who are you?" Sallie demanded from Brubaker. She quickly set her lantern down, pushed her cloak away from her arms and grabbed Amos' flailing legs, attempting to steady him. Shocked by Amos' red face, she shouted angrily at Brubaker. "You're hurting him. Let him down!"

"Fuck, lady," Brubaker muttered. "You're spoiling everything."

Sallie ducked beneath Amos' legs and stood up, her shoulders providing support. She wobbled beneath his weight.

Brubaker, flustered, couldn't decide what to do. There goes the suicide idea out the door. He'll have to kill them both.

"Loosen that rope. Let him down," Sallie ordered, gasping for breath.

"I can't do that, lady. It's gone too far." Brubaker pulled out his gun. This will be the easiest way."

The outside door opened and Lapp burst inside.

Brubaker reacted, pointing the Smith & Wesson at Lapp's chest. "Jesus H. Christ. Not you, too."

It took a moment for Lapp to comprehend the scene.

"Back off. Or you're dead right now."

Lapp ignored the order, stepped to the coat peg, pulled at the knot and loosened the rope allowing Amos to collapse on top of Sallie.

Sallie, flashing anger at Brubaker, cradled Amos in her arms.

Lapp took two steps toward Roy Brubaker before being stopped by the click of the gun safety being released.

"Get those hands up high and keep'em there," Brubaker ordered. "For all I know, you just might be carrying some little off-duty number in that coat pocket. If you are, the smartest thing you could do would be to drop it on the ground."

"I'm not armed," Lapp responded, raising his arms and hands, palms out, above his head.

Brubaker, flustered and frustrated, shook his head sadly. "All I wanted was the money. I never would have killed Jacob if he hadn't recognized me. And the same for this idiot here," he said, jerking his head at Amos. "I wouldn't be here if he hadn't seen me."

Amos pulled away from Sallie and stood up. Sallie rose and placed her arm protectively around his shoulder. Amos pulled away. Sallie addressed Roy Brubaker. "We will pray for you."

"Oh you will, huh," Brubaker snapped back with sarcasm. "How nice of you. I think you'd better pray for yourself and the idiot. Oh, and let's not forget your hero here," he said, jerking his head at Lapp.

An unearthly guttural groan rose from Amos' throat. At peak pitch, head down, he threw himself full-force into the gunman. Brubaker grunted in surprise as the gun flew from his hand and clattered on the concrete floor. Brubaker grabbed Amos' arms and tossed him aside like a rag doll. Before Lapp could grab the gun, the blade of Brubaker's hunting knife flashed in the light.

"Take one step toward that gun and your guts are gonna feel this knife," Brubaker snarled.

While Brubaker turned his attention to finding his gun on the straw-covered cement, Lapp quickly shoved Sallie and Amos down the row of cows.

Amos ducked behind the third cow. Lapp whispered at Amos to "come on," but Amos remained frozen next to the cow. Lapp pushed Sallie toward the end of the tunnel-like barn.

"There's no door out this way," Sallie warned with a harsh whisper. "Just a big ventilator."

They ducked behind a cow halfway to the end of the barn and looked back. Roy stood in the entryway, waving the gun. "It's hunting season," he taunted. "Here I come." A few steps later, he called with a peek-a-boo voice, "here's one. Amos, I see you." Brubaker slowly stepped behind the cow and leaned down to look for Amos. He raised his gun and was lined up to shoot the cowering Amos when suddenly he reacted to a stunning, painful blow to his leg. "Son of a bitch. What the hell?" The cow had aimed a perfect left back leg at Brubaker. "Jesus Christ!" He hopped back to avoid the second kick.

Lapp and Sallie exchanged approving glances as Brubaker stood clear of the cow, rubbed his leg, winced and hopped in pain.

"That's number eight. She's a kicker. Amos knew that," Sallie whispered.

"Stay here. I'm going around the other side."

Sallie grabbed his arm. "Wait."

Lapp and Sallie watched while Brubaker weighed his next move. To their surprise he turned and limped back into the feed room. They heard the crash of glass, followed, moments later, by a wave of smoke that rose and was blown further into the stable by a draft from an open door.

They heard the slam of a door. "Is he gone?" Sallie asked.

"Be careful. He may be waiting." Seconds later. "We've got to get out of here."

He grabbed Sallie's hand and pulled her cautiously down the row of cows, toward the rising black clouds. The cows, aware of the smoke and burning smell, began shuffling and snorting.

"Amos!" Sallie called. Almost like an apparition, Amos appeared at their side. In the feed room, the scattered flames, fed by the fingers of spilled kerosene, spread across the straw-littered floor.

Lapp, ran to the door, fully aware that Brubaker could be waiting outside to pick them off. He squeezed the door latch and pushed. It was propped shut from the outside. Lapp slammed his shoulder against the door. It wouldn't budge.

Sallie, moving quickly, grabbed a bucket of oats and spread them on the flames. Lapp stamped out small patches of fire. "We've got to keep it from spreading," Lapp yelled. The cows' bellowing became louder and more pathetic.

The bale of straw which was to have been Amos' execution platform burst into bright orange flames. Lapp, Sallie and Amos backed away and shielded their faces from the intense heat. Flames crawled toward the stalls.

Sallie yelled, "Amos. The fire extinguisher? Wo ist es?"

Amos, confused at first, edged along a low field of flames and through the stable arch.

He returned holding a red canister fire extinguisher.

Lapp grabbed it, and with experienced hands, sprayed the burning hay bale, then the area toward the stables, and finally, extinguished the flames by the door. White smoke filled the room and attacked their throats. Holding their hands over their noses and mouths was not enough to stymie the coughs. The smoke swirled to the ceiling. The fire was out.

Amos rushed into the stalls to quiet the cows by patting their rumps and talking to them by number. John Lapp approached Sallie Stoltzfus and wrapped his arms around her. She did not resist.

The moment was broken by the crack of one, two, then three shots. She pushed back and screamed, "the children!"

Chapter 36

John Lapp pulled back and forth on the door latch of the outside door trying to shake loose whatever was holding it shut. Suddenly it opened. Ten-year-old Samuel, burst in.

"The door was propped shut with a two by four." He added proudly, "I kicked it away," before being swallowed up in Sallie's arms.

"Are Lydia and David all right?" she asked, her voice choked with fear.

"I made them hide upstairs," the boy said, his voice muffled by the black apron.

He turned to Lapp. "The man shot your machine."

Sallie and Lapp exchanged glances of relief.

"Which way did the man go? Did you see where he went?" Lapp asked urgently.

"Ja, he went across the corn field. It goes to the highway."

Lapp made a quick survey of the area to make sure the fire was out, then ran outside.

Jolted by the cold air, he raced toward the truck with Queenie nipping at his heels. The dim light of the quarter moon revealed front tires flat to the rims. Inside the truck, the keys were missing from the ignition and the speedometer had taken a bullet right on the 50 miles per hour indicator.

Lapp slammed the door in anger. Sallie, Samuel and Amos ran up, puffing. "He killed your machine," Samuel said, pointing to the tires.

"Forget the truck," Lapp said, breathless. "How do I catch up with Brubaker? I need to contact the State Police, but you have no phone and no motorized transportation. I've got to get back to the highway." He thought about running down the lane to the road to hitch a ride, but chances of a car passing by at night were slim.

Sallie spun Amos around and pulled away the rope wrapped around his wrists. "Amos, get up to the house," Sallie ordered. "Put some of that horse salve on your neck. It's scraped up pretty bad." As an afterthought, she yelled, "or try the bag balm. And see that David and Lydia are all right."

Amos touched the bright red rope scrapes around his neck, nodded his head and did as he was told.

"Can I borrow a horse, quick?" Lapp asked.

"A horse?"

"And a buggy," Lapp added, knowing that Amish did not have riding horses and if he tried to ride one, he'd probably fall off and break his neck.

Sallie picked up on the urgency. "Samuel, fetch Blackie and bring him to the shed. We'll hitch up Papa's buggy."

The dog sensed the excitement and began barking. Sallie yelled, "Queenie, ruick," as they moved quickly to a shed where Sallie threw open the left side of the double door and pointed to Lapp to grab a wagon trace. They pulled the buggy outside.

Samuel ran toward them, leading the gleaming black standard bred horse who was already outfitted with bit, bridle and horse collar. Lapp grabbed the oiled, black leather harness from the buggy seat, and, as though he had never been away, worked with Samuel and Sallie to complete the job by attaching the trace.

"You'd be better if Blackie had blinders." Sallie smiled with pride over the efficiency of the three working together. Within two minutes the process was complete.

Making sure Samuel could not hear him, he ordered, "Sallie, get me Amos' 22 rifle. Quick."

"I don't know where he keeps it. Some place away from the children. The bible says ..."

"That bastard tried to kill us, Sallie. I could use a little help."

Surprised at his anger and words, she capitulated. "I'll try to find it."

"Never mind. There's no time."

Lapp jumped onto the buggy bench and grabbed the reins that Sallie handed through the open front window. "If you can get to a phone, call 911 and tell them to send the State Police to the EXXON station on 340. Use my name. Say it's an emergency."

Sallie reached through the door and switched on the battery powered side lights. "Can you still do this, Johnny?" She asked, with some trepidation.

"I'll remember once I get started. Don't worry. Go take care of Amos." John Lapp snapped the reins and yelled, "giddup". Blackie reacted immediately, jerking him forward.

The gelding picked his footing until the buggy wheels were comfortably in the wheel tracks of the rutted lane.

Seated on the bench of the boxlike carriage for the first time in 15 years, John Lapp's shoulders relaxed as he became more comfortable. When they reached the road, Lapp loosened the reins. Blackie was raring to go.

For the first five minutes, the fast, rhythmic clopping of hooves and horse-shoes on the macadam road were exhilarating.

At the corner of Route 30, he watched the heavy traffic, made up mostly of 18-wheel tractor-trailer trucks, roar by. He had no choice. Route 30 would take him to Soudersburg, where he could use a small two-lane road that was more direct to Roy's garage.

Even with the highway's wide shoulders, built to accommodate horse drawn transportation, Lapp felt like he was entering the Indianapolis 500 race driving a go-cart.

Edging onto the right shoulder, he snapped the reins and Blackie took off, quickly settling into a fast pace. Lapp squinted through the blinding glare of the steady steam of headlights as he fought to keep Blackie to the right, away from the traffic lanes. The motor and tire noise was deafening.

For two miles, each heavy truck that passed the horse and buggy created strong side and back drafts that rocked the buggy down to its suspension springs. Lapp gripped the reins and hoped Blackie was more confident and secure about being there than he was. He was almost beginning to trust the beautiful black horse when a strong side draft pulled Blackie and the buggy to the left into the right lane of traffic. Lapp fought to pull him back to the shoulder as a truck's deafening air horn blast rang through his ears. Involuntarily, Lapp shouted "Jesus Christ". His heart pounded and his arms shook as Blackie settled back into his pace.

Lapp's pulse finally stopped pounding when he turned the horse and buggy right onto the quiet, two-lane, Soudersburg Road.

Roy Brubaker pushed the speedometer to 70 mph on Soudersburg Road. In ten minutes he'd be back at the trailer, hitched up and ready to get the hell out of there. The pain in his shinbone was excruciating. That goddamn cow had pushed him over the edge. Otherwise, he would have finished off that idiot Amos, the woman, and that pain-in-the-ass cop. With any luck that damn barn burned down to the ground, and everything inside was nothing but uni-dentifiable bones and ashes.

His developing plan called for getting out of Pennsylvania and the jurisdiction of the State Police by crossing over into Maryland just below Gettysburg. An hour, maybe less from here. He could be free. The cops still had nothing on him.

Roy Brubaker was feeling quite smug when two shining eyes from the center of the dark road reflected back from his headlights. By the time he could react to the full-sized white-tailed doe, frozen in the light, it was too late. He hit the anti-lock brakes and gripped the steering wheel tight. Without the restraint of seat belts, which he defiantly refused to wear, the impact of the crash slammed him chest-first into the steering wheel.

Even though Blackie was pulling the buggy along at a fast pace, Lapp worried that he would not get to Roy's garage in time to stop him from leaving. He had been so wrapped up in his and Blackie's survival on Route 30 he hadn't stopped at one of the hotels or homes along the road and called the barracks for help.

His eyes searched for a public telephone or even the sign of telephone lines leading down the lane of the farms that were spaced out along the road. Nothing. His best chance of catching Roy was to keep going.

Roy Brubaker's left leg buckled as he stumbled out of his truck . He grabbed his rib cage and winced in pain from the impact of the steering wheel and the damage to the front end of his new truck. Goddamn grill was all smashed in. He couldn't see any water on the road from a damaged radiator, so it appeared to be drivable. Goddamn it! My beautiful new truck!

The brown deer with white markings had staggered a dozen feet ahead before collapsing. Flooded by the headlights, the animal's two-toed hooves thrashed in the air as it attempted to roll over into a kneeling position and regain its feet. The antler-less doe's ribs and belly heaved desperate breaths and blood oozed out of the side of her mouth. Roy was thankful that her big brown eyes were glazed, rather than staring accusingly at him. There was not enough room on the narrow road to drive around her, so he had to end her misery. He debated over whether to use the shotgun, but decided it would be too noisy. Holding the .40 handgun in his right hand, he aimed between her eye and ear and pulled the trigger. The doe's head bounced up then fell back. Her legs continued to twitch. He aimed again, this time at the white diamond on the doe's head. That did it. He stuck the handgun back into his belt, grabbed the deer by the hind legs and, cursing that the damned thing weighed a ton, strained and pulled her into a shallow gutter by the side of the road. His ribs and his leg hurt like hell as he wiped his hands on his pants and wondered if the doe had any kind of ticks or disease. A little late to worry about that now.

He reassessed the damage to the front end of his truck and shook his head in anguish. It was insured, but he had a $1,000 deductible. "Always fucking something going wrong. The story of my miserable life." Climbing into the driver's seat, he heard the all-too-familiar clop-clopping hooves of a fast moving horse followed by the clatter of the iron-belted wheels of a buggy on the macadam road. Jesus! Not another Amish man. He twisted the ignition key. The engine turned over but wouldn't start. Now what the hell was wrong? He tried again, stopped, and pressed the pedal to the floor until the engine roared to life.

John Lapp saw the tail lights of a vehicle ahead and wondered why it was stopped here on this lonely two-lane road. The red beacons, four feet above the road were judged to be either from a truck or an SUV. There was room to pass on the left, so he did not rein in Blackie's quick-stepping pace. From twenty feet away, he saw the fire engine red truck. It was too late to stop.

Roy Brubaker waited until the horse and buggy passed on his left side. Instead of the hat and beard of an Amish man or the black bonnet of an Amish woman holding the reins, he saw a man in a plaid wool shirt. It was that damned State Trooper!

John Lapp reacted to Roy Brubaker's surprised face by cracking the reins across Blackie's rump to drive the horse even harder.

The engine caught. Intent on taking care of that damn cop once and for all, Roy Brubaker shoved the automatic transmission into drive. The big tires screeched as he tore after the buggy.

John Lapp looked into his side view mirror and saw the truck bearing down on him.

There was no place to go!

Roy Brubaker aimed the bashed in front end his truck at the reflective triangle on the back of the buggy. He smashed into the back wheels that extended behind the buggy box, then backed off to assess the damage. The buggy was still moving, but the triangle was knocked cockeyed and the back wheels and axle were bent beneath the carriage. The right wheel no longer turned but was being dragged and the iron rim was throwing off sparks "One more time," Roy said aloud, "ought to take care of it." He aimed the right chrome bumper at the left rear wheel this time, ripping it from the axle. Ten yards ahead, he slammed on the brakes and jumped out of the truck. The horse kicked and dragged the three-wheeled buggy a few feet further, then gave up. Roy grabbed his lantern, switched it on, pulled the handgun from his belt and walked cautiously toward the still shining battery-powered lights on each side of the buggy. He gave a wide berth to the wild-eyed black horse, skittish and nervous, jumping and kicking, trying to free himself from the trace.

He was ready just in case the cop tried to jump him but he fully expected to find him slumped inside, gravely injured or dead. He shone the light through the open left side of the windshield and could see nothing but his own reflection. He flashed up, down and sideways.

The inside was empty! That goddamn cop has nine lives! Roy ran around the back and waved the light back and forth across a field of knee-high wheat. No sign of him. He was in there someplace. But where?

The urgency of getting to his trailer, hitching up and getting the hell out of there cut short his desire to flush out the missing cop and finish him off once and for all. He paused briefly by the horse and considered putting a bullet in its brain so that he couldn't be followed, but decided against it. That smashed-up buggy wasn't going anywhere.

The smooth engine of Roy's new truck revved up, the tires screeched, and then it could no longer be heard. Except for the shuffling of Blackie's restless hooves, the area was dead quiet. Gathering strength, Lapp turned his face and lifted his head high enough to scan the area for any sign of movement. Satisfied that Roy was gone, he collapsed back into the dirt.

With considerably more effort, he pushed his body up and rested on his knees. A sharp pain shot through the kidney area of his lower back and a burning sensation troubled his left shoulder. His fingers traced a trickle of sticky liquid from above his left eyebrow. A sniff of his fingertips confirmed it was blood. He wiped the residue on his pants, brushed the caked dirt from his shirt, and struggled to his feet.

Slightly dazed, he stumbled through the wheat field shoots to the macadam road.

There was little hope of a passing vehicle on the two-lane country road.

At first it sounded like the rumble of distant thunder. Then he recognized the measured hoof beats of a high stepping horse and the rumble of buggy wheels. The orbs of light beaming from the buggy's side lights became clearer and brighter.

Lapp stepped to the middle of the road and waved his arms. The horse was reined in and the buggy came to a stop. Lapp moved to the side door and pulled on the handle.

"Johnny? Are you all right?" Sallie's voice was high-pitched with excitement.

Lapp's eyes widened with disbelief. "Sallie. What are you doing here? How did you find me?"

Sallie Stoltzfus jumped out of the buggy and dabbed at his bruised forehead with a handkerchief. "You're bleeding. What happened here?"

"Roy and I got into a demolition derby. His truck won"

"I went next door like you told me to use the phone, but nobody was home. So I decided to chase after you." She wiped loose dirt from his chin.

"It's a miracle. How did you know where I'd be?"

"You told me already back at the house where you were going."

Lapp was enjoying the tender pats on his forehead, but decided he'd better get back to stopping Roy Brubaker.

Sallie read his face. "Get in. I'll drive. We'll find a place where you can call the police."

Lapp responded with a mock tone. "Sallie, I am the police."

"I know. But it's still hard for me to think of you that way."

Sallie cracked the reins and the buggy jerked forward.

Roy Brubaker pulled his red truck into the gravel driveway, swung around, and backed up to the coupler on his trailer. He jumped out of the truck cab to check the alignment when he noticed a Ford Taurus parked at his far-right gas pump. Who the hell is that and what are they doing here? Kids making out? He was tempted to roust them out, but decided getting the trailer hitched and getting the hell out of there was more important.

A couple of inches to the right and he'd be lined up. But a second attempt was still off-line. Roy swore and spit on the ground before getting into the truck and trying again.

With Sallie handling the reins and concentrating on the road ahead, John Lapp stole admiring glances at her beautiful profile. They exchanged smiles.

She spoke first. "This reminds me of those times when we would ride together. We didn't talk much, but we always knew what the other one was thinking. I feel that way just now."

"I know. It's almost unreal."

"It's real enough." Sallie breathed a long regretful sigh. "I know you're a policeman, but you shouldn't chase this man alone."

"If only I had a weapon. Some kind of equalizer."

Sallie frowned. "I don't like it. Reach around in the back of the seat."

Wearing a quizzical expression, Lapp twisted his arm behind the driver's bench and tried to ignore the painful alerts being sent from both his back and shoulder. But it was worth it. His hand found cold steel as he pulled out the .22 caliber, single shot rifle.

"Is it loaded?"

"I hope not. I found it after you left."

Lapp pulled back the single bolt action and an ejected cartridge flew onto the floor. "It was loaded."

"It shouldn't have been. That Amos is a dumkopf."

"You got any more bullets?"

"I grabbed the box. They probably slid under the bench."

Lapp grunted with pain as he groped the floor until he fished out the prize: a cubed box of bullets.

When Sallie's speeding standard bred brought them within a quarter mile of the gas station, Lapp touched her arm and said, "We're almost there. Slow him down to a walk. We don't want the noise from the buggy to alert Roy."

Lapp's head was clear and the adrenalin was pumping strength into his bruised body as the EXXON sign came into view. Strategies and options flowed through his brain. The new red truck was still there and a dim light beamed from inside the Airstream trailer.

Sallie grabbed Lapp's arm. "Johnny, don't do this by yourself."

Lapp pulled away and weighed the .22 rifle in his hands. He opened the buggy door and climbed out. "It's personal. I've got a score to settle with Roy Brubaker."

The horse, now restless, pranced noisily on the macadam road and let out a loud whinny.

The light inside the trailer was snuffed.

Lapp ordered, "get out of here, Sallie. Now!"

The strong tone of voice took Sallie by surprise. Holding back a verbal response, she pulled on the left rein, turned and walked the horse and buggy back down the road.

Lapp surveyed the scene. The truck and trailer were hitched up and ready to go. If a gunfight broke out, Lapp had no cover. Lisa Robinson was most likely sitting in the Ford Taurus parked at the gas pumps. No way he could use it for cover. The gas station garage building was beyond that and not reachable without crossing the wide open driveway. The moonlight was just enough to reveal a moving figure. The high windows in the front and back would not be big enough for a man of Roy's size to climb through.

Lapp kept his eyes locked on the side door, the only exit from the trailer.

He was startled by the sensation of a human presence next to him. "Sallie! Damn it, I told you to get out of here."

"I want to help. I'm afraid for you."

"You're not helping! You're only … shhh …" The side door of the trailer opened and Roy Brubaker stepped out. Lapp grabbed Sallie's arm and pulled her down before wiggling into a rifleman's prone position.

Roy, his face dimly lit by a burning cigarette, peered out into the darkness.

Lapp aimed his rifle at the bulky figure.

"Johnny. Don't shoot him," Sallie pleaded softly.

Lapp opted to try for surrender. He yelled, "Roy! You're surrounded and in our sights. Give yourself up. Now! Drop your weapons and step forward."

Instead, as Lapp feared he might, Roy did just the opposite. He jumped into the cab of the truck and revved up the engine. The weight of the trailer made for a slow start.

The headlights beamed brightly over Lapp and Sallie.

Lapp, from his prone position, took aim and squeezed off a shot. The bullet shattered the windshield, but the truck and trailer kept coming, steered in their direction.

Sallie, shading her eyes, screamed, "don't kill him. It's wrong to kill."

Lapp deftly reloading, responded, "someone should tell Roy that. Come on."

Lapp pulled Sallie from the ground and led her 50 feet to the right of the truck.

The truck would have to change its path to the highway in order to illuminate them.

When he judged the cover of darkness was sufficient, he remembered his Police Academy training and took a rifleman's one-knee position.

The truck stopped.

Lapp waited and listened. The truck door slammed. Lit by the taillights of the truck, Roy appeared between the trailer brace and the truck pointing a shotgun in their direction. Roy had a big edge in firepower.

Lapp took aim and squeezed off another shot. Instead of the thud of bullet hitting soft tissue there was a metal clang.

Roy responded with a blast in their direction. A hail of pellets danced on the ground around them.

Lapp, certain he was not hit, looked to Sallie. She brushed a spent pellet from her bonnet and responded, "I'm okay."

"Now will you get out of here, please!"

"No. We're together on this."

He wasn't so sure he could protect either of them. He quickly reloaded.

Roy, the lit cigarette drooping from his mouth, yelled, "how do you like that, cop? You got the missus with you? Can't do the job yourself? I got more where that came from."

Lapp trembled with anger. He took a deep breath to steady his aim and fired.

An explosion rocked the front of the trailer. His shot had hit the propane tank mounted on the tow triangle. Scattered flames engulfed the area. Lapp reloaded and charged forward in time to see Roy slapping with his hands at the sea of candle-sized flames that covered his body. He kept his rifle leveled at Roy while the killer rolled and writhed on the ground trying to snuff the flames.

"Sallie!" Before he could stop her, she pulled off her heavy wool cape and ran up to Roy, throwing it across his chest. She ignored the smelly white smoke and frantically patted down the flames.

A faint cacophony of police sirens rose in the distance. Out of the corner of his eye Lapp saw Roy's hand disappear beneath his coat. He withdrew it, gripping the handle of his Special Forces Survival knife.

Lapp reacted quickly by driving the butt of his rifle into Roy's arm with enough force to send the knife spinning from his hand. Lapp kicked it another three feet away.

Sallie had not seen the knife that was meant for her and, responding to Roy's howl of pain, chastised, "did you have to do that? This man is in pain."

Lapp shook his head and did not reply.

Roy's head flopped back in defeat.

Warren Moyer, dressed in his usual black raincoat and fedora hat, stood next to John Lapp and Sallie Stoltzfus and demanded to know what had gone on here.

Roy Brubaker, his face red from the fire flash, moaned in pain. A paramedic gave him a shot of painkiller then was joined by a second EMT who helped lift Roy onto a gurney. As they passed by Lapp, Moyer and Sallie, the second EMT handed the pock marked black wool cape to Sallie and said, "this looks like it belongs to you."

When Sallie accepted it, Lapp noticed a tremble in her hands and arms. Was the cape still hot? Before he could ask, Moyer took over. "I want to know what went on here."

Lapp responded, "how did you find us?"

"Got an urgent 911 call."

"From who?"

"A woman."

Lapp's eyes found Lisa Robinson, standing a respectable distance away, holding up her cell phone. When Moyer looked in her direction, she stepped forward.

"Who the hell are you?" Moyer demanded.

"Lisa Robinson. I'm with the Lancaster New Era." She did not acknowledge her friendship with Lapp.

"How did you get here?"

"Just following a story."

Moyer snarled. "Whatever that means. Look, Miss, you can't stay here. This is a crime scene."

"I know that. When can I get a statement?"

"When I find out what happened here. And when I'm good and ready. I want you out of here."

When Moyer turned away, Lisa exchanged an understanding smile with Lapp. She surprised Sallie by holding out her hand. Sallie nodded, but did not return the gesture.

Lisa spoke with admiration. "I want you to know I think you're very brave. I hope we can meet again sometime."

When Sallie did not respond, Lisa shrugged and backed away into the darkness.

Lapp, relieved that Lisa was gone, said,. "Lieutenant? Can we enter the trailer and look for the money?"

"I'll have one of the troopers do it. You and I are going to stay here and you're going to do some explaining. You okay? You look a little banged up."

"I was a victim of road rage."

"Explain."

"Roy Brubaker, the guy I was telling you about, was at the Stoltzfus farm trying to execute Amos to keep him quiet. Then he set the barn on fire with Amos, Sallie, and me inside."

Moyer shook his head. "I don't think I got all that, but go on."

"I chased him here in a horse and buggy."

"You drove a horse and buggy?"

"Until Roy ran me off the road, and tried to kill me. Thank God, Sallie showed up and brought me the rest of the way."

Moyer's attention was diverted by a call from a Trooper coming out of the trailer holding up the blue and white gym bag and announcing, "it's full of cash."

The anxious expression on Sallie's face told Lapp she no longer wanted to be here. "Lieutenant, can we finish this after I see Sallie back to her carriage?"

"Yeah, go ahead."

Sallie pointed to a clump of trees. "The buggy's back there."

The bright lights from the crime scene behind them paved the way. Before they took a dozen steps, Lapp put his hand on Sallie's arm. "Show me your hands."

"Why?"

Lapp pulled the mottled cape from her hands, stuck it under his arm, and held out his hands, palms up.

Reluctantly, Sallie did the same.

He held her long fingers in his and examined her red palms. Small white blisters were forming. "Sallie, they're burned. Do they hurt?"

"A little. Some salve will fix them up." He noticed her eyes staring at the gold band on his left hand. He caressed her fingers before pulling his hands away.

They walked, side by side, toward the horse and buggy that would take her home.

Except for her nose and chin, Sallie's profile was covered by her black bonnet.

Lapp was hesitant to interrupt her thoughts. "So much happened here tonight. The shooting ..."

"You did what you had to do. You're a good man, Johnny Lapp. You always were."

"You surprised me out there. You weren't afraid. I should have known when you stood up to the men in the barn, that you weren't afraid to speak out. Not many Amish women do that. I was proud of you."

Sallie grinned broadly. "I bet your wife speaks her mind."

Lapp smiled. "I guess she does."

"I knew it, because you're the kind of man that allows that."

Lapp took her words as a compliment and a further proof of his separation from the Amish ways.

They stopped by the buggy door. "Let me drive you home. It's pitch black out there. Can your hands hold the reins?"

She held up her hands and showed how she could open and close them. "The hands work and I've been on these roads many times. I'll stop and pick up Blackie and take him with me."

The sleek brown standard bred snorted loudly and shuffled his feet as if to say, come on, time to get back to the barn.

"Sallie, what happened here tonight … I don't know what to say …"

She interrupted. "We'll need some time to figure it out."

Sallie shivered and opened her arms. "Good by." Lapp stepped into them and pulled her slim body tightly against his. Her head was turned. A kiss was not expected and not offered. She pulled away. Another shiver rocked her body.

Lapp pulled the zipper on his jacket and began to shrug it off. He pointed to the pock-marked cape in her left hand. "That smoky, burned up rag won't keep you warm."

Sallie's hand stopped his movement. "I'll be warm inside the buggy. Don't you remember how cozy it is inside?"

Lapp remembered all too well as he watched Sallie guide the horse and buggy onto the road and into the darkness.

Epilogue

John Lapp parked his patrol car in plain view along an open one mile stretch of Route 30 between Ronks Road and Soudersburg. Some drivers still insisted on breaking the 35 mph speed limit, so he conscientiously turned on his flashing lights and chased them down.

Approaching the noon hour, he had written three tickets and issued one warning. This was his last day in a patrol car. Starting Monday, he would begin a training program that would lead to his promotion to detective grade.

Lisa Robinson's two-part, eye witness account of the shoot out and arrest of Roy Brubaker made headline news. In her appearance on a CNN report, she was beautiful and spoke eloquently.

Roy Brubaker's trial for the murder of Jacob Stoltzfus and the attempted murders of Amos Stoltzfus, Sallie Stoltzfus and John Lapp was set to begin March 18.

The morning following Brubaker's arrest, Lapp, in pressed uniform, polished buttons and shined shoes, stood next to Joe Handleman, of the Public Information Office, Warren Moyer and Captain Vernon Phillips while they faced the press on the barracks front steps. Lapp wore his official face while Phillips commended his detective work in leading to the arrest of Roy Brubaker, now in jail for the brutal murder of Jacob Stoltzfus. Phillips also announced that Lapp would be invited to become a detective, unless, of course, he didn't want to give up his life as a patrolman. Lapp thanked him with a modest smile.

Over the next several days, Lapp took the congratulations and ribbing of his fellow officers in stride. Betsy called to congratulate him and to ask, again, when he would be moving out.

He did not contact nor hear from his father or any other Amish. They were only too glad that the whole matter was closed.

Sallie was constantly on his mind and he was sorely tempted to see her. He had driven past the Stoltzfus farm several times over the last three months, but, at the last minute, could not find the courage to move up the lane. Their worlds were once again separate and apart.

Sick of fast food, he craved a juicy smoked sausage with mustard on a hard roll. Lapp turned the patrol car south on Route 501 toward Lancaster. The streets were clear and dry, but the curbs still had snow piled three-feet high from a succession of late December storms. Circling historic Penn Square, he pulled into the parking lot behind the impressive red brick 1880's building that housed the Central Market, the oldest publicly-owned market in the country.

On a cold January day like today, there would be a scarcity of fresh, locally grown produce, although the local apples and root vegetables like celery, carrots and potatoes, would be excellent. Living alone, he did his own grocery shopping now.

Betsy had not been entirely honest with her answer as to whether or not there was someone else in her life. He just hadn't expected it to be a woman. Dr. Leila Gordon was now her "best friend". In retrospect, Betsy's change in preference was a possibility he had never considered even when she dyed and cut her hair shorter and shorter, never wore dresses, and starved her thin body.

Leila's husband kicked her out and she moved in with Betsy after Lapp moved out. The divorce proceedings ended smoothly. They completed their third and final counseling session and a "mutual consent" divorce was granted. Now, nearly three months later, he lived in a small apartment in Landisville, just west of Lancaster, closer to the State Police Barracks. His stay there was only temporary. His new home, a single story ranch-style log house on a half acre, was in escrow. It stood adjacent to a stand of woods, and had a sour cherry tree, two Winesap apple trees and a large lot for growing vegetables in back. He had plans for more trees and was anxious to get his hands back into the dirt.

Lapp entered the market's glass-domed building and made his way along the aisles. He acknowledged the smiles and greetings prompted by his uniform from side-stepping senior couples, pairs of women carrying cloth bags, and young women with toddlers at their sides, pushing carriages with babies bundled up to their eyeballs against the cold. He examined the produce stands for good prices and quality before buying a peck of Russet potatoes and a small basket of Winesaps.

At his favorite lunch stand, he received a nod of recognition from the bald-headed, overweight short-order cook who took his order and pointed him to a round plastic table.

Lapp ate quickly and hungrily. He swallowed the last bite of sausage and bun, wiped the mustard from the corner of his mouth, washed it down with the dregs of cold cider, and stood, ready to face the real reason he'd come to the market today.

To see Sallie.

He wandered the market's aisles, sorting out the many white and black bonnets of Amish and Mennonite women that stood behind long tables.

Then he saw her, her face in profile, partly covered by the black bonnet. Jars of honey, jelly and apple butter with red-checked labels were stacked on the table. Half-bushel and peck baskets of various varieties of apples surrounded the stall. Sallie handed a small brown paper bag to a middle-aged woman who dropped it into her net shopping bag. Sallie smiled, took the money and said "thank you" as she returned some change. The woman hesitated a moment as if trying to decide on another purchase, but finally drifted away. When she did, Lapp took a deep breath and, with a dozen measured steps and a wide grin on his face, stood in front of her.

Sallie's face lit up with surprise and she literally jumped with joy. "Johnny!"

Lapp, fighting his emotions, smiled and spoke in a strong, clear voice. "Hi Sallie. Wie bisht? Alles is gut?"

"Alles is gut. It's wonderful to see you," she beamed. "Amos and I wondered why you hadn't been out to check up on us."

"I should have," Lapp admitted, "but a lot of things have happened since I last saw you."

"All good, I hope." She nervously wiped her hands on the white apron.

"Mostly," Lapp replied, choosing not to explain.

Acknowledging the bags he carried in each hand she noted, "you've been shopping."

"Just picking up a few things," he said, refusing to confess that the bags were a cover-up for why he was really there.

Nodding at his uniform, she said, "you're still a policeman."

"That's true. But starting Monday I'm off patrol and starting my training as a detective."

"A detective," she said approvingly. "They saw how good you are. Ja?"

"I won't be wearing a uniform anymore. I'll be in a regular suit."

"Like Lieutenant Moyer?"

Lapp nodded. "Just like that."

"I like you better that way."

Lapp noticed that two grey-haired elderly women appeared to be intimidated by the uniform and confused by the obvious friendly conversation he was having with an Amish woman. Lapp stood aside and said, "don't let me interfere with your shopping." The lady with the wrinkled Grandma Moses face replied with a creaky voice, "that's okay. We can come back." The two old ladies edged away, heads buzzing.

"I think I'm bad for business," Lapp confided in a lowered voice.

"Don't worry, they'll come back. And if they don't," she added with a toss of her head, "it's their loss."

"How are the children?"

"They're good."

"And Amos?"

"Amos is good, too. The children tease him, like everybody. I make them stop when I catch them. Otherwise, he's getting better all the time. He's almost given up smoking cigarettes. Or so he tells me."

It was hard to imagine that Amos could take the place of their father, being so different from Jacob. His mind raced with questions he wanted to ask but couldn't. Questions like: would she ever consider remarrying; or, could she foresee any kind of a relationship between them.

Lapp followed Sallie's eyes and turned to a pair of stalls across the aisle where four Amish and Mennonite women, behind a vegetable stand, were tittering and whispering among themselves over Lapp's visit with Sallie. Lapp felt a warm glow cross his face as he turned back to Sallie, who smiled in amusement over their attention.

She sensed the reasons behind his hesitation and broke the ice. "We must always be friends," Sallie said warmly.

"I know." Lapp agreed. "Sallie. Roy Brubaker's trial starts on March 18. There's a good chance you'll be called to testify."

"If I must, I must. Maybe you can come out and help me get ready."

"I'd be happy to do that."

And then there was nothing more to say.

He offered the feeble excuse of having to get back to work. An elderly couple handed Sallie a jar of apple butter they wanted to buy. Lapp backed away and when he caught her eye, he waved goodbye. She waved back.

Next time he would tell her about his divorce.

978-0-595-40427-8
0-595-40427-8

Printed in the United States
97472LV00003B/112/A

9 780595 404278